A
REIGN
OF
ROSE

A REIGN OF ROSE

KATE GOLDEN

BERKLEY ROMANCE
NEW YORK

BERKLEY ROMANCE
Published by Berkley
An imprint of Penguin Random House LLC
penguinrandomhouse.com

Copyright © 2024 by Natalie Sellers

Book design by Daniel Brount
Interior art: Flower background © sokolova_sv/Shutterstock.com
Original map design by Jack Johnson

Library of Congress Cataloging-in-Publication Data

Names: Golden, Kate, author.
Title: A reign of rose / Kate Golden.
Description: First edition. | New York : Berkley Romance, 2024. | Series: The Sacred Stones ; 3
Identifiers: LCCN 2024011515 (print) | LCCN 2024011516 (ebook) |
ISBN 9780593641941 (trade paperback) | ISBN 9780593641958 (ebook)
Subjects: LCGFT: Fantasy fiction. | Romance fiction. | Novels.
Classification: LCC PS3607.O4523 R45 2024 (print) |
LCC PS3607.O4523 (ebook) | DDC 813/.6—dc23/eng/20240321
LC record available at https://lccn.loc.gov/2024011515
LC ebook record available at https://lccn.loc.gov/2024011516

First Edition: October 2024

Printed in the United States of America
1st Printing

For Taylor, Sam, and Kristine,
my Flora, Fauna, and Merryweather.
Thank you for making all my dreams come true.

A world of lighte blessed across the Stones,
A king doomed to fall at the hands of his second son.
A city turned to ash and bones,
The fallen star will mean war has once again begun.
The final Fae of full blood born at last,
Will find the Blade of the Sun inside her heart.
Father and child will meet again in war a half century past,
And with the rise of the phoenix will the final battle start.
A king who can only meet his end at her hands,
A girl who knows what she must choose,
A sacrifice made to save both troubled lands,
Without it, an entire realm will lose.
A tragedy for both full Fae, as each shall fall,
Alas it is the price to pay to save them all.

LIGEIA, THE SEER OF LUMERA, 113 YEARS AGO

EVENDELL

N
W · E
S

VORST
REGION

CARRUS

PEARL
MOUNTAINS

Kingdom
of Citrine

AZURINE

SLEETCLIFF

JADE
ISLANDS

BITTER
WASTES

Mineral Sea

GARNET
KINGDOM

LUMERA

THE
DREADED
VALE

SOLARIS

AURORA

Salamanders' Gulf

Prologue

ARWEN
Thirteen Years Ago

I'M NOT GOING IN THERE."

I willed the words into reality by digging my heel into a balding patch of grass beneath my feet.

Bad things happened in Powell's work shed. Things that hurt my back and made me cry.

"Fine," Ryder allowed, releasing my hand to cross his arms. "Suit yourself."

Whatever "suit yourself" meant did not sound promising.

My brother didn't wait for my response. He raced into the brisk night after Halden and the two of them picked the shed's rusty lock with ease before slipping inside the thatched structure.

All the while, cold air licked at my face and shins. I shivered violently in place. My favorite nightdress was rife with holes and worn cotton. Too tattered to protect me from the night's chill. I needed a coat. Or to go back inside. But if I ran home, Halden and Ryder would think I was scared.

Which I was, but . . .

They didn't have to know that. My brother and his best friend were never scared. Not when they got into trouble arriving late for classes, nor when lightning struck so loud it sounded like the crack of a belt. Not when they snuck out on dark, windy nights like these.

Brave, strong, confident boys, my mother always cooed.

And . . . me. Chasing after them. The runt of the litter.

Why couldn't they have just invited me to join them? When I'd heard their hushed laughter and tiptoed from my room to ask them what all the fuss was about. If they'd just invited me then, I could have uttered a polite *Oh, no thank you* and gone back to bed armed with the knowledge that I hadn't been excluded.

A wolf somewhere in the distant woods howled at the huge white moon above, and I ground my teeth together. I wanted to go back to bed. It was probably still warm. I could stay there, under my quilt, until the darkness was gone and it was sunny and morning and Mother was awake.

I spun on my heel, crunching a dry leaf under my slipper to do just that. They could mock me tomorrow, call me a coward—I'd let them. Or maybe the shed would swallow them whole and they wouldn't make it home at all.

I'd only made one stride toward our cottage when a loud clatter and a yowl of pain warbled out into the night.

Owls hooted. Leaves rustled. My blood froze inside my body.

Another agonized shriek—

And I sprinted without thinking.

Not for my rumpled bed, but for that looming work shed. Like a little goblin's house, stark and solitary in the starless night.

"What happened?" I breathed, slamming the door open. "Wolves?"

Sawdust and varnish filled my nose and my back hurt in phantom memory.

"It's Halden . . ." Ryder's voice wobbled. "We were playing soldiers. Halden grabbed the saw. His hand, it's . . ."

I squinted in the darkness at the pool of blood. Slick, like oil. And above it . . . Halden—the boy that was always smiling—drenched in tears.

I'd never seen anyone cry like that.

"It's all right," I whispered, though I didn't know why I'd said it. His hand didn't look all right one bit. "I'm going to get Mother."

"Are you stupid?" Ryder snapped, yanking me back by the sleeve. "She'll wake Father, and we'll all be punished. Just stay put while I think of something."

Ryder's eyes, illuminated in a shaft of moonlight, cut sidelong to Halden. Ire flickered off him like candlelight, and I thought he looked a lot like Powell when he wore that expression.

It turned my stomach into tangles.

Halden had cradled his injured hand up to his chest, thick tears and snot bursting forth from his face. "This is your fault," he wailed at my brother. "I told you we shouldn't have come in here."

And Halden was right. The shed was horrible. So rickety and small. Always locked. I was only ever brought in here to be punished. My heart was already beating too fast just standing inside its four dusty walls. My lungs felt tight, like I'd forgotten how to breathe.

In, out. In, out.

I wanted to run. As far from here as I could get in these muddied slippers.

But my brother always landed on his feet. He always knew what to do.

And Halden was sobbing like an animal, and . . . my fingers hurt.

No, not quite hurt. They *tingled*. Like I'd spent an afternoon lying on them wrong, and now they were filled with sparkling needles.

"Can I see it?" I asked my brother.

Ryder contemplated my question. Halden held his tongue for a long, tear-drenched minute before Ryder nodded once.

"Come here," I said to Halden.

He didn't argue. Under the bleary moonlight I inspected the gash down the center of his palm, jagged and torn like fabric. The needles in my fingers intensified. My heart was beginning to pound too hard, like a bird was trapped inside my chest.

"I think I hear something," Ryder said. "You both stay here, let me go see . . ." He maneuvered around Powell's craft table in a rush, sending screws and bolts toppling onto the floor.

My chest seized even tighter. Powell wouldn't like that. Those screws were ordered by size. The bolts in a line to match.

"Well?" Halden sniffed. "What does it look like?"

"I've done this for Mother," I told Halden, stretching on my tiptoes for the rickety shelf just out of reach and dragging him with me. "Sometimes her legs don't work so well. She gets a lot of cuts and scrapes."

My hand found the rag I'd been aiming for, and I pressed the soft cloth into his wound and held it there.

Halden's sobs guttered into sniffles. That wolf howled once more beneath the blanket of night outside. "He's not coming back, you know."

Ryder? Sure he would. I opened my mouth to tell Halden so, but those needles in my fingers had become so frenzied I couldn't think. They stung and fizzed. Even though I didn't particularly want to see the gore again, I found myself asking, "Can I look once more?"

Halden nodded but turned his head as far as he could angle, back toward the dirt-flecked windowpanes that nearly blotted out the moon. Then he screwed his eyes shut for good measure.

The cloth had slowed the bleeding some, but . . . then it was back, spilling forth in rivulets and onto the floor. The cut was deep. I could see stiff white peeking out from underneath his skin. Bone, and layers of muscle. I touched the serrated edges gingerly, and a dawn-pale glow emanated from my fingers and into his hand.

Shock stilled my heart. I yanked my fingers back.

Halden's skin began to stitch itself together before my eyes.

I blinked them closed. Once, twice—

But there it was. A wound, closing on its own.

And that curious, panicky feeling in my chest, the one where I forgot how to breathe right—it was gone, along with the pesky needles. I pressed my fingertips against my palm, searching for that absent tingle.

"Are you done?" Halden's eyes were still closed.

"Almost." I touched the wound again, and this time my glow was smaller, less like a star and more like a matchstick. But after a minute his palm held only fresh pink flesh.

Was I a witch? Would Halden think so? Would he tell Mother and Powell?

Oh, Stones.

I cringed. We weren't supposed to curse.

I was doing everything wrong tonight.

"Don't look yet," I said to him, suddenly very tired. I wrapped his hand in the cloth once more, tying it in a knot to hide the evidence. "I think it'll be better by morning."

"Thanks, Arwen." Halden wiped the tears from his cheeks with the back of his good hand. "You didn't have to do that."

Did he know what my fingers had done? Did he know that whatever it was had made my whole body feel calm and on fire at the same time? I swallowed hard. "Do what?"

"Stay. Help me. You could have run off like Ryder did."

I wiped down the saw the boys had been playing with, sliding its bloodied edge along the hem of my nightgown. Then I placed it back on its nail, and knelt to pick up each screw and bolt Ryder had knocked to the floor. It would take me an hour at least to put them all back in their right order.

"You were hurt," I said around a yawn. "I couldn't leave you."

"Yeah," Halden said, though he was already moving past me for the door. "You could've."

PART I

The Ashes

1

KANE

I KNEW THIS TIME IT WAS MY RIB THAT HAD CRACKED.

Each inhale sent the mismatched shards straining from one another and pain radiating into the pummeled muscles of my back. Sitting up was marginally less painful, and I sucked in a slow, bracing breath.

The scent of pine and blood filled my nostrils.

When I blinked my eyes open, they raked down the cascading wall of solid, glinting ice that I'd plunged from—its peak still hidden behind thick white clouds, the smooth face marred only by the cracks and dents where I'd jammed my fists and feet, unsuccessfully attempting an ascent.

First you failed them. Then you failed her. Now you're failing again.

Anguish pierced my heart anew. Fresher, every fucking day.

Wasn't grief supposed to dull with time?

I stood, chest still constricting with two very different types of pain, and brushed snow and dirt from my backside. The motion aggravated deep scrapes along my palms. Whatever protective ward the White Crow had cast around his home atop that glacial mountain was inhibiting all aspects of my lighte—barring me from shifting into my dragon form, halting my accelerated Fae healing . . .

I trudged through near-blinding white back in the direction of the town at the base of the mountain. I'd only made it a few feet when the bruises, scrapes, and blisters across my body began to fade. My toe cut across the snow, demarking where the ward appeared to end.

I winced with the movement. The rib was going to take longer to heal.

If I were smart, or patient, I'd retreat down to town, get a room at the unsavory, sleet-coated inn, and lie still in devastating silence until I recovered.

But I wasn't smart.

I wasn't patient.

And I didn't mind the pain.

I was so cold these days it was almost preferable, feeling something ache inside my bones.

Pressing my palm to the radiating volleys of pain in my side, I appraised the ice-cold mountain range for the hundredth time. Beyond bare ponderosa branches thick with hoarfrost, and snow prints from hares and caribou, that towering rise of jagged hunches rose and rose and rose, gobbling up the skyline.

"You planning to become a dragon and fly at it again?" a crotchety old voice called from behind me. "That almost worked."

Gods damn it.

"No," I growled.

And that hadn't almost worked. It had only gotten me high enough into the air to spy the tiny stone cottage that topped the peak, observe the elderly sorcerer tending to a flourishing root vegetable garden, and then, as soon as I flew for him and through his wards, shift against my will midair and plummet to the ground.

That fall had yielded me one crushed kneecap, a concussion, and two dislocated shoulders. None of which had rivaled the experience of waiting days for my knocked-out teeth to grow back—nothing humbles a man quite like teething in adulthood.

My body shattering against packed snow hadn't been all bad. In some ways, I'd welcomed the pain. It allowed me to feel what Arwen had felt—that same gruesome powerlessness. Sailing through the air, instincts screaming at me to fly despite my brain's roaring that I *couldn't*—

"You're not going to die." That's what I had told her.

A grimace twisted my face at the memory.

So I'd tried again the next day. And the next.

The second time I fell out of my dragon form, I'd broken my back in two places, and lost the use of my legs. I'd lain there for half a day, inside the White Crow's wards, unable to heal, unable to move, until *this* mouth breather had stumbled across my prone form and, upon my very clear instructions, dragged me back toward town until a tingling in my calves told me I'd started to heal.

I appraised him now as he stood expectantly with that yoke across his shoulders. The wrinkly, crumpled do-gooder was named Len and had a long face and thin lips that he used to smile far more often than necessary. A dishwasher in the town's only tavern, Len climbed up the hill for fresh water from the well each morning, and once told me he was all too used to seeing sorry assholes like myself up here, trying and failing to reach the White Crow.

"Don't beat yourself up," Len said, eyes crinkling. "It's a feat when someone can even track the old nutter down."

Pressing against my aching, splintered rib, I cut a glance at him. "On your way now, Len."

The older man raised his hands in mock surrender. "All right, all right. Come down to the tavern if you need to refuel."

"Will do."

But I wouldn't.

"FUCK." I GRUNTED, SLIDING DOWN THE FACE OF THE MOUNtain, hands clawing for purchase against the rocks I'd driven into the smooth ice to serve as handholds. My chest slammed into one and I spasmed for air, landing hard against the snow. Through my blurred vision, I watched several brown rabbits scatter for the powdery brush.

"You're going to kill yourself before you do whatever you came here to."

"Why are you always here?" I croaked to Len through a mouthful of ice.

"This is where the damn well is!"

I craned my neck. Len gestured at the water source, yoke balanced across his back, twin pails spilling water from either shoulder. "Help me bring these down the mountain and I'll buy you a pint."

"There isn't time," I said, ragged, bearded cheek growing numb in the slush.

It had been months. If Lazarus had destroyed the blade already . . . then actually I'd have nothing but time. A miserable, aching eternity.

I swallowed a dry heave at the thought and sucked in more frigid air, rolling onto my back with a groan.

Don't think like that.

That sick, wounded yearning took root in my chest as it always did when her voice resonated in my head. Like bells. Like sweet music.

Arwen would tell me that I couldn't know anything for sure until I made it to Lumera and found out for myself. And I couldn't do that, couldn't confront my father until I, too, was full-blooded and had a chance of destroying him.

Which was why I had to get up *the fucking mountain.*

Up there—where the impenetrable clouds met an icy summit.

I squinted. If there had been a sun to see, it would have sunk behind those peaks hours ago. I could tell by the dim, cerulean light dulling the snow, and the cold seeping into my bones.

In the first days of my journey to the Pearl Mountains, a few residents told me I'd just missed the bright, clear-skied summer. It was cold year-round in the floating kingdom—something about the altitude, or the magic that kept the city hovering among the clouds— but it was especially brutal in both fall and winter months, when there were fewer than eight hours of daylight and near-nonstop snowfall. It was even worse here in Vorst, the region that served as home to the White Crow.

Meanwhile, Shadowhold was probably just reaching the tail end of autumn, the Shadow Woods likely replete with toadstools and blackberries.

Another swift kick to the gut. That's what thinking of my keep felt like these days. Not because of how much I missed my people, or Griffin or Acorn. Not because I longed for the comforts of lilac soap and whiskey and cloverbread.

But because even if this treacherous, frostbitten climb was possible, even if I reached the White Crow, convinced him to turn me full-blooded, stomached whatever anguish that might entail, and somehow still arrived in one piece back to my shadowed, familiar castle . . .

Arwen wouldn't be there.

Her books, filled with flattened petals, unopened. The side of my bed I'd so foolishly hoped would be hers, eternally cold. I'd never hear that peal of laughter again, nor smell her orange blossom skin.

I'd watch my home become a crypt.

I rolled over, burying my face in the snow, and roared until flames ran through my lungs. Until tears burned at my eyes and my chest rippled against the ground, the agony, shredding me, the guilt, the untenable sorrow—

"*Stones alive*," Len breathed. "You need a break."

"No," I grumbled, spitting ice and pushing myself up from the ground. "It helps. I'm fine."

"It's almost nightfall. You can't scale a mountain of ice in the dark with a broken rib and a punctured lung. Are you trying to die, boy?"

I'd asked myself that same question so many times I'd lost count. "Depends on the day."

Len offered me a flat expression. "One pint, a hot meal, and you'll be back to falling off the mountain again by sunrise."

Perhaps he was right. I was slinking dangerously close to that tipping point. The one wherein my own death was looking just a bit too attractive. Where I'd either join her or stop having to live each despicable day without her. But then her sacrifice would have been for nothing and that—that I couldn't allow. In life, or in death.

Dry wind bit at my skin as I limped toward Len with a grunt. Alarm erupted on his face as I drew near, but I only lifted the pails from his shoulders and moved past him, prowling down the mountainside. Len's sigh of relief was audible as he stomped through the snow after me.

Vorst was barely a town. It was barely a village. That aforementioned seedy inn, a nearly bare general store, a temple, and Len's quiet stone tavern were all it had to offer. Populated only by those passing through, solitary lifelong merchants like Len, and the rare scholar or priest who sought remote corners of Pearl to study or serve the Stones in peace.

Len's tavern—which he made clear to me three different times on our trudge over was not *his* tavern, but his cousin, Faulk's—was a frostbitten slate-gray hovel on the outskirts. I had to duck to enter, and, due to the low, slanted ceiling, hunch once inside, which sent currents of pain through my still-bruised abdomen.

With few options—the grim space had only a handful of mismatched stools and one bench with a man snoring beneath it—I sat down in a back corner beside the tavern's hearth. My table was built from an overturned pig trough. A single pillar candle melted atop it, stuffed into an empty wine bottle and flickering for its life.

"What can I do you for?" Len asked, prodding at the crackling fire.

The heat permeated through my stiff, wet clothes. Remnants of ice and snow were melting beneath the layers. I removed my gloves, brushing frost from my beard and flexing my hands closer to the flames. "I'll take that pint. And whatever you have to eat."

Len nodded once, returning minutes later with a foamy ale and a lukewarm meat pie. One bite told me it was mostly gristle but I ate the entire thing regardless and then asked for a second. Being this far from the White Crow's wards had bettered both my appetite and my injuries. I twisted to loosen my rigid spine.

"Want to know what Faulk tried to name the tavern?" Len asked, pulling up a low stool across from me and draping some animal's hide over his knobby legs.

Irritation pricked at my neck. I couldn't tell the elderly man to scram when he had offered me the first hot meal I'd had in days. But I really, *really* would have liked to.

When I remained silent he said, undeterred, "The Frozen Yak."

"Yeah . . . that's terrible."

"I told him every patron will think of rock-hard vomit when they eat."

My eyes found the soupy pie before me, and I lowered my fork.

"You're obviously not from here, but in Vorst, yaks—"

"No offense, Len, but I'd prefer a bit of—"

"Solitude?"

I let my silence answer his question.

Len only leaned forward. His cracked lips spread with a curious grin. "What do you want with the old Crow anyway?"

The fire popped beside me and the snoring man bathed in shadow rolled to his side. I sighed like an ox. "Is it even him up there?"

Len sniffed, the wrinkles on his face creasing with ease, as if he did that all too often. A chronic dripping nose from chronic winter. "It's him, all right. He's come down once or twice. Bought seeds for his garden."

"Does anyone in Vorst speak to him? Is there any way to send word?"

Len shook his head.

"Not even for—"

"The king of Onyx?"

I choked on a piece of lard-laden crust.

"People talk," Len said, leaning back. "Even in towns as small as these. Your land's been missing a king for the last two months. And not so many men can turn into dragons. Only two, by my last count."

Suspicion ground my jaw shut. "What do you know of my father?"

Len made a face. "This whole kingdom is made up of scholars. He's a Faerie, right?"

I said nothing, back rigid, narrow fork mangled in my grasp.

"Why'd you abandon your kingdom?" Len plucked the knife from beside me and twirled it across his crooked fingers. "Are you not at war?"

The rage that spiraled through me nearly blew out my fists and into the thin man. He was only spared by the equal rage directed back at myself—the truth in his words, all my mistakes, being forced to travel here and leave them all behind.

"I didn't abandon them," I growled. "My men are preparing for battle. I'm here to retrieve something we need in order to win."

"And what's that?"

Len's curiosity had graduated from mildly irritating to deserving of a fork through the throat.

"C'mon," he pried. "Who am I going to tell? The rodents?"

I took a breath. "The man I seek to destroy can only be killed by a certain type of Fae. I need the White Crow to make me . . . able to beat him." I said the next words very slowly, as to infiltrate Len's feeble mind. "Can you help me reach the sorcerer?"

Len's eyes softened, and for a moment, I thought he might actually answer me. "Why now? When you've been at war for years?"

I stabbed my warped fork into the soft center of the pie, ignoring him. Two more mouthfuls and I'd head back up—

"If you answer me, I might be able to help you contact the wizard. I have lived beneath him for sixty years."

I didn't want to talk about her with this toad. I didn't want to talk about her with anyone.

Len's eyes held my glare like he hadn't a fear in the world. If I left now, I'd never know if a single ounce of kindness to this man might have made all the difference. It's what she would have encouraged me to do.

"We had someone else who could kill the man," I finally said. "Someone very dear to me. She died."

Len nodded slowly, as if my coldness to him finally made sense. "My condolences, boy. I recently lost a woman I cared for myself. Hadn't seen her in many years." Len sniffed again. "Still hurts."

The unmistakable scuttle of rats' claws tinkered against the low roof and drew a grunt from the man still sleeping under the rot-holed bench beside us.

Len leaned back again, even closer to the hearth. "What would you give to bring her back?"

Anything.

I only finished my ale.

"C'mon, boy. What would you give?" Len pushed.

This dishwasher's hunt for companionship was grating my last nerve down to a fine thread. "Why ask such a thing?"

"Why not?"

"I don't dwell on hypotheticals."

Len snickered, toying with the knife still in his hands. Then he reached for my supper, and broke off a piece of crust, crumbing it in his hands and scattering it at our feet.

The fat, wiry rat crawled out of the floorboards, tentatively at first. Drawn to the scraps, but no fool. The rodent waited with practiced patience until Len scooted closer to the makeshift table and turned his back on the scene.

"What are you doing?"

"I don't want you to dwell, boy." Len had faced me, but his eyes were on that rat, grasping at greasy crumbs with reedy pink hands. Before I could stop him, Len lashed at the creature with his knife and speared the thing clean-through in a gory *crunch*.

"For Gods' sake, Len . . ." The man was senile. And all alone in this icy, lonesome town. I stood to leave, wondering if there even was a Faulk.

"Sit," he commanded, laying the impaled rat on the table. Its meager blood pooled around my half-eaten pie.

Mists of shadow twined around my fists. Though irritated, I had no real desire to hurt Len. But this was—

"And none of that," the old man said, jerking his chin at my hands. Len removed the knife, placed it on the table, and waited. I had no reason to stay, but some curiosity, perhaps some long-buried loneliness of my own, kept my feet from moving, and I watched as Len drew one wrinkled hand across the rat's plump corpse.

With no incantation, no lighte, no otherworldly glow, the rat twitched. And twitched again. Len hadn't said a single word when the rodent's curved spine reattached with an audible *crack*. The long-tailed vermin released a disturbing, harrowing squeak before rising and scampering across the table. It crawled to the ground and back through the gap in the floorboards from which it came.

My heart rattled my broken rib cage. It was more than Briar Creighton herself could do.

Necromancy.

My eyes shot up to Len once more. That crinkle at the corner of his eyes. The smirk playing on his lips.

"It's you. You're . . ."

"Now answer me, boy."

Knees loose, I dropped back down into my seat.

The White Crow had been with me all evening long.

I was a fucking fool.

And now I knew his question for what it was.

A test. One which I didn't have the right answer to. I knew the truth—that I'd give anything, any limb, any life, any realm, to bring Arwen back. That I would shear the skin from my own bones, tear the world to pulp to hold her in my arms even just one more time—

But I had no idea if it was the response the White Crow sought.

"I'd give more . . ." I managed on a breath. "More to bring her back than you could ever know."

"What if it spelled your own death?"

"In a heartbeat."

"Yes, that's an easy one, isn't it? What about an innocent's? What if her resurrection demanded an equal debt paid—"

Suddenly I was back aboard a ship in the heart of the Mineral Sea, reaching for a tear-stained, blood-soaked Arwen. *"I knew I couldn't go through with it. Not even for the good of all of Evendell . . . Do you hear me? I was willing to sacrifice the entire world to keep you alive!"*

"Yes," I admitted. Shame thick on my tongue, eyes down on the drying river of rat's blood, tacky and near-black on the tabletop. "I'd kill for her. A thousand times over."

"And if I raised your lover from the soil, brushed her off and made her new, and gave you the full Fae blood that you seek? If I said neither of you had to die, then what would you do?" The White Crow's teeth flashed in the fading light, breath swirling in a room now icy cold. I hadn't realized my bones were chattering.

"Would you still take your new skin," he continued when I

remained silent, "reborn as full-blooded just as the prophecy required, and slay your father? Knowing you were fated to die, as she once was? *Knowing* you could have lived a near eternity beside her? Would you still sacrifice yourself for the good of the realm?"

No.

If the Gods were that cruel, and somehow this wily, wicked sorcerer could turn me full-blooded Fae *and* resurrect Arwen . . . Then, no, I wouldn't leave her side ever again. There was no use lying to myself. Pretending to be some selfless man I wasn't, and could never be.

"A great disappointment."

The breath shot from my lungs. "I didn't say—"

Another swipe of that wrinkled hand and the old, nameless tavern of Vorst transformed.

When the spots cleared from my vision, my hands were braced on a rich maple dining table. Clean, polished, *sparkling* in gentle candlelight. The room glowed with dozens of the waxy, lit pillars.

Not a tavern anymore, but a bachelor's den: plush periwinkle settees, layers of mismatched cream rugs, exotic bottles of wine, and crystal decanters filled with spirit. Wood and leather and the smoky, spiced aroma of incense.

I hadn't even noticed how earsplitting the endless howl of wind whistling through the mighty trees had been until it was gone. Until that roar was replaced by indulgent silence.

And that veil of frigid cold—gone. Instead, a light, warm breeze rustled loose curtains. It felt like honey in my lungs. Despite the elevation and season here in Vorst, Len's magic had doused the entire hideaway in temperate air.

And still, my blood chilled as my mind stuttered to a halt.

Not magic.

And before me . . . not Len. Or, still Len, but perhaps as he'd looked thirty years ago. Virile, wise, angular. The kind of man you'd trust with your life, but perhaps not your woman.

Len, the White Crow . . . whoever he was, was no mere sorcerer.

"What *are* you?"

2

ARWEN

I SCREAMED LIKE A BANSHEE, SQUIRMING AND WRENCHING away from my guards, not bothering to contain a single ounce of my rabid, roiling fury.

Not even because it hurt. It didn't, so much. Not anymore.

After all these weeks, having my lighte harvested was more of a violation, more mentally distressing than it was painful.

"Hold still." Maddox grunted, his silver armor rippling with his taut muscles. "You're not making this any easier."

That was why I screamed.

"Good," I spat at the blockheaded kingsguard and his insuffer-able square jaw. I kicked my legs haphazardly and got Wyn in the kneecap.

"Ow," he groaned, soft dark hair falling in front of his baby face.

"That wouldn't happen if you knelt like I did," Maddox hissed at his underling from his low position, holding me to the chair. Then, under his breath, "Feeble in more ways than one."

"Let me go," I demanded. "Both of you sniveling, subservient—"

Octavia cut me off. "How greatly I despise that voice."

I could have said the same for the sorceress presently scraping the lighte from my veins. Somewhere between the first time she'd harvested me, when I'd sobbed like a little girl, and the fifteenth—the day I successfully spat in her eye—I'd decided Octavia reminded me of an aging female python. An apex predator whose scales had begun to lose their shine but who was determined to prove her power, the scope of her viciousness, to anyone who cared to listen. Sometimes even more fervently to those who didn't.

She also spoke with the same viper-like hiss. "Imagine if I just *snatched it*."

I opened my mouth to swear at her—but nothing followed. Silence, no matter how I screamed or rasped or whimpered.

"Much better."

Octavia returned to the gory task at hand, adjusting the tubes affixed to the backs of my hands and creases of my arms. When I winced, I swore her smile bared fangs. She studied the pale white lighte that dripped through her contraption and into the great glass barrels at her feet. Her graying, hip-length hair grazed my legs as she worked. The sound of Maddox's sinister hums reverberated in my ears. Sick glee at my pain worming itself through his vocal cords. I wondered if he was even aware of the grating noise.

I slouched back into my chair, strands of hair fluttering up from my face with my sigh of defeat.

The same oversize velvet chair I'd sat in almost every day. In the same lavish room I'd awoken in two months ago. Which was perched atop the same suffocatingly high tower in the same palace in the same capital of the same nightmarish Fae Realm it seemed I'd never, ever leave.

~✦~

ONCE OCTAVIA HAD PURGED EVERY OUNCE OF LIGHTE FROM my veins, Wyn laid me, depleted and still unable to speak, across the deceivingly sumptuous bed. My arms collapsed across my body and I crumpled myself into a ball. I didn't care who saw.

And maybe it was that notion exactly—that acceptance, that acquiescence to her power—but as Octavia strolled from the room, she offered me a serpentine grin and a flick of her wrist. With my next cough I found my voice had returned.

The kingsguards had walked in just as she'd left. Their armor reminded me of the exoskeleton of a rare silver crustacean—no leather or steel in sight, but a shinier, scalier alloy rippling over their joints. The helmets so skin-smooth it was as if their skulls had been dipped in the stuff. Only a sheer red visor covered their faces, and I had the errant thought that if I were ever in a position to fight one of these men, it would be the only entry point for my blade. I was sure no man-made weapon could penetrate whatever their breastplates and greaves were made of.

Maybe the Blade of the Sun could have. My blade, long gone now.

The muscled guards carried weighty barrels of my lighte from the room, which produced a peculiar shame deep in my stomach. I tipped my head toward the ceiling and that floating, pearl-crusted chandelier.

When I heard the doors slam behind them, I finally allowed myself to sit up, my legs tangled in layers upon layers of gentle petticoats.

My two shadows had lingered behind as always. Maddox, with his cold beady eyes, carved jaw, and cropped straw hair, stood ramrod straight by my door, same disturbing tune floating absently from his nose. Wyn had shuffled to the washroom and was just now returning with a cold compress for my forehead. His knee was worse today, since I'd kicked it.

I turned my face from his offer. "I don't know why you bother." My throat was hoarse from Octavia's spell.

"I don't know why you fight it every time," he said, dabbing the cool rag across my head anyway, the damp fabric soothing my clammy temples.

It was a strange order Lazarus had given my two guards all those weeks ago: keep me here, in this mighty looming tower, high above the rest of the palace—even farther above Lumera's walled capital city of Solaris, which I knew I was held within but hadn't seen any of, aside from the staggering view from my one window. Even at the expense of my health and theirs, as I learned in my first few weeks here, when I'd nearly scratched Maddox's eyes out trying to escape and he'd punched me so hard in the jaw it had taken a week for my face to regain its shape.

And yet, also, *serve* me. Make me comfortable, ply me with quince tarts and juniper perfume and delicate fans of osprey feathers at the tail end of summer. Light those stifling, revoltingly sweet sandalwood candles each day. So long as I never left the suite, make sure I was *pleased*. Entertain me with repetitive card games and fruit wine and stacks and stacks of books rife with the same propaganda extolling the *commanding* and *righteous* Fae King Lazarus Ravenwood. *A pinnacle of heroism, fairness, and vigor. As beloved as he is feared.* What a load of shit.

A bound captive and honored guest. The prisoner who was soon to be queen consort.

Wyn was better at doting than his brutal counterpart. They might have made a good team, if only they didn't despise each other almost as much as I despised them both.

Wyn dotted the cloth along my collarbone with care. I would have shoved him off had I had a scrap of strength left. To his credit, Wyn never allowed his caretaking to grow inappropriate. Or, he was as appropriate as one could be when imprisoning someone and allowing them to be drained of their bodily fluids against their will.

Even as Wyn kept his hands to himself . . . I still fought him ferociously. And Octavia, too, even knowing I'd never break her torment. Because stopping—stopping would mean I'd given up. And I refused to lose hope that one day, even if it were centuries from now, I might know what it felt like to be free.

And when doubt crept in as it had so viciously today, I thought of Kane's crooked smile. When I screeched so loud they plugged their ears, or bit so hard I drew blood, his words were the ones that rang through my mind like a temple bell. *That's my vicious bird. Such claws. Such violent, gorgeous claws.*

I'd only resorted to actually *hearing* him a few weeks ago. Or, what I thought must've been a few weeks ago. I'd lost all sense of time here, holed up in this marble-floored, scarlet brocade suite. Drained of lighte, lonely beyond fathoming, pale from lack of sun—sleeping and scowling in a constant, dizzying rotation . . . Kane's imagined voice in my head was all I had left.

My suite door creaked open, and with it my blood froze in my veins. Maddox poked half his head outside to converse with someone, and I held my breath.

A minute ticked by.

Another.

But in the end he only nodded and closed the heavy anthracite doors once more.

I didn't allow myself to ask what was coming next.

"She's arrived a few days early," Maddox snipped to Wyn. "His Majesty requires more guards. Stay with her while I aid them?"

"Of course," Wyn said.

But Maddox only scowled at him. "Without fucking anything up?"

Wyn gave a single resolute nod, no eye roll in sight, which would have been hard for me, personally.

The thickheaded guard deserted the ornate doors and the lock clicked outside as it did each night.

My strength had finally returned a bit—likely from the spike of adrenaline that came with the interruption—and I snatched the compress from Wyn's hands. Patting it along my arms and down to where my veins were wrapped in bandages, I willed my voice to be casual. "Who arrived early?"

Wyn limped, favoring his right leg, over to the carnelian curtains, stitched with that gold-and-ebony detailing. He drew them open and allowed hazy afternoon light to slip in and glimmer over his warm-hued bronze skin and pulled-back dark curls.

With some difficulty, I pulled myself to sit on the edge of the bed. "Early for what?" I pressed, still unanswered.

Wyn only gazed out through the high windowpanes, clearly trying to spy whoever had arrived.

"Why do you let him speak to you like that?"

"He's my senior," Wyn said to the glass. "In both age and rank."

Flipping the now lukewarm cloth in my hands before patting it along my neck, I racked my brain for a question that might reward me with another real answer.

Wyn winced as he maneuvered back to sit in the armchair across from the glossy fireplace, though he positioned himself to face me. With a grimace, he lifted his leg onto the velvet ottoman.

I'd noticed the lame limb the first day we'd met. My heart

lurched despite all the unfathomable things he'd allowed to be done to me. "I'm sorry about your knee. I wasn't aiming for it."

"It's fine."

I assessed him as he massaged the joint. "How young were you?"

Wyn's expression was one of great surprise. Lowering his brows again, he said, "Three."

"What happened?"

"I fell from a cupboard. Never healed quite right."

"What were you doing in a cupboard?"

The corner of Wyn's mouth ticked up as he appraised his raised leg. "My mother sells hairpins."

My brows furrowed. I waited patiently for more.

"She crafts them from metal, and solders little hand-bent flowers onto them. It's how she fed and clothed seven children."

"That's a lot of hairpins."

"Indeed. I was sleeping when I fell. Sleeping in a cupboard because there was no room left on the floor."

My heart thumped again and I had to reprimand myself. Why should I have any sympathy for this man? Even if he was more boy than man, really.

I told myself it was the principle of the story that hurt my heart, not Wyn's suffering. Kane had warned me that the vast majority of the Fae Realm lived in poverty worse than anything I'd known as a child—and Abbington was barely more than farmland and a handful of cottages. Based on the bits and pieces I'd gathered in my time here, outside the glittering walled city of Solaris were conditions worse than squalor.

Years ago, Lazarus's men had reaped both coin and lighte from all major cities until they were shells of their former glory—mere slums—and then used their yields to further fortify the king's own capital from all those that would seek what he had stolen. Shelter, resources, safety. But also glamour, amenities, excess . . . He built another set of walls around the coasts of Lumera, prohibiting any mortal or Fae in the land from fleeing to Evendell. The channel—the only route between realms if you weren't lucky enough to know a powerful witch to portal you out—was guarded day and night. Kane had said in passing once that Lazarus had plans to seal it off completely.

"You must hate Lazarus as much as the rest of us, then," I tried.

Wyn's eyes were sharp on mine. "He is my king."

I fiddled innocently with a loose thread on the duvet. "The two are not mutually exclusive."

"King Lazarus has given me the opportunity of a lifetime, despite my injury. A chance to bring my family to the sanctuary that is Solaris. If you're in his kingsguard long enough, he allows your loved ones within his court. That is a leader of generous heart."

"I have a hard time believing Lazarus employed you despite your disability out of sheer altruism." *Don't roll your eyes, bird,* Kane's voice rumbled inside my mind. I nearly sent chills up my own back. Maybe I was finally losing it.

Wyn pursed his lips. "I'm a skilled fighter. I had to be, to survive outside these walls. Growing up . . ." His hazel eyes found his knee. "I've earned my place in his guard."

"Is Maddox also hoping to buy his family safe passage to Solaris?"

"Maddox?" Wyn sneered. "Maddox was raised here, and by nobles no less. His first day in the regiment he wore gilded Solaris finery. He'll lead the lot soon."

I looked out the lofty window. I couldn't see much from the dizzying heights of the tower. All of Solaris's industry and production clogged the cityscape with thick gray clouds that reminded me of clumps of lint you found in high cabinets and old drawers. An unpleasant reminder of all the grime you never knew was floating around your home.

A knock at the door sounded and Wyn lifted his sensitive leg off the ottoman and hobbled to answer it. The knocks didn't frighten me. Only the servants knocked. The guards weren't that polite.

Wyn returned moments later with a teacup and fresh pot of tea and, after placing them on a shiny, varnished armoire, poured me a cup and limped back over. I sipped the fragrant rooibos and licorice in silence, allowing it to soothe my raw vocal cords. All that soundless screaming . . . When the ivory was drained, the little tea leaves formed a blurry image in the liquid's wake. I thought it looked like a lamb.

"Why does she despise me so much?" Wyn frowned at me and I rolled my eyes. "I can't imagine whatever vendetta Octavia has against me is some court secret. Is it my affiliation with Kane? Everyone in Solaris knows him as a great betrayer, right?"

Wyn's soft curls fluttered with his sigh. "Most have forgotten the rebellion ever even happened. Lazarus ensured that." He adjusted his leg, clearly debating how much more to share.

I held my breath.

"Octavia, like Lazarus's late wife, is more witch than Fae, but she does carry the blood of both. I think . . ." Wyn's eyes met mine with a wince. "I think she coveted the role you're being primed for."

That tea rose up like acid in my stomach. "*She* wanted to be queen?"

Wyn only nodded. "But she can't bear him full-blooded heirs."

I almost asked what gave Octavia the idea she could rule beside

Lazarus in the first place, but a new question had formed in my mind.

"Why hasn't Lazarus come for me yet?"

I'd been here months, and hadn't seen the Fae king since my first day in Lumera. Since I'd been impaled high above Hemlock Isle, stolen away, and awoken tethered to that luxurious, stifling bed.

Wyn sighed. "Is this your last question?"

"If I say yes, will you answer it truthfully?"

He seemed to consider my question before saying, "You cannot conceive without your lighte."

"Why drain me then?" Wasn't that the sole reason Lazarus was keeping me alive? To impregnate me with more true Fae that only the two of us could create? "What does he need my harvested lighte for so urgently?"

Wyn remained quiet, though his eyes weren't displeased. Maybe just tired. Either way, I knew my probing was futile. I'd squeezed every answer I could from him.

My gaze found the golden spires peeking through smog outside my window. "Is it winter yet?"

"I thought that was your last question."

When I remained silent his shoulders sagged. "No. The winter solstice is a week from today."

I nodded at my palms. "That means tomorrow is my birthday."

I would be twenty-one.

Twenty-one, and a prisoner. Held in a tower so high I might never see the ground again. Awaiting a fate worse than death, each day dragging me closer, and without a bead of lighte, single ally, or even halfway-plausible escape route.

Twenty-one, and wasting away.

And later that night, like all nights, I fell asleep to nightmares so ferocious, so abhorrent, I'd come to resent my own mind for crafting them. Leigh, weeping over our mother's body. Spiders with women's heads and wolfbeasts and gray, scaled dragons. Kane, soaked in blood, sputtering for life.

When I awoke, sweaty and panting, there was something new obscuring my vision. A nondescript brown box tied with twine, sitting atop my pillow.

With less caution than I should have employed, I wiped the sleep from my eyes and pried it open.

Inside was a delicate, carved hairpin.

Two identical iron spears met at the top where three daisies of different sizes curved around the outstretched wings of a swallow in flight.

The smile that cracked my lips was the first I'd felt in months.

3

~❖~

KANE

MY FISTS CRACKLED WITH OBSIDIAN THORNS AND SHAD-owed scales as I beheld Len, no longer on a worm-rotted wooden stool, but now seated in a sleek upholstered leather chair. Fit for a king rather than a man. Or a witch or a beast—I still didn't know what Len was. He hadn't answered my question.

"What *are* you?" I snarled once more. My rage sent the flames of the white candles around us flickering.

"Would it make a difference? I can't help you."

Fury—blazing fury—radiated through my chest. "Why *not*?"

"I serve the many realms. Not heartsick boys."

Serve the many realms . . . "Do not lie to me."

The man that wasn't Len frowned as he stood, his chair scuffing along the luxe rug beneath us. "About which part? The heartsick boys or . . ."

My mouth was inexplicably dry as I watched him pour himself a glass of whiskey from an ornate carafe. "A God? You're a Fae God?"

He dipped his chin. "Frankly, I thought you'd get there quicker, boy."

Was it possible that a God truly stood before me? I jerked my head around as if I could shake the shock away. "What is a Fae God doing holed up in Vorst?"

Irritation crested in his depthless eyes. "Do you have no fear? Most used to bow before me."

Used to. My mind scattered and realigned itself twice over. "A disgraced God. A banished one," I murmured. "What did you do?"

The man that was not the White Crow took his seat once more, now with a swirling amber drink. "I interfered with the lives of mortals. Who knew compassion for lesser beings was an existential sin?"

I had come all this way. Flown through hail and wind and ice. Topped clouds and peaks and pines higher than the stars. I'd scoured the Pearl Mountains for the White Crow. Scaled a mountain—and plunged from it—for days trying to reach him. And now I beheld a true Fae God. I knew, without a shadow of a doubt, that this was the only chance I would get.

"You know what I seek," I said, so low I hardly heard myself. "Can you make me full-blooded? I'm nearly so already. My father, Lazarus—"

"I don't require your recounting, boy. I watched your father rock in his cradle."

"Then you know what a monster he is. You know that blade may be gone already. Turn me, and let me rid this world of him."

"The blade cannot be destroyed," the God said, bored eyes on his drink. "Not by anyone."

"That won't stop my father." I would have tied a thousand

weights to the thing and sunk it to the bottom of the Ocean of Ore. Or fed it to an ogre, the blade safe within its monstrous gut.

"It didn't stop him. But the blade always found its way back. If the Blade of the Sun cannot be with its master, it will find a new one, mortal or otherwise."

Adrenaline and lighte both recessing, I slumped into my own plush leather chair across from him. "Where is it now?"

"With your father. In Solaris."

"Turn me," I said, heart in my throat. "I will do anything you ask."

"I did ask. You answered incorrectly."

"Your questions don't matter," I bit out, slamming my hands onto the heavy table between us. "She isn't *alive*."

The God only tsked. "Your intentions are what matter to me."

He had said he served the realms. Perhaps it was my integrity I needed to prove.

"You can decree the future, I'm sure. See all, know all . . . Tell me I am not the best chance we have to rid this world of my father. Tell me I don't wish to save the lives of those threatened by him more than anyone alive. *Nobody's* intentions are more pure."

The God only laughed. "Hers were."

"Arwen's?" I hadn't said her name aloud in over two months. The syllables slid cruelly across my tongue. Profound grief I thought I'd buried rose up my throat and coiled around my jaw.

And I couldn't stand it—couldn't stand another moment on this earthly plane knowing she wasn't here, too. Here was my only chance at giving her death an ounce of meaning and I couldn't convince him my intentions were pure? "I carry her will inside my heart. Consider her virtue, her morality, my own."

Whether he detected the tenor of pain in my voice, I wasn't sure. The God's unflinching gaze only burrowed into mine.

Despite how I was breaking, I pushed on. "Look inside my soul. Tell me I don't mean it."

The Fae God considered me.

His judging gaze seared across my tensed brows, my burning eyes. My fingers, splintering the wooden arms of the extravagant chair. A sensation stirred in my chest, and I wondered if the man had the ability to somehow dig his hands through my ravaged heart.

The Fae God's jaw stiffened. A breeze rustled the gauzy curtains. The wisps of smoke drifted from the incense over to the table until ash fell softly on the rich mahogany. I tried to draw in one single even breath.

When his glare found mine again, a sliver of hope sparked in my chest.

"You must swear on everything you own. Your kingdom, your coin, your people, that you will—"

"I will *kill him*. I swear it more ardently than anything I've ever sworn."

"Swear on her. That he will perish, one way or another."

The urge to bark out a laugh almost knocked me from my chair. "I swear on Arwen's grave. I will do it *for* her. In her honor."

The Fae God only scowled, but triumph soared inside my chest. I had him.

"I must warn you, boy, even if I were to try, I have never done such a thing. In the earliest days, when there was only Lumera, full-blooded Fae were born when Gods copulated with mortals . . ."

That was how Arwen had been conceived and born full-blooded—the mating of a Fae God and her mortal mother.

"But," he went on, shaking me from my recollection of that rainy night outside Mariner's Pub, "I have never taken a Fae and rebirthed him for the sole purpose of turning him true."

I wasn't clever enough to trick a Fae God. I was a mere blunt instrument. "Try."

"There may be grave consequences."

"I know what I am asking."

"The risk—"

"Do," I gritted out, "your worst."

A single wave of that hand once more and an elegant, elongated wineglass appeared at the table before me. Not wine, but thick, bone-pale liquid inside.

His eyes were vicious. "Drink."

That color— "What is it?"

The God only smirked. "You know what it is."

Lilium.

I knew better than to say what echoed in my mind like a death knell: *That will kill me.* Instead, I took two bracing, fortifying breaths—

And I drank.

It was as if I had guzzled liquid lightning. Charring my throat, seizing my body as it oozed down my gullet. I choked on most of it, sputtering half up, collapsing, knocking the chair out from under me. It clattered somewhere behind me, shattering some bottle . . . I didn't know. I couldn't think. Couldn't *breathe* as agony shrieked through me. As my soul fled my body, digging through layers of earth for her—

CONSCIOUSNESS FOUND ME SPRAWLED ACROSS THE POLISHED wood floor. Alive, it seemed. And still in that sleek den belonging to a God. Bergamot incense and pungent spirit filled my nostrils. I choked back a gag.

My mouth ached. My very skin . . . weaker, somehow. The pulse sliding along my veins, so quiet I couldn't hear it. I grasped at my body, my jaw, my thundering heart. "What did you do?"

My muscles, as I stood, sore though I'd barely climbed today. My tongue, heavy in my mouth. My eyesight, blurred . . .

"It's only temporary—"

But I couldn't hear past my own horror. "I'm . . . *mortal.*"

"All rebirth demands death. Now you are a slate, cleared and readied for a new inscription."

"How?" I hardly grit out.

"A weapon forged with not only my own power but the other eight Elder Gods' as well. A relic to grant you the blood you seek."

"The blade . . ."

"Touch the steel once, and you will regain your lighte tenfold." Len's eyes gleamed with victory. "You will be reborn, full-blooded."

Despite accomplishing all I'd set out to, relief evaded me. I was a mortal man. Mortal, until I got my hands on the blade. "That was not the agreement," I breathed.

The God stood from the table. "It's already been done."

"You knew all along, didn't you?"

For the first time, remorse crossed his eyes. "I had an inkling."

I thought I might hurl myself at him. Claw the skin clean off his face. But I was no longer Fae. I shouldn't have risked the wrath of a God when I was, and I certainly wouldn't now.

"And if I never touch the blade?" I asked around my splitting headache. "If I can't find it?" A simple fall down the stairs could kill me now. I'd never make it through Lumera. I'd never locate the blade in the palace unscathed.

"The realms will be doomed."

No, no, *no*—

Why had he done all of this? He knew I could never destroy my father if I wasn't Fae. Why did I need to swear to complete the prophecy in her place? Why did my intentions matter to him at all? How could he—

A singular, near-juvenile hope blazed in my mind. "Was this all a test? Are you . . . Will you bring her back?"

Ice in that voice as he regarded me with less than pity. "No."

"Could you?" I had to know. "Are you choosing not to?"

"I would have," he said, pushing his chair neatly back into the table as if finishing up supper. "If it were possible."

"Why? *Why* isn't it possible?" I was pathetic, and I knew he was sneering at me, and that nothing I said would work. Knew that I was weak and broken, covered in my own sickness and sweat, and *still*, I couldn't stop the words from shoving past my lips. "I'll bring you her body. I'll scour the realms for it. I will pay any price you demand. Obey any request."

"Go, boy. Find the blade."

"Please." I knelt to the floor, my mortal knees cracking against the wood. "*Please.*" My throat was so tight I could barely speak around it. Tears burned in my eyes.

"Please," I begged, wrung out. "Please bring her back to me."

"Find the blade, Kane."

When I lifted my bleary eyes to him, the Fae God was gone. The polished walls replaced by that grim cobbled stone. Bone-deep chill where there had been warmth. And my inedible meat pie, growing cold beside a dying hearth.

4

ARWEN

I KNEW MY LIGHTE HAD RETURNED THE MOMENT I'D OPENED my eyes. It had only been four days since my last harvesting. Usually it took a week. This was some kind of record.

The days in which my lighte regenerated were the most hopeful, and thus the very hardest, and I took steadying, soothing breaths to remind myself of that fact before I got carried away.

Just the tingle of power at my fingertips was enough to send my mind down a thousand varied, unorganized paths: *Set the entire room ablaze and make a run for it when they come for you. Use your round lighte shield as a battering ram and bowl yourself through the locked doors. Hold Maddox hostage with those long strands of white sun and force the guards to let you leave.*

I'd lost days swept up in those fantasies. Breaking free. Running all the way home. Scooping Leigh into my arms. Mari's bright hair, Dagan's loving scowl . . .

And then I'd have to remind myself of the reality: by the time my lighte regenerated even close to enough to enact any of those plans, I'd be harvested once again.

But the lighte in my veins didn't only mean power. Life, strength, *energy* returned to my body and the urge to take off running, to move and stretch and *fight* was just shy of agonizing. I hadn't run in months—maybe the longest stretch I'd gone since childhood—and I missed the meditation most on days like this, when I knew I actually *could* move if I so chose. It was like being given sacks of coin and sent into an overflowing, glittering candy shop only to learn the sweets tasted of someone else's spit.

Conjuring a similar taste in my mouth, Maddox smacked my doors open and leveled a glare at me. "The king wishes to see you in the baths."

My heart darted like a hare from a hawk.

"Now?" A stupid question.

Maddox's expression told me he agreed. "Yes, now."

I crawled from the bed, still in one of the fussy collared night-gowns I'd been gifted. When I'd searched the suite my first week here, I'd found drawers upon drawers—an entire closet—piled high with finery of every dense fabric and opulent, jewel-toned color. Teal and caramel and emerald dresses, gold-threaded shoes, diamond drop earrings.

I'd never wanted to set so many nice things on fire so badly.

Swatting away the fog of sleep, I made my way to the armoire and scrunched my nose up at the scent of apricot syrup that permeated the wardrobe. I could only imagine the entire castle had been spelled to make all the dust and cobwebs smell like pungent fruit, and I'd come to despise the fragrance. I missed mothballs.

I'd just wrapped a hand around one dresser knob when Maddox called out, "You won't need to change."

I sucked in a shaking breath, still facing the armoire. *Don't give that gargoyle the satisfaction of your fear,* Kane's voice commanded in my head.

Maddox and Wyn escorted me down a hallway I'd only pictured for two months on end. I'd been stored in that tower like supplies for the winter—and the new sights were as unnerving and exquisite as I'd imagined.

A feat of industrial power and intricacy: wheels and cogs, iron and steel, gold and diamond and rubies. The marble floor, red and reflective as glossy blood. Impossibly high ceilings, interior archways that served as bustling bridges from one wing to the next, balconies and windows offering glimpses into elegant, manicured courtyards absent of flowers, ringed instead with immaculately sheared hedges. Not a single leaf out of place.

The scent of ash was thick in the air. My nostrils stung as I asked Wyn, "Was there a kitchen fire?"

His limp appeared to be bothering him today. He favored his good leg as he struggled to keep up with Maddox and me. "Sometimes it rains right after dawn."

I blinked at him, though he kept his soft hazel eyes ahead of us. "Sometimes it rains . . . ash?"

Wyn shook his head like that would've been ridiculous. "Fire."

Of course. Of course it *rained fire* in Solaris. I didn't even bother to ask how Lazarus convinced his court that it was nothing to concern themselves with. How the people outside the walled city protected themselves. I didn't care to hear the truth or the lies.

I'd noticed handmaidens in those dark uniforms slip through passages that blended seamlessly into the walls, or open doors that were made to look like bookshelves, or move aside statues that sat atop entire hidden sets of stairs.

A winding palace of tricks and lies. I shouldn't have expected anything else.

But after being bound like veal in that suite, I was grateful for the exposure. I was grateful even for the long distance between wings. The castle's bridges and pathways were like a twining labyrinth and must've spanned more miles than all of Abbington. My tower seemed at the very opposite of wherever these baths were.

Baths. And Maddox telling me not to change out of my nightgown . . . The time had likely come. Despite the roiling nausea, I kept placing one foot after another. I had to be strong if I wanted to live.

But Maddox's atonal humming didn't help. It rang through the now-empty, echoing halls like a death march as the three of us walked, my soft-soled slippers light next to Maddox's and Wyn's heavy boots. I waited to be led before doors that would open to a damp, darkened bathhouse like the one where I'd grown up. Waited for the smell of stagnant water and sweat and furtive joining.

Instead, I was brought before an entire wing guarded by at least twelve more kingsguards.

Maddox and Wyn guided me past the silver sea of men, and the wing yawned open for us. A sterile glass atrium—cold and spare. A few marble pillars, to hold the impossibly high ceilings upright. Iron bookcases. Twin white chairs without a single divot or stain, made of the fur of something once woolly and tufted and thick. Likely a creature I couldn't conjure even with my imagination at its most boundless.

And five glossy black doors inside all that glass. Each with one ruby-red handle that made me think of a bloodied hand desperately attempting to pry it open. That, and a different golden symbol affixed to each door's center: a moon, a sun, a wave, a leaf, and a flame.

We walked toward the middle door, the one with the wave insignia, just as two kingsguards passed us by, each with a hulking glass barrel of white, shimmering lighte. I could have sworn the essence was humming through the drum, and the meager lighte in my veins pulsed, as if like could call to like.

My lighte. That was *my lighte—*

My neck craned so I could watch them heft the barrels through the entry affixed with the marking of the sun.

"Lazarus keeps all the harvested lighte in his own wing?"

Neither guard bothered to respond to me, and I was ushered inside.

Lazarus's private baths were nothing like my childhood town's bathhouse. Where Abbington had one single rectangular bath under stone pillars and faintly mildewed wood, before me sprawled dozens and dozens of steam-hazed, opaque blue-green pools of water, stretching on and on like rolling hills. Some as still as a frozen lake, some undulating despite their emptiness of bodies, a current gently rocking the water's surface from deep below. Some even bubbled raucously, sputtering droplets into the moist air.

We stood on a white stone balcony, and I inhaled minerals and sulfur and marble and soap as my eyes pored over all the milky turquoise water. Like everything I'd seen in Solaris, the baths were a showy, excessive extravagance. I'd take Kane's peaceful porcelain tub any day.

The balcony split on either side into two sets of hazy stairs that wove deeper and deeper through the baths, working their way around to its center, where the largest pool lay. Rippled and misted with steam, the pale blue water was held without edges and cascaded into all that surrounded it.

And in the heart of all that effervescent, peaceful jade water— Lazarus.

His undeniable beauty was possibly the most vile thing about his appearance. He had Kane's granite-carved jaw and piercing slate eyes. After a millennium alive, his thick, dark hair had grayed a bit, but he still wore it confidently overgrown like his son. But Lazarus had none of Kane's warmth. None of his joy. That grim-set mouth, steely lowered brows, and broad rippling chest made my stomach heave. I was grateful I hadn't eaten this morning. I would have retched.

"Arwen," he said, and though he hadn't spoken loudly, the echo of the rushing water carried his words right up to the shell of my ear. "Care to join me?"

I set my jaw. "I'd prefer not to wet my hair, thanks."

He said nothing from the center of that enormous, undulating pool shrouded in steam, and Maddox and Wyn dragged me down the set of stairs closest to us despite my flailing, depositing me at the overflowing lip.

Warm water seeped into my slippers, and I curled my toes as if I could spare them from the heat.

"Join me." His voice was deeper than when it summoned me in my nightmares. Harsher than even my own fear could replicate. His silver eyes bored into my own, and I tried not to dwell on the physical similarities between him and his son. Neither to mar Kane's beautiful image in my mind nor to endear me to the beast I beheld.

Would Lazarus truly force himself on me here in these baths? In front of all these men? My eyes cut to the handful of silver-clad guards standing watch. To Wyn and Maddox behind me, the latter's hand still a vise around my arm.

"Don't be modest," Lazarus cooed. "You've nothing they haven't seen before."

With a nod of his head to one straight-faced guard, my frilly nightdress and undergarments were sliced down along my back. The guard's lighte scented the air as satin and errant buttons pooled around my ankles on the wet floor.

I clenched my fists until they ached.

He *wanted* me to squirm. Wanted to strip me of not just my clothes but my dignity.

Yet so much had changed since the night I was mortified to take my mere tunic off in front of Lieutenant Bert. All those months ago—knees wet on a blood-soaked cottage floor . . .

I let that weak glimmer of lighte I'd woken up with zip through my body as I resisted the urge to cover myself. Instead, I stepped from the puddle of garments, wholly bare, and glowered at the Fae king as I entered his bath.

5

❦

KANE

I WAS SETTLING MYSELF AGAINST A LONG-AGO OVERTURNED wagon half buried in snow, readying my pathetic mortal body for sleep, when a branch snapped.

All the hairs on my body rose.

Snap. Another.

Whatever was hunting me was heavy-footed.

Exhausted irritation—not fear—fogged my gaze as I squinted into the moonlit tree line. I'd been without my lighte for less than four days and already it was more infuriating than anything else. Had I known I'd be stripped of my power, I'd have taken a horse or sled through Vorst. But I'd relied on my dragon's wings to carry me through the region's skies and now . . . now as I slept in ditches and trekked on foot through miles and miles of silent, blustering ice, it seemed the only real gift the Fae God had bestowed upon me was a near-constant urge to jerk my chin over my shoulder.

On my way from bleak, gray Vorst to Pearl's capital, Carrus, I'd narrowly avoided snarling white leopards and lumbering grizzly bears.

Animals I wouldn't have batted an eye at a week ago. I'd taken a mixed approach of hiding, distraction, and the occasional hunter's trap, but this thing . . . whatever snapped that branch, it had been tracking me.

I'd heard the sounds a few miles back, but kept moving until night sunk the temperature so low my breath crystalized in the air before it was halfway out my nose. As the daylight withered away, this decaying wheelbarrow had beckoned to me like a mirage in a desert of ice. Now, as I crouched behind it, its termite-laden wood was all that stood between me and whatever was out there.

Another branch snapped, followed by the rustle of scarce pines. Wind howled at my neck and I pulled my hood up in protection from the sting. Every layer of snow between my thick winter leathers and fur-lined cloak nudged me that much closer to frostbite.

Without making a sound, I stood and unsheathed my sword. Moonlight glinted off its shining surface. A bright harvest moon. For some inexplicable reason the otherworldly glow reflected in my steel made my chest tighten.

A bleak moan as something broke through the tree line was my only hint.

And then, she was shuffling toward me through the snow, her hobbling, disfigured feet facing backward. Matted white hair hung around her ghoulish face, lit by heavy moonlight.

A snow wraith.

I scrambled back on rocky ice, heart in my throat.

My skin was far too thin over my muscles. My breath too shallow sawing in and out of my lungs.

I'd never felt much empathy for mortals—not out of malice, I'd just never had the errant thought. But now . . . I'd never look at a mortal man the same. Each new day they woke up alive was nothing short of a miracle.

Fishing for the dagger in my boot, I careened over the wheelbarrow I'd thought might serve as my roof. The wraith moaned, unhinged jaw creaking with the force of her fury. My hands tightened on the hilt. Perhaps a straight shot through the head—

Before she could draw any closer I hurled the weapon at her skull.

And missed by a mile, my dagger landing in a mountain of fresh snow. The skeletal undead woman didn't even flinch.

Fuck. No Fae strength. No Fae aim. I'd been reliant on my abilities my whole life—I wasn't sure who I was without them.

I tightened my grip on my longsword. The frosty blade didn't waver, even as my mortality became weighty in my grasp. This simple sword—carved of plain steel and brandished now by human arms—was all that stood between me and an undead witch hungering for my soul.

That was what they'd always assumed wraiths were. Witches who had died in tragic, inhumane ways. Who had screamed so loudly in their final minutes that the raw, broken moan carried over to their afterlife.

The wraith before me released another guttural howl, those twisted feet shuffling her forward, and I decided the folklore was true. Ancient, rageful, and wretched. Lolling tongue and gray flaking skin. Her weather-scarred belt and necklace threaded with human bones. A barbaric practice—the jewels of her kill.

When she charged me, I drove my sword clean through her heart. Sure, and straight. Not a quiver in my form, despite the way the ice-cold air funneled through my aching lungs.

The wraith howled. Her inky-black mouth wrenched open, that long gray tongue twitching. I twisted the blade and shoved it farther, cutting through brittle bone and old, leathery tissue.

She moaned again, and a sick foreboding curled low in my gut.

She was . . . not dying.

Not weakened in the slightest.

In fact, as my heartbeat rattled my ribs, and true, punishing fear wormed through my clenched jaw, the snow wraith wrapped her hands, both missing more than half their fingers, around the blade and *pulled it deeper.*

Dragging herself closer to me, reaching that venomous, lethal tongue toward me again.

If it reached my face—my mouth—

I wasn't sure how much of a soul I had left after losing Arwen, but whatever scraps were buried inside my heart this wraith would surely unearth and devour with her kiss.

I yanked the sword back, trying to extricate it, and was reminded once more how little power I held as a mortal.

The sword was lodged too snugly inside her chest.

I yanked and tugged, dodging her stumped fingers and unhinged jaw. Her breath washed over my face—no warmth, as no blood pumped in those reanimated veins—and the stench . . . like carrion piled high in the sweltering sun. Like death, stolen from its peaceful void and forced to wander and search for eternity.

Stark understanding brought my eyes back up to the savage, frozen witch. The talismans and bone relics hanging around her neck. Tokens from a past life. And her sorrowful cloudy eyes . . . the unbearable, unending pain there.

The wraith released a viscerally unholy moan and lunged, faster now—

I recoiled too fast and landed on my ass, crawling backward as the wraith threw herself over the wheelbarrow, landing even farther onto the sword and eliciting another low, guttural sound.

Too close, too close—

Righting myself, I lurched up and back, fighting to keep that gap between us as wide as I could. I'd never outrun her, she'd never grow tired . . . and my only two weapons—one deep in the endless snow and the other lodged inside her body. One more step backward slammed my spine against the trunk of a tree, and I didn't think as I spun and climbed.

Didn't think, didn't *breathe*, as I dug one foot after another into bark. Up and up and *up*. Not as my hands grew raw and stiff from cold, burning and numb at once. Nor as pines and ice and bark cut through my vision and into my eyes.

Some voice in my mind, sunny and bright, pointed out that had I not climbed that wall of ice over and over, I'd never have the muscle memory to make it this high. That all my hard work had not entirely been for nothing.

Fair point, bird.

Up and up and *up* I rose as those desolate moans grew fainter. Higher still, as the snow wraith wailed, begging at the base of the tree for one taste, one *lick* of my soul.

When I was sure my hope had been proven true—that the wraith could not climb up behind me—I nestled myself between two branches spread in a V and sucked in lungful after lungful of freezing air.

That blur of matted white hair moaned from the ground, my steel shooting up through her back. Devastated. Brokenhearted. More sorrowful than I could bear to listen to. The earsplitting bellow of pain was too familiar.

Hours and hours passed.

The night grew from cold to frigid. Owls hooted. Snow fell.

My face was so numb the flakes that landed didn't melt.

At some point my shivering became a hazard to my position in the branches, and I tied myself to the narrow trunk with my belt in case I passed out. But sleep never came. My adrenaline too insistent on my survival. That still-wailing wraith too ravenous at the base of the tree.

And no sleep—no sleep meant hours on hours of wretched thoughts. Gutting memories. Imagined conversations that hacked at my heart.

"I can't live like this."

Her full lips turn down. "I know."

"Are you in pain?"

"No. I'm happier here."

I reach for her warm, soft skin, but all I feel is night. "Are you lying, my little bird?"

"Do you want me to lie?"

By the time the sky lightened to a dull, barren gray—the only color of daylight in Gods-forsaken Vorst—I'd lost sight of the ground altogether. Everything had blurred—the white of fresh snow, the white of the wraith's thick hair, the white of the clouds that misted across the peak.

But her wails had ceased and I knew that meant she'd abandoned me. For the wraith would never stop moaning. She'd wander these barren, frostbitten lands eternally. Stumbling through each day and night and day again. Sobbing for the life she'd lost. Begging for a soul to share. A mournful, weeping husk with a thick steel sword lodged clean through her heart.

I sighed, exhaustion and misery weighing heavy on my mind and thick on my tongue. My foot maneuvered to the nearest branch below to guide me down—

And missed.

Fuck, fuck—

Grasping at pines and branches, arms flailing, I fell—

And landed with a *crack* atop the capsized wheelbarrow.

The pain that radiated through my back and side was nauseating. So much so, I rolled over and heaved twice into the fresh, new snow. Nothing came out. I hadn't eaten in days.

If I didn't reach Carrus before sundown, I'd have to kill my dinner with my hands.

I stood on weak legs, body screaming, and scanned the dim morning on the mountainside.

No wraith. No creatures.

Just a sprawling, hostile ocean of stark white snow.

As I trekked, dawn slipped into early morning, and unfamiliar sunlight blanketed the simple mountain pass in prismatic, near-blinding white. That unfiltered sun—the clearing of those soupy, constant clouds—meant I was drawing closer to the capital. I traipsed farther, willing my legs not to collapse in relief or fatigue.

On and on, through billowing, gentle clouds like freshly spun cotton, and down trails that I'd noticed were now marked by droopy-headed snowdrops. And then . . . cobblestone. Sturdy, merciful cobblestone.

And cheery brick storefronts. The scent of hot breakfast rolls, and gardens of crocus and hellebore. The temperature now a pleasant winter chill, with snowflakes that melted along my sleeves. Genially grunting oxen with wings drifted through the skies above—jolly patrons with satchels of groceries at their saddles.

Finally, *blessedly*, I'd arrived in Carrus.

The floating kingdom's capital was like a wonderland—a jolly, bustling town of wooden cottages and flowerpots and cozy brick chimneys. All built into the tallest peak of the kingdom's floating mountains.

I ducked under an archway overflowing with bunches of ethereal winter hydrangea, each leaf dripping icicles that sparkled like clean diamonds. The ancient temples I passed were gilded by golden sunlight. Elegant swans drifted under their tea bridges and across glittering, clear ponds.

And while I appreciated the safety that came with candy-pink clouds and ruddy-cheeked children, each dainty, snow-tipped flower or winged animal . . . all of it only made me think of her.

I had the disturbing thought somewhere between a cart selling warmth elixirs and a sprawling ice plain tinged by the afternoon light that if I were left alone too long with my thoughts anywhere, I'd suffer similarly. Every brunette tree would conjure her hair. Every ray of sunlight, her generous power—

By the time I reached Carrus's sky docks—the wide planks held by sturdy, white rope and burnished supports—my mood was almost as wrecked as my body. The port, which hung staggeringly in midair, was hewn of some shiny white stone and dropped right off into violet sunset clouds. Burly dockhands helped townsfolk bundled in so much fur they looked like precious packages onto woolly, winged oxen—luftalvors—which took off into the skies below, one after another. Each luftalvor in flight sent senseless envy through my bones and an aching where my wings used to sprout.

"Excuse me," I called over to the stationmaster, though it came out like a grunt. The man's eyes cast down to my feet, and I realized my boots had lost their soles. "I need to sail for Onyx Kingdom."

The gruff man that turned had thick hair and an even thicker beard, with the dry, cracked lips and dulled eyes of someone who'd spent the last three decades whipping through arid skies.

"We don't fly there," he said, as if I should have known as much.

"I have coin. I'll pay triple your going rate."

"I said," he grumbled, turning back to his luftalvors and their low, fussy bellows, "we *don't fly there*. Now get. No peasants loitering on the docks."

It didn't seem worth explaining to him that, despite my overall disheveled, frozen appearance, I wasn't a peasant, and in fact had more coin to offer than he'd know what to do with.

"How can I get to Willowridge?" I said, each word a true effort.

"Nobody in Carrus will fly you there," he growled between the impenetrable bristles of his beard. "Onyx's nasty creatures will eat these guys out of the sky." He motioned back at the fluffy white luftalvors in their pen behind him. Two of the winged oxen gave me plaintive looks and a third shuffled over, feathered wings brushing against coiled fur as it licked its friend's face. "Maybe the captains in Sleetcliff, but I can't say for sure."

"Where is Sleetcliff?"

The stationmaster coughed up a wad in the back of his throat and spit it onto the iridescent white stone at his feet. "About a fortnight from here."

My teeth fused together. "Can one of your captains fly me to Sleetcliff?"

"We don't fly there."

"Where the fuck *do* you fly?"

"Watch your *tone*," he snapped, drawing a gleaming dagger from his scabbard. I reached for my own. I'd make this simpleton crawl on his knees and *beg* to fly me anywhere he'd be allowed to keep his balls.

My fingers grasped around nothing and my heart sank. *Right, no dagger. No sword.*

"Now," he growled. "Get off my *fucking* dock."

I sized up the captain. Likely in his midforties. Strong from years of flying and handling hefty luftalvors. If I'd eaten anything in the last three days, or slept at all, or had a weapon, or fewer injuries . . . even then I'd give my mortal self a fifty-fifty chance.

Without another word I shuffled out of his way.

Sleigh bells rang through the busy town as I rounded a tavern. Rosemary and bay leaves scented the air and my stomach turned on itself. The vivid alpenglow cast the surrounding mountaintops in shades of clementine and carnation pink.

It would be night soon. I'd have to spend another night away from Shadowhold, wasting time, withering—

"You get kicked off the docks, too?"

I jerked my chin toward the voice and found a kid, scuffed and tattered and far too pale, sitting on the ground. He reclined against the brick wall of the tavern, feet folded beneath him.

"Yes, actually," I replied, wary.

"They think we'll toss ourselves off the edge. Wouldn't be good for business, I guess." He shrugged, picking something off his filthy pants. "I just like the view."

But the peasant child had given me an idea.

"Any interest in helping me with something?"

SCREAMS SPLIT THE HAPPY, WINTRY TOWN. THEY BLEATED out from the sky docks—begging for someone, anyone, to save the little peasant boy from his own impending death.

"Come any closer," the kid vowed, somewhere past the thickening crowd, *"and I'll jump!"*

He was a marvelous actor. Perhaps using true pain and fear—the injustice of living on the streets—to power his performance. Too bad, then. With the amount of coin I'd given the kid, he'd spend the rest of his life fat and warm and perhaps thus untalented.

My assumption that the stationmaster wouldn't let a boy off himself on his dock was correct—not for any noble reason, but simply for the optics. I watched from behind the tavern as the bearded, panicked man pushed through throngs of onlookers craning their necks in both fear and fascination.

On brutally aching legs I curved through the crowd until I reached the luftalvor pen, hopped the wooden gate, and climbed atop the first one I could find that was awake.

"Come on, buddy." I grunted. "Let's go."

The winged ox didn't even stir.

"Let go of me!"

They'd caught the kid.

I'd only have minutes—seconds—until the stationmaster returned.

"Up." I kicked at the creature once. "Off!"

He only snorted.

But he had wings.

And I'd had wings once, too. And nothing sent me flying like—

I wrapped my hand around a plume of the luftalvor's feathers and gripped, yanking them back toward me.

The ox shot into the sky so fast I nearly rolled clean off and plunged to my mortal death. But my hands—as if still imbued with some Fae instincts—wrapped around the reins with a stronger grip than I'd ever exerted, and I held myself to the creature.

Inhaling the first real breath I'd taken since I left that Fae God in his enchanted hovel, I watched as the cheery, elevated capital of Carrus became a speck among towering white mountaintops, and then watercolor clouds swallowed the kingdom whole.

6

⁂

ARWEN

Lazarus didn't so much as smirk as I joined him.

His eyes were unreadable, trained on mine, and I remembered he could read my thoughts as plainly as if I'd screamed them at him.

He said nothing as I stepped one foot down into the shallow steps, and then descended until my body was submerged. The rush of flowing water and bubbling of springs filled my head and I dipped myself under.

Enveloped by warm silence, all I could hear was my own pulse in my eardrums.

Liquid, peaceful stillness.

When I emerged and wiped my eyes, Lazarus wasn't even looking.

"Quite the performance," he said, his back to me as he surveyed his steamy, water-lush domain. "I'd title it *Woman Proves She Is Different Now.*"

I only scowled.

A gnarled scar cut down the muscled planes along his spine. The damaged skin undulated, rippling as he spread his arms across the water's surface. Kane had bestowed that upon him. Wielding the Blade of the Sun, all those years ago.

I stilled my mutilated heart into submission. Lazarus wouldn't hear my longing.

But I could channel that rage. Could try to use any minutes alone with him to my advantage.

"Was it your own revenge? Back at Hemlock . . ." Despite the agony, I allowed myself to think of Kane's roars of anguish. "Making him think you'd killed me?"

"Nothing of the sort." Lazarus turned, expression still unreadable. "My son has always been ruled by his emotions. I only sought to heighten them. However, it appears I got more than I bargained for—your prince hasn't been seen in months. Perhaps I succeeded in breaking him completely. Perhaps he's gone mad from the loss. Or perhaps . . . a fate far more tragic: death at his own hand."

Even as dread curled around my lungs, I didn't break from his unflinching stare. "Kane would never abandon his people."

Lazarus reclined against the pool's edge. "Your love is enviable. My own wife died many years ago."

I could have screamed. "You *killed* her."

"Spoken like someone who's never been forced to sacrifice for a greater cause."

I would have sacrificed my very life to end you.

If he'd heard my thoughts, he didn't comment. "But you will. You and I, Arwen, are the last two of our kind in existence. Together we will repopulate an entire race of strong, powerful true Fae. No weak halflings, no dirty mortals. That sacrifice will be your legacy. You should be on your knees, thanking me for such an honor."

Before I could spit at him, Kane's voice snarled softly through my mind. *Don't play into his game, bird. That's what he wants.*

"There are only two of us, we'll never have an entire realm of true Fae. They'd have to—"

It was his smug, pleased expression that silenced my words and sent my stomach churning.

"Inbreeding?"

"Many great monarchies kept the bloodline pure with such practices. Ancient Fae and mortal alike."

The revolting thought was too much to comprehend. My own children, forced to breed with one another. With their own father, surely. "You foul, repugnant—"

"Those burns." Lazarus motioned to my torso. "Are they from my sergeant, whom you murdered?"

I fought the urge to cover myself as the memory of Halden's blistering iron sizzled against my skin. "Yes."

"And the one across your collarbone, or those down your back, are they all from him as well? A bit of a sadist, my sergeant." Lazarus tutted as if it was a shame. "Scarring my property . . . I'd take his other hand for that, were he still alive."

Revulsion twisted in my gut at the thought of Lazarus studying my naked body with such careful precision, like I was some prized specimen. Those scars were my memories. My strength fighting his wolflike mercenary. My will, unbroken by my stepfather's belt.

I sneered at him.

"Don't," he chastised. "You'll wrinkle the face of my queen."

When I curved my mouth down farther he only smirked and waded to stand under a steaming marble spigot shaped as the mouth of a fanged fish. He angled his neck, allowing the steaming fresh water to cascade down his marred back. "Maddox tells me you've been questioning Wyn about my motives."

My eyes betrayed me, slamming into Maddox's cold, unflinching gaze. Why I felt surprised was beyond me. He was snide and callous and would clearly lick the ground Lazarus walked upon for a chance to move up in his ranks. But to have spied on Wyn and me . . . listened to our private conversations . . .

Maybe what upset me was the realization that I'd not had a single moment of true privacy since I'd been brought here.

But Maddox's smug lips curling upward had no effect on me now. Not compared to the fear in Wyn's dismayed hazel eyes. His bobbing throat sent waves of lighte rippling down my spine. Some strange instinct that confused *heal* with *protect*.

"I assumed you would have summoned me to your bed by now," I admitted to Lazarus, bracing myself. "But that's why I'm here, right?"

"Close those legs, eager girl."

Over the rush of water I heard Maddox cease his incessant atonal hum to snicker.

"The Lumerian Solstice is in a few days time. We celebrate the bountiful harvest at the end of autumn with a ball each year, and I'd like you to attend as my betrothed."

I scowled at him. "Could you not have just forced me? Why bring me here and ask?"

"That would not be very befitting of your future husband, would it? Have you been treated poorly while here, Arwen? No dungeon, no torture, no suffering. Frankly, I'm still waiting on your gratitude."

I opened my mouth to tell him he'd be waiting a long damn time for that, but—

He *needed* me. He needed me to behave beside him. To attend *willingly.* Maybe I could use this audience, this slight power I held, for information.

"What is it you celebrate? There is no harvest. There are no crops for the people of Lumera *to* harvest."

Lazarus's grin was withering in its cruelty.

What had Kane told me all those months ago in his wine cellar? That lighte was a resource born into every Fae from Lumera's earth, and if it was overused—either from the reaping of Lazarus's citizens or the influx of crowded slums—the land itself suffered.

I pointed to my bruised veins from months of harvesting. "Your land is dying because of this. It's why the air outside my room is choked with dirt. Why it rained *fire* this morning. Because you are juicing your own people to the pulp."

His teeth gleamed through the steam as he jerked his chin toward my veins again. "Perhaps that *is* the bountiful harvest we celebrate here in Solaris."

Of course. Lighte. All the lighte that allowed his people to live in excess while everyone outside the capital suffered.

And all the lighte he was gathering for his war.

"You'll change your mind on my practices soon enough," he added. "When we take Evendell and raze it of all the useless mortal lives, you and I will have fresh land for our offspring. We'll build Evendell into something grander than even Lumera's former glory. And one day only the truest Fae will inhabit that realm. Don't you want a world of creatures just like you? Isn't your power, your lighte *lonely?*"

Rage gripped me, bruising my heart with its iron grasp. "All those people, murdered . . . I will never aid you in such a quest. I will *never* bear you offspring. And I will never attend some ruthless, barbarian ritual disguised as a phony celebration."

Interest, not irritation, flickered in his depthless silver eyes as he prowled closer through the water. In a low, rough voice he said, "Octavia has been insatiable over you. Just dying to see you crawl over her coals. And with burns like those"—he ran a single pruned thumb across the top of my breast and I jumped backward, my skin writhing—"I'd imagine you have a particularly strong aversion to open flame on bare flesh. Shall we find out?"

No sooner did he say the words than the bath doors flew open with a calamitous crash. I flinched despite myself.

Octavia strode in, dreary gray dress hanging loosely off her bony figure and mopping up water as she walked across wet floors.

"Out," he instructed me, voice harsher than it had yet been.

Despite the heat from the bubbling springs and the steam rising off my skin, my veins had filled with ice. I paused, shivering. I could stay put and be forced from the water, or climb out of my own accord and voluntarily suffer Octavia's torture. And not just any torture—not a beating or a whipping—but the burning of my flesh.

I—I couldn't do it.

Smoke-scented visions of Halden's white-hot iron pressed against my abdomen in a damp Peridot jungle sent my fingers trembling.

I had a little bit of lighte—I was not completely powerless.

But when I stood from the water, cool air veiled in steam kissing across my neck and breasts and thighs . . . I wondered if I was not even *more* helpless than I had been before. Equipped with shreds of my power and unable to use any of it. It was barely a spark. I'd be overpowered immediately.

With as much courage as I could muster, I walked to Octavia. She was only a few inches taller than me, and I lifted my chin as she appraised my dripping body.

"You can't imagine," she hissed, "how long I've waited for this."

And I understood why now. She saw me as ungrateful for the only thing she craved: the throne at Lazarus's side. I wished I could tell her she could have it. I'd never wanted anything less.

With a soft whisper of words I didn't know and a whirl of earthly wind around the marble and suds, a bed of crackling coals presented themselves at my feet.

Each hiss that sounded when a bubbling pool nearby spit a drop of water atop them reminded me of the sound I'd hear—the sounds I'd *make*—when I was forced to kneel, still utterly naked. My skin, melting—

"Or," Lazarus said from the opaque turquoise pool, undulating as he waded through it, "you could attend the Solstice."

Hatred etched itself into my heart, my neck prickling as sweat gathered along my brow and underneath my arms. My body knew the agony. It knew, even as I chose now to let this happen, how desperately I'd fight the minute the glowing red coals touched my flesh.

How completely exposed and humiliated I'd be. Already was.

But if he wanted to announce me as his queen to the court—if he needed to show his power, his *bounty*—then I couldn't let him. Not under any circumstances.

So I said nothing.

"Goody." Octavia grinned.

Bravery failing me, I flinched as she moved for my head. Her snake smile grew as she grasped my hair, my scalp already screaming.

"Wait, wait," Lazarus drawled casually. Bored. "This won't do."

Oh, Stones, what now—

"Octavia, start with her hobbled guard, will you?"

"What?" My thin voice gave my horror away.

The kingsguards across the baths shifted. Maddox's eyes flashed with delight.

"Your Majesty," Wyn stammered. "Why?"

"You didn't think you'd go unpunished, did you? For what you revealed?"

Wyn opened his mouth, but to say what, I'd never know. Octavia's ruthless magic snatched him where he stood at the base of those sprawling alabaster stairs and yanked him toward the coals.

"Stop," I cried, clawing at Octavia. Lighte rippled beneath my skin, but my body froze. With some kind of enchantment, the sorceress brought Wyn down to his knees and held his face near the coals. Ready, *eager* to plunge him against the blanket of sizzling rock below.

Wyn was shaking. Stoic, but shaking nonetheless. He gritted his teeth as Octavia lowered his face.

The pleas ripped from me. "Stop, *please—*"

This couldn't happen, not to him. I couldn't stomach the awfulness. My imploring eyes shot to Lazarus and once again found his glare laced with more intrigue than anything else.

That . . . that was why he was doing this.

Because I couldn't stand the awfulness.

Why Lazarus was punishing Wyn. Not for his indiscretion. But because he knew I'd never let someone else suffer for my choices. He was using my morality against me. Waiting for me to fold—

And as Octavia pressed Wyn's clear, golden skin into the sizzling coals . . . I did.

"Fine, fine, I'll go!"

My voice rang out, loud enough for them to hear over the snap of the embers and the rumble of the hot springs somewhere deep down below our feet. Wyn's cheek hovered not an inch above the rocks. "I'll attend. I'll be good. Please, just *stop* this."

Octavia slid her eyes to her king.

I did the same, though nausea churned my stomach. I swallowed with a wince.

"How good?" Lazarus asked, one graying brow lifted.

"Whatever you need."

With a brief, curt nod from her king, Octavia released me and Wyn from our spells and the coals evaporated into mist.

Wyn didn't look at me as our matching exhales rent the room.

"I know you think yourself very courageous," Lazarus said, wading through the water to stand from the pool. His chiseled shoulders and powerful, thick legs did not look like they belonged to a man his age. They looked like he could crush me with one hard stomp. "That your prince will come to save you, or like some sword-wielding heroine you'll surprise us all and save yourself. But whether you grin and take it like a proper queen, bejeweled and draped in Solaris finery, or you're bound and muzzled in my dungeons like a sow for breeding, you *will* bear my heirs."

His eyes shredded me as he drew near, and I fought the urge to squirm.

"You are no champion. You are no brave heroine. You are no prophesied savior of realms. You, Arwen, are just a womb. That is all you will ever be, until one day, you are dead."

Octavia hadn't needed her coals. His words might as well have been a brand.

Somehow, I thought, *I will watch you die before that day comes.*

But Lazarus said nothing at all. He only slipped into a silk robe held by a kingsguard of his own and strolled out, leaving Wyn and Maddox in his wake, stiff as corpses.

Maddox's eyes held a carnivorous grin, and my neck and cheeks heated with shame. I looked down at my useless bare body, and my powerless hands, still tingling with lighte.

"Let's go, womb," Maddox hissed.

Wyn, still kneeling on the wet floor, said nothing at all.

The easy gurgles of the baths and rush of the water fountains filled my mind, replacing all the anger and self-hatred. All the loneliness and despair. I walked on unsteady legs, slipped my damp, ripped nightgown back on, and followed Maddox up that stone staircase. Wyn limped quietly behind us.

Out in the atrium, Maddox hummed a pleased tune to himself as he strolled past. Beside me, Wyn had slowed to a pace that resembled a crawl. I'd never seen his gait so slow and fitful.

Octavia had known what she was doing when she forced him to kneel. Hot, fresh ire filtered through me.

"I'm sorry," I said under my breath.

"What could you possibly be sorry for?"

"They used you to get to me."

Wyn shook his head, every step sending his armor jangling and curls rustling across his face. "I should never have shared with you what I did. Someone is always listening here."

Those words clanged through my mind.

Lazarus had so thoroughly ignored every single barb I'd flung at him in my thoughts. It wasn't like him. A man who made a point to show how deep inside your brain he was, and how powerless you were to stop him. I'd never forget how utterly horrifying it had been to be so invaded the first night we met in Siren's Bay. How even my own thoughts belonged to him.

"He didn't read my mind today." I barely murmured the words. Handmaidens and guards passed us as we strolled down the black-

and-white-walled halls, and Maddox was only a few feet ahead of us, that incessant tune filtering through his lips.

Wyn shrugged. "Perhaps he didn't find your thoughts worth listening to."

I had threatened him. Told him I'd watch him die. He hadn't even smirked.

Was it possible he was weaker today? Maybe ill?

"Wyn, why does he need *my* lighte?"

Wyn bared his teeth in a way that told me the pain in his knee was worsening. These hallways were endless—winding and rife with dizzying mirrors and hidden passageways. And those ornate ceilings with their arches and fine molding so, so high—all of it, built to inspire vertigo and aching, restless eyes.

"The lighte he reaps fuels everything," Wyn said with a wince. "This city. This palace. His mercenaries. His weaponry. The entire Lumerian war machine."

"But he drains me even though he needs me full of lighte to conceive. He must need *my* lighte specifically."

"You're full-blooded. Your lighte is more potent than anyone's, other than his."

Hadn't Kane told me many Fae and mortals alike in Solaris had become addicted to lighte once they'd begun to intake more than their body made? Had Lazarus become dependent on it? I was the only other full-blooded Fae alive. Maybe he needed my lighte to support his own.

He *was* weak. That must've been it. Why he wouldn't allow me even enough lighte to conceive. *He* couldn't produce an heir, either.

"Wyn . . ."

But Wyn's grimace told me what his next words confirmed. "Enough questions for today."

"Just one—"

"I *can't*."

I stopped in my tracks.

Wyn winced as he did the same, rubbing at his leg. His greaves were still wet where he'd knelt on that slick marble.

Of course he couldn't discuss this with me. Physically, mentally— I thought our burgeoning friendship might actually be killing the kingsguard.

And it was foolish of me as well. Hadn't I learned my lesson? I had no allies here. Someone was always listening, always ready to use you or your vulnerabilities against you. I couldn't confide in Wyn. I was thoroughly alone.

"Right," I said, my eyes finding the floor, my own reflection bloodred and warped. "I know."

"I'm sorry, Arwen." When I lifted my chin, Wyn stepped closer, eyes flickering with more sorrow, more guilt than I could stand. "Really. I am." He grasped at his knee once more, grimacing.

"Stay still." Before Maddox could notice, I knelt to the ground and pressed both my hands into Wyn's lame leg. Eager lighte jumped from my fingertips, thrilled to do *something* before it was ripped from my veins once again.

The cartilage beneath his armor was old and scarred, but with what little power I had, fresh muscle and sinew sprouted beneath my palms, reinforcing the weaker joints that had been sore for decades.

When the last meager drop of my power had permeated Wyn's skin, I stood.

"What . . ." Wyn flexed the limb in disbelief. Bending the joint and redistributing his weight. When his eyes found mine again, they welled with tears. "Why did you do that?"

I swallowed against the emotion in my throat. "I couldn't watch you limp anymore."

"Yeah." He held my eyes with quiet intensity. "You could have."

The words felt familiar to me, though I couldn't place them. But the memory faded as we walked back in silence to my gilded, velvet prison.

7

KANE

BY THE TIME MY BOOTS TOUCHED SHADOW WOODS SOIL I wasn't surprised to find tawny leaves and a pleasant chill in the air. Crisp and clear, scented with rain-soaked moss and fresh soil. Arwen would have loved the patchwork of russet, crimson, and bronze overhead—it would've reminded her of her mother, her childhood. In Amber, the trees shed vivid leaves like these year-round.

I'd arrived in time for one last sunny autumn day before winter blanketed my keep. Summer had slipped away while I'd been free-falling through both snow and unending grief, and I'd made it back just in time for the tail end of the season that conjured my murdered—

Get a hold of yourself. You can't rage at the seasons.

The luftalvor loosed a low grunt and cocked its pink snout at me. His eyes softened with something I couldn't place. Perhaps it was pity. I offered the creature a benign pat on his rump, and with a snuffle the woolly, winged white ox took off into the skies above.

His wings flapped against bright, clear blue.

Envy soared in my own chest. Longing. Sharp, splitting anguish. What I'd give for detachment.

And the decaying leaves crunching loudly underfoot, fragments of red and gold like faded confetti. And the sun too bright on my weak eyes and cracked lips.

And . . . perhaps there was no point in taking another step.

Nothing would bring Arwen back. And I was a selfish fucking bastard. I always had been. What shit did I give about the realms or my father or any of it?

I didn't want to be alive. I wanted to be with Arwen, and live if that was the only means to do so. Perhaps I'd end myself right now and let the worms feast. Perhaps I'd find her in the nothingness.

Despite how achingly appealing oblivion sounded—how my boots had stalled, how my hands had begun to shake from sheer exhaustion—I stalked for the sentry towers on reticent legs.

It would be an insult to her memory to give up now. An insult to her bravery. Her hope.

Shadowhold's walls were surrounded by the sentries—raised stone turrets that were manned all day and night, poised and ready to sound the alarm against anything meandering in my woods that shouldn't be.

"My king?"

The soldier that called down had found me before I'd found him.

I squinted up into the vibrant canopy until I could make out the stone battlement and the dark, skeletal face poking out of it. The man lifted the vicious helmet from his head and appraised me with something like awe.

Did I look that broken down? Had they not thought I would return?

Did I blame them?

A blaring horn sounded. Boomed through the forest and into the keep ahead. When I moved past a copse of dark, gnarled trees, wrought-iron gates wrenched open before me with a creak. That wrenching sounded like the first notes of a song I'd memorized long ago.

Behind them, my gothic castle loomed.

Shadowhold.

All the stained-glass windows lit from within, my banners and spires and stonework, etched and carved with such care. The sea of colorful wartime tents. A fortress I'd made into a home not only for myself, and for her, but for so many innocent mortals and halflings. Men and women and children who had built full, satisfying lives here.

And some ego, some pride didn't want them to see me limp through the gates.

Didn't want all of those people who'd relied on me to protect them, some of whom had crossed the channel with me and fled Lumera for a better life, to see their king ravaged by heartache and frostbite. Bruised and starved and damaged.

So I stood at the keep's precipice, frozen anew, my feet unwilling to propel me forward nor back as the horn's tune blared, signaling my return.

Still as death itself. Weaker than I'd ever felt.

The men in the barracks lowered their swords and crossbows and legs of meat. The women and children with apples and gourds halted at the brutal sight of me.

Silence rent the brisk autumn air.

One single glossy red apple toppled from a dropped wicker basket and rolled across the dry grass.

Thousands of eyes held mine. Not one person moved, or spoke, or so much as shifted. I wondered if they, too, were holding their breath.

And then, though I couldn't fathom why, one thick, heavy-browed soldier in only half his full armor knelt. A single knee pressed down to the dirt, helmet in his hands, eyes focused on me.

Before I could react, two soldiers beside him followed suit. Kneeling, removing their helmets. Gazes steadfast and unflinching.

Like a mighty ocean wave, cresting slowly and then crashing all at once—the entire barracks stooped to their knees before me. A sea of men, women, children—soldiers, nobles, farmhands—bowing before their wayward king, returned home to them. *For* them.

And it was that truth that moved my feet down the wide avenue between all the kneeling faces. That truth that made my eyes burn and my throat bob.

Arwen was dead.

I'd not traveled to Pearl nor made my way home for her. And perhaps I hadn't wanted to admit that to myself—that no valiant act of mine might bring her back—but I had found the White Crow, and I would slay my father, not for Arwen, but for these people. These people who deserved a king that would fight for them no matter what he'd lost.

I'd spent decades driven by revenge. But Arwen had only known of Lazarus for mere months, and had still given her life in hopes of protecting the citizens of Evendell. She, too, had loved these people. And even if I did want to join her—to end myself and see if our souls might inhabit the same realm once more—I wouldn't. Not yet.

Not until I could take Lazarus to his grave alongside me. I would not leave these innocent people in his clutches.

Shame should have been what coursed through me as I beheld their steadfast faces—I'd spent so long fighting for the wrong reasons, I'd not accomplished what I'd set out to do when I'd left them all, I'd not returned full-blooded . . . But it was unwavering duty that filled my veins instead as I walked past the hundreds of kneeling men and women. That was what propelled my stiff legs forward.

Past each unyielding gaze. The uncompromising resolve in their eyes.

My people, who I'd gone to the ends of the continent for. I was like them now. I knew what it meant to be vulnerable. I knew how desperately they needed me. And though I hadn't known it, I'd needed them, too.

"You're alive."

A slight pinch tugged the side of my mouth up as I turned to find my commander standing just outside the, pitch-black war tent. Standing, among a sea of kneeling men. Rigid jaw, cropped hair, hulking black armor glinting in the sun, his sea-green eyes as resolute as his soldiers around him.

I didn't trust my voice not to crack around the tightness in my throat as I said, "Give me a little credit."

Griffin nodded, as if I hadn't been joking, and then he, too, knelt before me. "Welcome home."

MY MUSCLES BARKED WITH EVERY STEP ACROSS THE CASTLE grounds, past thick picnic blankets and baskets piled high with the harvest. I was sore from the journey. *Mortally* sore, which was even less pleasant than usual and made me feel all too breakable.

Griffin swung the thick door of his cottage open and I stepped inside. A couple of years ago he'd built the place himself, nestled at the edge of the keep. He'd never liked sleeping in quarters made up each day by servants, nor having guards man his hall at night.

I sat down at his kitchen table with a wince. The marble tabletop was clean save for a heavy-looking sword and whetstone. Griffin loved nothing if not a solitary, tactile activity.

"Where have you been, Kane?"

Though he was my oldest friend, I'd likely spent less than two hours of my life in Griffin's austere cottage. The walls were crafted of bare, whitewashed wood. The bed, on a loft above us, folded with care. Simple white cotton sheets. No books, no leafy greenery, no art. No clutter at all. "What are you, a monk?"

Griffin ignored me, closing the door and sitting backward on the other pale wooden chair to face me—two chairs. Griffin had two chairs. "You stopped sending ravens a week ago. I had a convoy ready to leave at first light."

"We need to get you more chairs," I said, twisting to scan the space.

"Kane," he bit out, voice low. "What happened?"

I wiped a finger down Griffin's cold table, alongside the dull sword. Not a lick of dust. "I found the White Crow. He wasn't so much a sorcerer as a Fae God."

Griffin's jaw tensed. "What the fuck."

"I had similar sentiments."

"And what? He helped you?"

"He stripped me of my lighte."

My commander did not show emotion. Not even when his own parents had been hanged before him. But at my words, Griffin's sea-green eyes practically churned. "Kane—"

"Not permanently." I heard air flee him in relief. "If I touch the Blade of the Sun, I'll be reborn as full-blooded Fae. I can take her place in the prophecy and kill my father."

"Another hunt for the blade." Griffin sighed. "Why do I feel like we've done that one before?"

"*We* aren't doing anything." My eyes fell over his bland glass-fronted hutch and unlit hearth despite the autumn chill. "I'm leaving tonight for Willowridge. I'll have Briar open the portal for me. Unless our magically challenged witch is fixed?"

Griffin made a face. "She's still with Briar. The progress hasn't been excellent . . . But I don't really know. She doesn't speak to me much these days."

Any part of me that wanted to jest about his Mari problems withered with the look of true regret in his eyes. "How come?"

"She blames me. And you. For Arwen."

My blood turned with the mention of her name. "You had nothing to do with . . . what happened that day."

"I told her I knew about Hemlock. And that I let you both go alone. She has every right to hate me."

Guilt slammed into me like a hammer across an anvil. *I* was the only person who had allowed Arwen to jump from that platform. I'd regret it every day of my now stunted, mortal life. Griffin didn't deserve that same fate.

I opened my mouth to tell him as much, but his flat look told me he wasn't interested in my pity. Changing course, I lilted, "When you say *not excellent*—"

"No substantial magic, last I heard."

"It's been almost two months."

Griffin's jaw went rigid. "She's terrified."

"Of what?"

"Failing everyone, I think," he said, eyes on his knuckles, stretched white across his chairback.

"And what of the little seer's father?"

It'd been a promise we'd made to Beth, the girl who could divine the future, back in Crag's Hollow. To rescue her father, Vaughn, from Amber's clutches, if he was still alive.

"We found him, actually. He was being kept in the same encampment Halden and his men brought Arwen to, back in Peridot."

Again with her name—ice shards against my heart. My fingers curled around the edge of the table.

"On her parents' urging we brought Beth back to Shadowhold for her safety." His mouth twisted into a knot. "She's a little . . ."

"Yeah. Any visions?"

"Nothing yet."

The sun flecked through the half-moon-shaped window above the stony kitchen, turning the clean marble table between us into a glowing sprawl of light.

"You know I'm coming with you," my commander said after a minute.

"No, you'll stay here. Ready the troops for war in case I fail."

"In case you fail? You mean in case you, a mortal, are killed in Lumera? You will be."

"It's nice to feel so supported."

"I'm not fucking kidding, Kane." A muscle feathered in Griffin's jaw. "You should have six armies backing you. Or thirty."

My blood simmered. "We don't have six armies, do we? Unless there's been any word from Citrine? Or the traitor?"

"Yeah," he said, scratching the back of his neck. "A few things have transpired."

I readied myself. "Wonderful news only, I'm sure."

"Amber Kingdom is no longer stationed in Peridot. Amelia was reinstated as the rightful queen. She's rebuilding Siren's Bay, and sent you a letter saying her army won't fight alongside us. I don't think they'll fight at all."

"She sent a fucking *letter*?" If I had my lighte I might've obliterated Griffin's spotless kitchen.

"She did."

"Queen of the Peridot Provinces . . ." I hummed to myself. "Is Eryx furious? Usurped by his own daughter?" I could only imagine the look on the vainglorious bastard's face.

"Eryx is dead."

The already cool stone home dropped in temperature. Perhaps it was my new, mortal constitution, but I fought a shiver.

Amelia. Capable of deceit, betrayal, and now patricide. Some queen Peridot had earned.

"When our convoy arrived at Fedrik's ship in Sandstone, to send the king to Citrine as we'd planned, Eryx was found poisoned in the back of the carriage."

"And Citrine?"

"Broderick and Isolde think we tried to frame Fedrik for Eryx's murder. It's . . ."

"Absurd," I growled. "They're imbeciles."

"Maybe we sail there once more. See if begging on our hands and knees changes anything. I'm not above it."

"Ha," I said without humor.

"We should find out."

Griffin had been my closest friend since childhood. My only real friend, the past few decades. Not only that, but a loyal, self-sacrificing, and trustworthy commander of my army. He'd been there for me through everything. For Arwen, too.

And I knew it wasn't fair to saddle him with this. I'd be leaving him with nothing. Worse than that—a legacy of loss and broken alliances. An unwinnable war on the horizon. But the people out there who had knelt before me—the people of this entire continent—they needed Griffin. They deserved a leader who was moral and steadfast. Who was good.

"*You* should find out. I'm going to Lumera. It'll be your problem either way, Griffin. When I'm gone . . . I want you to take my place on the Onyx throne."

"Don't." He sighed, lowering his head to rub his temples. "Don't say that."

"You're the only one I trust."

When Griffin's gaze met mine, it was mournfully grim. "I have no interest in ruling a kingdom."

My smile was faint. "That's why you'll be great at it."

"What if—"

"There are no what-ifs. I'm either going to succeed in finding the blade and kill my father, which will grant my death as well, or I'm going to die trying."

"So, what . . . ?" Griffin swallowed audibly, the barest hint of emotion flashing across his face. "You're saying this is it?"

My gaze found the stony floor, safe from Griffin's eyes. "Yeah. This is it."

8

~◈~

ARWEN

I'D NEVER ATTENDED A BALL.

The closest I'd come was probably the banquet Kane had thrown at Shadowhold for King Eryx and Princess Amelia. My memories of that night were dusty and drenched in birchwine, but some remained etched into my psyche nonetheless, impervious to time or drink or grief: Kane telling me I looked beautiful in my black silk dress; his body caged over mine as he protected me from a hail of wine barrels; the way, even then, he knew exactly how to distract me from my panic . . . At the memory of his words—*death by bird*—a laugh broke from me.

"Something funny?"

Maddox wore his usual silver armor, but the steel mask affixed to his face mimicked the bones of some sort of primordial predator and only served to amplify his brutality in the spare candlelight of my suite. He hummed a haunting, dismal tune that reminded me of a wheezing organ.

"What's the purpose of the masks?" I asked instead of answering as a tired-looking handmaiden strung a loop of diamonds tightly across my neck.

Behind me, Wyn answered, "Legend requires we hide our faces from the Fae Gods so they do not grow envious of our plentiful harvest."

I swore his words were laced with irony, and I peered down in an attempt to meet his eyes through the mirror. They gave nothing away, hidden beneath a bronze mask with curved horns and slight ears like those of an antelope. I looked over the dimly lit suite behind him through the glass. A red glow from the candle's reflection on the duvet, and the thick curtains and crimson settee . . . it was a room bathed in blood.

The handmaiden instructed me to purse my lips and finished applying rouge and charcoal to my face. The glossy vanity was cluttered with powders and creams, and the mirror before me ringed with a fuzzy white glow—powered by some kind of lighte that lit my face too brightly. The white marble was cold against my arms as I leaned forward for her. I wasn't sure I'd seen a single beam or plank of wood in all of Solaris. The entire city was a reflection of Lazarus's stony, unmoving heart.

I longed for the hundredth time for Kane's warm, cozy bedroom in Shadowhold, and those clean, dark cotton sheets. The way they smelled of lilac soap and him. I missed all his unexpected clutter, and those fat history books, and even the scratches Acorn had left across the wooden floorboards.

"You almost done?" Maddox asked the woman from his post across the room. "If we're late, it'll be my head on a stake."

"And wouldn't that be a shame," I muttered.

"Yes, sir," the woman replied to Maddox, pinning up another strand of my curled hair with Wyn's artful birthday gift. I'd asked her to include it and she'd been kind enough to comply, though I got the sense if I'd asked her to put a fork in my hair she would've. I'd never seen anyone so deeply unenthused.

I focused on the hairpin as the handmaiden worked my curls around it. The daisies at its tip were the only things on me that felt like *me*.

I despised my gilded dress. It was bare of any straps or sleeves, and corseted into oblivion, flattening my chest and pinching my stomach and ribs. The liquid gold skirt offered even less flexibility. Both made my heart panicky, only calmed by the fact that I knew if I really wanted to, I could rip the damn thing clean off. It wouldn't be the first time I'd stood naked before the Fae king.

The gown was completely sheer. In direct candlelight any lascivious eye could see the entire outline of my nipples, and the high slits on either side left nothing of my legs to the imagination. Another strategic maneuver aimed at my humiliation. A reminder of what I was inside these palace walls. What I'd become, so long as I remained in captivity.

"*You, Arwen, are just a womb*," he'd said.

My skintight gloves crawled all the way up my arms, hiding the bruises clustered along my veins, and my shoes bound my feet and wound up my ankles with unbending cord. My hair had never been piled so high, nor my face been so caked, only to be covered by a mask anyway.

All of it to drive me further to the brink of discomfort.

Once the handmaiden pressed the gold-threaded mask flush against my face, I studied the two red droplets under the left eye—made to look as if I were crying tears of blood.

"Hurry up," Maddox hissed. "Or I'll drag her there by those damn curls."

"Maddox," Wyn cautioned behind me, and my brows rose against the fibers of my tragic mask. Wyn never spoke up against the higher-ranking guard.

My handmaiden hurried her work, securing the back of my corset and looping diamonds through my ears. I could feel her fingers trembling.

Behind us, Maddox pushed off the doors and prowled toward Wyn. "You've gotten a bit too bold since losing your limp. Might be a favor to crack you a new one."

I watched through the mirror as Wyn didn't cower, but didn't argue with the taller, broader guard, either.

Maddox's lips cut a harsh line. "Your service in the kingsguard is a disgrace. Everyone thinks it. You do know any of us could *demolish* you if we so desired, right?"

He said the words with such promise. Such intent. Wyn's expression remained as rigid as a bowstring. My handmaiden didn't breathe, and the room crackled with intensity.

I scrambled for the crystal perfume bottle and I pumped it once, primrose filling my nostrils, before I stood abruptly. "I'm ready."

Like undertakers guiding me into the afterlife, Maddox and Wyn stalked alongside me through the winding, laborious hallways of the palace. At night, I found the red marble floors and glinting obsidian décor even more insidious. The stuffy, too-warm air for early winter was suffocating, and the pulsating, sickly sweet aroma of vanilla that scented it turned my stomach in on itself.

How had Kane grown up here? The palace didn't suit him at all. Maybe the isolated, lofty ceilings and depthless black walls were new additions, after Kane's rebellion. I couldn't imagine his mother, such an elegant and thoughtful soul as Kane had described her, had lived somewhere so cold. Like dwelling in the heart of a primordial beast.

Raucous music and dissonant voices alerted me to the ball before we rounded the sharp-edged corner and found the grand staircase. Dozens of those silver soldiers lined the hallway on either side—a display of power, or a necessary protection, I wasn't sure—and spare partygoers lingered in hallways, some trying to curb premature inebriation, others hunting for a hidden washroom, and others still exchanging secrets or affection in shadowed alcoves.

The celebratory, opulent veneer might have had the desired effect if it weren't for all the masks.

Most were twice the size of mine, headpieces covering the entire face of the wearer—reaching high above their heads, or hanging low down to their necks as if their jowls were melting. Everyone appeared to be in on some unspoken competition: the larger the mask, the more affluent the wearer. Some were beautiful—a crescent moon beside a sun; dainty, silken butterfly wings spread wide; a weaving of bronze beads across an entire face—but most were not. Most were crafted to terrify: maws wrenched open, pearl teeth dripping carnelian blood; moonfaced owls with translucent white-blue eyeballs or dozens of heavy golden chains hanging from noses and sagging mouths and ears.

A black leather bird mask with an elongated, pointed beak swooped in too close and I flinched. The wearer ducked toward me again, cackling, and I recoiled from a whiff of something much more potent than wine or ale.

Righting myself, my heart immediately slammed into a stone wall at the sight a few feet down the hall.

Leaning casually against a black marble pillar was an impossibly tall, broad-shouldered man with a dark head of rugged hair. His hands were folded into his pockets with ease as he leaned close to a petite woman in a revealing magenta gown and a mask that glistened like the scales of a fish in sunlight.

It's not him. It can't be—

But my stupid, thumping, pulsating heart didn't listen. Not for a second.

And I found all my breath was stored tightly inside my lungs as we passed the hulking man and he let out a loud, grating laugh.

The air fled from me in a rush, disappointment and sorrow flooding my now empty lungs.

Not Kane. Not his laugh—

Maddox tugged my arm back, halting my still-moving feet. We had reached the top of the bifurcated stairs, and my heart stopped cold once more against my immeasurably bound, gilded chest. The poor organ could not catch a break, and I blamed months of seeing so few people, so little life or movement . . .

And now—a gargantuan throne room sprawled before me lit only by red pillar candles and a ceiling rife with glittering faux stars. The walls were bedecked with intricate metal-hewn garlands and bouquets spare of any real flowers, and beneath them, a shiny black-and-white-checkered floor fit for dancing, packed with hundreds of revelers.

All of it, absurd excess with no soul. No spirit.

But the dark, joyless décor was not what stole the breath from my lungs.

Nor the sheer number of people in Lazarus's court, willing to dance the night away, ignoring the beast they served or the heinousness that spanned outside Solaris's walls.

Nor was it even the dais, and the banquet table that stretched across it, populated by rich nobles. Or Lazarus, dark and triumphant, seated at its center—his throne behind them covered in some swath of velvet as if he didn't wish his court to see the thing if he was not sprawled across it.

No, what sent me lightheaded was the empty chair beside him.

Waiting, impatiently, for me.

"I can't," I heard myself say.

"You must," Wyn replied.

"The queen is coming," Maddox grunted, ushering us away from the staircase. "We'll proceed after her entrance."

My brows pulled together under my mask. "What queen?"

A herald wearing a red-and-black-checkered uniform cleared his throat twice, silencing the high-pitched chatter and low horns of the band. The expectant room's attention landed squarely on him, and he announced at a blaring decibel, "Queen Amelia of Evendell, Ruler of the Peridot Provinces."

Shock—utter *shock*—weakened my legs and forced me against the slick banister to remain upright. I'd thought it would be revulsion, or fear, or horror that brought me to my knees tonight. But this—

Queen Amelia. Welcome in Lazarus's court as a guest.

Amelia was elegance incarnate as she made her way past us and down the broad, glittering stairs unattended. Legs as long as a heron's, her ivory gown the same color as her braided hair. Like a second skin on her exquisite body, it rolled on and on behind her as she walked, a train others would have to be wary of all evening. A power play, as was everything Amelia did. No jewelry, save for the dozens of colorful gemstone rings on her long, lithe fingers.

But that mask.

A garden of vibrant, bejeweled flora and fauna that began at her high cheekbones and climbed to a corona of stems atop her head. The embroidered plants and creatures—wings and claws and petals and stems—formed more of a headdress than a mask, and though I could only imagine the weight, Amelia held her chin high, accentuating her fine jawline and elegant neck.

What in the Stones could have compelled Eryx to abdicate his throne to his daughter? Nothing of this world. He was either coerced or dead. But Amelia, here as Lazarus's ally . . . It must have been Kane's doing. A plan of some kind.

Hope like I hadn't allowed myself to experience in months fluttered aimlessly in my chest. I had to speak to her somehow.

But Amelia was already halfway down the steps, on her way to mingle among the crowd, and eventually take her seat at the elongated banquet table.

"I need to use the washroom."

Wyn and Maddox both turned to me, an antelope and a beast. Prey and predator. "No," the latter growled. "We're already late."

"But I think . . ." I gagged. "I'm going to be sick." I heaved again and clutched my stomach.

"Oh, Gods," Maddox cursed, scanning to see if anyone had noticed. "Fine, retch quickly. Wyn, take her."

I heaved again and Wyn dragged me back down the hallway toward the ladies' salon. "Do you need me to come in with you?"

I shook my head and dashed inside.

The ladies' salon was unlike any washroom I'd ever entered. Conquered by women appraising themselves in those same glowing vanities I had in my suite, adjusting straps on shoes and fussing with belts and earrings. Gossiping and sipping fizzy wine. Two women were admiring each other's masks before they traded, giddily evaluating their new looks side by side.

I sped over to them. "That's just what I've been looking for!" I bubbled to the wider-hipped woman, her new mask rife with snakes in place of hair. I pointed to my own. "My husband loved this one, but it's so boring."

"No," she cooed, drunk. "It's lovely. Mine was hurting my"—a hiccup—"cheekbones." She nodded to her younger friend, who was struggling to hold the offending piece against her face.

"Here," I offered the young partygoer, taking mine off. "Trade me?"

The other woman, too inebriated even to speak, gave me the hefty mask without argument and took mine in return.

Without as much as my thanks, I hurried deeper into the salon. I wasn't sure how long Wyn or Maddox would believe I was sick, but I doubted I had more than a handful of minutes.

The new mask—two hands pressed across my eyes with fingers tipped in long black nails—wouldn't be enough to slip out without alerting Wyn. My dress was too recognizable.

I scanned the washroom. Faint pink wallpaper. Porcelain and gold sinks and shelves replete with linen hand towels. No curtains I could steal . . . no throws or blankets—

An older woman with ringlets of white was nearly snoring in a blush settee in the corner, a chalice dangling from her fingers. Tossed to her side, a vivid, floral fur coat.

Hideous. And *perfect*.

I prowled over and gently pulled the thick, dyed hide from the couch, careful not to wake its sleeping owner. Her head drooped, and I held my breath—but only a slumbering grunt drifted out.

Thank the Stones.

Wrapping it around me, I moved for—

"What are you doing?"

I whirled, heart in my throat, to find a woman in a badger mask. "That's my mother's coat."

"Of course it is!" *Well done, Arwen, that's a response.*

The badger appraised me, crossing her arms.

"And . . ." I continued, grasping at nothing. "And she was kind enough to offer it to me while she rested because I am *freezing*." I mimed being very chilly. "Isn't there something so special about women making friends in the ladies' washroom?"

The badger's frown cracked slightly. "She is generous. That's what being a mother of six will do to you."

I laughed too hard. "I told her to come find me whenever she needed it back. I'll be sitting up on the dais with the king."

"Oh my," Badger Mask said, leaning in. "You will?"

"Mhm." I nodded. The clock was ticking and I needed this badger out of my way.

"How did you land that seat?"

"My sister. She's a duchess."

"A duchess! Of what territory?"

Bleeding Stones. The badger's mother snorted in her sleep beside me and rolled to the side, pressing her face flat against the rosy fabric.

"Pirn?" I tried. I told myself that sounded like a real territory. Or maybe this would be the end of this half-baked, poorly planned—no, *unplanned*, ridiculously unplanned—

"I love Pirn," the badger cooed. "Especially in the spring. So beautiful."

"Indeed." I grinned, narrowing my eyes at her. She was bluffing as well. I'd almost forgotten that Lazarus's court was filled with self-serving, lying social climbers.

"Might you introduce me to your sist—"

Before she could utter another word I hurried out the door, directly past an unaware Wyn, arms folded patiently as he waited.

I wouldn't have much time before he broke into the women's washroom to look for me. I needed to find Amelia.

Nearly bashing into dapper, rich men and elegant women plied with too much wine, I hurtled down the staircase and into the madness.

Revelry reined. Blaring music, bodies sweating, laughter that sounded like weeping. Bumped by imposing Fae, toes trod on by dancers, I scuttled across the checkered floor like a beetle on a battlefield. It was too dark, and my vision was obscured under the hands of my mask. My corset too tight, the fur of this obscene coat itchy on my neck and chest.

When I finally saw that pristine ivory dress, I uttered my thanks to the Stones themselves. Amelia's white silk train was unmarred by a single shoe print. If I were a beetle, the new queen of Peridot was a dove, high in the sky, untouched by the boisterous chaos.

"Queen Amelia," I cut in, despite what seemed to be an engaging conversation with some mustached noble. "It's been too long."

She turned, the intricate ornaments of her mask whirring and tinkering with the movement like real creatures might. "Who is that? These masks are such a pain."

"Mari." Though I knew it was ridiculous, saying her name made my eyes burn. "Mari Branton."

Amelia faltered only briefly before pulling me into a stunted embrace and hissing against my hair, "Arwen?"

I nodded until she released me, though she only stood there, gaping.

I turned to the mustached man across from us, whose expression said he knew his odds of bedding a queen tonight were rapidly deteriorating. "I haven't seen my dear friend since her coronation. Would you mind terribly if I stole her away to catch up?"

"Of course not." The man bowed.

"There's . . . a courtyard this way," Amelia whispered, finally finding her voice. "Follow me."

"I don't have much time."

"You've a lot more than I thought."

Amelia dragged me past the swarm of revelers, across that checkered floor, past the sixteen sweating musicians playing a frenzied piece, and through a wide set of doors.

My racing heart stilled with the fragrant breeze. I hadn't been outside in months.

I inhaled fresh night air. Or whatever served as closest to it here in Solaris. Dry, slightly sweet, a little thick. But fresh air nonetheless.

Amelia yanked me past a few more relaxed soldiers—still on duty, but with the visibly less demanding domain of the courtyard—and toward a shallow, dark reflection pool, its still water topped by fat lily pads but bare of lilies and glinting in the light of nearby curved lamps.

"How are you alive?" Amelia's words were hushed as she tipped the monstrosity from her face and across her head like a hat. I did the same. Not-quite-cool-enough air washed over my face.

"Lazarus healed me. It was all a ploy to get to Kane. He never wanted me to die."

Her eyes were still wild with shock. Her breaths rushed as she said, "But the prophecy—"

"I know. He destroyed the blade. Now he can't be killed."

"And he kept you here because . . . ?" The moon's light was spoiled as it was every night by those immovable clouds of putrid gray, but some thin, determined silver glow still cast Amelia's tan skin in delicate shadows.

I sighed and lowered my voice even more. "He wants me to bear him full-blooded Fae children."

Amelia's eyes widened even farther. *"What?"*

I resisted the urge to shake her and only said, as calmly as possible, "Amelia. You need to get word to Kane that I'm here. That I'm alive."

"Arwen . . ." She was shaking her head as if trying to sort through the onslaught of new information.

"I think I can convince one of my guards to—"

"Arwen." She sighed, eyes finding that rippleless reflection pool. "I can't reach Kane."

My stomach twisted. "Why not? Isn't that why you're here? Aren't you two—"

"No—I . . ." When her sunflower eyes found mine again, they welled with regret. "I'm the one who gave you up."

9

KANE

SHADOWHOLD WAS NOT A PLACE PARTIAL TO GOODBYES. Barracks of soldiers meant the majority of those who lived here had calloused against the word years ago.

And that suited me just fine.

Griffin would tell Dagan and Lieutenant Eardley and all the rest where I'd gone. Better to spare them the discomfort and false encouragements of a formal send-off.

The hot water had barely registered across my skin as I'd bathed.

The pork and cider tasted like sawdust as I'd swallowed each bite.

Acorn slept in my quarters while I packed, and I didn't bother to wake him. I didn't know who that farewell would be more painful for.

But this bedroom—

Her melodic voice filtered in with every crisp breeze through my balcony. Her delicate movements—her arched back, those strong legs—conjured every time the gossamer around my bed shifted in the wind. I couldn't spend another moment in this hollowed-out room. The heart of it had been scooped out like guts from a gourd.

I braced myself against my writing desk and the wood groaned under my weight.

The only loose end that itched at my conscience was Leigh.

She would most likely hear from Dagan that I'd returned and left once more without saying goodbye. I'd never see the little one again and she'd think I'd orchestrated it as such.

The thought guttered through my mind. She didn't deserve that.

But the last time I'd seen her—

I couldn't even make out her face when she'd launched herself in my direction. Heart in my throat, I'd pulled Leigh tightly into myself, felt her arms wrap around my waist, gripping the back of my leather armor, sobbing for her sister, begging me to tell her it wasn't true . . . It had destroyed me. I couldn't face those huge blue eyes now and admit I was leaving her, too.

I'd been so numb that day, I'd hardly muttered soothing hushes as I held Leigh, promising her all would be right.

And the truth was, it would be, for her.

Leigh would grow up in a world unthreatened by my father. I would make it so. She'd always miss her sister, of course. But soon she'd find ways to store that grief deep within herself. Or expel it in constructive, useful outlets. When I was gone, Griffin would purchase her and Ryder a cottage somewhere in Willowridge or a smaller, quieter town outside the capital. Or they could stay here, where Dagan could teach her to wield her sword like Arwen used to. Show her how to push the pain outward.

And one day Leigh would move on. She'd still cry occasionally. She'd tell her close friends, and teachers, and first love of her sister, the bravest, kindest person she'd ever known. The fabled savior of Evendell, and the girl who had run back into sure peril for the mother they both loved.

And one day Leigh would realize it had been months since she'd last thought of Arwen's contagious smile or her chocolate-brown hair tied into a braid as she ran.

Leigh would be all right.

Mari, too. Dagan. Ryder.

And I—

I'd never wake up the same again. And that would be all right for me; I didn't particularly want to. It would feel like a disgrace—a profound betrayal—to feel at ease. Laughing, grinning, joking when Arwen wasn't here with me. It wasn't something I'd ever be capable of.

So I wrote Leigh a letter. A short one, because I'd never had much of a way with words, and even if I had, there was no way to explain that truth: that she'd just have to wait for the grief to run its course.

I left it for her on my desk and headed for the stables.

I'd have to ride for Willowridge on a horse, since I couldn't shift. By the time I drew near, my vacant chest—whatever space my heart had once occupied—had been encased once more in resolute, un-feeling steel. And I was grateful.

Inside I found Ryder, leaning against one of the stalls, smoking a cigar, thick smoke curling into the flared nostrils of the horse above him.

"Inflicting your filthy habit on the steeds?"

Ryder spun, shock winning out over fear in his eyes—but only by a hair. "You're back."

Before I could respond with a dig at his observation skills, the high-pitched squeals of girlish laughter pierced the air. My chest ached with Leigh's voice, filtering out into the night like seeds of a windblown dandelion. *"Ryder!"* she sang. *"Ryyyyder!"*

"Maybe he's in the library." Beth's voice, too.

Guilt and quiet wrath rippled through me. Mostly at myself, but also at this weasel, who was flattening himself against the raw wood and holding in a gasp of tobacco smoke.

"Are you *hiding* from little girls?"

"I just need a minute, all right?" Ryder said as a cloud of swirling gray escaped from his mouth alongside his confession.

Ire spasmed in my neck. "You are their only remaining protector."

"Well, that can be a lot of pressure, Kane." Another thick run of smoke billowed out.

I sneered. *"King Ravenwood."*

"King Ravenwood," he agreed, alarm flickering in his eyes. "Of course." Ryder backed up a step onto a pitchfork, his elbow clanging against the wood as it flew up, sending the horses around us into fits and grunts.

"So Arwen dies because of *your* stupidity, leaving you sole guardian to Leigh and her seer friend after two decades of barely lifting a finger for anyone but yourself . . . and you cannot handle one iota of that responsibility?"

"Hey," he said, eyes clearing. "That's not fair—"

"Whatever will you do without your abused older sister to pile all your obligations on?" If I had my power, obsidian shadows would have spun off my body in rivulets. It would have been a terrible effort to keep myself from pummeling his lazy mug.

Ryder swallowed a gulp. "I love Leigh. You know I do. But Beth is an odd one. Doesn't talk much. Doesn't make people feel . . . comfortable."

"She's *a child.*"

"Yeah," Ryder said, hands raised in defense. "I know. But they're inseparable. They require constant entertainment. And I've got to hone my skills before the war, and—"

I could have laughed myself hoarse. "As if you would lift a single finger in battle." Arwen had sacrificed everything for her family. For this entire continent. I was mere hours from giving my life, too. And this *insect* couldn't take care of the one person I'd leave behind who needed him most. "I always knew you were as selfish as they came. But now I see your condition is far graver: you're a *coward*."

He staggered back a bit with my vitriol but I was too incensed to stop. Anger I thought I'd long since moved past barked through my bones. "Those two little girls have seen more brutality in their combined eighteen years than you have in all your living days. You'd be lucky to protect them with your life. At least then it would be fucking worth something."

Fuming, I pushed past him, my back itching where my wings once spread.

BY THE TIME I REACHED BRIAR'S THE SKY WAS AWASH IN muted shades of blue, the night too new for stars.

Her sprawling lawn was bare of lavender—the precipice of winter meant all those rows had been harvested, dried, and pressed, now likely filling antique crystal jars and thin satin sachets.

My footfalls were heavy on the veranda and I swung the iron knocker with more force than necessary, still acclimating to my mortality.

Cori, Briar's handmaiden, didn't seem surprised by my arrival as she welcomed me inside. I wondered if Griffin had sent a raven, or if she'd simply spied my horse tethered to the wrought-iron gates.

"Briar's upstairs in the library," she said with a well-mannered smile. "May I get you anything?"

My eyes lingered on the polished maple staircase. The paintings in their ivory frames. The last time I'd been here . . . Slick, soft skin and discarded white silk flashed across my mind. My heart gave an agonizing tug.

"No." When I realized how ragged I'd sounded, I added a gruff, "Thank you."

Cori just nodded primly and I prowled up that beckoning staircase. The hallway was shadowed in fuzzy-edged slants of periwinkle as twilight filtered through the banister.

It was no shock that after all these months, I'd find Mari with her freckled nose embedded in a book. Her copper hair was pulled up with a single quill as she lay prone on the patchwork quilt of Briar's least accommodating bedroom: the one so swollen with books that the sorceress affectionately referred to it as her library.

Briar was bundled in the corner in a dark silk robe, dewy from bathing, her hair still dripping on the hardwood floors. As Mari read in comfortable silence, Briar's long back dipped to scan one of the many shelves crammed with grimoires.

"Welcome, Prince Ravenwood." Briar spoke without turning, her voice like a razor coated in honey. "How nice to see you've made it back to Onyx Kingdom in one piece."

I gritted my teeth, leaning against the doorway. So she was in a mood. "Evening."

Mari gasped, though she remained on the bed. "Kane?"

She didn't appear glad to see me. Startled, perhaps, but not glad. Griffin hadn't been lying when he'd said Mari blamed us for Arwen's death. Strangely, though, I'd missed the witch more than I'd expected to. Somehow we'd actually become friends. And because of that, I knew better than to ask how her tutelage was going.

"Briar," I managed. "As usual, I need your help."

Briar only continued to scan those shelves for something that eluded her. "Mari can help you."

"I can't actually," Mari said to Briar pointedly. "Not without an amulet that a certain sophisticated yet very disorganized witch refuses to make for me."

"Not with that attitude," the sorceress lilted.

I pushed from the doorframe and strolled into the room, stopping at the foot of the bed before the unlit hearth, also packed with parchment and leather.

"Well, one of you needs to try." I studied Mari, her legs kicking lazily behind her as she returned to her book. "Mari, I am your king."

Mari looked up, pinning her punishing gaze on me. "You are my dead friend's lover," she said. "Possibly her murderer, depending on one's perspective."

Briar turned at that, violet eyes flaring. *"Mari."*

I bit my cheek, an axe lodged in my heart. "That's cruel."

Mari's eyes burned hot on mine. "It's true."

When I said nothing—the word "murderer" hacking into my mind repeatedly—Mari added, "And even if it weren't, I can't help you anyway. I haven't done any real magic since Peridot."

Briar scoffed, sitting down on the bed beside Mari. A familiar, comfortable gesture.

"If I'm so unhelpful, why are you reading the grimoire I gifted you? And for the third time by my count."

The nearly fossilized pentagrams on the cover told me Mari was not flipping through any common spell book. The one in her hands was a relic of some sort.

Mari looked up from the pages to glare at her mentor. "Because I'm bored. The better question is why you think anyone has need for this cloaking spell. Invisibility: the most useless of magic for the most useless of witches." She turned another page, eyes finding mine. "I don't know why I'm still here."

"Griffin told me you were feeling as much."

At my commander's name, Mari's legs ceased their rhythmic, leisurely kicks behind her. "I might feel better if I had another *amulet*."

"Don't whine, little witch."

"Mari," I tried again.

Like a child, she flipped another page of the book.

I reached out and snatched it from her hands.

"Hey!"

"Be careful with that," Briar snipped.

"I need one of you two to open a portal to Lumera for me."

Mari's russet eyes lifted to mine under long, morose lashes, and she righted herself into a sitting position. "Why? Where are you going?"

"The capital. Solaris."

My gaze slid to Briar, and I handed her the ancient book. The immortal witch's expression had turned grave. She'd been the one to tell me of the White Crow. She knew what my return—what going to Lumera—meant.

Mari frowned. At Briar. At me. "Well, I just told you—I can't do basic magic. Not even an invisibility spell, let alone opening a *portal between realms*."

"If you need aid there," Briar said, putting the grimoire down and tying her robe more tightly, "the Antler coven serves the rebel king, Hart Renwick. They travel through the Dreaded Vale, never in one spot for too long lest they be found by your father's army."

I nodded my thanks. She finally understood why I'd come.

"Who's Hart Renwick?" Mari asked.

"A Fae leading a revolution against my father," I said. "He's spent the last few years building up quite the army, and now apparently he has a coven fighting for him, too."

I'd never met the kid, but my spies spoke highly of the powerful half-Fae who had, over time, amassed an army of dissenters and had taken to calling himself the rebel king. He and his army stole through the realm, marauding lighte outposts, freeing fringe and border cities from Lazarus's reign, and inciting small yet formidable acts of revolt across the realm. The sheer feat of evading capture the last few years was impressive in its own right.

"What are you going to do there?" Mari asked, voice small. She was bright. She had an inkling.

"I'm going to avenge Arwen."

Mari's eyes cast down to her hands.

"You were right," I said to her, and only her. "It's my fault she died."

When her eyes found mine, they were swimming with sorrow. "Do you regret it?"

Whether Mari meant Hemlock Isle, or bringing Arwen to Shadowhold in the first place, or anything that happened in between, I still said, "Yes. Everything. I regret giving her hope. Having it myself . . . Thinking somehow we had a future."

Foolish. All of it.

Outside beyond the small, rickety balcony, the cool evening had become a starless night of pure pitch. I sucked in a breath that did nothing to quell the sorrow in my gut.

"Goodbye, Mari," I said.

Briar closed her eyes and began to chant the words I'd heard her utter only a handful of times. The sheets on the bed fluttered, the balcony curtains rolling on an earthy wind.

I braced myself for the split in time and space . . . but no such thing occurred.

"Briar?"

"Quiet," she shushed. "It's not coming readily. The realm is growing more untethered. I don't . . . I can't . . ."

The walls of the miniature library shook, molding cracking and beams groaning overhead. Mari and I exchanged one panicked look before the enchanted wind halted and Briar's eyes flew open.

"I can't do it alone, Kane."

My heartbeat had started to pound in my ears. "What do you mean? You're the—"

"I know what I am," she sniped, more shrill than I'd ever heard her.

Both of our eyes fell to Mari.

"No way," she said, scooting back on the bed, curls falling behind her shoulder. "Don't look at me like that."

"We're of the same coven," Briar said. "It's the only way."

"I have a lot of faith in you," I added.

"That faith is tragically misplaced," she said, chewing her lip. "Arwen would be so disappointed in me now."

"No," Briar said. "She wouldn't."

"None of us—*especially* Arwen—could stop believing in you if we tried," I said, kneeling so our eyes aligned. "That's not how friendship works."

"I'm going to fail you both. I know I am." She cut her eyes to Briar. "Without the amulet . . ."

"Your magic was never born from the amulet," Briar said. "As I've told you nearly every day, little witch. The amulet was a mere crutch, but you can access that power all on your own."

"You're wrong." Mari shook her head at both of us. "I'm not worth anything alone."

I didn't have endless time to play psychoanalyst. I had a father to kill and a woman to die for. I ran a hand down my face, over my bearded cheeks and chin. "None of us are. That's why I need your help."

But Mari didn't seem to hear me. Her wheels were turning. "Even if we opened a portal . . . there won't be any way back to this realm unless you take us with you. We'd have to do it again."

Briar's words held an edge of foreboding as she said, "He won't need one."

We both cut our gazes in her direction.

"What?" Mari's voice had ratcheted up an octave. "Why?"

"He's full-blooded now. It's a one-way ticket he's after."

In an effort not to hide how wrong she was about her first belief, I schooled my face.

But Mari only stared me down. "That . . . that shouldn't be possible. *How?*"

"A sorcerer," I said. "In the Pearl Mountains."

Mari's head shook softly as she processed the weight of my words. Then her eyes landed on mine once more. This time they welled with remorse. "Kane, you can't."

"No." My laugh was a mere rasp. "Not without your help."

"That's not what I mean and you know it," she snipped, but her expression was one of horror. "It's a suicide mission."

"Mari," I said softly. "This is what Arwen died for. This is what I need to do—what *we* need to do, so that her death is not in vain."

"That is some faulty logic. Your death won't bring her back, Kane. It won't right that egregious, universal, catastrophic wrong. And you." She turned to Briar. "You're just going to let him do this?"

Sympathy emanated from Briar as she studied Mari's pained expression. She lifted one elegant hand and brushed a curl from Mari's face, a strangely maternal gesture. "Lazarus must die. For what he's done. For what he plans to do. For Arwen. This is how we end his life."

"I've already lost Arwen . . ." Mari said, her voice hoarse. "I can't lose anyone else."

"If you don't help us now"—my next words stung more to imagine than to utter—"we will lose them all."

Mari said nothing to that, and I couldn't think past the truth I'd laid bare. How much more suffering was in store for all of us if I failed.

An owl hooted from beyond the balcony doors. Somewhere farther away, horses and their carriages stomped rhythmic noises into the city's cobblestone, and a slight breeze brushed curled strands of red around Mari's chin.

"Together?" Briar asked.

"Fine," Mari muttered in the end, standing from the bed and chewing her lip. "I can try."

Briar stood, too, and lifted her arms to the wooden beams across the ceiling. Mari copied the movement. They began to utter a low, practiced spell, and I wondered if Briar had already attempted this with Mari before to no avail. Perhaps in hopes—or with faith—that I'd succeed in finding the White Crow.

A static charge rent the room and sent every hair on my body standing on end.

"You're not controlling the magic," Briar said to Mari, though both their eyes were closed. "You're letting it play with you."

"I am trying my best," Mari bit through gritted teeth.

"You can do this, little witch," Briar soothed. I didn't think I'd ever heard her talk to anyone with such warmth. "Do this for your friend. It's what she would have wanted. Honor her, with your power."

"I *can't*," Mari cried. "It's too—"

A rumble of thunder struck outside, though the night sky sparkled, dark and clear.

And though tears had begun to fall steadily down Mari's cheeks, and my stomach twisted with the awareness that I was witnessing something too personal, or that I'd brought this sorrow upon Mari myself—

Pages rustled across the room.

Clearly bolstered by the progress, Mari whispered the incantation more fervently. Those tears, falling freely now, as she chanted. Like an oath. Like a prayer—

All the books in the compact library—cracked and old, pulpy and new—fluttering, whirring, spinning around us.

Mari's eyes snapped open and then shone. A little awe, a little pride, a little fear . . .

Briar gave her a nod of encouragement and the air, crackling with texture as they chanted, wrinkled around us.

The space between the two of them bent and retreated, yawning outward and splitting in half, edges rippling in translucent light.

Mari swallowed a gasp. Books tumbled to the floor.

My own heart raced at the sight. I'd never grow accustomed to time carving itself open in this way.

Briar's eyes pierced mine. The inky-black portal undulated between us, warped matter reflected in its rift. "Go, Kane. Go and finish what we started."

10

ARWEN

HOW COULD YOU?" THE WORDS DODGED PAST ALL MY shame and pride to hurtle from my lips. "And *why*?"

To her credit, Amelia didn't flinch or shift on her feet. She didn't gaze back to the glimmering reflecting pool. She didn't reach for me. "My entire kingdom, all those lives . . . To me, they were worth one Fae. Even someone I liked. I'm sorry, Arwen. It wasn't a decision I made lightly."

Loneliness had swamped me so thoroughly the last two months. Stifling loneliness that poured out though shameful midnight tears, and yet it had never felt more crushing than in this very moment, standing in front of someone I thought I knew. I had no words for her.

"As you can imagine," she continued, "I haven't spoken to Kane since."

"He'll kill you."

"I'm sure." Her eyes finally cast downward. With remorse or fear I couldn't tell. "But he won't wage war on Peridot's people for my mistakes. And that's all I care about."

"So Kane still thinks . . ."

"You're dead? Yeah. I'm sure they all do—I did."

"And you're here in Lumera only as Lazarus's ally." Not a plot, then. She was simply a guest of honor at a Fae masquerade.

"My deal with Lazarus was that my land would remain neutral. My armies won't fight in the war for either side. And if he wins, and takes all of Evendell, he won't decimate us."

"After everything he's done, what could make you think he'll uphold his end of the bargain now that he has me? Had he killed me, as you thought he did, he would have been unstoppable."

"Peridot is worth more to him preserved. Our fresh water and produce and livestock . . . He'll need all of it when he inevitably turns Evendell into this." She gestured to the ashy, sickly sweet air. The clipped dry hedges and trees bare of leaves.

"Amelia, you have to help me get free of this place," I tried. "They drain me of my lighte every few days. I think Lazarus might need it for some reason. Could he be weak or ill?"

"I doubt it. But . . ." She angled her head in thought. "The Fae assassins that can shift into those horrible creatures, Lazarus's mercenaries . . . They're his most valuable asset, and a dying breed. I wonder if he's pumping his best soldiers full of your lighte to create more."

I shook my head, my mask rattling. "You know I can't shift."

"You're a full-blooded Fae. Of course you can."

Desperation was clawing its way into my throat. "Is there anything else you can tell me? Anything you know of his plans?"

"Even if I somehow *could* help you flee the castle . . . you have no lighte, and this realm is a fucking hellscape. Earthquakes, thieves, beasts, harvesters . . . It's a mess. Even if somehow you braved all that, the journey back to Evendell would take you months and you'd never survive it alone. Nobody travels between realms without a portal anymore. And to find a powerful enough witch in these lands to open one up for you . . . there are probably only six or seven in the entire realm."

Tears stung behind my eyes. "I cannot just give up."

"That's the wrong way to look at things."

I must have made a face, because Amelia sighed before saying, "At least you're alive, Arwen. There's real power to be had at Lazarus's side. You can still help people."

"What are you saying?"

"You could change this realm, and Evendell, too, when he takes over. You'll be queen consort."

"I will not roll over and be *mated with* so I can have a meager slice of symbolic power."

Amelia's stern expression didn't waver. "You'd get used to it."

I recoiled. "Could *you*?"

"In some ways I did. For a while, at least."

My stomach hollowed out with her implication.

"My father made it clear before I was grown that my value to him—to my kingdom—would be found between my legs. He spoke often and crudely of how I'd be married off to please a royal man one day. Of the children I would bear, and the security my union would bring our kingdom. I was a token. A piece of meat, for the majority of my life. Eventually I learned to live with it."

Her voice was callous and detached but not even Amelia's unfeeling exterior could hide the pain laid bare in her words. The shame and sadness there. Despite everything, my heart ached for her.

"I got used to telling myself that one day I'd inherit my father's kingdom or my husband's and would put my *symbolic power* to real use."

I nodded, thinking of Powell. I'd told myself all kinds of things to make it through each lash of his belt. I'd survived, despite the pain and shame. It dawned on me that Amelia and I had both been thoroughly failed by the men who'd raised us.

"I'm sorry."

"It's fine. I'm just . . ." She sighed. "Trying to offer you the best advice I can."

"Even if I could survive it . . . Lazarus already wishes to see all the mortals in Evendell exterminated. Once he has enough full-blooded Fae heirs, he'll force them to repopulate both realms. Eventually he'll have halflings killed, and then all other Fae that aren't full-blooded, too. We can't allow any of that to happen." I took her cool, ring-stacked hand in mine. I'd been away too long—if Wyn had gone looking for me in the salon . . . I had to hurry. "You're one of the smartest people I've ever met. You're tough and decisive. If there's anything you can do, just try, all right? I believe in you."

Amelia jerked back as if struck, wrenching her hand free from my grasp. "How can you say all that? After what I did to you?"

I pulled my mask back over my face. "We're more powerful together than at odds."

I turned to leave—

"Wait." She grasped my arm. "If somehow you do get out of here . . . Will you tell your brother that . . . I'm sorry? That I never meant to use him?"

Ryder? What did he—

Oh, *Stones*. I'd told Ryder we were going to Hemlock Isle. Had he been the one to tell Amelia? I didn't even know they spoke . . .

She didn't wait for me to answer her before she said, "Good luck, Arwen."

I didn't look back at her icy eyes, covered once again by that remarkable mask, as I dashed through the courtyard and back into the boisterous ball. Up the sprawling stairs, my heels clacking in time with the music, and down that bustling hallway, to the doors of the women's salon.

No Wyn in sight.

Not good, not good—

Inside, it was even more packed than it had been before. I shoved through peals of laughter and gossip-tinged whispers until I found the latrine stalls and locked myself inside one. Itchy coat and mask shed, I breathed until my heart rate had slowed.

Only then did I emerge—

And spot Wyn backlit by gauzy pink light, prowling through, scaring women right and left.

"Wyn," I croaked. "Over here."

Even under those curled horns I could see his eyes light with relief. "Where were you?"

"Terribly sick. It got all over my mask . . ."

He appraised me, eyes narrowing. "I checked each stall. You weren't here."

"Where else would I have been vomiting for the last ten minutes?" I sucked in a breath.

An excruciating pause as he appraised me.

Then the stalls behind me.

I didn't exhale. Couldn't as his lips pressed into an even line.

"Come on," he said at last, pulling me by the arm from the salon. "I'll find you another mask."

Wyn led me back down the stairs and across the throne room. By the time we reached the dais I'd managed to loosen the unbearable tightness in my lungs just a bit. He guided me to my seat at the banquet table, and I found Lazarus's chair beside mine empty.

"Here," Wyn said, handing me a great gilded mask to match my dress. Solid gold and glimmering like the sun. Near-blindingly shiny, and as heavy as a slab of granite, the inside padded with sorrowful, mottled moth wings. The feel of them against my face as I slipped it over my head told me they were real. *Cruelty.* Everything in this palace—

"I'll be watching from back there." He motioned to where the other guards stood and I merely nodded, still a little shocked I'd gotten away with my deceit.

Nobody at the table spoke to me, and I was grateful. My mind was a whirlwind, and I needed . . . I needed . . .

I had no idea what I needed as I gripped a chalice filled with some bitter spirit.

Nobody was coming for me.

Kane, my family, my friends—all of them still thought I was dead.

I had no options. No plan.

I beheld my distorted reflection in the medley of sweating refreshments. A glistening, fatty spread stretched across the banquet table. Gold-flecked peas, bowls of spiced milks and stews, garlands of mulberry pastries—all of it oily and odious and pointed toward a whole roasted peacock, sitting directly before me, plumes of its magnificent, delicate tail feathers still intact.

Maybe I really would be sick.

A laugh that strung me as taut as a harp string ripped from my left. Lazarus wrapped up whatever conversation had brought him such mirth and took a casual seat beside me.

"Where have you been all night?"

He wore no mask, as if he were the only man in the palace—in the city—on equal footing with the Gods. No mask, but the richest golden coat and pants I'd ever seen, stitched with care and precision, and fit to his muscled body like a glove.

We matched perfectly. Nausea swirled in my gut.

"I wasn't feeling well."

"I'm sure." His tone sent my stomach plummeting down a ravine.

"Your Majesty—"

Lazarus turned to greet a heavyset man who ambled over to the banquet table with surprising grace given his size. He bowed to his king, and under layers and layers of rich green robes his large body jiggled with the movement.

"My truest apologies to have missed the gift-giving. But I did not arrive empty-handed."

"What kind of gifts?" I asked them both.

Knowledge was the only currency I'd be able to spend on an escape.

The weighty man's already-pink cheeks deepened their rosy hue. "My son is young, but already shows significant strength. The missus and I were able to juice him of almost a gallon."

My face held no neutrality. Not a drop. I knew it was not only shock—but repugnance—that contorted my expression. "You and your wife . . . drained your own child of his lighte?"

Interest sparked in Lazarus's eyes when he cut them to me.

The man in question didn't falter. "But of course! 'Tis the Solstice. And we had an abundant bounty."

Lazarus gave the man a generous nod.

"But *why*?"

The man's fuzzy brows lowered as he considered me, eyes sliding back and forth between Lazarus and me. The Fae king nodded at me as if to say, *Go on, tell her.*

"His Majesty has built a sanctuary here in Solaris. His court is bountiful and lush. He will conquer new realms for us to grow and become stronger . . . It's the least we can do, for our king."

Bountiful and lush? I'd only noticed the lack of flowers, of wood, of cheer, but now my eyes found the hanging, glittering stars of lighte, the decadent banquet spread, the extravagant clothes and jewels . . .

The portly man took my stunned silence as dismissal and bowed once more before leaving us. Lazarus only released a brazen laugh and returned to his chalice.

He wasn't just stealing lighte from his people. His own subjects were giving it to him *willingly*. I almost hurt for them, falling for his fantastical lies. His power reviled me, of course, but the *abuse* of such staggering power . . . Such a malicious, smug display of utter control. Such brainwashing of his stupidly loyal court.

"They think you're going to save them from the wasteland that is Solaris. They're sycophants, and fools, but you . . ." I studied his clean-shaven, coldly handsome face. "You plan to start an entirely new world without them. You feed off their *hope*."

Lazarus shrugged. "I only make promises I intend to keep. I will rebuild Solaris to its former glory. And I'll craft Evendell into the same for our offspring. The Fae here will throw themselves at my feet for what I'll have built them. What *we* will have built them."

"At what cost? Look at what your attempts here in Solaris have already done! All your finery and weapons and palaces with baths large enough to wash ten cities . . . Your greed has *ruined* the realm. How can you not see how wrong it all is?" I gestured at the banquet, the dancers—an entire celebration for reaping resources from innocent people.

Lazarus didn't even balk. His eyes only skated over me, rife with pity. "I'm sorry that's how you see it."

I fought the urge to gouge at his eyes with one of my three forks. "Go for the snail fork. Sharpest prongs of the lot."

Nausea engulfed me.

He was inside my mind again.

Which meant—

Lazarus didn't unleash his gloating, gleaming grin. He didn't raise a full graying eyebrow in my direction. He only nodded once, confirming my fears before turning to the noble Fae across the banquet table in jovial discussion.

Lazarus had regained his lighte. And I—

I couldn't feel anything yet, but I had no doubt I'd recover my lighte tonight, too. It had been three days since my last harvesting. And I was getting stronger. Every time they took my essence from me, it was as if my body was so angry, so fueled by rage, it replenished itself that much quicker.

And Lazarus was the most calculating, shrewd monster I'd ever met. He'd planned patiently for *decades* to wage war on his last living son so that he could ensure his win.

He'd taken a dose of lighte just as mine had regenerated.

Which meant now we were both powerful enough to conceive a full-blooded heir. He'd waited for the right moment like a toad eyeing a fat, fuzzy fly until *snap*—he latched his tongue around his prize. And tonight—I understood with perfect clarity and mind-numbing horror—that prize, that *harvest*, wasn't lighte.

It was *me*.

11

KANE

RETURNING TO SOLARIS AFTER HALF A CENTURY AWAY was not dissimilar to revisiting a childhood classroom as an adult. I couldn't deny the comfort, the familiarity—the soles of my feet knew the pebble-dashed streets of the walled city better than they'd ever know Shadowhold. I'd been raised here. Had played my first game of chess with my brother under that awning outside the noisy toy shop. Had broken my first bone climbing those still-mismatched stairs to the southern tower—the guard who'd allowed me such freedom was whipped the next morning in the city center until his back peeled like a late-summer peach.

These paved stone avenues only served to remind me that I'd never be that boy again. I could sail or fly or run anywhere—the highest peaks of the Pearl Mountains, the lowest depths of the Mineral Sea—but I could never truly go home. Not to the walls that had sheltered me in boyhood. Not to the life I'd built in Shadowhold. I was a nomad, with no destination, and everything still to lose.

Think on the bright side, I told myself. *You'll be dead soon.*

And it was true. Soon I'd spare the greater good from the monster that was my father, and in doing so, find my home there. Perhaps my coffin might serve as some new foyer. A mantel of graveyard soil. A roof of inching worms.

The brassy twangs and pitchy strums of an orchestra plucked me from my gruesome fantasies. I craned my neck up toward the looming palace flickering with glowy red light and the shadows of exultant bodies.

He was celebrating. Hosting a ball of some kind.

My father experiencing joy should have sent my dragon hackles straight up. The vacant ridges only served as a reminder of how egregiously underprepared I was to stalk inside those walls.

As I neared, the palace entry became visible, and I could just narrowly make out revelers wandering in and out amid the merriment, donned in elaborate masks.

The Lumerian Solstice. I'd been gone so long, I'd forgotten what had once been my favorite day of the year. More memories of Yale and Griffin, not even ten years old—unwilling to dress as anything other than stately guards. We'd fight my mother, who'd handcrafted brilliant masks of rich leather and real lion's fur to turn my brother and me into decorative, regal beasts.

This was good, actually.

A mortal in the palace of Solaris hunting for the Blade of the Sun? My full week in Pearl traveling across pillowy, silken clouds and endless snow had not offered me a single intelligent idea on how to accomplish that without dying. And swiftly.

But the masquerade was a godsend. Perhaps literally—I'd never know.

Once inside, finding a mask couldn't be too difficult. Knowing the Solstice, there would be fewer sober patrons than I could count on two hands. The real obstacle would be slipping inside in the first place.

Crouching behind a stationed carriage, I appraised the palace entrance.

Rows upon rows of those bone-white gates with their red-and-black filagree stretched on. Hordes of silver-clad Fae guards milled between every layer. And beyond them, deep inside the heart of the castle walls, I knew each invitee was being checked against an elongated scroll with at least a thousand names scribbled down its face. An infestation of thick silver armor would monitor that, too.

Perhaps . . . perhaps I wouldn't need a mask at all.

That silver Fae armor—molded carefully to each guard, sealing off everything but their face under a red visor—was as powerful a disguise as any headpiece or costume. One on one, I couldn't physically best a Fae soldier with my new mortality, but with a bit of creativity and the element of surprise on my side . . . I'd at least have a shot.

But I'd never get my hands on one of those men at the castle's entrance.

I hurried from the bustling gates toward the back of the palace. Around carts selling masks of monsters and dragons and exotic birds—I fought the trivial ache that stirred in my chest at the wings and scales—and through cobblestone alleys with decorative garlands of Fae lighte strung high between buildings.

It wouldn't be spare of guards, but I'd have far fewer to contend with. And I'd have the gardens—tall, strict hedges and precisely cut grass—as meager cover.

I kept my face buried in my cloak. I knew it was an unnecessary precaution—no mere citizen would recognize me after all these years. And even if they did, the fallen prince would have to be mad to return to Solaris without an army, and in his human form no less. They'd assume their mind had been playing tricks on them—nobody could be that foolish, right?

Wrong. So very wrong.

I was as foolish as the night was dark.

The dry, clipped gardens surrounding the back entrance were closer to the rich Solaris neighborhoods that hugged the city's walls. Those nearest to the palace were the most noticeably grand and stately. If I found myself outrunning Fae soldiers—or trying to—I'd at least have a chance of hiding in some noble's courtyard or lofty agate doorway.

I slipped behind a crisp, sheared hedge. Back here, only one spear-tipped gate stood between the gardens and the palace. Heart beginning to ratchet, I pulled my sword from its scabbard and threaded it under my arm and through the fabric of my tunic. From afar it made for a convincing stab wound. And my clothes were dark enough that they'd be unable to discern whether I was bleeding or not. I lifted my cloak's hood over my head.

Kneeling to the sharp blades of grass, I sucked in a mouthful of muggy Solaris air.

"Help," I called out with an exhale, crawling out from the hedge into clear view of the castle. Moving toward the suburban, pebbled streets, I writhed back behind another row of low, dehydrated bushes. I slid across the dirt, cautious not to actually slice the tucked blade right through my rib cage. "Dear Gods!"

I crawled even slower. Then I croaked out another garbled plea.

One set of footfalls sounded a few feet away. Hurried, but in no real rush. "Sir, this is royal property."

Victory sang in my ears. I only moaned, my face blocked by my hood. The soldier sighed, kneeling to inspect my grievous wound.

"What happened to you?"

I overtook him in one swift movement.

My cloak served as a fine noose, wrapped tightly around the flailing soldier's neck—working both to subdue him and silence his screams. I grunted as I rose to my knees, heart spasming, and kicked us both back behind the nearest towering hedge. Looming over him, I pulled the fabric tighter, and tighter still. His face—a round one slackened by shock and lack of oxygen—was turning a ghastly shade of purple. My muscles strained, my brow dripping sweat. The soldier clawed at me, nails scraping entire chunks of skin from my neck and cheek. The pain hardly registered.

An eternity crawled between us. He gasped and spit. All I could think was that his silver helmet would prove even more useful now that my face was marred by scratches.

"Please," he gasped, hardly audible. "Just let me—"

Death stole away with his final words.

NOW, *THIS* WAS A PARTY.

An upbeat melody blared through my eardrums, steady drum line like a heartbeat in my chest. Women danced with abandon, dressed like works of fine art, men drunk and drooling after them. Roasted bird and hot buttered rum scented the air. I swiped a full chalice of crimson birchwine from a server as I ducked through the throng and toward the banquet table.

Arwen's chocolate hair and endless eyes filling my mind, I raised the glass slightly and drank the rich spirit to her in one long swallow.

It was a beautiful night to die.

If I could commend my father on anything at all, it was his tremendous forethought. The man had always been six steps ahead of me. Ahead of everyone. Of course, once he realized the blade couldn't be destroyed he'd have it guarded night and day. Probably by the fiercest creatures known to man.

Which meant it was in one of the lairs.

The monsters Lazarus chained beneath these floors . . . they made my nightmares look like sleeping aids. Where they were kept were the only catacombs in the castle Griffin and I never dared explore. Not even at our most rebellious . . . or most inebriated.

The best route to the lairs would be past the raised banquet table atop the decorated dais, through the castle kitchens, and down into the—

"Honored guests."

Layers of skirts heavy like sodden mops slowed their swirls all around me. Shiny leather shoes stopped midtap. Bile pitched in my gut.

I hadn't heard my father's voice since Siren's Bay.

My head swam with startlingly vibrant memories of Leigh's and Arwen's screams. Sand that had grown heavy with blood. The clash of metal, bleeding into the band's quieting harmony. I tucked my chin down and pushed faster through the crowd, my heart slamming. The silver helmet covered my face, I knew, but it wouldn't be the first time he'd picked my thoughts out of a crowd. Though I'd found ways in my youth to quiet my mind around him, I didn't dare look to that dais and run the risk of letting my emotions get the best of me.

"What a triumphant celebration of our plentiful harvest," Lazarus announced.

The crowd of trashed noble Fae cheered.

Rat brains. Fucking imbeciles, all of you. How could they fall for his manipulative swill?

My eyes suctioned to the scuffed, checkered floor of the great hall.

Ten more feet. Maybe twelve. I could slip into the kitchens while he addressed his subjects. Make it to the monster lairs in the next few minutes, if I was fast.

I hurried past buxom women and potbellied men scarfing down enough food to nourish the entire starving realm. At every too-quick step that drew an odd look from a guest I slowed my pace until my legs moved rigidly, as if wading through a swamp.

Five feet now.

"I couldn't conjure a better night to announce, in the greatest union our realm has yet seen—"

I could just make out the oil lamps that lit the hallway that led to the kitchens. The chefs and servants and dishwashers fussing like hens to get each appetizer and drink out to the crowd. I dodged one such speeding server, steadying his tray of emptied glasses with a muttered, "Sorry."

"I present to you," my father continued, "the beautiful last full-blooded Fae, who has agreed to be my queen."

I stalled at his words, my eyes still on that bustling hallway, my blood turning to solid ice.

My first thought was that my father was lying to his people. He'd done it before. Countless times. He was the kind of leader—the kind of man—who would tell his subjects anything so long as it served him. He'd tell them all to slit their throats if it would award him more lighte, more power, more coin . . . Certainly he wasn't above dressing some unassuming Fae girl up and presenting her to his court as the captured full-blooded Fae?

Within a fraction of a second, a different, far more horrific thought drifted in: *He's going to display Arwen for them. Her rotting, impaled corpse. His crowd will cheer as he—*

No.

I was sick. Sick, twisted, depraved—that kind of barbarity permeated only my mind, not reality. He wouldn't . . . even *he* couldn't—

As the masked revelers around me boomed their cacophonous cheers, and morbid curiosity won out, I lifted my head to the banquet table.

A gold-draped woman stood in an elaborate matching mask beside my father.

It's not her. Don't do this to yourself. It's not her.

But . . . the woman's curled brown hair falling softly down her back, and the gentle shape of her jaw, and those full, worried lips . . . so similar. Standing there, body bound tightly in some garish gold monstrosity that hugged her hips and too-thin limbs and displayed her chest as if it were a feast for any lecher's eyes. Her lovely flushed cheeks. Her long, elegant neck. Her chest, rising and falling—

Everything inside of me halted.

No mask—not even the lavish gilded one that covered half of her delicate face—could hide those warm olive eyes from me.

Alive. She was alive.

Where devastation had run rampant—all of it, cleared out in a single instant. My vision blurred with hot tears. My knees buckled, and I locked them to stay upright. Was this real?

I took in the sweaty, delighted faces and grotesque piles of food and barrels of spirit. I was here. In Solaris. And so was she.

Arwen—*my Arwen*—was alive.

Even with the White Crow, I'd never allowed myself to have hope. But I doubted the woman I beheld now had ever given up on me. That thought alone—how she might recount the days she spent steadfast in her belief that I'd come for her, soft hand laced in mine as she spoke—it nearly sank me to my knees.

But I stood firm, holding her shadowed eyes as she observed the roaring crowd with nothing but loathing.

"In honor of our sacred Solstice," my father said beside her, "we swear a hallowed oath to bear heirs worthy of this palace."

His words slammed me back to this plane. This reality—*heirs*.

The crowd, still hollering with glee, cheered louder as Lazarus edged toward her. "True Fae heirs that will restore this great realm. Heirs that will bestow more lighte, the *strongest* lighte, back into its soil. And we'll begin our quest . . ."

Arwen flinched as he reached for her. Stroked her cheek. Her neck. Her arm.

I dug my toes into the floor to keep from launching myself at him. From becoming a human barrier between her and his fucking hands. He was *touching her* with his fucking *hands*.

Lazarus grinned as he cupped her backside with familiarity before a rabid audience. "Tonight," he promised.

No—*no*.

A harvesting ceremony.

That's why he'd put her in that vile, degrading costume. Why he'd fondled her before his entire court.

I pushed past a squealing woman in a ghoul mask as Lazarus grasped Arwen's face in one hand. Not gently. Not a touch between a king and his queen. But with malice. So tightly I could see the flesh of her cheeks draw inward, could see her recoil from his touch and try to yank herself away. But he was stronger, and he jerked her toward him.

I was barreling through a grunting, squealing crowd when he planted his lips on hers.

My stomach coiled into feverish knots, and I froze.

My eyes, locked on a more gut-wrenching sight than I had the stomach for.

He was *kissing her*. Not chaste, not kingly. A vile, vicious kiss. A promise of violence to come.

Arwen squirmed. Tried to withdraw from the intrusion.

And the sick, sycophantic members of his court all around me were still *cheering*, as if beholding a harmonious union.

I would *annihilate* him. I had to. And if I could, I would have killed each member of his court, too. Slowly. And with euphoric pleasure.

Lazarus released Arwen and motioned for the crowd to quiet down. In the absence of their hoots and claps I could hear only my heart pounding. My lungs, shallow with breath.

But I had to be smart, first. For her sake, I had to drown those volatile, impulsive parts of me for the time being.

Arwen was *alive*. She had survived the fall. Survived *impalement*. And not only was she alive, she had likely spent the last few months here. In Solaris. With my father. Betrothed to him. He had probably beaten her. Harvested her lighte. Done . . . unspeakable things to her.

And I would not be able to save Arwen, to shear the skin from my father's bones—to feed it to him as it regenerated for a thousand years—until I'd been reborn as full-blooded. If I charged the dais now, I'd be dead in the next minute, if not less.

And then he'd conduct the harvesting ceremony before his entire banquet of nobles without incident. An archaic practice performed at midnight every Lumerian Solstice. One which my father and his court believed would help him conceive the full-blooded heir he'd always hoped for.

All those men and women, watching in polite silence as he rutted—

I couldn't—*wouldn't*—allow that to happen.

I pulled my eyes from the now-seated Arwen, staring at her plate piled high with dead peacock, and moved swifter than I ever had in my life. Not for the dais, nor the monster lairs, but for my only hope of getting to Arwen before my father could.

12

ARWEN

I THOUGHT I'D DESPISED MY BLOODRED SUITE, BUT THAT room was a full, beating heart compared to the skeleton I stood within now. The harvesting ceremony wouldn't take place in my suite nor Lazarus's private quarters. The revolting tradition, which Maddox had so generously explained to me on our walk over, was held in this sterile, ceremonial bedchamber.

Glinting white marble floors without a speck of dust. A single dazzling, dark-iron chandelier hanging overhead like a guillotine. And a bed.

A large, sprawling bed.

Clean, silken white sheets. Prim. Folded neatly. Just enough pillows.

And crowding around the bed—at least fifty nobles, dignitaries, and esteemed members of Lazarus's court. Mostly men with round, greasy faces, drunk and stuffed from the ball still raging below us, sneering at me and revering me in turn. All of them—waiting. Waiting to watch me taken by their king. In clear, bright candlelight. Naked as a newborn mouse and just as helpless—

Alarm bells rang throughout my body. I couldn't stand still—fury and revulsion and undiluted fear writhed inside me so violently I was shivering.

Wyn offered me a bleak expression, but I couldn't bear to look at him. He, too, was accepting this sickening tradition. But there was no room for betrayal in my heart right now. Only urgency: I had to think of something.

One glance at the stately marble grandfather clock told me I had only a handful of minutes to do so. It was almost midnight. Lazarus would be here soon.

Though Wyn told me most near-full-blooded Fae women flocked to this chamber eagerly each year, hoping to bear their king a full-blooded heir, it was still a more revolting ritual than I'd expected, even of Lazarus.

A mistake, to underestimate his viciousness.

Between Powell and Bert, Crawford and Killoran . . . I'd come to expect the very dregs of human rubbish from most men I encountered. But it was the women who stood around this ceremonial bed—the wizened, crinkly Fae ladies who had surely seen their fair share of *harvesting*, who had the gall to shoot judgmental glares in my direction, or, even worse, appear flat-out bored by the iniquity—their gazes were the ones that truly shattered whatever might have been left of me.

If given the opportunity, I would have scraped the gleeful expressions from their high-boned faces with my blunt nails.

I shuddered again, jumpy and sweating. A hand brushed against my back and I nearly jumped through the stark white ceiling.

But it was only Wyn. "You're going to be fine," he whispered.

"I'm going to kill him." I sounded as ill as I felt.

"If I could," he said, hazel eyes simmering, "I'd do it for you."

Maddox prowled closer and hissed at us both. "He's coming."

Oh, Stones, oh, Stones—

The clock, ticking. So loud my ears rang. Two minutes—

I'd tried to slink down into someplace buried deep inside—to submerge myself somewhere untouchable, somewhere only my mind could find me, somewhere I could weather this as nothing but a mere husk of myself.

But my heart was thrumming like a caged bird and my limbs were *screaming* at me to fight, and the images skittering through my mind—I couldn't face them.

And if I didn't have enough lighte to protect myself from Lazarus, then I needed to flee.

"Can I use the washroom?" I asked my guards, blinking under the bright white reflection of all that lamplight. My face, hot and clammy.

It had worked for me once tonight.

Maddox opened his mouth, surely to tell me no, when an elderly Fae bathing in pearls craned her neck out from the crowd. "Holding it in will make you more fertile," she offered.

I recoiled in disgust.

"And," she added with a wry smile, "it'll feel better, too."

"Go," Wyn said before I could snarl at the frail woman. "You only have a minute."

I didn't know if that was a warning or merely the truth. Regardless, I hurried from his grasp and into the washroom before he or Maddox or any other voyeur in the crowd could say a word against it.

The door closed behind me and my chest nearly caved in from the silence. From the privacy.

Don't break don't break don't break—

I had no time for that. Nor enough time to tear my sweaty gloves off or rip the heavy mask from my face, nor to rinse my mouth with soap, scrubbing my lips until they were raw and plump and bleeding.

Still, that's what I did. The thought of Lazarus's saliva, his imprint being anywhere on me, made my skin crawl. It was enough that I'd have to live with the memory of his lips on mine. I would not allow him to touch me again.

My hands found the damp creases in my forehead and bridge of my nose where the mask had dug into my skin, and rubbed until my mind settled.

Think, Arwen.

My desperation was crystalizing into resolve. The spark had returned to my veins, that buzz of powerful lighte, as I knew it would. Sun and air and warmth sparkling deep within me. The rush of adrenaline that so often fueled my panic also fed my lighte. It had always brought me back when I was on the brink. Halden's poker, Reaper's avalanche of rocks—how many times had the fear I'd thought made me weak actually, physically, made me *strong*?

And Lazarus was using that strength against me. Allowing my lighte to regenerate so he could birth something sinister between us. Force himself on me, inside me—

The Fae king had been right: If I stayed here, I was a sow for breeding. A *womb*, as he had said. A womb with an audience.

So I wouldn't stay here. I'd put that fight-or-flight to work somehow—

Flight. *Flight.*

What had Amelia said? *"I bet he's using your lighte to create more of the shifting Fae."*

The porcelain of the washroom sink was cool and steadying against my palms as I braced myself to stay upright.

But when I'd fallen from that cliff in Peridot, hadn't a bizarre itching pricked at my shoulder blades? *Needles buried under my skin.* That's what I'd felt.

And when I plummeted from Lazarus's back toward his out-stretched claw, it had been *like points trying to break through my flesh.* As if they could hold me, suspended in air.

Had I been like Kane, and Griffin, and the mercenaries all along?

Heart buried in my throat, I hurried for the one rectangular window that reached the paneled ceiling and ripped the thin lace curtain aside to expose the glass panes behind. This wing was lower than my tower, and beneath the foggy clouds I could make out a glittering city of stars and lights and homes. Rolling hills bathed in moonlight, peppered in pines and oaks. A twinkling river curving in the distance.

I was suddenly ravenous for that cold, dry night air whipping at my hair and sending gooseflesh across my arms. My pulse raced for it. Even if it was thick with smog and ash. Even if it might be the last thing I felt before I flattened against the cobblestone below.

Shuffling sounded from somewhere. Either the roof above me or outside the washroom door, I couldn't tell, but I had to move. Had to *now.*

Now, now, now—

I crossed the washroom and snatched the gilded urn, embossed with the image of a wild horse rearing up on his hind hooves and filled with delicate hand towels. Then I turned on the water and let the rushing sound mask what I could only hope I'd be able to do next.

Feeling the urn's heft in my hands, I dumped the linens to the floor and lifted it once before smashing it against the glass of the window.

Nothing but a resonant *smack*. As if the glass was not glass at all but steel.

Spelled glass.

Sweat prickling under my arms, I cut my eyes back to the door of the washroom.

Waited without breathing.

Prayed to every single Stone that nobody could hear over the sound of water spraying against the porcelain basin—

And when nobody barged in, I slammed the gold bowl into the glass over and over, each slam of the urn more violent, less careful. My rage poured out through the gilded piece, through its brutal smashing. All that I had left—every last drop of hope—I slammed into that window.

Not caring as a chunk of the horse's gold mane broke from the carved piece. Not caring as my palms ached and my arms, weak and fatigued, began to shake.

I had to be free.

I *had* to.

Sweating and gnashing my teeth, I slammed again and again, until with both hands and one final blow carried by an arc of white, resplendent lighte from my palms—

Glass rained down.

As did the lovely nightscape before me.

What had been a lush, tree-dotted countryside beyond Solaris painted in silver by a full, white moon high in the sky was now . . . barren. No countryside. No riverbed. No uneven, green hills rising and falling. Beyond the walled city was . . . nothing. Miles and miles and miles as far as my eyes could see of emptiness. A few lone structures—possibly lighte outposts or slums—but nothing more.

Lazarus must've had Octavia spell all the windows in the palace. All of it—false.

Well—it didn't matter to me.

I'd figure out where to go next once I was free of this palace.

I would have rather wandered a desolate desert and died of starvation than stayed here, waiting for Lazarus to make me his before a room of shameless spectators.

I'd rather fail, falling to my death, than bear his children. I was sure of it.

Still, that assuredness didn't do much for my racing heart or my plummeting stomach as I climbed onto the windowsill. The ceremonial room was on the highest floor of the palace, which meant the soldiers and city folk below—the storefronts and cobblestone and lamplight—were so small they all blurred together.

My stomach dipped as muggy air swept along my face. Glass crunched under the soles of my shoes. My hands trembled on the jagged window frame I clung to.

The muted din of revelers echoed from the city streets as they left the ball. I could almost make out their figures as they bled out into the streets below me. Pointed roofs of noble homes and swirling streets and alleys below. The height was worse than dizzying. My vision yawned out and blurred. Burrowed into a single pinprick and tunneled. I held on with hands like claws.

A gory, final image of myself charged into my mind's eye: a splatter of bone and flesh upon the manicured Solaris hedges directly below the window. My heart spun in my chest.

More shuffling and thumping sounded from somewhere above or in the next room. No, it was definitely resonating from above—there was someone on the roof. Crunching, nearing. Drawing closer to the window I was practically hanging out of.

I couldn't be sure. I couldn't think, let alone listen closely—

So I didn't dare look up. Not even when I swore I could smell Kane's cedar scent invading my senses. I was losing it—the unsound mind of a woman seconds from free fall. I had to jump. Now. *Now.*

My last thoughts were, *Please let me be something that can fly. Please let me shift at all.*

And then I leapt—

Only to feel the frantic grasp of a warm, sturdy hand around my arm . . . but too late. Whoever had reached down from the roof and grabbed my wrist I'd pulled down with me.

We fell rapidly, his words lost as the wind shattered in my ears.

But that touch.

That touch that never wavered—that pulled me close to him, cradling me in his arms even as we plunged, prepared to insulate my fall with his own limbs . . . That cedar and leather scent in my nose, those silver-ringed hands on my bare back, the dark, sable hair clouding my vision—

Kane.

PART II

The Spark

13

ARWEN

I HAD NO TIME TO THINK AS THE GROUND SURGED TOWARD us both. My heart barely pumped a full beat. But I still had my lighte, and it coursed through me on pure animal instinct—

The bubble of sun-flecked power blossomed around us just in time to cushion our fall into the shrubbery below.

We still landed with a thud, Kane's hands around my waist and the back of my head.

My bubble fizzled quickly—far too much shock spinning in my mind—and thin sticks and leaves swallowed us whole.

Before I could utter a word around my astonishment, Kane climbed off me and pulled us both farther behind the hedges. We crouched, away from the prying eyes of soldiers drawn to the ruckus, twin breaths racing in our lungs. Tiny twigs had lodged in his dark hair and unruly beard, his face was gouged down the cheek, and his neck red and splotchy from where I'd all but strangled him with my grip— but that signature Kane half grin was undeniable in the moonlight. And those eyes, welling with tears, simmering softly on my own—

My heart gave out completely.

He must have seen it in my eyes, because he only brought a silver-clad finger to his lips as we observed the guards in shaky silence. Not a breath between the two of us as they peered at the bushes we'd nearly died atop of and decided the brief ruckus was nothing more than a fox or stray dog.

"You'd think plummeting to your death once would have been enough," he murmured once they were out of earshot.

That voice. I'd yearned for that voice. It was even better than I'd remembered: choked raw by emotion, and yet still a deep, confident rumble. One I had once described as thunder and a caress.

When he brought his hand to my face, I realized my cheeks were wet.

Kane was here, in Solaris. Grinning at me.

I flung myself into his arms like a kite in the air. I was sure I'd topple us both farther into the bushes, but Kane only loosed a muffled groan as he held me to him tightly, steadying us both. Those massive hands spanning the length of my back was enough to set tears free like a river rushing away.

And I couldn't help it as I cried into the spot where his neck met his shoulder. Buried myself farther into him. His scruffy beard against my cheek. Despite the Fae armor, he still smelled of leather and mint and sweat and skin. His breath was hot against the shell of my ear and my fingers twined in the strands of his dark, clean hair as I cried.

"Shh." His words muffled against me. Those lips. That dark, bearded chin. "My love," he murmured. "I'm here."

I couldn't inhale enough of him. His lips found mine in a daze of tears and I broke again. Choking out a weak cry as he kissed me so gently, so reverently, shrouded in brittle leaves and shrubbery. A kiss for all the times he couldn't. For all the nights I'd stayed up wishing for just a minute like this. A single second of it.

Kane tipped my face up to his, angled my chin and brushed his large hands across my neck and my shoulders, dusting off leaves and thorns. Picked them carefully from my hair. Those searing quicksilver eyes shadowed as he said, "Whatever you experienced, whatever you went through, whatever made you want to . . ." His jaw was rigid as a glacier. "I promise, together we can—"

"I wasn't trying to kill myself." My voice was like gravel.

He narrowed his eyes at me as if he didn't want to be cruel but knew that I was lying.

"Really," I promised, pressing a hand to my cheek to dry my tears. "I was trying to fly."

Relief swamped me as that pain in his eyes blossomed into awe and then male pride. "You can shift? Into what?"

"Well, nothing yet," I admitted. "Someone distracted me."

"I thought I could catch you before you leapt."

But . . . he hadn't shifted. We'd been falling to our deaths, and he hadn't shifted . . . "Why didn't you transform?"

His gaze devoured my own, filled with sorrowful understanding. "I don't have use of my lighte right now. And I don't have my Fae strength, or my heightened senses . . ."

"Kane, you're . . ." I couldn't fathom the words.

"Mortal. For the time being, yes."

He moved us deeper in the bushes until we could stand. A long stick scraped along my thigh, still exposed in my scant gown, but I hardly noticed. Kane . . . the most *Fae* being I'd ever known—was *mortal.*

My dragon, unable to shift.

"Do you miss it?" I couldn't help the question.

His breath shuddered out. "Terribly."

"How did this happen to you? Why did you come here? What were you even doing on the roof?"

"A piss-poor attempt at a rescue, clearly. Though, in my defense, I hadn't expected you to fling yourself out a window."

I tried to smile but my lips split where I had scrubbed them raw.

"What did you do to your lovely mouth?" he asked, reaching to stroke my bruised bottom lip with his thumb. The sensation sent sparks along my veins.

"He kissed me." The memory curdled in me like sour milk.

Kane's nostrils flared with thinly concealed rage. "I saw."

"You did?" I angled my head toward the castle roof, towering high above us. "How did you even know where to find me?"

He sighed tightly. "Every Solstice they hope the most fertile Fae will bear my father a full-blooded heir. I'm familiar with the ceremonial chamber."

I winced.

Kane marked my reaction, and wrath—*blistering* wrath—rippled from that stare. "Which is why you need to go. It won't be long before they realize you're no longer in the washroom."

"How, though?" I peered through the dense shrubbery as best I could. We were outside the castle, but in the heart of the city. Soldiers surrounded the perimeter, wealthy homes were gated and the streets too wide to offer cover.

"You're going to cut through that leftmost alleyway. The one to the right of the marble fountain in the center of that courtyard. Run until you reach the city's eastern limits. Then you trek for the next city over. Aurora. Once there—"

Horror was beginning to patter in my heart. "Wait, Kane—"

"*Once there,*" he pushed on, "ask around for Hart Renwick. Find his compound. How much lighte do you have right now? Was that protective sphere the last of it?"

"Kane, I'm not leaving you. No chance."

His eyes gave his remorse away, and for some reason that was worse than if he'd argued with me. His hands tightened where they rested on my shoulders. "You're going to have to, bird."

No, no, no—

He released me—misery, pure *misery* being parted already—and fished through the dirt for his helmet.

"Why?" I knew I sounded desperate. "Where are you going?"

"Back inside to find the blade and hope none of those weasels realize who I am before I do so."

"The blade is gone, Kane." I'd gone through this in my own mind a thousand times. "He destroyed it."

"It can't be destroyed. It always finds its way back to a master, and he wouldn't gift it to another. Not when it can be used to kill him. The blade is in the castle, trust me."

All this time my blade had been here? Waiting for me?

"How do you know all this? Why did you come here if you thought I was dead?"

"It's a long, deeply unpleasant story," he said. "If we make it out of here alive, I will regale you with the entire thing and you can tell me all the ways in which I'm an absolute moron."

"Kane—"

He drew his attention back toward the city beyond the bushes. "You'll look like any other partygoer to the soldiers out there. You're fast, you'll outrun anyone who catches on. Worst-case, you may have to—" He cut himself off to study me. "But we both know you can take care of yourself."

"What is your master plan here? Sneak back into the palace, steal the blade, and meet me in some other city?"

His silver eyes crinkled with warmth, but there was something else there. Sorrow? "Doesn't sound so hard, does it?"

"Kane." His jaw was tense when I reached to cradle his face in my hands. His beard rough and unkempt. I was going to cry again. "Don't do this."

"Don't worry about me." One dimple revealed itself with his crooked grin, and my stomach flipped anxiously. "The armor will do half the work."

"Do you even know where the blade is?"

"At first, I thought it would be in the monster lairs."

"Monster? What kind of monster?" I was braver now . . . brave enough to launch myself out a window with nothing but gold heels and a dream, but still—the word "monster" didn't do *nothing* to me.

"*Monsters*," he corrected. "Plural. Their lairs are peppered all throughout the palace catacombs."

"Wonderful."

His large hand encircled mine and squeezed. I could feel his muscles, taut and ready for the bloody fight to come. "I figured he'd have the blade guarded by the fiercest creature in Lumera." He gestured down to the impossibly tight heels laced around my legs. "You can't run in those."

"Right," I muttered.

"Then I realized," Kane continued, kneeling to the ground, "I was right." He gently slipped my foot out of the heel and all the blood rushed back into my toes and arches. I flexed my foot gratefully. "Lazarus believes *himself* to be the fiercest creature in Lumera."

"You think he keeps the sword in his own wing?"

When Kane stood back up, his frown was almost a sneer. "I think he's the kind of person who gives an order and then does the job himself before anyone can fuck it up. I bet it's in his very bed."

I shuddered at the thought.

Kane's eyes shot down to me and I clocked the grimace he fought to hide. "I'm sorry . . . I didn't mean to—"

"It's fine. I'm—"

"Ready?" he asked, eyes grim.

I wasn't. It was all happening too fast. Too soon. Kane was mortal. We'd just been reunited, and now to be split apart so soon once more . . . What if we never found each other again?

But I knew this man better than I knew the rhythm of my own heart. He wouldn't budge.

"Fine," I breathed. "Go. And I'll meet you at that compound."

With a nod he slid the helmet down over his head. In the suffocating dark night, he really did look like one of them. I tried to focus on the familiar shape of his nose and dip below his lips. I lifted to my toes and pressed a single kiss to the slice of his neck that wasn't covered in weighty Fae silver.

A resigned sigh ebbed from him. It was bereft, actually, but I could barely see his expression under the silver helmet. "I love you, Arwen," he said, the silver rings on his hand scraping gently across the skin of my back where my dress hung open as he pulled me close.

Before I could say it back—before I could get in one full inhale of his warmth, his smell—Kane slipped from the bushes, fitting seamlessly in with the other soldiers milling about the street.

Something cold and prickly crawled down my spine, gnawing through my stomach and limbs. A sensation I'd felt too many times.

He was keeping something from me.

14

KANE

THE BLOODRED MARBLE FLOORS OF THE PALACE HAD AL-
ways given away my brother and me as kids. The snapping of
our feet, haphazard as we ran and roughhoused and sent expensive
sculptures toppling with our boyish glee. Too many lashings from
my father and his enforcers had taught me to walk heel-toe to hide
the noise. I stalked quietly past the dozens of soldiers. My heart
thundered in my pilfered Fae armor.

In stark contrast to my slow, methodical steps, my mind was
spiraling. In the shock and relief and sheer *joy* at holding Arwen—
feeling her piled-too-high hair tickle my chin, inhaling her orange-
blossom scent, kissing those lips . . .

Lost in all that honeysuckle and warmth, I'd forgotten what I'd
come here for.

To die.

To kill my father, and thus, to die.

"And if I raised your lover from the soil . . . gave you the full Fae

blood that you seek? If I said neither of you had to die?" Len had asked. *"Would you still sacrifice yourself for the good of the realm?"*

And what had I thought to myself?

No. Absolutely not. I'd wanted to tell him, *Fuck no, and frankly, fuck you for even asking.*

And he had granted me my request regardless.

Perhaps he knew what I, in that moment, still hadn't yet.

That if by some wretched, cosmic joke I found the other half of my heart still alive, that perhaps I'd choose not to give my life for the good of the realms. That I was a selfish, greedy bastard and I wanted nothing in this world but her. Not justice. Not revenge. Not to save the lives of millions of innocents.

Just. *Her.*

But that in a *second* cosmic joke—one surely the Fae Gods were beet-red with laughter over—I was incapable of being selfish with Arwen.

She'd never be able to let Lazarus live. Not before he'd captured her, and surely not now. She'd never let him conquer and maim and destroy. What was I to do? Hold her hostage? Force her to live a long life with me while everyone else suffered? Force her to live knowing that suffering was our fault, because we wanted to be happy? I'd never do that to her. And I'd never let her pay the ultimate price for Lazarus's death.

So I'd have to instead, in her place.

Perhaps the man that wasn't Len hadn't known it all then. Perhaps he'd only hoped.

But I knew for certain—if I managed not to fuck up somehow—that my brusque, hurried *I love you* would serve as our last goodbye.

Arwen would make it to Hart. I had more faith in her than

anyone. The rebel king would get her home safely. Across the channel or with a portal cast by the Antler coven. And I'd find the blade. I'd kill my father—fulfill the promise I'd made to that Fae God.

I'd die for the realms. I'd die for my people. I'd die for Arwen, so she could go on living.

By the time I'd reached Lazarus's bedchamber—the door in the tiered glass atrium marked with the sigil of the moon—not one guard had even cast a glance in my direction. I raised a hand to the red stone handle, pulse thrumming.

"Hey," a husky voice called to me.

I said nothing, jangling the handle.

"Hey!"

Open, damn it, open—

"I'm talking to you." The silver guard drew nearer. A short, stocky oaf, his armor a little too big. "Are they still fucking?"

Acid singed my tongue even as relief loosened my shoulders.

"Yep," I said.

The guard nodded, impressed. "Good on him. I'd go for days with that little thing, too."

I nearly bit through my tongue.

"What'd he send you for?"

"Fresh trousers. Old man doesn't have the self-control he used to."

The kingsguard stared at me like I'd spoken sacrilege.

I didn't inhale.

My sword burned through the scabbard at my hip. I reached for it . . .

Until the small man broke out in a braying, boisterous laugh. The imbecile wheezed over and over, until tears had gathered behind red glass that covered his crinkled eyes.

"Off you go," he barked, patting me hard on the shoulder and sliding his lighte across the spelled door handle.

I let myself into my father's room without another word. For a moment, bathed in near-darkness, all I could hear were my own shallow breaths and my heartbeat slamming too fast inside my head.

My father's bedroom was dark and stagnant. A window had been left open, night air sending thin black curtains around like wisps of smoke, but the Solaris breeze did nothing to ease the thick air.

I squinted in the darkness—his bed was perfectly made, as always. Not a crease. Not a fold out of place. The vaulted ceilings and stone floor made for a chilling echo as I strolled through.

My hands raked over the face of his marble desk feeling for hidden cubbies and drawers. I combed through his orderly bookshelves for false walls, and then his armoires for the same. Past each rich tunic and robe, hunting for hinges or the smell of lighte or glimmer of magic. Under obsidian ottomans to inspect each marble tile, I crawled beneath the heavy bed, palmed atop shelves for latches or keys or safes. I even dug through the pristine fireplace that hadn't been lit in millennia. Nothing.

The room was bare of any blade.

He's your father, I told myself while lodged under a leather reading chair. *Where would he keep the only weapon that could kill him?*

The sound of his voice in the doorway stalled the breath in my lungs. "On me, of course."

My blood ran cold in my veins.

Slowly, I eased out from underneath the stiff leather. "Father."

"Son," he answered, closing the door behind him and peeling off his black-stitched formal coat. When he hung the refined piece on the coatrack, a mighty, glinting weapon shone from his scabbard.

Sheathed at his waist—the Blade of the Sun. Its hilt a dead give-away, ornately encrusted with the nine Holy Stones.

Focus tunneled my vision.

Four feet from me—three, perhaps—was my ability to become full-blooded Fae. To regain my dragon form. To take Arwen's fate away from her, save her life, solidify her many thousands of years of living along with millions of other innocents . . .

"So that's where you went," Lazarus almost hummed, prowling toward me, so slow I wasn't sure he was actually moving.

I fought every urge to scramble backward. "Get out of my mind."

Lazarus unleashed a repellent smile. "It seems I've been stood up. Any idea where my harvest has run off to?"

My mind guttered into stillness. Utter silence. I knew better than to think of her or where she was now.

"I'll kill you for that," I vowed. "For what you tried to do."

"With the blade strapped to my body? That would be some trick."

"That it would." My lips curled from my teeth in a menacing grin. "Want to see?"

I prowled closer.

Lazarus's deep laughter halted my movements. My father sank comfortably into a velvet chair. He unsheathed the Blade of the Sun, winding the weapon aimlessly between his hands. "In all your fool-ishness and impulse, my dragon child . . . have you not realized what you've given me?"

I said nothing. Thought nothing.

"A true Fae heir, my boy. The only one I ever wanted."

Oh, Gods—

Me.

"I'll never sit on the Lumerian throne."

He only smirked. A game—it was all a game to him. "If not you, and not Arwen's child, then who?"

"Hart Renwick." The rebel king could have the realm for all I cared. I wanted nothing to do with it. "He's been building quite the army."

Lazarus only cackled—genuinely, bafflingly amused. "If you think I'm threatened by the rebel king, you haven't been paying attention. The boy is little more than a halfling." His teeth gleamed in the spare moonlight. "When I am gone, the only man who shall sit upon my throne and call himself King of All Realms will be true Fae. If not you, son, then you must understand why Arwen's womb is my only option."

I will kill you. I am going to fucking kill you. "You will not touch her. Not ever again."

"How can you be certain she isn't already with child?"

I flinched, and hated myself for it. "She would have told me."

"Perhaps." He stood and circled over to the bed, smoothing out a crease I couldn't see. "Or perhaps she was ashamed, son. Perhaps it was painful for her at first, but . . . All those scars along her back, and burns across her stomach . . . Women like that." He shook his head at the memory. "Eventually they start to like it."

I lunged for him, sword raised, aiming for his cracked, shriveled heart.

Steel met steel with ferocity, and a furious growl ripped from him. The Blade of the Sun rippled with frost in his grip, sending icy sparks splitting where our weapons clashed. My mortal muscles barked with the force of his blow.

My next strike knocked the blade from his hands. We both watched in dismay as it scattered across the room.

I lunged after it, but spears of solid ice shot from my father's palms.

Narrowly dodging the shards, I dropped down to the ground and scrambled behind the iron bed frame. Glass shattered behind me, raining down in bursts. Books clattered to the floor, a thick paperweight toppled. I could taste my fear. Could feel my hands shaking like they'd never done before. I'd never been so . . . *fragile*. One of those spears—just one wrong move—and I'd be dead.

"How long have you wished to do this?" I croaked.

Lazarus launched javelins of solid ice in my direction as I clawed my way across the floor. A single spear shot past my head, and wisps of my own black hair fell to the floor between my hands. But the blade glinted on the thin, gray rug by a leather chair—I just had to wrap my hands around it. Just *once*—

Disdain clouded my father's voice. "You have never understood a single thing, have you, son?"

I dove, one arm outstretched, reaching, *straining* to touch—

But a mist of suffocating cold slammed into my chest and sent me flying backward atop crushed glass. My helmet flew from my head, teeth biting into my tongue. Hot blood filled my mouth.

"You think I want to kill you?" Lazarus thundered. "You're my fucking son."

For a moment, only our ragged breaths rent through the room.

My voice was so low I could barely hear myself. "You actually want me to rule alongside you?" My throat tightened with some emotion I could only attribute to a far, far younger version of myself.

My father's silence spoke a hundred years' worth of words between us.

He did not want to kill me. All this time.

Furious breaths heaved in and out of his lungs.

But his labored breathing—I'd never heard my father pant. Not when using his lighte, not ever . . . This . . . it seemed difficult for him. Something was wrong.

With a bracing breath I stood and lunged for him once more, throwing my body into his. We slammed into the floor with too much force—my chin rebounding off his sternum, his head smacking the stone with a *whack*.

I braced for the ice. For his power—but nothing came.

Instead, pain bloomed across my face as his fist—the iron fist of a true Fae—collided with my jaw.

My vision blurred, my ears rang . . . and yet . . .

I laughed.

He had *punched* me. My own father.

Because he was out of lighte.

I reared my fist back and delivered an answering blow. My father's nose crushed beneath my fist, and the feeling—the sensation—was so cathartic I did it again. And again.

He sputtered blood.

And then pain cut through my side. My ribs, my kidney—as his fist slammed into my body.

Across the floor my knuckles grazed a candlestick. One that must have fallen in the hail of ice spears. My fingers wrapped around the pewter and before my father could slam another fist into my face, I brought it down across the crown of his head.

The *crunch*—and his pained groan—sent adrenaline into my bones.

"Where are my Gods-*damned* guards," he bellowed. "*Guards!*"

I wondered the same. We'd been making enough noise to raise alarm bells. I could only hope something had stalled them. And would continue to.

"Guards!" he screamed again.

"Scared to fight me like a mortal man?"

He didn't answer as blood leaked from his nose, brows furrowed in both fury and concentration. He'd never looked so old to me. So tired.

My nails dug into him, scratching across his wrinkled face, the paperlike skin of his ancient neck, drawing blood—

His blow to my liver was like being run over by a stallion. I hadn't experienced physical pain such as this in my life. Mortal pain.

But our brawl—

We'd landed within grasping distance of the Blade of the Sun. My eyes cut to its glinting face on the thin, gray rug beneath that leather chair, bathed in darkness, mocking me—

Another blow from his fist smashed across my face.

Pain sprang behind my eyelids and in my shattered jaw.

His fist collided again and the world expanded and pinpricked around me. Nauseating and unfiltered. Time slowing. Something wet spilling from my nose and down the back of my throat.

I swung with my free hand, but each punch of mine was weaker, and weaker still.

Until I blinked through swollen eyes to find him brandishing my own sword above me. Double-bladed, vicious point hovering just over my throat. That steel an oath of death.

But my fingers . . .

They'd just barely reached the clean-cut edge of the gray rug.

With the last dregs of strength I had, with cords of muscle I hadn't ever used before, I wrapped my hand around that thin edge and *pulled*.

"Goodbye, my boy."

Lazarus hefted the sword up and brought it down just as the Blade of the Sun's hilt kissed the skin of my palm.

And in that moment, the one in which the blade met my flesh—

All noise hollowed out to a single ringing silence. The ground beneath me spider-webbed out with jet-black shadows—my shadows, folding and constructing themselves into my *wings*. Metallic lighte filled my nostrils as I sucked in the first deep breath I'd been granted since the moment Arwen jumped from that platform in Hemlock.

And then I was beautifully, horribly, mercilessly ripped apart.

15

ARWEN

BACK IN THE BATHS, LAZARUS HAD SAID I WAS DIFFERENT. Or that I thought myself as much. Well—he was right. I was different now. Braver, less trusting—stupider maybe. Whatever it was . . . I never ran for that alleyway.

I'd stood, in my horrid gilded dress and bare toes, hiding in the bushes where Kane had left me. I'd told myself, *Just long enough to see him come back out with the blade.*

And when I couldn't hear my own thoughts over my raucous heartbeat a minute longer, I'd gone after him.

"Excuse me," I said to the first guard I found on the cobbled road, making my voice sound innocent and lost. "I'm looking for my king?"

He only eyed me, sweaty under his bloodred visor, sizing me up. Another strolled over, hand on his pommel, shiny in the moonlight. "Fae girl, did you run?"

"No." I shook my head, willing my eyes as big as dinner plates. "I got lost. This corset is just so tight." I shimmied around in it, pressing my breasts together. "I only needed some air. If you would just bring me to my king . . ."

They were silent as they studied me, attempting to make sense of my vaguely flirtatious babbling. Another, more stately guard with a prominent mustache wandered over, and the three clustered around me like moths to a naive, busty flame.

"Take her to the king," Mustache said. "He's on his way back to his wing now."

Jackpot.

Inside the palace the candelabras were dimmed, the music had ceased, and the faint peals of laughter and singing had been silenced. The ball was over, and any remaining members of Lazarus's court were upstairs, waiting to watch me be defiled. We sped through an arch that looked out onto a courtyard, and ashy night air called to me through the glass.

I'd been free. Now I was back in this nightmarish, poisoned palace. I should have listened to Kane. I'd surely be deposited right back into my suite, trapped once more.

Do not panic now. Find Kane. Work together.

Freedom outside these walls while a mortal Kane suffered inside them was not any freedom I was interested in. I just needed to get to Lazarus's wing. I'd use my lighte then. I still had some rolling through my veins. Enough to defend myself.

Finally we arrived at Lazarus's atrium with all its strange doors and their symbols.

"Is he in there?" The sweating guard beside me called to the other armored men in the atrium. I counted five. More than I could likely take alone, but with Kane's help, wherever he was . . .

"Indeed," one replied, intrigue drawing him nearer. "Is that the girl?"

"Yeah, she—"

A single crash rang out from Lazarus's bedroom. Like glass shattering. The guard beside me stiffened, reaching for his sword.

Shit. *Shit*.

That was Kane. It had to be. In there, mortal, with his father—

I moved before I could think.

My lighte flung from my fingers in ribbons of hot, white fire. The power lassoed around the two guards nearest Lazarus's bedroom door before they could get inside. Their screams echoed off the domed glass ceiling. It was the surprise that had doomed them—

But I wouldn't be as lucky with the others.

Lighte like a vicious, honed wind flew from the sweating Fae guard's hands and I dropped to the ground mere seconds before it could ensnare me. I could shoot my own power back at him, but thought it better to conserve what I had left.

Instead, I crawled for the unconscious men I'd charred, brandishing a dagger taken off one just in time to slice it through the neck of another soldier, snarling as he lunged for me.

An older, haggard guard's cloudy gray lighte snapped through the air and sent me back down to the ground. Agony radiated across my shoulder. When he raised his hands once more, I rolled to the side, drenching myself in the blood of his fallen comrade.

I raised my hands as he hurtled for me—

But his blow never came.

He clattered to the floor, body sizzling on impact.

Sizzling, as flames from *my palms* engulfed him, until the embers were snuffed out entirely by his peer's wet blood.

Triumph and hot, thrumming *power* lit me from the inside. Nobody would stand between Kane and me. I'd topple this whole palace to get back to him. And as if my lighte understood that, the power funneled out of my hands in jets of fire and sunshine, casting the wing in blinding rays of light and gilding the night-dark hall.

And that's what it was. Power. I was more powerful than these men. I could see it in the way the remaining two approached me cautiously. Rabidly angry, embarrassed—but cautious. Fae soldiers or not, I was true Fae. And they . . . they were *scared*.

The dagger I'd nabbed flew through the air toward a new, incoming guard—someone who'd heard the noise or seen the feathered licks of fire brightening the pitch-black atrium—and lodged in his visor, carving its way through his eye. Gory gurgling spewed out as he crumpled to the ground.

Kane would have liked that one.

The last men appraised me. A shorter guard, wheezing furiously, and the sweating man who'd brought me here, clearly regretting his choices.

I stood, sucking in a breath. The muffled shouts of Kane and his father echoed through the door behind me. I had to be quicker—

The sweaty guard unleashed his own stormy lighte at me, and the other soldier ran for Lazarus's bedroom. Strikes of needle-sharp wind stung my legs and face—but my white flames engulfed them too quickly, protecting me as mightily as they destroyed.

Before he could advance with a stronger attack, my lighte swallowed the sweating guard whole.

Even his screams.

Until—

Until a *hand*—a firm, thick hand—closed around my throat from behind and the other gripped my arms behind me in a vise.

I gurgled for air, kicking at impenetrable silver armor.

Every limb—every *nerve* in my body—protested as I fought and fought and fought to breathe. Joints and tendons straining. My elbows writhing into his chest.

I could hear in his growls and grunts as I squirmed. "Don't fuss," he ordered, his meaty hands squeezing me closer and closer to unconsciousness. Pain whipped through my chest. I was running out of air.

With the last of my energy I closed my eyes and tried to focus on all Dagan had taught me about my lighte. He'd always said to focus on my emotions—that therein lay my power. And Kane—

He was likely on the brink of death if he was alone with his father this whole time.

That thought alone—

A whirl of conquering sunlight shot from my mouth as I threw my head back toward the guard and *screamed*.

Air rushed into my lungs as I fell to the floor. And while I heaved in precious lungfuls, I took in the still-twitching crisp on the marble floor behind me, his flesh sizzling in my nostrils.

I had no time for relief nor to thank the Stones—

I leapt over scorched, distorted bodies and shoved against the door to Lazarus's room.

My fists slammed at the anthracite with every ounce of energy I had left. Slammed and slammed and *slammed* until the bones in my hands had surely cracked and splintered and pain radiated up my arms into my already throbbing shoulder blade.

I used all that was left of my lighte blasting strike after strike at the door's handle and hinges and frame to no avail.

Spelled. The door was spelled shut.

"Let me in, you *coward*," I screamed at the unflinching, ugly black stone. Thumping my now swollen fists against it.

A mighty crash sounded from the other side. Grunts and heaves.

Kane was alive. And I nearly broke—

I'd been so scared. So scared to lose him.

I had to find another way inside before our luck turned.

My eyes landed on the door marked with the insignia of the sun. The one I'd seen soldiers carrying those massive barrels of my lighte into the day I'd been brought here for the baths.

A terrible, *terrible* idea coursed through my mind.

If I wasn't getting in with my own power . . . I'd just need more. *Much* more.

I moved, exhausted, inhaling the seared flesh of men I'd practically cooked alive. Smoke was still curling off the now charred fur settees. The atrium was destroyed—books and vases, frames and debris, all of it dripping blood and sizzling. Bodies and limbs fanned out like a gruesome mosaic across the floor—

I'd *massacred* seven people.

Killed them like animals—

Inside that room now, bird. Analysis of ethics later.

After everything—that voice inside my head was still his.

I threw myself inside the room marked with the symbol of the sun and slammed the door shut. It was too dark to tell exactly what I shared the space with. But the smell—a bit metallic, a bit astringent . . . like coins and spirit and something else too potent to describe. That was all I was hoping for: *lighte*.

Sounds of violence filtered in through the wall. Thumping, roaring. The crashing of some weighty stone furniture.

Hurry, hurry—

I felt around in the darkness. Round glass containers filled the space. Each about the size of my torso. I slammed my fist into the glass, and the barrels *glowed*.

The entire room, cast in an eerie yellow, like a vengeful sunrise—

Before me were not just a few vats of lighte. Not the handful I'd seen carried inside days ago . . . No, Lazarus's reserves were rows and rows and *rows* of these barrels. Rising high up into vaulted ceilings. Enough lighte to power a city.

To win a war.

Or . . .

Or to destroy the walls between us. Enough lighte to get me to Kane.

I pressed my hand against the barrel. The lighte whirred and shook, glowed brighter, *angrier*—

Heavy footfalls and the clamor of guards' shouts sounded in the distant hallway. After using nearly all my power to eviscerate those soldiers, this was the only chance I was going to get.

I gathered every last ounce of strength I had left in my bones, sucked in a ragged breath, and slammed a ferocious blast of white-hot fire into the barrel before me.

A single vicious *crack* sounded in the half darkness.

And in the span of a heartbeat, some deep, base instinct formed a weak bubble of shimmering illumination—the very last lighte I had—around my huddled body before I was engulfed in a hurricane of blinding fire.

HEAT.

Incessant heat swamped my body.

Sticky. Prickling. So hot it was flashing cold before burning up again.

Kane. Where was Kane?

My face was so hot the tears were drying on my cheeks as they shed. Not tears from pain, but from the debris in my eyes. Glass and dust and shards of stone.

Ringing filled my ears alongside shouts of horror, agony—

And *roaring*. A dragon's roar.

Lazarus?

I scrambled to sit upright, but my legs . . .

My legs wouldn't move. I couldn't feel them.

Not good. I blinked and blinked and blinked until the world came back into focus.

At first, the blur before me was hot and bright and tinged red.

Then it clarified in an instant, and if I'd had any moisture in my throat I would have screamed.

Fire—all around me. Licks of it still heating my face. The entire lighte repository was gone, and in its place a gargantuan blaze of pure heat. The door had been blasted open—no, blasted *off*—and outside, where the glossy walls of the atrium once were . . .

Scurrying bodies climbing over a mere foundation—rubble and silver armor and uniformed handmaidens. Some tending to injured guards, others running from falling scaffolding and glass. Collapsed pillars, dangling, charred chandeliers, candelabras impaling—

If this palace had been filled with life—potted plants and gardens and *wood* and *wicker* as the fortress at Siren's Cove had been—the entire place would be pure ash.

My eyes squeezed closed. I couldn't hear my own breathing over the tumult. The marble beneath me was cracked in half. Smoke filled my lungs as I tried to crawl forward, dragging my immobile legs with me. I'd either suffered a spinal injury in the explosion or my legs were numb from impact, and I'd need time to regain feeling. I prayed to the Stones for the latter.

Either way, I had to get away from that heat before I was broiled alive. Had to find *Kane*.

Outside of the receptacle was only marginally cooler. Bits of fabric from the settees and rugs were still lit with low flames and in-candescent cinders yet to be extinguished.

And out here, too much night—

That smoggy air and filtered moonlight slunk through my hair and along the skin I could still feel—my arms, my neck. The bare back of my ridiculous gold dress.

The entire ceiling of the atrium—that soaring arched glass dome decorated with wrought iron and filagree—just *gone*. The walls, too. The few left behind broken in half and charred and scorched with soot.

And Lazarus's bedroom—blasted into oblivion. Dark, rich bedding and expensive rugs alight with flame. Books on fire, ashes swirling.

Empty. No Lazarus, and no Kane.

Heavy feet thumped toward me.

Blessed, sturdy footfalls.

Kane—

Thank the Stones. Consciousness was slipping away and my body hurt so thoroughly . . .

And then, like a ship's horn in blinding fog revealed a behemoth sea creature: slow, resonant *humming* . . .

A callous, calm sound as those boots drew nearer. Like a finger pressed on a single out-of-tune key. A dissonant, stagnant pitch.

That noise sent my blood to ice as I peered up at the face looming above me.

Not Kane.

Maddox.

16

ARWEN

Maddox snarled as he took in my wounds. My undoubtably pale face. The dead guards and toxic flame and glass-strewn chaos reigning over the atrium. "What the fuck happened?"

"We were attacked."

He knelt, his eyes narrowing. Flames crackled behind his thick head. "Lying whore."

"No," I pleaded. Tried to stand.

Mistake.

Wobbling on bloodless limbs, I fell to the floor, palms barely extending fast enough to catch me. My body screamed in pain.

"You did this." His voice sliced through my dizzying thoughts. "You fucking did this."

An unstable balcony in the hallway clattered down in a crash of smoke, sending nurses and handmaidens screaming. A column followed suit. The palace was collapsing.

Unbothered by the disintegration around us, Maddox grasped

my shoulders and yanked me up with his meaty hands. I scratched and tugged away to no avail.

"Stop." My voice was too hoarse to hear over the shouts and pleas and screams.

Then I got a decent look at him.

Maddox's face was covered in ash. His ear, blown clean off. His nose was bleeding. "You're going to be sorry." Maddox swore, wrapping a single hand around my throat and squeezing, eliciting an involuntary whimper from me. "I am going to make you so," he said, grunting and tightening his fist, "*so* sorry."

I clawed and choked, my limp legs dangling, leaden beneath me.

"Let her go," someone called. "Let her go, Maddox!"

But Maddox was too rageful. I could see it in his beady eyes. His grimacing, blocklike face. Nothing would stop him from ending me. And it would be easy. I already had no air. A concussion, I thought. Some spinal injury, and burns. So many burns . . .

I could barely process Wyn as he barreled into Maddox and sent the three of us flying toward the stiff, unforgiving stone floor of what was left of the atrium.

My entire body wailed with the impact. I cowered—none of that brave, last full-blooded Fae left in me—as someone delivered blow after blow after bone-crunching blow beside me.

Please let it be Wyn.

I pried one stiff, blurred eye open.

Soft dark hair plastered to his head, face contorted with real, true conviction, Wyn knelt over Maddox and pummeled him with more fury than I'd seen from anyone in a long, long while. Years of fury. A lifetime's worth. And something in my smoke-filled chest broke at the tears that slipped down his face as he raged and drove fist after fist.

"Wyn," I croaked eventually, crawling toward him. "He's dead."

But Wyn did not falter. He slammed one bloodied, ashy hand after another into his rival until teeth scattered across the floor. I was never squeamish, but even I couldn't bring myself to look at what remained of Maddox's face.

"Wyn, please."

Finally, some vengeance-spell broken by my ragged plea, Wyn released Maddox and stared at what his hands had done.

Eventually he climbed off his fellow guard and lifted me to stand. I swayed on my numb legs and Wyn course-corrected, allowing me to lean into him. "Arwen." He sounded worse than ragged. "We have to get you to—"

"Why?" I asked.

His voice drifted off as he observed the chaos. The devastation. The few guards funneling out past walls of fire, desperate for a reprieve from the growing blaze.

"Why . . ." I croaked again, finally casting my eyes over Maddox. The bloodied guard was a nauseating lump of blood and soot.

Feeling was finally coming back to my legs. Not my spine, then, thank the Stones. I held my palm to the burns across my back and neck. No lighte yet. It would be a while before any of my lighte regenerated. I'd used more tonight than I had in months.

"All I ever wanted was to do right by my mother," Wyn said as I righted myself to stand. "She wouldn't be proud of the things I allowed to happen within these walls." Wyn shook his head. "The things I allowed to happen to you."

The crash of something—a pillar, or lofted ceiling—sent us careening back and down into the ground. Soot and wreckage filled my mouth and eyes. And heat. More fire, more ruinous flame.

"We need to go," Wyn managed around the thick, gray air.

"Where is Kane?"

Wyn's bloodshot eyes locked onto mine. "He's here? In the palace?"

As if on cue, somewhere, a dragon roared.

Before I could make sense of it—had Kane regained his lighte? Had he found the blade? Or was that a victorious, celebratory Lazarus?—a wild lick of fire lashed out at us. Supernaturally hot and scalding my flesh. Engulfing us, burning—

And then we were moving. Running, as best I could, before the flames could maul us. *Sprinting*, despite the pounding in my head and all my sizzling burns.

"Wyn," I panted as we ran past burning columns and melting flesh, "what is the fastest way out of the palace?" He knew what I meant. *Where no guards will see us.* I had to get out, had to find Kane—

"There isn't one," Wyn shouted. "They're already hunting for you."

Flames blazed through my vision. Walls of it tunneling, blooming around what was left of Lazarus's atrium. Swallowing the carcasses of the settees, melting every candle, warping the shards of vases and frames.

"Gods above," Wyn breathed.

The heat was unbearable. Eons past discomfort. My heart slowed, tired of pumping so fast for so long.

"*Think*," I urged him. "You've been a kingsguard here for years. There has to be something. One of those hidden passages?"

"The broom closet," he said in the end, already moving toward a nondescript door that might have otherwise blended into the bloodred walls, and dragging me behind him.

I dodged over groaning, melting men in silver armor. "It won't protect us forever. Eventually we'll be kindling."

"Trust me," he called back.

But the door was locked. Wyn readied his hands at the frame, lighte curling—

"No." I seized his wrists. "If you blow the door we can't defend ourself from the flames."

"Gods damn it," Wyn cursed. "Then there's nothing else, Arwen. Not if we can't get inside without blasting it open."

But I'd watched my brother and Halden pick the lock of Powell's shed a hundred times. I sank to my knees, heart racing, and fished Wyn's hairpin from my curls. The metal glinted in the glow of the surrounding flames, and I nudged it carefully into the keyway despite my shaking hands.

Agonizing seconds ticked by in which I wondered if this was the worst possible detour to being burned alive . . .

"Arwen . . ."

"I can do it," I bit out, "I just need one more—"

But then the door clicked open and Wyn and I tumbled inside before slamming it closed.

Darkness engulfed us both. And cool, trapped air. Dusty and stale but still—*cold air.*

Wyn and I sighed in unison.

The closet wasn't really large enough for us both. It only held three brooms, propped against a wall of shelving stuffed with cleaning supplies, buckets, and rags. The cramped space was lit only by the warm, flickering light of the blaze outside, slipping in through the crack at the bottom of the door.

"Now what?" I asked, willing my fear to quiet its ringing in my ears—I couldn't panic. Not now.

"There was a false wall in here years ago . . ." Wyn's warm, ragged breath fanned over my face in the small space. "One that led to a tunnel that took you to the city center. An escape route for Lazarus in case the castle were ever breached."

Dust filled my lungs and I swallowed a hacking cough, my heart rate already picking up inside the tight, suffocatingly dark enclosure. My fingers drifted along the cold stone wall, the one bare of shelves. No hinges, no break in its smoothness. I could hear Wyn digging through the feather dusters and soaps.

"But maybe . . . I don't know, maybe it's been sealed . . ." Terror was slipping into Wyn's voice.

And with each scream that sounded outside, doubt crept further into my voice, too, even as I said, "He's too self-serving. He'd keep a private way out just for himself." I crouched down to palm the molding where the wall met the marble floor. My hands scraped around lint and rodent droppings.

Wyn nearly toppled over me trying to feel the opposite shelf. Pitchers and linens toppled to the floor and an errant sponge rolled off my back. "Arwen," he sighed. "I'm sor—"

Before he could apologize, a creak split the shallow closet.

The entire wall of supplies wrenched open, more materials tumbling down, until we were rewarded with a small, unlit corridor.

Air I'd stored up fled my lungs in a rush. Wyn thanked the Gods.

Then we stood and walked out into the abyss.

The corridor was inky black and silent. More and more silent the farther we walked. I could only tell we were heading downward by the slight pull of my thighs and calves. A quiet dripping sounded from somewhere. Up or down, I couldn't tell. Footsteps thundered every once in a while high above us. But no doors. No light. No ladders or windows or ways *out*. None as we marched deeper and deeper into the bowels of the castle.

My mouth had gone bone-dry. My hands trembled at my sides. My burns stung.

When I heaved for no reason at all, Wyn finally turned back toward me. I only knew he had from the echo of his feet shifting in the gritty dirt floor. "What's wrong?"

"Nothing," I said, walking past him. My heart had settled itself in my tonsils. I dry heaved again.

"What is it?"

Tightness seized my chest with the scuttle of *something* across my foot. "I get anxious in enclosed spaces. It's fine."

No sooner had I said it than a simple turn yawned the tunnel open widely before us. The rocky catacomb was dimly lit, but where the light was coming from I wasn't sure—not moonlight from above us, not candles—but I sucked in great heaves of air regardless. I nearly leaned over to brace myself against my knees.

Critters scurrying and the sound of shifting sediment echoed, but I was too relieved to have some space, some light, some *air* that I hardly noticed.

Moss—or perhaps severely mildewed fabric—lay in tufts in one corner. A stone well crumbled in the opposite one. I couldn't imagine how stagnant, how putrid that primeval water might have been. And from some other corner, a clatter—

Dinner scraps clinking. *Bones—*

Wyn drew in a breath.

Either this had not been the right route, or Lazarus had employed some kind of safeguard to block his only exit to the city center. Some kind of—

A withering, earsplitting screech rocked the cavern and silenced my thoughts.

"We need to go back," I heard myself say. "Now."

Wyn grasped my hand and we ran for that tunnel. To go back the way we'd came, back up that immortally dark corridor and back out into the flames.

But we weren't fast enough. The creature was already there, waiting for us.

Grinning.

17

ARWEN

WE HURTLED FROM THE MONSTER LIKE ARROWS THROUGH a thick veil of mist. Practically blind, utterly senseless, but quick. Deadly quick.

Wyn dove behind something before I could see what, and yanked me after him. We landed beneath a jagged, rough-hewn boulder just as a raging shriek rent through the cavern.

No, not a cavern. A den.

One of the monster lairs.

"Is this not an exit?" I managed around my racing breaths.

Wyn shook his head. "I have no idea."

But that light . . . that light was coming from somewhere.

The feathered creature spread its hunched, heavy wings and roared, fanning our faces with the pungent scent of rotten meat. Through the darkness, I could just make out the tips of each giant, plumy appendage meeting either stone wall with ease—brushing, *stooping* against the ceiling. This creature, whatever it was, had even more power, even more strength than could be used in this dank, dripping den.

Those claws—stemming from long skeletal arms, hidden underneath the demonic wings—stained red from tearing into years' worth of prey, prowled toward us, talons scraping across the dirt. Despite the owllike wings and legs, those rippling feathers, and angled, pointed ears, the creature's face was . . . eerily *human*. Or, humanlike. A flat, gray, misshapen nose. Bony, low cheekbones that nearly jutted into a lipless maw. And when it shrieked—rows of teeth. Not fangs, but *teeth*—dozens and dozens of them.

And yet it was those narrow blinking eyes that told me what the behemoth goblin bird was. Eyes I'd seen go around before a rubber ball or drift shut at the foot of Kane's bed. I knew what we beheld even before Wyn uttered, "It's a strix."

Not quite like Acorn. Far larger, far more angry . . .

And this strix appeared to have been driven completely mad.

We scrambled back when it lunged, narrowly avoiding those treacherous claws. The close call offered me a glimpse of the strix's eyes. Not brown and warm like Acorn's, but milky white, with pale, gray scars over thin eyelids. Scarring that carried across the bridge of the strix's nose and protruding brow, where no plumage grew at all.

This strix was blind.

It wrenched open its bestial mouth and roared, spit and flecks of whatever rancid meal it had last eaten flying toward us. Wyn leveled his hands at the strix, soft, velvety lighte brimming in his palms.

"No," I hissed, seizing his arms in my own.

Confusion rippled from his hazel eyes, which I could only make out due to the light spilling in from the other side of the rocky lair. Not moonlight, but yellow *city* lights. The exit Wyn had spoken of. I could almost hear the cries of citizens, likely witnessing their grand palace swallowed up in flame.

"They're not violent creatures," I told Wyn. "Not unless they have to be. This one's been blinded. It's afraid." If I didn't despise Lazarus for all he'd done to me, to Kane, to his people—the blinding of this innocent creature would have cinched it for me.

With another shriek, the strix snapped those teeth not an inch from my face. Wyn and I dove backward, and watched the beast's milky, scarred eyes whir. The strix rammed into the wall where we'd just been and howled so loud the rock behind me shuddered.

Wyn and I scuttled over each other to stand. My guard frowned up at the disoriented beast. "We cannot let it kill us out of empathy."

"I'm not suggesting that," I breathed. "But we can get to the other side without harming it."

I'd been wrong. It wasn't a lair, but a cell. That corridor—far too small and too winding for the creature to get through, especially without its sight. But not so small that the smell of a city—chimney smoke and sulfur and meat roasting—couldn't waft through. Torture for this strix, unchained here but unable to reach the freedom it smelled and heard each day and night. Such utter cruelty.

I didn't wait for Wyn to agree. I sprinted across the puddles of what I knew from the scent were years of waste. Hurtling, dodging the flaps and claws—

But Wyn was not fast enough behind me.

The strix tackled him, leveling the guard to the ground with a garbled grunt and driving those claws into the arm Wyn raised to block the blow.

Horror blurred my vision into spots.

Wyn blasted the creature back with his swirling violet lighte. I raced for him, bracing my hands on his wet, sticky arm and feeling the skin there stitch back together. The glow from my lighte lit the entire cave.

Finally, some of my power had returned. Maybe just enough to—

The strix flew toward us with that horrible, many-toothed smile. It was the smell. The metallic smell of Fae power. The creature dove for us.

This time, though, I ran toward the feathered beast. I wasn't sure if enough power had returned to me, but I had no other ideas. I'd dig deep and see what I could mine . . . Aiming for one of those wings, I tried to grasp on to the feathers, dodging the claws—

But the strix must have sensed my footfalls or heard my racing breaths, and it clawed through my dress and sent me flying backward into cold, hard stone.

"What was that?" Wyn screamed, rushing to my side.

"I was wrong," I gasped on an inhale.

"You think?" Wyn spit blood onto the ground, his sweaty, dark brows highlighted by faint city lights.

"Its other senses are heightened." The strix shrieked again and debris rained down above us. "Do you think you can blast the passage open wider with your lighte?"

"Yes, but—"

"And can you distract the beast? I think I can climb its wings."

"Why would you do *that*?"

I gritted my teeth and pushed myself to stand. "I have an idea."

"An idea that will result in our dismemberment?" Wyn's voice was edging on hysterical.

I considered his question, backing up as the strix prowled closer, claws outstretched. "I hope not."

Wyn sighed and leveled his gaze at the beast. "Hurry."

I didn't give the kingsguard a chance to change his mind as I hurtled for the other side of the cavern. That exit, that corridor illuminated with streetlight.

"Here, birdy!" Wyn called out to the blind creature, his voice echoing against the cavern walls as he rapped his fists against them. "Over here!"

Another deafening shriek. That howl so violent it shook the bones beneath my skin. The strix took off after him, flapping wings that couldn't move quite well enough in the space, shuffling those deadly, clawed feet.

And I waited.

Waited, as my heart thundered in my ears, unable to inhale a single breath. Until the creature flung its wing out, scrambling toward Wyn with those terrifyingly gangly arms.

I dove, latching on to the feathered, owllike wing, holding tight as it swung me this way and that. I climbed, fingers digging through the plumes until I sat atop the howling beast. And as it thrashed and screeched, I held my hands across the strix's dry, empty eyes and pushed any lighte I had left through my fingertips.

The creature balked and stumbled backward, its spindly arm swinging up to swat at me and lash a single razor-sharp claw across my midsection, ripping me open.

Even as pain exploded in me—I held on to the creature's eyes through clenched teeth and felt my lighte bloom behind its eyelids.

This was what my power had always been for. Not destruction. Not fear.

My lighte glowed and I swore I heard the sharp intake of Wyn's shocked breath before the creature bucked once more and I toppled to the ground in a heap.

And then . . .

Silence.

Wyn's hurried footfalls sounded behind me. He fell to the ground and held a hand to my stomach, repeating over and over that he never should have listened to me. That we should have killed the beast when we had the chance.

But all I could hear was the silence. The sound of a strix that I knew—knew in my very soul—was blinking eyes open to see for the first time in who knew how long. That silence, that *freedom* continued to echo through my ears as Wyn scooped me into his arms. "Oh, Gods above," he murmured.

I knew what he meant, even as my eyes rolled back in my head. And try as I might, the more I pressed my own palms to the weeping tear in my stomach—there was no healing power left. Any meager lighte that had regenerated since I blew the receptacle had been used on the strix.

Unlike the Fae king, by all accounts, I was not immortal. My life was not tethered to the Blade of the Sun by prophecy, like his. And while full-blooded Fae lived longer than any other beings, and my healing abilities had gotten me out of more close calls than I could count, there were some injuries and ailments that took their toll faster than any Fae could heal.

I was half-aware of Wyn's flash of violet lighte. There was a mighty rumble and the sound of boulders groaning as he split the rocky corridor open. Once it settled, he carried me through the winding corridor until warm fog kissed my face and ashy, mild air funneled in through my nose.

And over the sound of my own labored breathing, my own teeth chattering—

Feathered wings flapping.

We peered up and witnessed the strix, with its newfound sight, soar into the muggy night sky, high above those smog-tinged clouds. Bright, jubilant shrieking echoed from its lungs.

"He's free," I told Wyn.

"It's a she," he said with a grunt. When I peeled my eyes open, Wyn's nose was bleeding down onto his lips.

I squeezed my eyes shut to quell the nausea.

Not squeamish.

I wasn't squeamish.

I was . . . dying.

That dragon's roar I'd heard in the atrium ripped through the cold night air once again. A roar of fury and anguish and pure night-black power. Rising up into the sky.

The rush of relief bowed my heart inside my chest. Such a beautiful, harrowing roar. The roar of a conqueror, the roar of a king. A grin that tasted of blood split my face.

Not Lazarus.

That was my dragon.

Tears burned my eyes.

Go, Kane. Do not come back.

"I don't think he can hear you," Wyn grunted before we stumbled backward.

The ground shook as Kane landed before us, and my eyes cracked open wide to behold the enormous night-black creature— blade-sharp, glittering talons, scaled obsidian wings, hooded silver eyes that gleamed like a harvest moon as he cocked his enormous head at us, nostrils flaring. Horrendous, spectacular, beauty and nightmares incarnate . . .

Guards in that thick layered armor were already hurtling toward him. They'd been waiting at the perimeters for me. The gilded arsonist who'd set their capital ablaze.

Fools, I thought. They were fools with their weapons raised high into the air—

Lighte flew out of their crossbows and swords and my dragon

reared up on hind legs and spread his marvelous wings wide. He bellowed out with each painful blow, blocking us from the assault.

But blackness spotted across my vision until all I could see was the darkness and all I could feel were Wyn's jagged, desperate inhales and his grunt as he deposited me onto something cool and textured. A small, pathetic noise split from me at the touch. My hands grasped aimlessly for Kane's familiar scales.

Those guards hastened toward us, roaring. Their heavy footfalls drawing closer and closer—

Wyn's pleading cries seized my stomach as he begged Kane to get me help.

With strength I didn't know I still had, I forced my hands tightly around Kane's back just in time for my stomach to hollow out at the sight below. We shot into the air, past the swarm of silver guards who converged on Wyn, and up into the night-dark sky.

18

KANE

Lazarus's mercenaries were gaining on us.

After touching the blade, I'd awoken from whatever Fae God power had made me full-blooded to find an inferno of firelighte. That, and my father gone, along with the Blade of the Sun. He'd left me for dead in the explosion I could only assume was Arwen's doing.

She hadn't gone to Aurora as I'd instructed her to.

But anger was the farthest thing from my mind as I soared from the palace.

Guilt was what punched through my gut.

All this time I'd fought to protect Arwen. But she was stronger than I'd given her credit for. She'd fought through an entire kingsguard to get to me. She'd freed us both. And I'd almost caged the bird I loved—had nearly clipped her wings. If we made it free from these mercenaries alive, I'd apologize for that.

I'd apologize for a lot of things.

Though I didn't think I'd get the chance. At least a dozen creatures had taken to the night sky behind us—harpies, manticores, sphinxes—scales and beaks and forked tongues lashing and whipping through the ether, high above the plumes of smog that covered the walled city.

A wretched, raging ball of fire whizzed past my hind leg, and though it missed, the heat still singed my talons.

My full-blooded Fae dragon form was every bit as powerful as I'd hoped, with a lengthier wingspan and sharper claws, and I was almost certain the incendiary ability to breathe fire. I could taste ash and flame in my lungs as if they were forged from my esophagus . . .

And when a foul, ghoulish rooster with long, scaled dragon legs—a cockatrice—squawked past and dove for Arwen, I reared my head back and gave my new lungs a try.

White-hot fire erupted from between my fangs. The cockatrice had no chance of retaliation. Its feathered crest and fierce beak sizzled in an instant, devoured by flames and reduced to cinders that rained down on the vast city below us. Arwen held tight to my ridged spine as I blazed another two creatures intent on torpedoing us downward.

Free of the closest assailants, I wound us lower, but not quick enough. The impact of one fireball cut through me like a knife in butter. I roared with the blow. Molten heat lit the membranes of my wing, and agony tore through and shuddered the limb.

Lower, and lower still I swept, fangs bared against the pain.

I couldn't fly back to Evendell like this. The channel was safest when partially flown—a journey I'd made only once before and just narrowly survived. There wasn't a world in which I didn't fall from the sky in exhaustion.

We'd have to lose these last few somehow.

Another rush of fiery hail sent me even lower, diving through the thick gray clouds of filth and curving my ravaged wings up to cradle

Arwen on my back. Her hand on the membranous fibers was both calming and invigorating at once.

Beneath me, through the pitch-black night, I could just barely make out the sentries and their fires atop the walls that protected Solaris from the rest of Lumera. Or, protected Lazarus from the atrocities he inflicted beyond his treasured capital.

Soon only barren land sprawled beneath us.

The harpy that led the remaining pack drew nearer. A maliciously beautiful Fae with the body of a hawk. Snarling, her claws cut through the thick air so violently I could hear the wind howl. Could feel the gusts carried by her feathered wings cast over us as she soared closer. That wind—awash with the promise of death.

In the distance, Aurora loomed.

The slum nearest Solaris. Bordered by the Dreaded Vale.

This would have to work.

Weaving through thick plumes of grimy fog, I plummeted, wrapping my wings around myself and Arwen like a tightly coiled bud yet to bloom. I sank down through the foggy sky, gaining speed, tumbling, until there was only the scent of ash in the air, the deafening, thrashing wind, and the heat from Arwen's body, held against my scales.

Shifting back into my human form, I landed with Arwen still gripped securely in my arms atop some kind of awning.

Pain radiated across my shoulders, and Arwen groaned. Whatever stand we'd sank through toppled under our weight. Potatoes and turnips spilled out into the quiet night street.

That harpy shrieked from the sky.

Quick, quick—

I righted myself to stand among splintered wood and shredded canvas and smushed, pale vegetables.

"Hurry," I urged.

It was only then I got a good look at her—

The paleness of her face, the tears at the corners of her eyes . . . and the deep red that had seeped into her thin gold gown, clutched between her fingers.

"Kane—"

No, no, no—

I had no time for horror. "You're fine," I gritted out, scooping Arwen up and taking off.

The impoverished slums only offered one long avenue, and without the walls of Solaris the entire road was shrouded in a thick, repellent fog. Crooked, stacked homes and half-toppling storefronts swayed into one another, most windowpanes streaked with dust, most roofs in desperate need of reshaping.

The building behind me shook with the weight of whatever creature had landed atop it. I wasted no time taking off down a thinner, dirt-lined alley. Arwen moaned as my footsteps echoed against the peeling walls.

My eyes caught a shadowed alcove and I veered sharply into it. When I peered down to set Arwen on her feet, I saw my hands were coated thickly in her blood.

"What happened to you?" I hissed.

"Monster's lair," she mumbled. Then, warmly, "You flew."

"I've been remade."

Arwen's response was a wet, hacking cough.

She was losing too much blood. And not healing herself. My heart rate quickened.

A sickly male groan sent a spike of adrenaline through me and I whirled to find a bundle of rags. A man lurking beneath them shared the alcove with us. Through a cloud of mosquitoes, he moaned again and I caught sight of the festering wounds along his cheeks.

A mortal, poisoned by lighte.

He grumbled again and I urged him to be silent. The thundering feet and shouts for our capture drew nearer. The Fae mercenaries had shifted back to their human forms.

"Please," the sickly vagrant begged. "More, I need—"

"Shh," Arwen soothed, leaning up against the wall to support herself.

We didn't have anything to help the man. No medicine, no coin, no lighte to offer him. My gut churned.

"Please," he moaned loudly.

"We have nothing for you," I hushed.

Mercenary feet shuffled outside in the fog-riddled alleyway.

"But I need—"

"Be *quiet*—"

"It's going to be all right," Arwen muttered, dropping to the man's eye level with a wince. "We just have to calm down—"

"Sir." His voice pitched to a near whine as he craned his neck up to me. "Sir, won't you please . . ."

I pressed a blood-soaked hand to his mouth.

"Kane—"

The man thrashed and spit.

My eyes peeled over the corner and into the street. A woman in nothing but a transparent shift that accentuated her wanton curves flashed sparks of pale blue from the tips of her fingers. A whore shilling her lighte.

And farther, around some crumbling corner—the wails of a baby. Even farther, the grunts of a brawl.

Nowhere safe to hide.

My gaze found the sickly man again. His eyes were unfocused and wild.

"Kane, release him," Arwen urged quietly.

"He'll give us away."

"You're going to suffocate him—"

They were sure to find us. I'd have to fight the mercenaries off, which meant leaving Arwen here. With him. And if she passed out from her wound, if he sensed her lighte—if he touched her . . . I didn't want to harm the vagabond. But I'd have to knock him out to ensure her safety.

"*This way*," a mercenary's voice echoed.

My hackles rose. The vagabond gnashed against my hand. I moved behind him, guilty, already regretting—

"In here," a small voice whispered behind me. Arwen and I spun to see the wall beside us open into a shop. We ducked inside just as the herd of mercenaries passed.

My relief was as tangible as Arwen, back in my arms, sagging breathlessly against me.

Inside the shop was both ashy and humid, and smelled of burnt hinoki. There were no shelves. No glass cases to display jewels or crates with fruit. Just three thick candles sputtering for life, and a threadbare carpet with too many dark red stains for it to be a coincidence. Only a minuscule break in the panic, as relief was replaced by nagging suspicion.

"Thank you," I said to the woman, who was wrapped in layers of dark fabric to keep out the heat and the rancid air. All I could discern were her sunken hound eyes and hunched frame.

"What is this place?" Arwen asked me too quietly.

The woman craned her neck to get a better look at Arwen's wound. "She's dying, your girl?"

I recoiled as if struck, cradling Arwen even closer. "No."

"I'm fine," Arwen coughed, grasping tightly at her abdomen.

The woman only nodded from behind her rags. "Soon, though."

"Do you have bandages?" I asked. "Any medicine?"

The woman shook her head.

A cold sweat broke across my neck. Not from fear—I was strong enough to best this meek woman mortal, let alone full-blooded. No, the weariness came from something else. From the realization that this place was not a shop at all.

Arwen stumbled into me farther, dizzy from blood loss. "I need to lie down."

"We'll give you fifty coin for her."

"She's not *dead*," I snarled.

"Soon," the woman said again. Like a promise.

My claws itched to shred through my knuckles. "Where is the Dreaded Vale?" I gritted out.

"South of here. You aren't far. Daybreak will arrive any minute."

I understood her warning: these slums were dangerous in the dead of night, but in the harsh red light of dawn . . . every soul in Aurora would be drawn to Arwen and me like buzzards to carrion. Lighte was the commodity in Lumera—the power in our veins the only currency that mattered. For addicts, for harvesters; to feed crops, to give power to those hoping to one day escape.

"Do you trust me?"

Arwen's eyes had gone cloudy, but she swallowed hard and nodded. "Always."

The alley behind the hidden door had been silent since we entered, and given the pallor of Arwen's skin, time was not on our side. I managed my thanks to the woman and ducked us back out into the muggy, forlorn streets.

~⟡~

THE DREADED VALE WAS LESS OF A VALLEY AND MORE OF A
winding maze of black, parched trees that rose so high into the night
sky I couldn't make out their tips from their trunks.

I couldn't risk shifting and drawing the attention of any mercenaries still on our tail, nor flying too fast and passing the rebel king's
hideout altogether. I'd been walking for at least thirty minutes, Arwen cradled in my arms. Her eyes had begun to flutter closed.

"Hey. Stay with me."

"I'm here," she murmured. "Though I'd rather not be. This place
is . . ." She wheezed. "Nightmarish."

A morbid grin twitched at my lips. It was true. Among the tangle
of parched trees, thick red ooze spilled from the creases where the
branches sprouted and some pooled down by the roots.

I nodded toward it as Arwen and I trudged onward. "When I was
young, my brother's brute friends would call that stuff 'viper
come.' It was an awful name, a play on a slur used for Fae that draw
their lighte from blood."

"Hemolichs," Arwen supplied.

"Good memory. Nastier boys than Griffin and I would dare
each other to eat it and find the consequences of that curiosity on the
other side of a two-week stay in the infirmary."

Arwen's weak laugh became a steady cough and I urged my legs
quicker.

As if sensing my rising anxiety, she reached a clammy palm up to
my neck. I brought my lips over to the back of her hand and pressed
them there once as I hurried. "It would be such a disservice to my
grief to say I've missed you."

"I know," she murmured. "I don't think I breathed properly the entire time we were apart."

I hadn't, either.

"What did you mean when you said you were *remade*? Why were you mortal?"

Was now the best time to tell her everything? Hunting for Hart's elusive compound, black, spindly trees around us taking the shape of lurking ghouls and foes? Stumbling through snapping twigs and the rustle of cracked leaves while she struggled to stay awake?

But I had to keep her conscious somehow. Distract her.

"I went to see the White Crow. Mortality was necessary for me to become full-blooded."

"You're . . . like me?" Her eyes fluttered at her own words. "A full—"

Arwen's words were swallowed by her violent shaking in my arms.

"Shh," I murmured to her as she convulsed, brushing dark hair from her clammy forehead. She was hot. Running a fever.

Fuck. *Fuck*—

Her lighte wouldn't regenerate for another few hours at least. It wouldn't be enough time—the wound was working faster than her Fae healing could keep up with. My pulse quickened.

"We need help," I called out into the empty Dreaded Vale. My voice was too low. Gravelly and hoarse. "Anyone?"

Silence, save for the wind snapping and sighing through cracked, brittle branches leaching red gunk. Silence, save for the squawking, hungry crows, and for my feet pounding on what was once grass.

Arwen went limp in my arms, passed out.

My mouth tightened. There was nobody here.

"Hello?" I called out again, louder this time, hefting Arwen more evenly into my arms. "Hart? We need help—this woman." I studied Arwen's too-pale face. Mouth slack. Eyes sunken. "This woman needs help."

My words were swallowed by that wretched dry wind. My lips cracked. My throat ached.

I said to her, "You're going to be fine, bird."

She didn't stir.

My legs moved faster. We passed more branches. More long, gnarled trunks of trees and shattered stumps. More roaring wind. No sign of Hart or his clan. No sign of any life at all.

"Hello? We need . . ." I was—I was *shaking*.

We were too far from Aurora now to go back. Nobody there could help Arwen anyway. It was unlikely anyone had healing lighte—a rare ability. And if there were witches in Aurora or any of the other slums, I didn't have time to find them. They could be anyone. Anywhere. Or nowhere at all.

The sun was beginning to rise.

Illuminating the skies bloodred and violent orange. The colors of daylight in Lumera. Panting, I ran deeper into the vale, my feet narrowly avoiding dried vines. When the rainless sky cracked bright with lightning, I only hurtled faster.

I almost missed the hiss that whipped through the trees.

"Hart?" I bit out through clenched teeth. *Please.* "It's King Ravenwood. We need—"

But it wasn't Hart.

I trained my eyes on the slithering creature, wriggling itself free from the parched ground. Hairy, like a boar; ridged tail, like an alligator. Bright yellow eyes, like all the beasts born from Lumera's ruined earth.

My breaths came faster as I backed away from the snarling creature. I couldn't put Arwen down. Somewhere, in some far-off corner of my mind, I knew that if I released her and killed this beast, when I returned to Arwen she might be dead.

But I couldn't—*wouldn't*—think like that.

Instead I roared at the thing as daybreak cast it in crimson shadows. Spittle flew from my lips as they curled back from my teeth. As my jaw ached. I bellowed again, the veins in my head bulging.

Screaming not just at the snarling, bug-eyed beast but at all the pain, all the suffering the woman I loved had been forced to endure.

The creature froze, observing me, before slithering away.

I could only drop to my knees. "She needs help," I begged, bowing over Arwen and holding her to me tightly. Rocking us back and forth. "She needs—"

Her skin was too cold.

"You cannot leave me," I commanded her pallid face, brushing my fingers across her cheeks and chin. "Do you hear me? You *can't*."

Her head only lolled lifelessly to the side.

I'd already lost her once. And then heartless fate had returned her to me, alive and warm, only to wrench her from me again? So she could die *here*, shrouded in hot red sunlight, in this fucking barren valley of pitch-black skeleton trees because I couldn't find a single soul for miles?

Despite the roiling, thrumming terror—I had to keep moving. When I stood and cast my eyes down to study Arwen, it was white powder that caught my attention, coating my knees and boots.

It was . . . chalk.

A boundary.

A *witch's* boundary.

I turned, something small and hopeful flapping inside my chest.

I dragged Arwen in the other direction, past whatever boundary I'd knelt on and roared again, my voice a fraction of what it had been hours ago. "Is anyone there? Hart?"

Movement shook the distorted trees before me.

A dozen women emerged. Dirtied hands wrapped in protective linens and feathers in their hair. And with them, slowly, as if the fabric of space were opening itself up to reveal what had been there all along—men in armor and children and horses and wagons. Crude huts and blacksmith tables and cabins and fires roasting plucked hens. The scents and sounds and sights of an entire encampment, hidden in plain sight in the Dreaded Vale.

Hart's clan. At last.

Any relief I might have felt was devoured by urgency. "Where is Hart Renwick?"

"Who are you?" the woman who had stepped forward asked. She was narrow and angular, like a praying mantis. "How did you find us?"

"This woman"—I jerked my chin toward Arwen's lifeless body—"needs *help*. She has a terrible wound. Her stomach, it's—" My voice broke. "She needs a witch or a healing Fae. I'm the king of Onyx Kingdom and rightful heir to the throne of Lumera. I'm a friend to the rebel king. Please—"

"A wound like that . . . she is likely dead, King Ravenwood."

"No. She's true Fae." Each word punched through gritted teeth. "You have to *try*—"

Before the lean woman could respond, the camp turned with the sound of lone heavy footfalls. Turned almost in union as a man emerged.

The man was soaked in blood. His chin, his half-open white shirt, his palms.

And he was laughing.

The loping man, too tall for his own limbs, hair swooping into his face with each step, came to stand before me, surveying us but not threatening. Just . . . curious. "*The* Kane Ravenwood? Could that really be you?"

"Yes," I said, breathing hard.

"Valery, help this man," he instructed the woman. Still with that playful smile. As if war were his favorite pastime. As if my grief did nothing to him.

The gaunt woman, Valery, with her many pendants, knelt before me and gently opened her arms to take Arwen. And behind her—

Their dark long skirts, the leather and beads on their clothes, and concerned expressions on their faces . . .

The Antler coven. As Briar had said.

It was all I could do to nod as Valery lifted Arwen's body up and away from me. I missed her weight in my arms and lowered my head to my hand to suck in steadying, fortifying breaths, turning that razor-sharp fear inward and swallowing it whole.

"My coven is highly skilled," Hart said. "I'd say she's got a chance at least." When I lifted my face he was tucking his hair aside, coating the bronze strands in red. His eyes met mine, and he flashed me a crooked, confident grin.

19

ARWEN

I HAD COME BACK FROM THE DEAD THREE TIMES IN MY LIFE, and was certain it had been three times too many.

It wasn't that I wished to die. Each time light sputtered from the darkness and breath yawned into my lungs, my first instinct was always to thank the Stones. But that rush of appreciation—the grasping of each of my limbs and swaths of flesh to make sure all was still where it was meant to be—never lasted long.

Each time, I was hit with a distinct sense of foreboding. A knowledge that each brush with that howling, bottomless void was just a mere taste of the looming inevitable. That fate was a mischievous feline, and my death was a ball of twine on the precipice of unraveling.

"Contemplating the nature of the universe?" Kane's ragged voice still broke shivers across my back as if he had whispered the words against the sensitive shell of my ear.

He walked in quietly, closing the door of knotted wood behind him. The makeshift infirmary was entirely crafted with rounded logs, like a crisp mountain cabin.

"More like my fragile existence." It was an attempt at lightness, but neither of us laughed.

Wisps of sable hair fell past his dark brows, and, despite his easy words, they were furrowed with pain as he beheld me. He'd changed out of his stolen Fae armor and was in a slightly frayed brick-red tunic and dark pants. His hair wasn't clean, his face still scuffed here and there with blood and dirt, but . . . he'd shaved. As if the most offensive grime that covered him was the beard he'd worn while I'd been gone. The souvenir of his grief.

Kane watched me from across the spare, warm room. Hollow bars of crimson sunlight drifted through the mismatched logs of the roof and painted his gracefully carved chin and folded arms. Kane made no move to join me in the stiff bed with its thin, moth-eaten blankets, and I sat up with a poorly concealed wince.

"Don't rush yourself." His eyes were a brand on my face, my bare shoulders—at some point whoever resurrected me had sheared my golden gown clean off. Good riddance.

Kane watched intently as my hand rubbed down my sore neck.

"Where are we?"

"A hidden encampment built by rebels." He sounded hoarse. Like he'd been screaming.

"Hidden?"

"Warded by a magic boundary, just outside that city I spoke of, Aurora."

"Where you told me to ask for . . ." My medicated mind couldn't conjure the name he had given me back in the palace. Back when he'd urged me to run. Guilt swirled in my newly stitched stomach. Had I listened, would he have had to endure whatever cast his face in such pained exhaustion?

"Hart Renwick," Kane supplied quietly. "He's a young Fae who's built up an army of insurgents. The citizens of Lumera call him the rebel king."

"Oh" was all I could manage.

Kane's cheek twitched. But yearning—longing and remorse and unfiltered regret—was all that shone in those eyes.

"Kane . . ."

"I can't," he said in a rush.

Horrible, ice-cold fear sank through me. "Can't what?" I whispered. Tears had already welled in my eyes. I was so, *so* weak when it came to him.

He shook his head, brows lowered in some kind of warning. "If I go to you . . . If I hold you . . ." His voice broke on the word and I began to cry in earnest.

"Arwen . . ." His next words were said so low, his tormented expression was the only proof I'd not imagined them. "It will *break* me."

Something like relief loosened my shoulders just a bit. I'd thought . . . assumed he was saying something else. And I wouldn't even have blamed him. To be together, when everything around us was constantly shattering . . . I wasn't sure *I* was strong enough. But this . . . this fear was something else. Something I could handle.

"Come here," I whispered, scooting to the side carefully. "And I will put you back together."

I could tell by the way his brows met that my words weakened his already flimsy resolve. He crossed the room in three strides and gathered me into his arms.

We breathed each other in. His warmth, like home. His ragged breaths—each one a rhapsody. His leathery scent and sweat seeping into my entire aching body—I swore my bones groaned in pleasure just to be held by him.

Kane pressed his lips to my forehead over and over. "I've almost lost you too many times," he said. "And each time . . . I lose a piece of myself each time, Arwen."

"I know," I replied, running my fingers up and down his powerful, shuddering back. "But maybe . . . if everything we face, we face together, the pieces will grow back even stronger."

Kane coughed out one wet laugh and I wondered, my face pressed against his chest, if he was crying. "Your optimism knows no bounds."

I smiled against his sternum, and murmured, "Isn't that why you keep me around?"

"No," he said, lightness finally returning to his voice as he tipped my head up and our wet eyes met. "I'm mostly in it for the banter."

This time, when we kissed, we took our time. Soft, and salty with tears.

When my lips ached and my body had grown too tired to move, we stayed in the dusty bed, holding each other in peaceful silence. I buried my head into the nook of his neck—I'd missed the comfort of his body more than I could articulate.

Kane's fingers curled softly around mine.

"Are you sure this is . . . all right?"

For a moment I didn't know what he meant. That maybe I was too wounded to be touched?

But his face—the unbridled misery carved into every one of his beautiful features . . .

"No." I shook my head, horror blaring in my ears at the realization of what he must have thought. "Kane, your father never . . ."

A single breath released from him and he pressed a hand to my cheek. "You don't have to tell me anything you don't wish to. I can't imagine what you experienced there. If I could, I'd go back and rip the rest of the palace to shreds. I might, still."

"He kept me in a tower for months, but aside from that kiss he never touched me—never even tortured me. They took my lighte every few days. His court witch did it."

"Octavia." Kane's eyes narrowed to slits. "That scheming, treacherous bitch."

I sighed. "Yeah, she's a monster."

"She's my aunt."

My eyes widened. How had I not put the pieces together? Kane's mother had been mostly Fae, but he'd told me long ago in his wine cellar that her grandmother had been a witch. And Octavia had Kane's same unruly dark hair . . . That's why she'd expected to be made queen. She had been the late monarch's sister.

"She was envious of my mother's throne and beauty, her closeness to Briar rather than her. Octavia always wanted to climb up the rungs of the court. But to serve the man who butchered her sister . . ." Kane looked as though his fury could capsize an armada.

I grasped for his hands and squeezed. "Your father is weak, Kane. That's why he needs her. Why he had her take my lighte. He's losing power, I think."

Kane considered my words, his head tipping to the side in thought. "He ran out of lighte fairly fast when we fought. He punched me."

"Your father *punched* you? Rather than using his lighte?"

"Perhaps he's been supplementing his power for years." A dark smirk curled at his lips. "Yours is more potent than anything else he'd find in Solaris. It might have made his dependance worse. Hart will need to hear this. I told him you might need some time, but . . ."

But every moment we stayed here we put Hart's encampment at further risk of detection. We needed to leave this place—this realm entirely—before any of Lazarus's men or his Fae mercenaries tracked us down. We needed to ready the Onyx army for war.

"No," I said, pressing off his chest and taking a steadying breath. "I'm all right."

I moved to swing my legs over the bedside, but he stopped me.

"Stay put. I'll bring them in here, to us."

"Them?"

"Valery, the witch who healed you. She's Hart's right hand and the high priestess of the Antler coven. They've pledged themselves to him and his resistance."

My raised brows must have revealed my surprise because Kane nodded. "Yeah, he's something else."

My burns from the explosion had already faded and I could feel my stomach wound healing rapidly. After filtering the dregs of replenishing lighte into my stitches, I brushed my fingers across all my jagged scrapes and multicolored bruises. I wondered if being in Lumera—the homeland that birthed the Fae race—heightened the regeneration of my lighte or the effectiveness of my healing abilities. I felt better than I expected to.

By the time Kane returned with the rebel king and his witch I'd even pulled on a worn-out cotton frock that had been left on the brass hook near my bed.

"For a woman who was clinically dead two hours ago," the handsome man striding inside behind Kane drawled, "you look *remarkable*."

The rebel king was not at all what I'd been expecting.

Not an old general, beat up and battle-scarred but . . . well, Hart Renwick was what Mari would have called a dreamboat.

He was tall in that lanky, masculine way. Not necessarily broad or muscular, but so lean and wiry you knew he could outrun a gazelle without breaking a sweat. He had the same slightly overgrown hair that Kane did. The kind that fell past his ears and hit midneck, bits drifting across his cheekbones unless he brushed it out of the way or tucked it behind his ears. Kane was always running a hand back through his hair to clear his face, but Hart just let the auburn strands cover his eyes like a shaggy, unbothered dog.

And that *smile*. Nobody's grin held a candle to Kane's, but Hart Renwick could steal runner-up. Despite the circumstances that had led us here, and no doubt the resources he and Valery must have expended to save my life, Hart's eyes crinkled around a pleasant, relaxed grin that showcased endearingly imperfect, pearly-white teeth.

"Thank you," I managed. Despite my accelerated healing, I didn't quite *feel* remarkable.

"Of course," he quipped, prowling past Kane and deeper into the room toward the only furniture beside my bed—a creaking wooden sideboard, which I assumed was filled with medicinal instruments and ointments.

Instead of leaning on the credenza, Hart leapt atop it in one graceful movement and let his feet dangle over the edge. "My father used to tell me, never miss an opportunity to tell a woman of her beauty."

Kane followed him inside and took a seat at the foot of my bed with a frown.

"I meant," I said, cheeks growing warm, "thank you for healing me." My gaze found Valery, still in the doorway, who made no move to enter the cabin. She was tall and sharp-boned, with the posture of a dancer. Her many necklaces cluttered a thin, narrow chest. When I offered her a grateful smile, her flat expression didn't change.

"You cleaned up." Kane's words were deceptively casual, though everything from his breathing to his posture was lethally focused on the mischievous rebel.

"Didn't want to scare your lady."

My stomach twisted as I contemplated what he'd been dirtied with earlier.

Kane raised a brow. "What had you gotten yourself into?"

"Just a Fae merc who'd followed after you. What can I say? I do enjoy the kill."

"How did you build all of this, Hart?" Kane asked, one hand falling casually across my ankle, still tucked under the threadbare blanket. His warm, broad palm over the sensitive skin—even through a layer of cotton—sent a shiver up my spine.

"I had a lot of help," the rebel king admitted, eyes finding Valery's.

Her expression warmed for the first time, and she entered the cabin in earnest, closing the door behind her.

"In the beginning, inspiring one man to find the courage to join the revolution was difficult. Then, amassing a handful of real, sturdy weapons. Training peasants and mill workers to fight like soldiers . . ."

"Sounds impossible," I croaked.

"I grew up in one of the worst slums in the realm."

Kane raised a brow. "Celeste?"

"The one and only," Hart said with a smirk. "Lost my parents to harvesters at six. Lost my sister to a pox a few years later." Nausea swamped me at the thought, and Kane's grip tightened on my ankle. If those tragedies still broke his heart at all, Hart didn't let it permeate his casual demeanor. Maybe that aggressive playfulness was as much a shield as the ward around his encampment.

"Somewhere between that and stopping a Celestian woman from smothering her toddler rather than fail to feed him, I figured nothing could be more impossible than making it as long as I already had. Somebody had to put an end to your father. Why not me?"

Kane's gaze was grim with understanding. "Where do you expend the majority of your manpower?"

"Valery and her coven keep us dissenters safe, and we focus on destroying his battalions and outposts in steady increments."

"The outposts," Kane considered, leaning forward. "That makes a big difference?"

Hart unleashed that crooked grin once more. "Huge."

"He can't pay his mercenaries, power Solaris, or fuel his army without the stolen lighte." It was the first Valery had spoken, her voice low and reedy. I searched her face for any hint of emotion and only found cold, unwavering resolve, eyes trained on her rebel king.

But it was Kane who grinned this time. A small smile, but those dimples and curve of his full lips still quickened the pulse in my veins. "Arwen destroyed Lazarus's entire repository. Engulfed half the castle in firelighte."

Hart leapt from his perch on the sideboard. "Well, shit—we've been waiting for an opportunity like this."

"And," I added, my voice still raw, "I think he might already be weakened."

"How so?"

I cut my eyes to Kane, who gave me a subtle nod.

"I'm not sure," I admitted to both of them. "But he can't seem to regenerate lighte as quickly, or hold on to his power quite as long. He seems to need to infuse some of the harvested lighte into his own body just to maintain his power." I swallowed acid. "He prefers my own, since I'm full-blooded."

"Magnificent." The corner of Hart's mouth ticked up with malicious glee. "The *all-powerful, true Fae* king of Lumera is a sniveling lighte addict."

Kane couldn't help a sly answering grin of his own. "I think it has more to do with the purged land. I can ask the researchers back in Willowridge to look into it further, but my assumption is that by destroying the natural balance of lighte in Lumera, he's weakened himself."

"And the more lighte he needs . . ." Hart said.

Kane finished his thought. "The worse he'll get."

Hart turned to Valery. "This is . . . fan-*fucking*-tastic."

Valery only raised an incredulous brow. Not a big talker, that one.

"But that means he has reason to take Evendell sooner than later," Kane added. "He'll need fresh land to begin again."

"Valery." Hart motioned to his witch. "Ready the others. We'll fly for Solaris tonight."

"Done." Valery spun with grace and made for the door.

My heart only leapt in my throat. *Tonight?*

"No." Kane released his hold on me and stood from the bed. "No attacks tonight."

Hart's brows lifted but Valery halted in her steps. That was the strange thing about Kane. No matter where he was, who he was with—friend or foe or stranger—he was always the commanding authority in the room.

"We must work together," Kane said. "You need Onyx's army to defeat him. You need us." Kane motioned to himself and to me. I didn't feel very violent and powerful under the covers of this thin, dusty bed, but I nodded anyway.

Hart only snorted. "You're going to cross the channel with thousands of men?"

Kane shook his head. "We'll use our witch. She's the one that sent us to you."

"You have a witch that can portal an entire army across realms?" Valery asked.

Hart smirked. "Do you also have a unicorn and a troll that will turn my shit to gold?"

Kane didn't grin this time and Hart's eyes flared with understanding. "Creighton?"

Kane sat back down on the bed beside me and gave a single definitive nod.

"Briar Creighton . . ." Hart mused, leaning against the scarred wooden sideboard. "A brilliant witch and an even more brilliant fuck."

A noise sputtered from me, and I realized I'd choked on my own spit.

Briar had been alive for hundreds of years; I guess I couldn't fault her for sleeping with some of the most handsome, roguish men alive. For whatever reason, my eyes cut to Valery before anyone else, and saw she had turned a little pink. I hadn't taken her for a blusher, but I wasn't surprised. Hart probably had that effect on people.

Kane ignored Hart's crudeness. "Once we're back, we'll rally our troops and return here, to your encampment. Then we can storm Solaris as one."

"With all due respect, your kingliness," Hart said, hopping back onto his makeshift perch and bending up a long leg to lean an elbow on. "There's nothing stopping me from hitting him tonight without you."

To my surprise, Kane only cocked his head appraisingly and asked him, "What are you, half?"

"My father was full-blooded. My mother mortal."

Kane nodded to himself, assumption confirmed. He wasn't a halfling—a mortal with trace ancestral amounts of Fae blood—but he wasn't nearly as powerful a Fae as, say, Griffin or Wyn. Or as Kane had been, before being remade.

"Hart, your following is impressive. The work you've done . . . Having led a rebellion of my own, once . . ." The rueful smile didn't reach Kane's eyes. "I'm aware just how impossible this must have been. How much trust these people have in you, and you in them. But none of that will matter when you face Lazarus. Weakened or not, he's full-blooded Fae. You're half. You don't stand a chance without us. In the end, only I can kill him with the Blade of the Sun."

"Or me," I supplied.

"No," Kane said, low and authoritative. "It will be me. And only me."

20

ARWEN

IT WAS SHAMEFUL HOW LONG IT TOOK FOR THE REALITY OF our new situation to dawn on me. Far, far too long. I'd been so distracted by my injuries and Kane and our reunion that I hadn't put the most obvious new piece of our complex puzzle together in my mind—

Kane had become full-blooded Fae, like me. Like his father.

He was now capable of taking my place in the prophecy.

Which meant the truth I'd spent so many months coming to terms with—that even though I wanted more than anything to live, I *would* die to save Evendell, to save my family, and my friends, and the man I loved—it wasn't the case anymore.

One of us would have to die to end Lazarus, as stated clearly in the seer's words, but now it was possible it could be *him*.

Which would mean I would live. A near eternity without Kane.

Knowing he had paid the ultimate price for my life.

I grasped at the stitches across my stomach as it heaved, Kane's reassuring hand stroking my ankle once more.

This time it did nothing to soothe me.

Before this war was over, one of us would be dead.

One of us would leave the other behind. Alone. A greater suffering than anything I could imagine. There was no other way Lazarus's reign could end.

While I bowed to this ruinous realization, the strategizing had continued around me.

"We don't need to kill him," Hart was saying. "Just to sack his city. Slay his army. Destroy his power source, which, thanks to your woman, has already been halved at least."

"I've been exactly where you are," Kane swore, deadly calm. "I know how this goes, Hart. All of your men will die."

Hart shrugged. "Perhaps, but is that not the risk each one of them signed up for?"

Oh, no.

Sometimes it surprised me how well Kane and I knew each other. We'd only met less than a year ago, and in that time gone with whiplash quickness from precarious allies to adversaries to friends, and now to something deeper, and much more profound than a couple. If I believed in such things, I would have called him my soulmate.

Which meant I knew what Hart's blind focus on beating Lazarus would elicit in the man beside me. What his own demons—the men and women, the *family* he'd lost when afflicted by the same thing—would bring out in him.

Sure enough, Kane stood from the bed in an instant, his lighte rumbling. Sharp shadows of black and wisps of nightshade twined around his knuckles and wrists as he snarled, "You smug sack of shit."

Valery crossed the room as quickly as I'd seen her move and placed herself in front of Hart and the sideboard. I sat up, my own warm lighte coursing down my veins and toward my fingertips in a way

I'd only ever associated with seeing someone who needed to be healed. Some corner of my mind wondered if I were to look down, if I, too, would see yellow rays of light wreath themselves around my palms.

"Are you really so eager to cash in the lives of those who have put their faith in you?"

"All right," the rebel cautioned, still seated atop his sideboard. "All right. Easy, everyone. Kane, your point is taken."

He might have been placating him, as I knew it was fear that filtered through Hart's viridian eyes, but Kane surprised us both by breathing out evenly and running a hand through his hair. Silently, the dark talons and thorns around his forearms retreated into his tanned skin.

"So," Hart tried, calmer but still guarded. "Where is this blade you need?"

Kane scratched his neck. Silence gobbled up the cabin.

My heart plummeted.

"You're fucking with me." Hart bit back a laugh. "Right?"

"Kane," I breathed. "You left it there?"

"When I awoke," Kane said, voice like gravel, "*remade*, he'd fled with it. I searched for him, and found you with that kingsguard . . ." A haunting, sorrowful expression contorted his face.

I fought the urge to scramble toward him and deposit myself into his arms. We had been apart for too long, and I wanted to hold him. Instead I said to Hart and Valery, "We may have one last card to play."

Kane cocked his head in silent question.

"Amelia is in Solaris."

His brows knit inward in sympathy. "Arwen . . . She isn't—"

"I know. She told me everything. I still think we can work with her. All she wants is safety for her people. She knows us winning this war is the best outcome for Peridot."

Kane was not having any of it. Cold fury burbled up where so much love had just occupied his silver eyes. "You want me to trust *Amelia*—"

"Another *great* fuck," interrupted Hart, who was examining his dirtied nails.

Once again Kane didn't bat an eye. "After she betrayed us to side with Lazarus? After she had her own father killed? After she signed your fucking death sentence?"

"Sheesh," Hart muttered. "What a bitch."

"Bird," Kane tried, softer this time. "I'm not trying to insult you. Your positivity is one of my favorite things *about* you. But don't you think it's a little naive to believe that—"

"I said *work with her*. Not *trust her*. Hart, do you think you can get word to Amelia somehow? To tell her that if she can find the blade and bring it back to Onyx, we swear to spare her life despite her betrayal?"

"*Arwen*—" Kane nearly raged.

"Wait," Hart interrupted. "You don't even have your alliance with Peridot anymore?"

"No," I admitted.

"So the only army we're waiting on is Onyx's?"

Kane and I remained silent and Hart loosed a long, irritated sigh. He was right. Onyx and Hart's rebels alone, as fearsome as both armies were, couldn't defeat all of Lazarus's Fae soldiers. Let alone their allies of Amber and Garnet, too.

"Do we have any other options to take Peridot's place?"

There were nine kingdoms in Evendell. Not counting Onyx and Peridot, or Amber and Garnet—who had long ago aligned with Lazarus—that left Jade, which was uninhabited; Pearl, which was army-less, too, its precarious location high above the clouds serving as defense enough; and Opal, which was a sprawling no-man's-land with only a handful of territories and a treaty that declared them neutral in all wartime affairs.

"Citrine?" Hart suggested.

"We tried," I said. "They won't fight with us."

"And Arwen broke their prince's heart," Kane added with a cruel smirk. "Which didn't help."

Hart grinned at me like that was a delectable piece of information.

"That only leaves the Quartz of Rose."

Kane shook his head. "The Scarlet Queen—"

"Now she," Hart mused, "was the greatest fuck. But the things she wanted me to do to her a—"

"Hart," Valery admonished.

He went wide-eyed. "What? People love that story!"

Kane rolled his eyes. "The Scarlet Queen is mad."

Hart waggled his eyebrows at me as if to say, *Yeah she is.*

I couldn't decide if I found him repulsive or adorable. A bit of both?

"And," Kane continued, "she's got her own unruly kingdom to keep an eye on. The southern dissenters still threaten to wage war on the north, and they've only grown stronger the past few years."

"Couldn't we try to convince her? Rose won't be spared by Lazarus. Hart, if you've had . . . intimate relations with the queen, wouldn't she be open to discussing with you?"

Hart shook his head. "Only if you were willing to tramp out her enemies in the south. Frankly, you'd have better luck tracking down Aleksander's army."

"*No.*" Kane's voice hadn't sounded so uncompromising the entire afternoon.

Aleksander . . .

My mind drifted to a conversation Kane and I'd had in his cabin in Crag's Hollow that rainy, harrowing night.

"I even convinced Aleksander Hale to join us, the leader of a peculiarly savage race of Fae called Hemolichs . . . they draw power from corpses, wounds, even their own injuries, making them unmatched warriors. Some drink the blood of animals, mortals, or other Fae to keep their lighte strong."

"Why not?" Valery asked Kane.

"He hasn't been seen in decades. And even if he had—I wouldn't trust that filthy Blood Fae for all the coin in this realm."

A smile leapt up Hart's face. "Lovers' quarrel?"

"I watched hundreds hanged because of him," Kane growled. "My own mother and brother among them."

It was Griffin who had told me that Aleksander's men, his army of Hemolichs, were enslaved by Lazarus and used like prized fighting dogs. That Aleksander had agreed to fight in Kane's rebellion, but instead gave them up to Lazarus in turn for freedom for his people. By the time Kane and a handful of Fae escaped Lumera and he went looking for Aleksander, the Hemolich was gone. The last they'd heard, he'd used his army to help the mad queen of Rose, Ethera, win her civil war against the south, and hadn't been heard from since.

"You didn't kill him?" Hart asked, as if it were expected protocol to eviscerate any man who betrayed you.

"He's been hiding from me for fifty years."

"Vendetta like that . . ." Hart shook his unruly head of hair. "Why'd you stop looking?"

"I had . . ." Kane tucked his chin down as if he'd almost faced me but thought better of it. "Other priorities."

"Well," Hart said, letting his leg drop over the edge of the sideboard. "He's in Rose, somewhere."

"What gives you that idea?"

"Ethera told me. When we were . . ." Hart jerked his chin toward me with a boyish smirk. "Having intimate relations, as you said. The two of them made a blood oath years ago. Probably right around the time he left Lumera and swore his army to her cause."

"What was the nature of the oath?"

Hart shrugged. "No clue."

Kane scratched his chin in thought. "I always assumed a mortal like Ethera never aged due to some kind of spell or curse . . . Seems it's the blood oath that keeps her so young."

"And so fucking crazy . . ." Hart said, eyes glazing over as if re-calling a specific memory. When Valery cleared her throat, Hart's eyes found ours and he schooled his face. "Look, betrayal a half century ago or not, Aleksander Hale's Blood Fae army is ten times more powerful than Rose's mortal one. They're *machines*. They draw their power from *blood*. Drinking it, pulling from people's bodies, corpses, necrophilia, lathering themselves in it . . . You know what that means? Carnage, war, losing a fucking limb—it only makes them *more powerful*."

"I know that," Kane gritted out. "It's why my father enslaved them in the first place. Both to fight for Solaris and to keep them from turning that power against him."

"You're going to let your hurt feelings stop you from using an army like that?"

Kane remained silent, though his jaw had gone rigid.

"He tried once," I said softly. "We have no reason to believe Aleksander wouldn't deceive us again."

"Gods, he betrayed the fallen son of Lazarus. Who's now full-blooded . . . He's a dead man anyway. He'd probably be thrilled to work off his debt to you."

Kane only said, "We'll get through to Ethera, somehow."

"So," I said, my mind swimming a bit with all the new information. "Hart will get word to Amelia to somehow extricate the blade from the palace in Solaris in return for her life, and we'll speak with the Scarlet Queen and convince her to rally her army for our cause? Without endangering thousands of southern Rose lives . . ."

The sharp-boned witch nodded in my direction, though Hart's expression darkened with doubt. And I didn't blame him. It was ambitious at best.

"Amelia won't believe you and I are aligned," Kane said to the rebel. "Her default is distrust. Here."

Kane pulled his mother's black signet ring from his pinky and offered it to Hart. "She knows what it means to me. Tell her it's a sign of my word."

Amelia, who had been one of Kane's closest friends. One of his only friends. Who knew his history, his suffering—my heart stirred for the bond they'd both lost.

Hart nodded, placing the onyx-and-silver ring in his pocket with care.

"Once we have our armies and the blade," I said, "we'll bring everyone back here. How long do you think it will take Lazarus to rebuild even half the lighte we destroyed?"

"Two weeks," Hart said. "Three, tops."

"We'll move quickly, then," Kane said.

I was way ahead of him, already easing myself from the bed and sliding on borrowed boots.

Kane motioned back toward me. "Thank you again, Hart."

"Don't mention it." Hart hopped down from his spot atop the sideboard. "Kane, once we win. . . ." For the first time, Hart appeared less assured. He shot Valery a look that I couldn't quite read.

"I don't want our good men to war over the throne, and I know it's your birthright, but—"

Kane shook his head. "It was my brother's, not mine."

An ache pulled at my chest with his words. With the memories I knew plagued him. Kane never wished to usurp his father. Not before he rebelled, not after when he inherited the throne from King Oberon in Onyx, and absolutely not now that he was full-blooded. It was his father's dream to have a true Fae heir on the Lumerian throne. Kane would never fulfill it.

Hart remained silent, showing a tact I'd yet to see from the spirited would-be king. He was waiting Kane out. Allowing him to make the first offer.

"Should we win," Kane said in the end, "as the son of Lazarus, I will crown you king of Lumera. You have the people of this realm behind you, and that's what matters. In return, I only require that you will agree to a handful of my political requests, no questions asked."

"A generous offer." Hart grinned broadly. "And one I'll gladly accept."

"You've proven yourself a decent man," Kane said. "Perhaps a pig, but . . ."

Hart only laughed, rough and genuine. "Perhaps so. But I love this land. I love these people. And each one of them deserves a life better than this one."

"Indeed." Kane nodded. "It will bring me great relief to see you take his throne."

"Me, too, friend."

Kane extended his hand and the two men shook.

For some near-indescribable reason, the simple act made my throat tighten with emotion. I wondered if I'd just beheld something very pivotal for the future of all realms.

Kane's bright eyes on mine told me he felt the same. "Do you have a steed to spare? I've always found the first few days of the channel easiest on horseback."

Hart shook his head. "We don't have that kind of time. Valery and her coven can open a portal between realms."

Valery nodded to us both and excused herself, and Hart followed suit before stopping in the doorway. "If we succeed, there will be ballads written about this afternoon."

Kane grinned that chilling, glittering smile of his and my heart thumped at his devastating beauty, multiplied only by his joy. "I hope they leave out how many powerful women you've fucked."

Hart beamed. "I don't."

The door closed softly behind him, leaving just Kane and me, alone again at last.

He took a tentative step toward me and leaned down, brushing his thumb across my cheek and cradling my jaw. The curve of his silver rings slid gently along my chin.

Those slate eyes were tired, his face bruised, his hair shiny and tousled around his face.

I'd never be used to his heartbreaking looks.

I tried to swallow them, but tears pricked at my eyelids and slid silently down one cheek and then the other. Kane's brows knit inward, worried.

But I shook my head and covered his warm, large hand with mine.

We were going home.

PART III

The Flames

21

ARWEN

THE PORTAL VALERY AND THE ANTLER COVEN HAD OPENED for us deposited Kane and me into the middle of the Shadow Woods. The gnarled roots that sprawled like dark veins across the forest floor had always been bathed in mild tufts of moss and tall rustling grass. Now they were dusted in a fine layer of snow.

I'd never seen snow.

It was one of the many things I'd been sure I never would.

And yet, here it was, like spilled sugar all around us. Where dewy patches of foxglove and daffodils had once sprung forth in the summer now grew only red-beaded holly and rose hips. The forest was even darker than usual, the softly falling snow a thin film between us and the daylight.

I must've shivered. Or maybe it was my lips turning violet and my nose rosy, but while I took in the dried branches poking through gentle clumps of white powder at my feet, a thick cloak, still warm from Kane's body, draped around my shoulders.

My weary eyes found Kane's, and he reached for my hand.

I didn't hesitate because of him.

When my gaze dropped to those long, outstretched fingers, all I wanted was to grasp them and pull myself into his arms. It was all I'd wanted to do for months.

But I could think only of the spires and turrets of Shadowhold, visible now through the snow and trees. That domed, decorated one, Kane's cozy study. The stained-glass tower—devoid of its usual vibrant colors due to the hour and the snow—Mari's precious library. That highest point there, with the wind vane, Shadowhold's temple, which I'd never stepped foot inside before.

Memories, people, warmth—all of it as it once was.

And yet I'd been through so much. I wasn't sure all my new edges and angles would fit through the doors the same way.

"Arwen?" Kane's voice was a bit raw.

We had been through more in the last day than I wanted to remember. He was worried about me, and that concern made me shiver again.

Kane's brows pulled together as he said, lower this time, "Let's get you warm, yeah?"

"Mhm." But still, I didn't move.

A dry wind rustled the few crackling leaves unwilling to fall from the trees above and swept snowflakes against my hair and the shell of my ear. The hind legs of a deer were visible, only briefly, moving through the dark green brush.

"Bird?"

"I'm not sure I can"—I swallowed—"can go back just yet."

If my words worried him further, he didn't let on. Kane simply stepped closer to me, his boots crunching against the snow, which blanketed twigs and dirt on the forest floor, and brought his hand up to my face before saying, "May I?"

My nod felt like an understatement, but it was all I could manage.

Kane's eyes flickered with something like relief as he brought that hand to his mouth and breathed warm air onto it. Steam filtered into the space between us, the scent of mint and cedar from his breath thickening the air. All the while his steadfast, quicksilver eyes never left mine. Kane exhaled into his palm once more before bringing his now warmed hand across my cheek.

So gentle I shivered again, though this time not from the cold.

Kane's eyes grew warm.

He brought that hand down to the bare skin of my neck, still exposed where his cloak was too big for my frame. Then across my shoulder, until he slipped underneath the garment as well as my blouse. When his rough fingers circled gently around to the back of my neck, I stumbled into him.

Warmth, and his heady male scent and broad, muscled body made my senses fuzzy and languid. One of Kane's hands fisted into my hair, the other dragged me closer, snaking around my back, my waist—

My lips found his chest through the thick fabric of his shirt, and my hands roamed over his ribs and the curve of his strong abdomen and subtle dip of his collarbone. When I reached up on my toes—

He was groaning my name. Again, and again.

Breathing it. Repeating it like a prayer.

"Arwen. My Arwen." And *"My bird, my love—"*

And then his lips were brushing—just barely *brushing*—against my own. His nose sliding gently along mine. His hands on my face near-shaking with restraint. Those thumbs, caressing my jaw, waiting for a sign from me. Some indication of what it was I wanted.

I pulled him down into me, closing every gap between us save for our mouths.

He was thick and hard against my stomach, and though it had been the last thing on my mind when we'd stepped from that dizzying portal into these woods, suddenly a pulse of need spread through my body, blaring as loudly as a bell tower.

That need pooled between my legs and low in my stomach, beneath where my stitches had healed. My eyes fluttered open to find Kane's simmering gaze on my lips.

His eyes were wholly black. Pure, pupil-black. Not a sliver of slate gray to be seen.

And his breaths—

Ratcheting out of him at a feverish pace. As if he'd been battling a great beast.

Maybe he had been. The raw, near-pleading look in Kane's eyes told me there was quite the beast currently roaring inside him, the one urging him to plunge his tongue into my mouth. To rip the clothes from my body and make love to me in the middle of these snowy woods, our bodies still slick with dirt and the blood of our enemies like frantic, war-torn barbarians.

Somewhere between one of my own shaky, choked inhales and a shallow grunt of his the beasts inside both of us emerged victorious.

Kane's mouth on mine tasted like pure desire.

The kisses we'd shared—in that Solaris garden, in Hart's infirmary— they'd been mere vessels in which to store months and months of misery and yearning. And relief at seeing each other again, when I was sure neither of us thought we'd ever be given the chance.

But those kisses had not been about wanting or lust. Or vicious, near-painful *need*.

They'd not made my bloodstream rush with liquid fire nor sent my heart racing so fast I could have latched on to it and been hauled away.

But this kiss did.

When Kane dragged his tongue across my own, licking at my mouth and sucking shamelessly on my lower lip, the whimper I released sent scandalized creatures skittering into the bushes.

Kane barely noticed. His warm breath swept over my neck and ear and jaw as he trailed rushed kisses all across me. Then back up to my mouth, and then down the sensitive skin of my throat once more—

Heat blared through me. He was going too slow.

More, more, more—

I whined at his indolent leisure and brought my hand down to grasp haphazardly at his pants. When I brushed his twitching, stiff length, we both groaned.

"Easy," he said, voice husky and low, though I could feel his lips grinning against mine. "Let me take my time with you."

With gentle care, and without removing his mouth from my lips, he lifted me into his arms and walked us back until we met the thick heft of a tree trunk. I sighed with the contact, luxuriating in the pleasant feeling of being pinned by him. Compressed wonderfully underneath his body with nowhere else to go.

I held him so tightly around the middle with my legs—my back balanced against the sturdy oak—that Kane released both hands and palmed my breasts roughly over my faded beige dress.

We hummed in perfect harmony.

Undoing each button with care, Kane slipped one hand under the fabric and pulled down my bodice just enough to brush a calloused thumb over my bare breast. I wasn't cold—we were still wearing all our clothes and his body heat was radiating off him and onto me in waves—but my nipples were pointed to near agony. That thumb, sliding across me in slow, languid circles sent a need that teetered on life-threatening straight between my legs.

I mewled, *aching*, and swore Kane chuckled through our kiss. "You really do love that."

My head was too dizzy to form an intelligible response.

Without halting his light caress across my nipple, Kane brought his lips down to my neck and sucked languorously, the soft scrape of his teeth sending stars into my vision alongside the falling snow. He held me to the tree with his fingers stretching across my side, thumb still petting over and over that pointed tip until I cried out, and even then he didn't relent.

The way he touched me . . . I thought I might come from just that thumb and the agonizing, pleasurable pinches he doled out whenever he saw fit.

Kane's other hand fished through the layers of my borrowed dress until his knuckles stroked the inside of my thigh.

Oh, *Stones* . . . "Kane—"

"Yes, bird?" he breathed against my neck.

But then his fingers were brushing against the thin cotton that separated him from the almost mortifying wetness that had collected between my legs, and once again I couldn't form an answer. Not while I could feel his fingers swiping across the fabric, soaked so thoroughly that he could barely create the friction I so craved.

His shoulders tensed under my hands as he touched me. I was so swollen for him, so plump and slick and ready, and knowing the effect that had—how ragged and wild it made him—only produced another senseless whimper from the back of my throat.

Those hands—

Those *fingers*—

Kane shoved the sodden fabric to the side and pushed his thumb rigidly against the spot I'd been shamelessly grinding along any part of him I could reach. I bucked from sheer pleasure.

"There you go," he murmured.

I nodded, panting, nearly contracting, *moaning*—

"Shh," he soothed. "Relax."

Deep breaths—I sucked in deep, bracing breaths.

Kane brought his hot tongue to my aching nipple—the one he'd been toying with—and dipped his mouth to suck on the tender bud.

The pleasure . . . It was *mind-bending*.

He snarled softly around my breast in deep satisfaction.

At the same time, he dragged a single finger through me to bring the slickness there back to the little bundle of nerves at the apex of my thighs. While my head emptied out completely, Kane rolled his fingers across the spot, pinching and soothing until I was pleading for more.

Disregarding his earlier instruction to go *easy*, I pressed down the front of his pants again, palming him, rubbing him, brushing my thumb over the head of his—

"*Fuck*," Kane ground out against my collarbone, and my skin might have gleamed with how wanton that noise made me feel.

"Please, please . . ." I mumbled. "*Please*—"

"Yeah," he breathed. "Yeah, all right."

Kane removed his hand from between my legs and I could have sobbed from the loss. But he unlaced his pants deftly and I whimpered when his cock sprang free, bulging with a desire that looked almost painful and leaking from the tip.

I ran my thumb across the moisture there, a little mesmerized, and Kane's whole body shook as he allowed me, patiently, to stroke him.

His grunts were raw and guttural, and sparks shot through me at the sounds, collecting in my chest and between my legs. I reached for his lips with mine, feeling only warmth and breath when our mouths brushed clumsily. Too distracted to kiss with any real skill, but licking and skating across each other nonetheless.

Closer—

I wanted to be closer. I wanted to be joined. And never parted. Not ever again.

When his eyes drifted, dazed, to mine, they turned just as impatient. Kane angled my body up slightly, lifting my skirts until we were aligned. His eyes found mine once more, those unwavering slate eyes brimming with love and just a sliver of worry. I nodded to reassure him—

Yes, *yes—*

Kane parted me with his length and nudged inside.

I was wetter than I think either of us had anticipated, and Kane groaned as he slid in to the hilt, stumbling into me a little, stretching me so fully that I clawed at the bark of the tree as I cried out.

"Did I hurt you?"

I shook my head.

But I couldn't breathe, couldn't speak around the obscene, magnificent fullness. Our bodies—it was like we'd been made for each other. Kane slowed his first thrust, allowing me to adjust to his size. When I opened my eyes, I found him staring down at me, that silver gaze *shining.*

I'd missed Kane beyond what I believed were the boundaries of human heartache. I'd seen his face in every tall, dark-haired male far away enough for me to squint at. Heard his voice in my head before my own. Smelled cedar and leather every morning as I awoke, remnants from my dreams bleeding into day. And each night, I'd fallen asleep to memories—the look of awe on Kane's face, lit by guttering candlelight as he'd touched me for the first time in Siren's Bay. His sensuous smirk when I slapped him in his own throne room. The way he'd held me in that rain-drenched clearing after Halden held me captive.

All of that misery.

All the agony of missing him more than I knew someone could miss *anything*—

And for him, it had been worse.

He'd thought I was dead.

That was all I could think of as Kane brushed stray hairs from my face, his breathing uneven, releasing the rare male whimper or sigh. All I could think of as he gripped my hips to angle me around him, grasping my breast through my shirt, burying his face in my neck and inhaling me.

I fisted my hands in his dark hair, damp and dotted with snow, and brought my lips lightly to his temple, pressing myself into him even farther, canting my hips around him, closing my eyes—

My Kane. Who had suffered so much.

Had endured such torment to find me—

Kane reared his head back and wiped a hand down his cheek before yanking it in front of him to examine the moisture there.

His cheeks were still flushed with exertion, lips full and parted and wet, but when his eyes found mine they were gutted. "Are you . . . crying?"

My cheeks heated. "Please, Kane, please don't stop."

That would have been more painful than anything. To be parted from him in this moment.

Kane's eyes welled with empathy and he slowed his hips but didn't withdraw. Instead, he brought his forehead to mine and closed his eyes, sucking in a jagged inhale.

"I'm here. You're here, and we're together," he mumbled, rocking his hips a little as if he weren't fully in control. "Arwen, I love you. I'm here."

"I love you, too," I said, beginning to ache around him, craving the rhythmic pounding once more.

I raked my fingers through his hair again and again, and arched into him a bit.

Kane needed no further urging. He resumed his thrusts, slower this time and more deliberate. He angled himself again until I was grinding against his body with each plunge, over and over and over—

My voice was rough as I said, "Harder."

He groaned. I whimpered with the sound.

Kane braced one hand on the gnarled trunk behind me and the wood splintered under his grasp. He pushed into me with unspeakable roughness. So hard, so brutal, it was just shy of painful.

"More," I breathed. "Harder."

"No," he grunted.

The place where our bodies were joined had drenched my thighs, my skirts, and I mumbled something incoherent around the wet, slapping noises that I was sure all of Shadowhold could hear. I shook and bucked, trying to wring myself out atop him, chasing that pleasure, that building—

"Please—"

"Just breathe," he soothed.

I tried to listen to him, tried to slow myself down, but the pressure was too great. I was racked with a need that was stuck at the top of a towering cliff, begging to plunge off the other side. My nipples were too tight, my core clenching and shuddering, the pleasure almost mindless, *merciless*, and still I couldn't, I wasn't—

"You're almost there, bird," Kane coaxed. "Don't force it." He thrust into me with a ruthless rhythm and brought a hand down to massage that spot where I craved him.

"Oh, Stones," I groaned, slamming my head back into the tree.

"Yeah?" His voice was so strained I wondered if he was fighting to stave off his own climax, waiting for me.

"Yeah," I whined in answer.

He slowed his hand and I nearly screeched.

I'd do anything to come. Deplorable things. I'd crawl through the snow below us, beg on my hands and knees like an animal. I'd—

"Just a little more," he breathed, taking my earlobe in between his teeth and biting just this side of roughly. Then he thrust into me once more and I *exploded*.

My climax seized me like a ferocious undertow as I tensed and spasmed, nearly ripping Kane's shirt from his body in my white-knuckled grasp. Shattering, sobbing, splitting in half—

Kane's fierce grunts as he finished inside me only pushed me further over the edge as we came apart together, sighing and groaning into each other until we were both heaving heaps. Thoroughly spent.

Even after our panting had subsided and he grew soft inside of me, we stayed like that. After we detangled just long enough for him to withdraw and tuck himself back into his pants. After I was empty and sore and could feel his release leaking down my thighs. Even then, he held me tight to his chest, leaning us against the sturdiness of the tree.

I scraped my nails softly down his back until he shivered. Kissed his damp brow and his ice-cold hands and his even more frozen silver rings. Felt more warm, salty tears drip down my cheeks and onto the thick wool of his shirt, though they were less insistent this time.

He brushed the hair from my face and pulled the cloak more snugly around my shoulders when the wind chill picked up. Murmuring into my neck how much he loved me. How much our separation had nearly killed him. Laughing that it did, in fact, kill him.

Until finally, he exhaled a mighty sigh and lowered me gracefully to the ground alongside the evening light as it faded around us. Wind howled gently through the gnarled trees, drowning out the rhythmic chirps of crickets. The moon's illumination cast the snowdrifts beneath us in veils of rich silver.

Kane appraised me once, his eyes the color of the winter that surrounded us. He brushed a thumb across my cheek and I nuzzled into the touch. "Well, bird," he breathed. "Shall we?"

22

ARWEN

THE FIRST PERSON TO RECOGNIZE US IN THE PALE DUSK
light was a young solider with a mop of stringy hair and an impressive height for his young age. As we strolled through the barracks, hand in hand, he scrambled over a fresh campfire to alert his
peers, sparked by the realization that his king had returned.

Kane stifled a grin, which produced a matching one across my
own face.

By the time we strode into the great hall, the entire castle was
abuzz with murmurs and hollers and the rare cheer.

I was touched—I loved the people of Onyx, of Shadowhold
specifically—but there were only a few faces that mattered to me, and
I scanned the bustling hall for them.

Shadowhold in the wintertime was the most magical I'd ever seen
it, and the great hall was no exception. The dark wood floors were
somehow warmer, friendlier in contrast to the sheets of white that
filled the windowsills outside. Each pillar and arch was dotted in garlands of bright red poinsettia, aspen leaves, and wreaths of mistletoe.

Cranberry and peppermint and roasted nut aromas wafted in from the kitchens, and the delightfully haunting chords of a lute and jingling bells played a winter carol somewhere by the roaring fireplace.

The castle was fuller, too, and busier, which I assumed was due to all the soldiers and families bundled inside to stay warm. Their chatter and laughter and the clinking of their glasses only made me feel more at home. Solaris had been so empty. So cold. Shadowhold bundled me up and placed me into direct sunlight. I already felt my petals unfurling.

A family erupted in exultant laughter and I blinked twice at them. Small blonde girl, older, gray-haired man . . .

My heart expanded, and Kane squeezed my hand tightly.

Sitting at that long, lovingly dented wooden table, replete with plates piled high and steaming mugs, was *my family*.

Leigh, pitching her head back as she laughed with unfiltered glee, and beside her, Beth—the little seer whom I'd not realized would be here—not quite smiling but eyes still bright. Ryder and Barney across from them. Dagan, with his nose in a thick book, at the head of the table ignoring them all.

My hurried stroll to them became an ungraceful sprint as I drew nearer and nearer and nearer to the table.

"Arwen?" Leigh's stunned surprise was cut off by my barreling embrace. I pulled her so close I could feel her heart beating against my own. Her small hands reaching for as much of me as she could grasp. Blonde curls filled my vision and my throat grew so tight I couldn't speak. But that was all right. I had nothing to say that she couldn't feel through my hug.

I'm alive. I love you. I'm sorry I was gone so long.

"How is this— How . . ." Ryder's awed voice cut through Leigh's tears.

When I finally released our sister and got a good look at him, his smile was soft, though unmistakable remorse swam in his eyes. "I never thought I'd see you again."

When I wrapped my arms around his neck and held tightly, he appeared more stunned than anything.

"I'm so sorry," he mumbled into my shoulder. "So sorry."

"It wasn't your fault."

He nodded against my shoulder wordlessly. If I'd learned anything from all the stupid mistakes I'd made—telling Halden things I shouldn't have, not listening to Mari about the amulet before it almost killed her, and about a hundred other awful errors in judgment—it was that life was far too short to be the last one to forgive yourself.

Ryder pulled back just enough to search my face, frowning as he beheld what I was sure were sunken eyes, pallid flesh, and weak limbs. I needed some sunshine, and to move my atrophied muscles. And to *eat* something. Nothing had done less for my appetite than captivity.

"I'm all right," I assured him. "I'm going to start training again as soon as I can."

A gruff voice behind me said, "I've heard that one before."

For whatever reason it was the soft, relieved smile on Dagan's wrinkly face—his uncharacteristically warm, crinkled eyes—that wrecked me.

My face crumpled and I launched myself at him, fully expecting the old man to back away and let me topple onto my face. I wouldn't even have minded. But he was surprisingly strong and sturdy, and his dry, knotted fingers gripped me tightly into his chest as I broke into soundless sobs.

Somewhere amid the tears I could just make out Griffin's out-of-breath voice beside Kane, as if he'd come hurtling into the great hall amid the commotion. "Holy Gods above. Is that—"

"She was alive," Kane murmured. "All along, she was alive."

THE WINTER SUN WAS NEAR BLINDING WHEN I AWOKE. Brighter, as it reflected off heaps of fresh, clean snow. It sliced through the curtains into Kane's room and directly onto my face, pulling my eyes open. I pointed my toes and let my knuckles brush against the smooth headboard.

Home. I was home.

I stretched again. All my muscles protested. Every single one.

From fighting, from healing, from Kane.

I grounded myself in the memories of last night. How, after Kane and I had eaten an entire pork roast and two full loaves of clover-bread with everyone and, over many glasses of birchwine, had shared our stories—both the gruesome and the hopeful—he had brought me upstairs. And when I'd complained I couldn't bathe because my limbs were too tired and my belly too full, he'd carried me into the bath. He'd washed my hair with the most delicious lilac and lemongrass soap, and then my entire body after that, kneading and rubbing every inch of me from my sore shoulders to the slick ache between my legs until I squirmed and sobbed with pleasure.

He'd brought me to bed and we'd made love again. Slower, more careful, less hurried. Less twined around the leftover thorns of suffering for so long without each other.

I'd still cried during. And after. And then blubbered to Kane that I was sorry for ruining everything and I didn't know what was wrong with me. And that I wasn't pregnant, or hormonal, or tired—although, in fairness, I *was* actually that last one.

He'd raised a single brow and asked me why in the world I'd felt the need to explain myself. Clearly he hadn't grown up as a teenage girl with an younger brother and one male friend—

But Kane had only laughed and pulled me close and assured me that it might take some time until we felt like ourselves again. And even though he was right and I knew it, I still wanted that time to speed by as quickly as possible. I was eager to get my old life back, even just for a little, before we went to war.

This firm mattress, Kane's simple dark sheets, and his warm sleeping body beside me were at least the first pillars of that old life I could grasp on to: a reminder that I was here and I was safe and this was real.

Even my toes, prodding into the slumbering body of Acorn at the foot of our bed, brought a smile to my cheeks. I sat up on my elbows to peer at his odd little goblin face and wiry, feathered owl wings. Some dream of his resulted in a snort that sent my heart racing, and I brought the covers up around me in reflex.

All right, so I was still getting used to the strix, but everything else—everything else was a relief.

Kane's muscular back rippled with his own snores, the lucky bastard hidden completely in shadow while I had taken the brunt of the harsh dawn light. I rolled over, hoping to chase the last thread of sleep before it evaporated from my grasp completely.

I'd need all the rest I could get—we likely had only another day here, two at the most, before we had to leave for Rose. Find a way to convince Ethera, somehow, and then . . . The thought that followed was like tripping down a flight of stairs.

We'd have to go back.

Back to Lumera. Back to Solaris.

Back to that Stones-forsaken, muggy, marble-filled, bloodred-and-ink-black palace. Like a dreadful bruise.

Nausea seized my stomach and I sat up with enough force to wake Acorn and produce a shriek from him. As soon as his half-opened beady little eyes realized it was only me, he yawned and returned to his sleep.

But I was suddenly far too awake to lie in bed another minute.

I found my leathers in Kane's closet, alongside my prized, well-worn copy of *Evendell Flora*; the black silk gown I'd been wearing when we'd been trapped in a wine cellar together; and the blue dress he bought me in Crag's Hollow. Some part of my still-healing heart ripped back open at the realization that he'd not disposed of any of my things in all the weeks he'd thought I was dead.

He'd kept it all. Artifacts of his love.

I changed silently, careful not to disturb either of my sleeping, winged boys, and found my way through the drowsy morning halls of Shadowhold. Down the grand staircase—that, too, festooned with wreaths of holly and little linked pinecones—and out into the barracks. Past the colorful tents that filled the front walls of the keep, now doused in lovely new snow. Past the gates, which creaked open for me as if I were some kind of royalty—guards in their shining obsidian armor and helmets shaped like eerie skulls waving pleasantly at me and wishing me a nice day. After lifting my arches against the trunk of a tree to stretch, I set off into the Shadow Woods at a brisk, jolting pace.

And I was not afraid.

There was nothing in these woods I couldn't face. No creature, no beast, no animal. I had survived beatings, loss, torture, Fae mercenaries, harvesting, confinement, impalement, explosions—

I had *survived*.

It was no indication of a flawless future, of course. Beth herself, a seer who had yet to be wrong, had told me point-blank that I would die. I knew in my bones, even after I'd survived so much, that it was true.

But I didn't brave so many horrors, defeat so much evil, suffer so deeply, to give up whatever joy I was left with. I was grateful for my life. Not the potential of it, or the purpose it served. Not for what I hoped one day, if every single miracle came true, it *could* be. But for how it looked today.

I rounded a bare beech tree and the two mighty stags that grazed below it—soft brown fur speckled with white spots, nuzzling each other in the dappled wintry sunlight—breath funneling pleasantly in and out of my tired lungs, glittering white snow at my feet.

And I thought, if we only had a day or so before Mari and Briar received the raven we sent last night and arrived at the keep, a day or so before we continued on our journey, which would inevitably lead to the war that would ensure my death or the death of the man I loved, I was going to enjoy the ever-loving *Stones* out of this run, in case it was my last.

It was right in the middle of that solid, strengthening thought, about ten yards from the North Gate of Shadowhold—I'd run an impressive half circumference of the keep and was feeling a little too pleased with myself—that I heard the unmistakable sound of Leigh's high-pitched yell.

23

KANE

I'D ONLY PANICKED FOR A MINUTE.

No, not even a minute. A second.

It hadn't helped that I'd awoken, breathless, from another dream in which I was chained in lilium, forced to watch Arwen purge widow venom from her thigh, writhing and screeching in excruciating pain. If Killoran wasn't already dead, I would have flown to Hemlock Isle and skewered him myself this morning.

Fresh from that nightmare, I'd rolled over, still bare from the night before, and grasped for Arwen, only to find empty, rumpled sheets. Had the worst-case scenario torn through my mind? That Lazarus had stolen her away somehow, or murdered her for her deceit, and I'd find her cold, lifeless body in my bathtub? Had I bypassed Acorn's squawking and hurtled into the hallway with nothing but a decorative pillow to cover myself, dark-winged lighte surging from my bare shoulders and arms, and roared at the guard on duty to tell me *that instant* where the *fuck my wife* was—even though

Arwen was not my wife and I'd never seen the shaking kid before? Yes, yes, and . . . yes.

To the quivering guard's credit, he had told me in one sentence strung together with no breaths that she'd woken early and gone for a run, that the sentries were watching her make a tight perimeter around the castle, and that she was actually keeping a pretty inspiring pace.

And I had calmed. A little sheepish, sure, but I fixed the kid's collar—I'd roughed him up a bit more than I'd meant to when I'd seized him, still acclimating to my full-Fae strength—courteously pretended I hadn't noticed that he'd wet himself, and strolled back into my quarters to take a long, hot, introspective bath.

I'd hoped when Griffin and I met not fifteen minutes later that he wouldn't have heard anything of the outburst, but of course, he had.

"Not even pants?" Griffin asked, incredulous, as we stalked through the training annex and toward the war tent.

"I'd like to see you manage to intimidate anyone wearing a velvet cushion. It was impressive."

His grin was worse than shit-eating. "Somehow I doubt that."

But we were both laughing now. Perhaps with the loose delight of a sunny, winter's day spent knowing all the people we cared about were safe and alive in the very walls of this keep. That would put a smile on anyone's face.

Griffin and I were on our way to be briefed on our position with Queen Ethera. We had sent word for Sir Phylip and Lady Kleio late last night. If there was any information out there that could help convince the Scarlet Queen to fight beside us—anything other than offering to crush the southerners who wanted her crown—my dignitaries would know about it.

Griffin's eyes took in the snow-veiled training annex. "Check it out."

I cut my gaze sidelong across the training field and found Leigh driving her sword into Barney's while Beth and Ryder sat in the snowy grass a few feet away. Given the collection of white flakes atop their heads, Ryder and the little seer had been sitting there for some time.

"She's decent." My eyes glued to the push and pull of Leigh's sword. She shouted with each blow, as surely Dagan had taught her to. Her bouncy blonde curls had been pinned back, and she was wearing dark training leathers. I'd only ever seen her in frilly Amber dresses. She looked just like her sister—bold, resolute, focused.

I couldn't conceal my pride. The little one had been through enough trauma to break a brutal thug, let alone a sheltered small-town ten-year-old. And there she was, making Barney work for his wins.

But her form was lacking. Defending without stepping, forcing her to lean over her too-planted feet. Overcommitting to her swings from far away and leaving herself defenseless. Barney was a great soldier—brute strength of a bison and more sword skill than most men his size—but he wasn't half the teacher Dagan was.

"Hey," I called to them, jogging over. "Less arms, more feet. You have to—"

Arwen's shrill voice cut through my words "Leigh!"

I turned, and found her sprinting toward us as if a rabid beast were on her tail, feet slowing to a walk as she took in our confused faces.

"What are you doing?" she asked her sister, breathless.

Leigh shrugged. "Not using my feet properly, I guess."

Barney wiped his brow and offered her a dismissive shake of his head as if to say, *You're doing just fine.*

Arwen's dark hair was tied in a loose braid peppered with fresh snow. Her nose and lips were blushing red either from the brisk run, cold weather, or embarrassment, which made my heart stir fondly in my chest. Already her skin had regained some of its pigment and her eyes some of their brightness since we'd left Lumera.

"What did you think?" Griffin asked, sympathy in his usually cold eyes.

She shook her head, puzzled. "The worst. I heard her yell."

"Nothing of the sort." I pulled Arwen's warm body into mine and pressed a kiss into her hair. "Your sister's become quite the swordswoman."

"I know you wanted to teach me, but . . ." Leigh's face dropped.

Griffin coughed. Ryder studied the blades of grass at his fingers.

"I know," Arwen said quietly. "But I'm back now. Swordsmanship is wonderful, isn't it?"

Leigh beamed. "Better than drawing. Better than riding a horse. I feel like a mighty beast."

"For a tiny thing, you swing like one, too," Barney huffed, hands on his knees. "I'm exhausted."

I offered Barney a half grin. "In that case, may I?"

Barney nodded, handing me his blade and plopping to sit beside Beth and Ryder, snow puffing up in his wake. Ryder gave him a good-natured pat on the back, while Beth said nothing. Then she offered him her jug of water, which Barney accepted with a wide-eyed nod, patting sweat from his shiny bald head.

Leigh gaped as she beheld me with Barney's sword.

"*You're* going to teach me?"

"Just a few tips."

Arwen beamed beside Griffin, who only raised a brow. "We have to meet Kleio and Phylip soon."

"Let them have their fun," Arwen teased, nudging my commander in the arm. "I'm sure she'll make quick work of him, won't you, Leigh?"

Griffin hardly concealed his grin at the little blonde's vigorous nod.

Arwen was right. We couldn't live like this—both of us, in constant fear that at any moment something horrific could befall the other. Or someone else we loved. We had to chase the joy when it presented itself to us.

"All right, Leigh," I began. "You've got a good foundation, but your assessment was correct. It all begins with your feet. Not your arms, like so." I feigned a few blows.

"Got it," she said, still breathing hard. "Come on." She lifted her sword at the ready. "Unless you're chicken?"

I couldn't see their faces, but I would have paid a hefty fee to know whose smile grew wider, Arwen's or my commander's. "Shall we make it a bit more interesting?"

Leigh's eyes lit up as they so often did when I enticed her with a wager. We'd made a fair few back on the ship to Citrine.

"I'll use my left hand. And I won't move my feet." I fixed them firmly in the snow beneath us. "And," I added, "I'll close my eyes."

Leigh grinned. "And all I have to do is strike you once?"

"Indeed."

Leigh didn't even wait to hear what was in it for her, if anything. She steeled her jaw and charged, leaving mere seconds for me to shut my eyes, toss my blade into my other hand, and plant my feet.

Her sword met mine in a pleasant crash over and over again. Her little huffs of frustration and exertion told me where she was at all times, which felt a bit unfair, but it wasn't as if I could avoid them. Even if she'd been silent, Leigh's blows were consistent, and I knew where each one was headed long before it drew near.

Despite Barney's shouts for her to *"Aim lower!"* and Griffin's low, mumbled, *"A gut punch would help,"* Leigh had only succeeded in deflecting blow after blow and not so much as slicing a fiber on my pant leg.

After parrying an offense which sent Leigh far enough away that I could no longer hear her panting, I stilled. She was good, the little one. Sly and cunning. I briefly wondered if I should let her steal a win, or if affection was clouding my judgment.

When the next blow sang through the air and my blade shot up just in time to spare my chin, fire heated my blood.

That was not the little one.

Another blow slashed, and this time the sharp tip dragged smoothly across my middle, nearly ripping my shirt, followed by a melodic half laugh.

I opened my eyes.

Arwen, blade pointed at the ready, gasped. "That's cheating!"

Leigh had taken a seat next to Beth, Barney, and Ryder, leaning back on her hands in the snow. Griffin had rested against the bare sycamore behind them, and at some point Dagan had come to join him, too.

"I'm the cheater?" I asked Arwen, incredulous. "You two pulled a bait and switch."

Leigh snorted from the sidelines but Arwen's eyes only gleamed.

I resisted the animal growl that spurred in my chest as the breath funneled in and out of her. She was ravishing like this. Determined, a little flushed, playful.

Shaking my head, I lifted my feet from their hold and prowled toward her.

Arwen darted back, feet sliding through the snow, as I advanced on her. Steel slammed against steel.

Griffin and Dagan were still supported against that broad syca-more tree as we weaved around it. They leaned into each other like furtive conspirators as they commented on our every strike and step. Griffin shot me an entertained look as we rounded, while Dagan's face revealed nothing as he watched, keeping a careful, concentrated eye on both our movements. Always a teacher.

When I lunged to sweep Arwen's leg and she deftly shot over me and nearly struck my spine, a sound I'd never heard rang through the bright snow-laden annex: the flutter of Beth's laughter.

Arwen and I both spun with the noise. A smile splitting the seri-ous seer's face was almost uncanny. But Arwen offered no warning as she attacked anew, grinning herself as she feinted and swung. We clashed, drawing close, and Arwen pressed an unexpected hand against my ribs and murmured through ragged breaths, "You're lucky I don't have a dagger on me."

"That I am." I grunted in agreement. Arwen's eyes flickered with heat. I hated to disappoint her, but I was nothing if not competitive. When I transferred the blade back to my dominant hand it was hard to fight the smirk that threatened at my lips.

Arwen's gaze colored with surprise. From the ground, Leigh re-leased a low whistle and Beth laughed once more until Ryder shushed them both.

Our near-evenly-matched sparring dissolved once I made the switch. My blade flew from me like another limb over and over, and Arwen could barely blink in time to keep up. Breathing rough and parrying sloppier, Arwen offered me the first real opening, which I ignored.

The second, though, I lunged for.

She had to learn, and time was not on our side—

I only understood the move for the trap that it was once my sword was too far from my body. Arwen slashed upward. My blade would never reach back in time, and I wasn't nimble enough to hop away. She had me beat.

Black, spindly shadows—thin and virtually harmless—split from my rib cage to guide her steel behind me. Arwen stumbled with the unearthly force and guilt tickled the base of my neck.

"You all right?" I breathed.

Arwen righted herself and tucked a freed strand of hair back into her braid. "New rules?"

Her twitching lips and rosy cheeks expanded something in my chest. My lips ached for hers. I managed to say, "It would make Dagan very happy, wouldn't it?"

"For Dagan, then," Arwen agreed, panting.

To our left the old man grumbled something that sounded like, "*Leave me out of it.*"

Arwen closed her eyes, sucked in a thorough inhale, and when she flicked them open once more, they gleamed.

The bubble of lighte that she bloomed around her body was as delicate as glass and as glittering as fresh water in the midday sun. It reflected the daylight and blinding snow around us in sparkling arcs. When I slammed my blade against its face, the blows reverberated into the calluses of my palm.

I allowed my darkness to advance, flirting with the bubble's surface, lashing at it playfully. But Arwen had moved onto the offensive, taking my tentativeness as an opening. She panted hard, sweeping her sword through her own shield with ease as if it were mere fog. Lustrous, glittering fog.

Arwen parried each of my blows, angled low, and ducked expertly, and with an expression that belied her own surprise, sent out a ribbon of white flame toward me that nearly singed the hair of my forearms.

"Woah," Leigh uttered.

Dagan grunted in approval behind us.

But my eyes pulled from our clashing silver up to her face. Her expression—so poised, so confident. So focused. I had been a wreck this morning over this woman, and here she was ducking and retreating and driving her blade with utter sureness. I had been going far too easy on her—she wasn't a finch, but a falcon.

I let my lighte loose, her whips of that strange, delicate firelighte sailing amid cords of my ultraviolent ebony.

Until one tendril of my darkness grasped her sword, and I wrenched her toward me, her feet skidding through the snow-covered grass until she landed against my chest. She was weakening, I could see it in the fading glimmers of her power.

Our rushed breaths mingled as I held her close, twin puffs of steam in the cold air.

And just like that, a flash of potent heat—not unpleasant, but not comfortable, either—bloomed against my chest. I peered down to find Arwen's hand pressed against my heart. Dainty rays of lighte tickling my tunic. Singing the fibers.

"Interesting." I hummed.

Arwen had a deeper well of power than even another full-blooded like myself could access. I'd sworn she'd been losing steam, but being cornered only allowed her to unleash a buried strength perhaps even she hadn't known she had.

Arwen wrenched her sword free and I released her, throwing out twin ropes of obsidian, satisfaction and adrenaline thrumming in my blood, until they met Arwen's raised blade and the air itself rippled. Our energy was a near-blinding clash of shadow and sunlight.

"Holy Stones."

Arwen's blade, twined in that vibrant, sunny fire, halted an inch from my cords of shadowed thorn. I yanked the shadowed tendrils back into my hands just in time and stumbled to a halt.

The crisp, winter wind scented of cinnamon and cloves, and I whirled in the direction of Arwen's eyeline, following the sound of Leigh's exclamations and my commander's hurried footsteps.

Mari stood there, draped in a warm green cloak with a fur hood. Her eyes locked onto Arwen's in shock as Leigh scrambled up from the ground to wrap the witch tightly around the middle. Griffin appraised Mari with a hesitant nod, which she barely acknowledged. But Mari, even with her arms wrapped around Leigh, couldn't stop staring at the sweat-drenched, red-cheeked vision across from me.

Leigh's sword—the one Arwen had been using—landed softly in the snow as Arwen crossed the training annex for her friend.

"I didn't believe it," she murmured. "You cannot imagine the noise I made when I got the letter," Mari said, arms still gripped around Leigh's back, eyes still glued to Arwen.

Arwen's smile was soft. "I probably can; I was there when you found that squirrel in the apothecary."

Mari laughed around her awe, and somewhere behind us Dagan chuckled at the memory, too.

Leigh finally released Mari just as Arwen swallowed the witch into a hug, her face diving into a mess of snowy red curls.

Moments passed as the women held each other, shaking silently with the onslaught of emotion.

I was pretty sure Barney was crying. Griffin had found his scabbard very compelling, but I couldn't tear my eyes away. It had been too long since any of us had experienced so many instances of joy, and in such quick succession.

Eventually Arwen released her friend with a sniffle. "How have you been?"

"Better." Mari grinned. "Much better. All better actually, now that you're alive."

I exhaled into the brisk morning air. Griffin found my gaze and nodded in similar relief.

"Welcome home," I said to the witch.

"It's been too long, Red." Ryder waved at her from the grass.

"This is Beth," Barney said to her. "She has visions."

Beth didn't smile and Mari's brows knit inward. "All right, great. Hello, Beth," she said warmly. "It's so good to be home."

Dagan huffed. "The library's a mess."

"Of course it is," Arwen said, taking her friend's hand. "Nobody can run that place like Mari."

The witch only faced Arwen again, eyes warm and a little tired. "Forget how I am. How are *you*? How's . . . not being dead?"

Leigh frowned up at her, and Mari shrugged.

But Arwen only released a wet laugh, gaze painting over the wintry annex—Dagan and his begrudging smile, Griffin with his folded arms, her brother, her sister . . . the bluebells, the fresh snow, Barney and Beth, and my steadfast eyes upon hers.

"You know, Mari, I can't complain."

24

ARWEN

"I KNOW IT'S IN HERE SOMEWHERE," MARI SAID, BLOWING A red curl from her face like a horse. "I purposely didn't leave it in the library because I knew how valuable it was."

Mari's bedroom rivaled the aftermath of a tornado. Not just books—of course the shabby, cozy, colorful space was *hemorrhaging* books—but also quills and partnerless shoes and half-melted rouges and various brainiac hobbies she'd started and then promptly given up on.

After our morning training session, Kane, Griffin, Dagan, and I had met with the nobles to discuss our position with Queen Ethera. The tricky monarch wouldn't be swayed by gold or land. All she really wanted was to keep the south from rising up against her. We'd discussed offering her battalions and convoys, but we couldn't spare the men ourselves.

We'd left the forum with clear orders: find *something* of value to offer Ethera in return for her army. When I'd filled Mari in, she'd dragged us to her cottage on the spot.

"I still don't see why the ledger is our way in with Ethera," Kane said coolly, stepping over a half-knit quilt to lean on Mari's childhood vanity. She'd never replaced the old wooden thing, and when she sat down to paint her lips and cheeks she looked like a glamorous giant. "If we give it to the queen, she'll track down every living name in that book and torture them. Doesn't seem like a plan anyone but Griffin would go for."

Griffin grumbled, eyes glued to a smear of lip stain on one of the four half-drained mugs on Mari's bedside. "Don't waste your breath."

I frowned at them both.

"I told you all," Mari said to us, fishing through her unmade bed. "I'll explain when we find the ledger. It'll make more sense then."

I'd forgotten Mari had even taken the book with her from Reaper's Cavern. The one that contained all the names of the men and women from the south of Rose who'd fought against Queen Ethera's northern army and lost.

"Are you going to help or . . . ?"

Chastened, I opened drawer after drawer and felt around for the tome, fishing unashamedly through Mari's unmentionables. The two texts I found sandwiched between all the dainty lace were both recipe books. One was entirely about pies.

I was *honored* to be this woman's friend.

I waggled the books at her. "I need to understand the organizational choices that were made here."

Griffin, far too tall and broad for Mari's cluttered room, paled beside me at the sight of all her lacy underthings. He turned, busying himself with a half-threaded embroidery hoop on her shelf. He'd mindlessly begun to sort the various spools when Mari shrieked at him, "Don't touch those!"

The commander's jaw went rigid. "This room is a cemetery of hobbies, witch. It's making me ill."

Mari's eyes devoured his as if prepared for combat.

Kane snorted, tinkering with a tiny music box. "Tread carefully, Commander."

Griffin shifted on his feet. He appraised the vibrant, tangled threads in his hands. "I could just—"

"I *dare* you," Mari sniped.

Any laugh that had threatened to bubble up my throat was swallowed hastily.

The commander sighed. "Someone let me know when she's found the damned thing."

Maybe it was because I'd spent so many weeks away from them all, or maybe I was still raw and a bit overly sensitive, but something in my heart cracked at his resigned expression. That he couldn't bear to be around her, nor without her. That he couldn't welcome an ounce of vulnerability into his generous yet walled-off heart.

It wasn't his fault. Nobody had ever taught him how.

Mari said nothing as Griffin maneuvered his too-big frame through her small doorway and out of the cottage. Through the window I watched Mari's father nod sternly at the commander. He'd been sitting on the front porch for the last twenty minutes. The sweet lumberman claimed no interest in getting in our way, but I knew he feared being in such close proximity to Kane. I'd seen sheer terror drip through his expression as soon as we'd arrived.

"So," I tried casually. "You revile Griffin again?"

Mari frowned. "Of course not. I just don't like people touching my things."

I raised my fistfuls of her underwear and heard Kane's elegant chuckle.

"Well, not *you*. You can dig your grubby hands through anything you want," she said with a smile. Then her eyes lit with some new thought. "Speaking of." She spun, searching. "Do you want to borrow my basil pots? In the spring you could—"

"Mari." I laughed. "Thank you, but—"

"Oh!" She pulled a dusty book from behind one of her pillows. "Or this book on the history of herbalism—"

"Let's find the ledger first? Then I will gladly scavenge this pigsty of yours for gifts."

Mari nodded brightly in agreement and moved to toss the dry leather-bound text back into one of the many mountains of cloaks and boots.

"Actually," Kane said, halting her with an arched brow. "I'll take it."

She grinned and handed the hefty book to him. Kane considered the tome in his hands, flipping through it casually, his hair skating dreamily over his forehead.

My chest expanded. My two bookworms—I loved them so.

Dropping to the floor, Mari slid underneath her bed.

I raised a brow at Kane, who only shrugged, one large hand still holding open his new book as he craned his head down to study Mari's sub-bed frame fumbling. "What are you—"

"Aha!" Mari scrambled out from the depths, her hair like a tumbleweed. "I knew I put it somewhere safe."

"Indeed," Kane drawled.

But Mari ignored him, plopping onto her unmade bed, and I did the same beside her. I'd missed her so much, I could have rested my chin on her shoulder like a faithful dog. But I settled for watching her leaf through the yellowed pages.

"This ledger was made by Oleander Cross!"

I peered up at Kane, expecting to share another confused glance. But his brows had met in interest. "It was?"

Mari nodded eagerly. "That means—"

Kane was apparently way ahead of her. "If he'd even do it."

"Sure he would. That's how he makes most of his coin now. He wouldn't even have to know what it was for."

"Somebody," I interrupted, "please clue me in."

"Oleander Cross is the finest historian and bookmaker in Evendell. He's old now, but still crafts historical texts and ledgers. He's most famous for recounting battles throughout Evendell's history. The kind of books that will be passed down from generation to generation or kept in the most exclusive museums."

"He crafts more duplicates than originals these days," Kane added, wrapping his hands around Mari's iron bed frame. "Because they go for so much coin."

I fit the pieces together slowly in my mind. "You want him to craft a decoy to bribe Ethera with?"

"She'd give anything for the names of those who waged war against her all those years ago. She's never been able to track down any of the generals or commanders. Not without this ledger."

"So," Mari added, "she won't even realize when all the names are fake. She'll hunt them down and never find a soul."

"We'd have Kleio use a low-level noble to contact him, say it's for a museum. He'd never know it'd be going to the Scarlet Queen."

"And by the time she learns the names were false . . ."

Kane finished my thought. "We'd have already used her army to beat Lazarus. We could handle her wrath then."

It wasn't a bad idea. Not at all. "Mari, you're—"

"Thank you!" She beamed. "I know."

"THIS IS PRETTY NICE," I SAID TO RYDER, AND I MEANT IT. I hadn't been inside the soldiers' barracks, other than the tented pavilion that served as Kane's war room and occasional forum. But Ryder's quarters were clean and relatively spacious, even as they smelled a bit of horse and woodfire and boy. I'd wanted to come see him before we left for Rose. Only a day after we'd found the ledger in Mari's room, Kane's messengers had contacted the historian and paid him generously. We were leaving tonight.

Ryder's hastily made bed could only fit one, and there was another across from his with simply folded sheets and a few errant crumbs.

"Who do you share the cabin with?"

Ryder walked to a barrel filled with fresh water and poured me a mug and then one for himself. "At first it was this utter lug head who would not shut up. I persuaded him to trade with Barney."

"How'd you do that?"

Ryder shrugged, though a bit of pride peeked through his eyes. "Used some carefully carved cherrywood to convince him we had termites."

I laughed. "You must use your powers for good, not evil."

He chuckled, too. And then, sighing, said, "Arwen—"

"I know—"

"You might, but you still have to let me say it."

I sat down on his bed. "All right."

"I think in Citrine . . . I fell for Princess Amelia."

That had not *at all* been what I was expecting.

"She was the most impressive, mean, knock-down-drag-out-gorgeous, cold-as-ice living thing I'd ever seen. Every time she spoke, I felt it in my—"

My eyes cut to him as if to say, *Don't you dare*.

"*Chest.* I felt it in my *chest*."

I stifled a laugh, kicking off my shoes and folding my legs more comfortably atop his bed.

"She didn't give me the time of day unless we were speaking strategy. All she cared about was Peridot. Freeing the kingdom, rebuilding, saving her people from warfare and conquest. All pretty noble stuff."

I nodded because I agreed. It was noble. She was cold and calculating, manipulative and harsh, but in the eyes of her people . . . She'd always been clear that she would do anything for them.

"While you lot were off finding the blade, we started . . . spending time together. She told me she'd have me assassinated if I told anyone, and I sure as Stones believed her." He laughed a little to himself at the memory and I suddenly felt that I was witnessing something too personal. I cast my eyes to the floor.

"She was so different when we came back to Onyx. I still don't know why. Maybe she had already made up her mind about . . . what she was going to do. But I missed her. Like nothing I'd ever felt, I missed her. And when you told me you were going to Hemlock—" He shook his head. "I thought it was the only way she'd talk to me like she used to, if I alleged to know more about the plan than she did. She probably played me. Knew how eager I'd be, how I'd tell her anything just to be in the same room again."

Oh, Stones. My brother was a lovesick fool.

I wondered if Amelia had ever even liked him. She had asked me to share her apologies, but I couldn't tell if that had been from honest remorse or something a bit more personal. My heart hurt at the thought of either.

"She behaved so strangely the rest of that day. I told myself it was out of guilt, I think, because it made me feel better. About myself and her. But I went straight to Griffin. Told him that I had a terrible feeling. We flew for Hemlock not five minutes later."

My brother sank down on the bed next to me and braced his forearms on his knees.

"Arwen, I'm sorry. Truly, I am. Had I known what she was capable of . . ." He scratched at his neck, finally bringing his eyes to meet mine. He had never looked more like a little boy to me. Like the kid I'd grown up alongside.

"You can't blame yourself. The only person responsible for what Lazarus did is Lazarus."

"That's not the point. I was only thinking about *me*. About what I wanted. *Who* I wanted, I guess." His eyes found his hands again. "It's all I ever do. Think about myself."

I struggled for the right words—he was right. He had been selfish, and I didn't want to fuss and lie and tell him otherwise like I might have in the past. But I also knew the unabashed hurt that was nagging at him wasn't doing anyone any good.

"I saw her in Lumera. She asked me to tell you that she was sorry. And that she hadn't meant to use you."

Ryder blew out a breath and cradled his head in his hands. "Will you kill me if I ask how she seemed?"

I mulled his question over in my head. Aside from her apology, I tried to remember if there was anything noteworthy about my conversation with Amelia the night of the masquerade ball. "She seemed resigned. Glad for her people but . . . remorseful. I don't think she's being hurt or anything, if that's what you're worried about. Lazarus sees her as an ally."

"I don't know if that's good or bad." Ryder pressed his face into his palms.

"For now, it's good."

"And when Kane tracks her down eventually?"

I tried to imagine Kane greeting his old friend in a warm embrace. All that came to mind was a vision of a pitch-black dragon, satiated and stuffed full, with wisps of long white hair hanging from his maw. "We'll handle that when the time comes."

"I won't say good luck," he joked with an exhale. "Didn't count for much the last time. But . . . be safe, Arwen. With the faux ledger and the Scarlet Queen. I'll be here, with the tykes. And Barney. My husband."

"Ryder." I frowned. "Do you want to come with us?"

I wasn't really sure why I'd offered. I knew he didn't, and that none of us—Kane and Griffin tied for least of all—wanted him to join, either.

"I don't," he answered, a little morose. "I'm so grateful *not* to be going. How's that for a burgeoning solider? Brave as ever, I am."

I stood to leave, but an errant thought pulled me back. "Can I offer you some unsolicited advice?"

Ryder cocked one brow at me but I took his silence for approval and plowed onward. "Try not to think so much about who you were supposed to be back then, or who you want to be one day, or what will impress which princess or librarian, and maybe just try to be . . . you. Today."

"That's very corny," he said after some time, though his eyes were elsewhere.

I shrugged. "I'm not as good at this as Dagan."

◈

THE QUARTZ OF ROSE WAS MORE INDUSTRIAL THAN ANY other kingdom I'd been to, but the steel and scaffolding didn't hinder its beauty one bit. I'd been surprised, during our flight over, to find myself comparing the kingdom's elegant homes to Willowridge's, or the capital city of Revue's busy streets to Azurine's. Surprised by my own knowledge of Evendell—my understanding of the nuances of different cities, different ecosystems, different social and political strata.

I'd been right, when I returned to Shadowhold, to fear that I'd changed. I had.

But the woman I was now—walking past wrought-iron fences wreathed in greenery and corner taverns adorned with flowerpots— this woman was all the things I'd hoped one day I would be: a little more worldly, a little less afraid to ask for what I wanted, sympathetic to the ambiguities of life and the complicated choices we all faced. Not necessarily brave, but aware of the fact that it was courageous just to get up each day when there was so much to fear . . . Maybe most importantly—this woman *liked* herself.

An issue I hadn't even realized might have been the worst offense of all and the most deep-seated.

The streets in Revue were replete with both monolithic factories pumping hot black smoke and vivid open-air markets. Warehouses with men slathered in dark oil and coal right beside antique-looking bookstores—The Rosecomb, Under the Cover. Beside bespectacled women pushing carts piled high with tools were poets reading to one another on storm-gray building stoops.

While Willowridge had a gothic, almost dreamy darkness to it,

Revue was vibrant. Bustling, and more sensual. More aggressive, too, and dirtier. People walked faster and with more purpose. The handrails and curbs were not polished clean like in Kane's capital. The air smelled of tobacco—though the pipes here were long and skinny rather than fat and curved like Ryder's.

Despite the chilly winter night and all the snow crunching underfoot, the women around us wore clothing I'd never dare to. Shimmery, shining dresses with long fur coats. Plunging necklines. Shorter hems than some of my nightdresses. My cheeks flushed at the sight of a sheer bodice with exposed boning worn as a top of its own, with nothing but a feathered scarf to keep its wearer warm.

I was so overwhelmed by the sights and wild display of skin I almost missed Mari as she ducked after Kane and Griffin into the inn. The sign out front read "The Empty Inkwell" in industrial block lettering, and I followed after them.

For better or worse, the reclusive bookmaker lived in a small neighborhood in the eastern hills of Revue. Better: once we had our fake, we were only minutes from Ethera's doorstep—after we'd devised our plot, we'd sent a raven and scheduled an audience with the queen for tomorrow afternoon. Worse: we'd have to keep a very low profile. If Ethera found out we'd met with the historian, our only bargaining chip would be wasted, and she'd never align her army with ours.

Which meant staying the night in this musty, unremarkable inn in the city center with a shoddy chandelier that hung so low Griffin had to hunch the entire time we stood, clustered inside. Twangy music that sounded a little metallic and filtered emanated from somewhere deeper inside. I wondered what kind of musicians wandered the halls of lodgings like this one.

"We only have the one room available, I'm afraid."

Mari shook her head. "There are four of us. I'm sure you can see why that won't do."

"And there are *two* beds," the innkeeper rebutted, pressing pointed spectacles that had slid down her nose back up the elongated ridge.

"And we are *paying customers* with quite a lot of coin." Mari was turning a bit red. "Can you please look once more?"

The woman's unmoving stare rivaled a brick wall. "I don't think so."

Mari placed an elbow on the wood counter and leaned close. "I'm not sure I like your tone. For your information, we are—"

"Very sorry to have bothered you," I jumped in. "The double will be fine."

Mari sighed like a horse and I swore a low chuckle rumbled from Griffin beside me. But when I turned my face up to his, the expression I found there was as stoic as usual.

The darkened stairs were carpeted in a red rug that hadn't been cleaned in some time, and cobwebs decorated each low, jutting overhang Griffin and Kane were forced to duck beneath. But the halls were adorned with oil lamps and well-worn yet cozy furnishings, like antique trays and portraits of somber rainy days and pale, contemplative women.

Our shared room was on the top floor, and had a peculiar handle in the ceiling that, when pulled, brought down yet another set of stairs that led to a private rooftop. The hardwood floors were dark and scuffed, and the two beds—one a rich artichoke color and the other a buff straw tone—looked plush and welcoming. Even the antique floral wallpaper was charming, and I decided I liked this strange, romantic inn.

"Arwen and I will take this one," Mari said, dumping her snow-soaked coat and bulging bags atop the green bed.

Kane and I shot each other twin glances.

I wasn't a child, and wouldn't make a fuss over something so trivial, but . . . Kane and I had been separated for months. And without being melodramatic—who knew how many nights we had left to share a bed together?

Not even for sex—we'd never attempt something in the same room as our friends. But that intimacy. That warmth . . .

"You two can take the other one," Griffin said bluntly, jutting his chin toward Kane and me. "I'll sleep on the floor."

"Don't be such a martyr." Mari huffed. "Why? Because you and Kane can't share a bed? That is the most antiquated, fragile, small-minded—"

"Because they want to fuck, witch," Griffin said, nodding at Kane and me.

I wasn't sure who flushed redder, me or Mari. I opened my mouth but she saved me an unintelligible response.

"Oh. Of course. We can give you some privacy, not a problem."

Kane only chuckled, the sound sliding along my bones, before he ran a cool thumb down my arm to my wrist. I shivered.

I could hear the roguish grin in his voice when he purred, "Shall we go see about a bookmaker?"

But Griffin cut through whatever playful energy had been thickening the air between us. "The replica we sent for won't be ready until tomorrow, a few hours before our tea with Ethera."

Mari plunked down on the hay-colored bed. "What should we do tonight, then?" Her eyes brightened as ideas began to crystalize. "The last time I was here with my papa, we visited this dark, quiet tavern where they played strange, sultry music and all the women wore short sparkly dresses, and they read these long poems that were more like stories that had no beginning or middle or end really but I loved them anyway."

Griffin appraised Mari once before turning to Kane. "I think we should train."

"Yeah." Kane nodded, releasing my hand and moving for his discarded swords. "We should probably train."

25

ARWEN

Mari flung herself back into the springy bed with faux devastation. "This is an outrage."

I covered my laugh with a question. "Where would we even spar?"

Griffin was already pulling at those unexpected, drop-down stairs and climbing up to the roof.

Kane scaled after him.

"I swear," Mari said to me as we followed. "His brain is just three lone words rattling around in the abyss: *eat, frown, train.*"

I smiled, climbing the stairs last, and when I reached the roof, the view that charged at me stole the breath from my lungs.

All of Revue—the entire city—*sparkled.*

A mountain range of towers and domes and balconies scattered with lights. Entire pillars lit up with them—flickering and sparkling like jewels in sunlight, commandeering the skyline. Rooftop gardens not dissimilar from the one we stood on now, set aglow with colorful lanterns and twinkling tea lights. All of it one richly warm, romantic, night-blooming sea.

From what Mari had told me, I knew those slopes and hollows were filled with art exhibits, literary salons, dramatic cabarets, and fine buttery meals. That those winding streets and grand avenues were flanked by elegant stone buildings and mansard roofs and luscious, ornate detailing. Slow, sultry melodies and upbeat bass lines misted out of the city below, blending with the chatter of sidewalk cafés and horse hooves on cobblestone and wheels rolling gently through snow.

And our little rooftop—encased in pretty wrought iron that Mari was already leaning over, her curls rustling with the breeze. A dried garden plot spread from one corner, where in the summer surely a stunning patch of flowers sprouted under the generous, uninterrupted sun. Two rusty chairs and a pebbled glass table with an ashtray and a desiccated cigar had been shoved to the edge by either Kane or Griffin to make room for their swordplay.

The men's blades clashed lightly, their lighte barely flaring in the night. They were just going through the motions. Waking up their various and ample muscles.

Kane's form was elegant. Refined, practiced. I imagined that came from studying under a masterful, by-the-book instructor like Dagan. And that otherworldly grace—I was sure that had been inherited from his mother.

But Griffin was a different kind of swordsman. Scrappy and brutal, as if his hulking body merely contained too much power to control. The unexpected moves seemed to dart out of him on a whim—a feint here, a sweep of the leg there. For a man that kept everything so internal, so closed up and private, I thought watching him fight might be the most intimacy he shared with anyone. Here, the commander was baring his soul to us, acting on each impulse and desire as it sprang forth, without a second thought.

"Shit," Kane uttered, looking down at his sword midparry.

They sprang apart and inspected his steel together.

"I'll buff it out," Griffin offered, taking the dulled weapon from his king.

Kane glided over to Mari and me and slipped his warm hand around my waist. Chills licked exquisitely up my spine at the touch, though my eyes roamed over the luxe gated palace where we'd meet the Scarlet Queen for tea tomorrow. I was grateful for the respite our night in Revue offered. I didn't have much desire to meet a woman who'd earned her nickname from the amount of blood in the streets when she took the throne. Nor much hope for how that meeting might go, or how soon war might follow . . .

"What are you thinking?" he asked me softly.

I was thinking of enemies and violence and things beyond my control. "Is there any chance Aleksander knows you're in Rose already?"

"I doubt it," Kane said, running a hand through his unruly hair. "We've covered our tracks."

Mari leaned forward from my other side. "Who's Aleksander?"

"The leader of a race of Fae called Hemolichs. They—"

"Oh, *him*. Blood Fae. Betrayer. Hiding in Rose from Kane." Mari nodded to herself and cast her eyes back out at the sparkling city.

Kane stiffened beside me, and I placed my hand atop his until his grip on the wrought iron loosened. "How do you know all of that?" I asked Mari.

"Come on." She shot me a withering look. "You weren't gone *that* long."

Kane leaned past me to say to Mari, "You ever hack that invisibility charm?"

"No," she said, frowning. "Given that I'm not hideous nor a pervert, I thought there were other, more pressing spells to master."

"All right, easy." Kane put his hands up in mock defense, and I missed his touch instantly.

I pulled his arm back around my waist. "I think invisibility could be valuable, Mar. You never know who you might want to sneak up on."

Mari worried her lip. "I can't seem to get it quite right."

"We are up here to train. You want to try?"

Mari abandoned the balcony rail with a sigh and stood still in the center of the roof. Griffin watched her carefully from his post buffing Kane's sword. Wind spun around her feet and rustled the few remaining dried branches in the dead garden. She whispered the words of her spell.

And then the wind ceased, and the light snow that had been lifted fell to the ground. Mari sighed deeply before opening her eyes to scowl at both of us. "See?"

"Have you tried adjusting your stance?" Griffin asked, coming up behind Mari to study her legwork. "Doesn't matter if it's light or magic, being centered is half the battle when drawing power into yourself."

He leaned toward her, his battle mind clearly taking hold, and, as his face neared hers from behind, brushed his hands across her hips and thighs to right her stance.

"There," he managed, as he stood, a little breathless. He was so close her hair fluttered with his words.

Mari's eyes went stark.

The silence around us rippled, and my *own* cheeks grew warm.

After what had to have been a full minute of him standing there behind her, nearly panting, hands still on her hips, Mari said, "Do you always breathe so much, Commander?"

He stepped back immediately and appraised his hands as if they'd been on fire. Then he cleared his throat and said, "Chronically."

I laughed, as did Kane beside me, and whatever tension had coiled between the two of them eddied out into the night.

"What about you?" Kane said, raising one graceful brow in my direction.

"What about me?"

"Kane tells me you tried to shift," Griffin said. "Back in Lumera."

Mari folded her arms in thought. "If you're something with multiple heads, will you tell me if each head has its own brain, or if you have one brain, and the other heads function more like ancillary limbs? I've always wondered about that . . ."

"You've *always* wondered about that?"

She shrugged. "I wonder about a lot of things."

"Don't deflect," Kane chided. "Now's as good a time as any to test your abilities. You have quite the arena here to practice in." He gestured to the broad, glittering night sky, the city lights below rivaling the stars that hung high above.

But that thought only made my gut clench. I'd fallen enough for many, many lifetimes. "It's late . . ."

"You know I'd catch you," Kane offered softly, his shoulders rolling back as if he could feel his wings behind him.

"Come on," Mari said with impish glee, as if encouraging me to eat sweets for supper. "It'll be fun."

"Fine," I sighed. I wandered into the middle of the roof, giving each of them a wide berth. Stones forbid I shift into something gargantuan. Once there, I closed my eyes and tried to channel Dagan. He'd instruct me to clear my mind.

Focus on whatever emotion I found in the wake of my churning thoughts.

Gratitude and hope, sorrow for all we'd suffered, fear, as was always there. I amended my stance—Griffin had been right about that—and concentrated on pulling from the atmosphere. The chilly winter air, the moonlight on my nose and shoulders.

Not a single sensation to be felt. Not in my back or anywhere else.

"I don't think it can be done unless . . ."

"Unless what?" Kane asked, silver eyes narrowing.

"I'm not sure. Unless I'm in some sort of danger, I think."

Kane's expression turned a little stricken, and I regretted sharing that. Reminding him of what I'd been through.

"We should take a break anyway," Mari said brightly, focusing her gaze on the city filled with light below us. "To be here, in the capital of a kingdom *known* for its music and taverns and cafés—"

"And brothels," Kane offered, his earlier amusement once again dancing across his mouth.

"Great," Mari said, exasperated. "Take me to a brothel. Honestly. Anything but more training. I spent the last two months doing exactly this for hours and hours on end."

"I've never been in a brothel," I mused before turning to Kane, moonlight glinting off the bow of his full lips. "Have you?"

I was sure he had. I could conjure seamlessly Kane's mesmerizing jaw and dreamlike silver eyes pulling the attention of every working courtesan in the sordid, solicitous place. So darkly compelling they'd offer themselves to him for less than their going rate . . .

"Many, many times. But never for the women."

"What for, then?"

"Far worse vices. Gambling, brawls, too much drink."

Griffin laughed to himself from his perch against the roof's edge. He'd picked up Kane's sword and begun sharpening it once again.

"One night, I had to hunt through three different Solaris whorehouses looking for him. Found the bastard underneath a featherbed, drunk as a fish in a wine barrel, talking some courtesan into quitting to become a seamstress."

Mari folded her arms and scowled. "I'm sure you frequent brothels often."

The sword nearly clattered from Griffin's hands. *"Me?"*

Mari's eyes flashed, curiosity more than piqued. But her arms stayed firmly locked across her chest.

A gruff laugh cracked out of Kane as he crossed the roof to stand beside his friend. "I don't believe my commander's ever actually had to pay for sex." He gave Griffin a loud smack on the shoulder followed by a jovial squeeze. "Though I cannot fathom why, women are constantly giving it to him for free."

Mari's eyes widened into shock. *"Constantly?"*

Kane failed to suppress a smirk.

"Don't listen to him," Griffin said to her. "I don't— I'm not—"

"No, it's fine." Mari swallowed. "Obviously." She sat down right on the rooftop floor and conjured a spell book to leaf through. "To each their own."

Griffin's glare at Kane was downright menacing.

I shot him the same one.

Kane plucked his newly sharpened sword from Griffin's hands, and sauntered over to me. "And what's that look?"

"Stop torturing them," I said under my breath.

"Why? It's very pleasing."

I rolled my eyes. "You're a nuisance."

But Kane's eyes were focused on Mari as she read over another spell. And Griffin, as he watched her like she was his very heart, twirling hair and folding down pages, right outside his body.

"It's painful, isn't it?"

"They're scared to give themselves over to it," I said. "I don't blame them."

Kane's smile was faint in the glittering night. "Would you scream at me if I locked them in our room until they just fucked already?"

My lips twitched. "I'm not much of a screamer."

"Really?" Kane's gaze sharpened on mine. "I could change that."

"Oh?" I smirked, even as my blood heated. "How?"

His silver eyes simmered. "On my knees."

Unable to help myself, I stepped a little closer, desperate to press all the pulsing parts of me against him. Kane grasped my fingers with feline precision as they crawled up his chest. Without lifting his eyes from mine, Kane said, far too low, "Arwen and I are going to bed now."

26

ARWEN

DRAGGING ME BEHIND HIM, KANE HURRIED US DOWN THE rickety steps before giving either of our friends a chance to reply. We slipped down into the darkened bedroom below and Kane closed the contraption with a flick of shadowed power.

"You can't leave them up there all night so you can bed me."

"Can't I?" Kane arched one elegant brow, and a slant of city light glowed across his ridiculously carved jaw. The portrait of kingly male arrogance.

I hid the curve of my lips as I pulled my boots off one by one. Then I lifted my blouse overhead. My hands found the waistband of my leathers and I shimmied them down around my ankles and then off entirely, tossing the garments into the corner beside our bags.

Through the red-hued room, lit only by one steady oil lamp under a crimson shade and the glow of the city through the dusty windows, I realized Kane hadn't moved.

Not a muscle.

He only looked me up and down, noting every curve of my body, every rise of my chest.

And I didn't meet his eyes. I knew, if I did, it would be over. Twin dams bursting at once.

So I just listened to his slow, rough breaths as I removed my bodice and let my breasts fall, full and aching. And then I knelt, the vertebrae of my spine pebbling as cool air slithered across them, and fished my nightdress from my pack.

When I stood and slid the silk fabric over my head, Kane stalked leisurely behind me.

And though I could smell him—his sweat and leather and the mint on his breath—and could hear his labored breathing, I still didn't turn.

"Bed?" My voice was thin. I swallowed.

Kane said nothing at all. No witty retort or sexual innuendo.

He only wrapped one warm, broad hand across my neck to gently cradle my jaw, the other snaking around my waist like a hot iron band, his fist bunching in the material as if he were one swift tug away from shredding through it—and pressed his length into my back with a heady, rough groan.

I shuddered out my own moan and liquid heat gathered between my legs.

"I thought you didn't sleep in undergarments," he muttered against the shell of my ear before sucking the lobe into his mouth. Teeth nipping, then licking the spot.

I couldn't gather a response around my blaring need. It was all I could do to shimmy the thin, now dampened fabric down my hips and to the floor.

"Good girl." The words wrung a whimper from me.

His hand drifted from my waist to my hip, lazing across my low stomach, and gathered the fabric of my nightdress until he'd grazed my bare flesh. I shivered, and he kissed my neck indulgently, the way he would my mouth. Tongue and teeth and lips. Slow, soft, suckling. He muttered something—

"Bird?"

"Huh?"

"I said," he purred, "are my hands cold?"

I nodded into him. "A little."

"Can I warm them against you?"

I nodded again, his silken voice like a drug. I would have nodded if he'd asked to swallow me whole.

Kane let those chilly, calloused fingers drift down. Down and down and *down* until he swirled them across the place I'd been waiting for.

I bucked against the feeling and he held me to him, easing me against his chest, helping me to weather the light brushing of his thumb and forefinger and the slow, wet circles.

"Oh, Stones," I breathed as my knees went weak.

Oh, Stones, oh, Stones, oh, Stones—

The creak of the stairs unfurling across the room was like the breaking of glass. I sprang from Kane, who hesitated to release me, whose lips briefly lunged back for my neck as if he were a man possessed—

But I shoved him away just as Mari scrambled down the stairs and Griffin after her.

Kane chuckled darkly as he turned away to adjust himself.

I knew I was fifteen shades of pink when I opened my mouth to apologize but Mari only scooped up her canvas bag and brushed past us both, slipping into the washroom and slamming the door loudly behind her.

Griffin made his way down the stairs slower, and when his boots touched the floor, he closed the rungs manually and locked them tight.

"Sorry to interrupt."

"What got into her?" Kane asked, jerking his chin toward the washroom. His voice was still a bit like gravel.

Griffin shrugged, but his eyes were hard. "Fuck if I know."

I wasn't sure which of the two of them could stand to be alone together less. Being up there, even for ten minutes, had likely been one impressive game of sexual-tension chicken.

I crawled into the tufted green bed and it sighed under my weight. Fluffy soft sheets enveloped me like the petals of a rose. Griffin pulled his shirt overhead, revealing a broad swath of hefty, chiseled muscle. Swiping a pillow from the bed across from us, he lay down on the floor.

Kane pulled his shirt off, too, and I watched through red-hued lamplight as he traded his dark trousers for thin cotton pants that hung low on his hips. The significant V where his waist cut down to his groin was highlighted by sharp shadows.

My toes curled under the sheets.

That body . . . That beautiful face . . . That even more beautiful soul—

Mari's intrusion was for the best. Letting things go further with Kane, while they had been right above us . . . completely inappropriate. I had no idea when I'd become so lust-addled—I'd been driven half-insane.

Kane's body compressed the bed beside me, shifting the sheets and sending a woodsy warmth across my skin. I tried not to hum when his large hands slid over to me and pulled me into his chest, one flattening down my back and drawing easy, slow circles there. My stomach pressed against the hard planes of his side, his neck only inches from my lips. He looped one leg across both of mine, the pressure soothing aches in my calves I didn't even know I had, and I inhaled masculine mint and cedar.

The washroom door opened with a noise that told me its hinges were in desperate need of oil, and Mari slipped out in her own dark cotton nightgown and matching robe.

She had to step over Griffin to crawl into her bed.

"Where is your shirt?" she whispered at him loudly, defeating the purpose of the whisper.

Kane, who had been stroking my back as we snuggled, snickered into my hair.

"I'm sleeping," Griffin said calmly.

"Without a shirt?"

"Yes."

Mari huffed, her body's plunge into the bed sending the sound of creaking coils and rustling linens through the room. She leaned over to extinguish the oil lamp and drowned all four of us in darkness.

I turned over, pressing my bottom into Kane and wrapping his broad hand tightly around my middle. Sleep was what I needed. Sleep to quell the frenzied way Kane was making me feel. He slid his other hand under my neck, tugged me closer to his chest, and nuzzled me from behind with his nose.

Arching into him a bit, my legs tangled with his. Our bodies, separated only by silk—

"You don't have to sleep on the floor," Mari muttered quietly.

Kane exhaled into my shoulder, the noise edged with frustration.

Across the room, Griffin sighed, too. "It's fine."

"I'm serious," Mari continued. "This is silly. What if I have to use the washroom in the middle of the night?"

"Then you'll get up and do so."

"It's too dark. What if I step on your face?"

"I'll live."

"Well, it can't be comfortable down there. And to be honest, I know this is selfish, but I feel a lot of pressure to offer you this blanket, because I know you're going to be cold."

"Keep it. I don't—"

"No, I knew you were going to say that, but now I'm supposed to say, *No, you have it, Commander, I insist*. But the thing is, there's only the one. And without it I will *freeze*. I'm not Fae like you three, so I really don't want to give it up, but I also don't want to be—"

"Go to sleep, witch. Please."

The silence that followed was a mercy.

For Griffin. For Kane and me. For Mari, who I feared would wring herself out completely if she spoke anymore.

Kane squeezed my thigh once. Just high enough that what was meant to be a playful gesture, poking fun at our friends, sent a shiver across my skin.

I stretched my legs, elongating my back, using the movement to bring us so close that there was not a single space left for doubting what either of us wanted. The warmth from his bare chest permeated into the silk of my nightdress. His breath fanned across my neck in hot, ragged bursts.

His length had hardened thickly against my backside. Need spun within me and my mouth watered with it. Those arms had become bars of pure heat across my chest and stomach, and his hands had begun to roam . . .

He stroked my collarbone gently, just his thumb brushing back and forth. Caressed the silk of my dress across my stomach, right below my navel.

Slow, indolent circles.

I ground my backside against his hardness, movements small enough that the mattress never shifted, nor the duvet wrapped around us. But each nearly imperceptible drag of my bottom up his length or press toward his own chest tightened his hands against my skin.

And drew more moisture between my legs.

Kane's lips hovered over my cheek. With each fluid movement his breath grew rougher. More raw. I nearly begged him, as their king, to order Griffin and Mari to busy themselves outside of this room for just an hour. Just ten minutes.

Fine, five minutes. I wasn't greedy.

Kane's fingers traveled down until they slipped easily under my short silk dress—skin touching skin at last—and all other thoughts eddied from my mind.

A moan lodged in my throat as he dragged a knuckle across the aching bud, swirling his finger over the utterly sensitive flesh, circling, teasing—

His breath ebbed and I felt him grin against my ear as he squeezed not quite gently. Bucking his hips—that throbbing length like granite—against my backside as if he weren't even aware he'd done it.

And then his fingers . . .

Finding what I knew would please him so—slick, slippery wetness pooling between my legs. His hand paused there, and a silent breath shuddered from his lips across my neck and ear.

If Griffin and Mari weren't asleep, they'd hear us for sure. And Kane—

Kane was done for. Dipping in and out of my plump, swollen folds. Running his fingers so lightly across that spot I craved I nearly cried out in desperation.

If someone were going to stop this, it would have to be me.

But the way he was touching me . . .

The ache that had built in my core—almost more pain than pleasure now—threatened to sweep me away like a whirlwind. I was seconds away from climbing atop Kane and finding my release regardless of Griffin and Mari. At this point the entire city of Revue could watch and I'd let them.

His finger finally curled up and inside me—

Before a truly wanton moan shot through my lips and echoed across the room, I shoved Kane's hand away. His fingers, soaking wet, fell to my thigh and remained there. He flexed his hand as his breathing echoed in my ear.

His entire body was as tense as my own. His cock pulsed against my bottom.

Griffin stirred on the floor and city lights painted his back as I watched him turn closer to the edge of Mari's bed. I took a shaky breath and blew it out quietly.

"Soon," Kane growled against my ear. His voice as rough as gravel and laced with unwavering promise.

Soon, indeed.

27

KANE

After the worst sleep of my life—filled with the most lurid, debased dreams—we left bright and early for the bookmaker. As we'd dressed, I could hardly look at Arwen through the haze of my own shame and pent-up need.

By the time we stalked down a charming avenue on our way to Oleander's home, I'd shaken off at least some of my mind-bending desire. We had an important day ahead of us, and I couldn't spend it fantasizing about Arwen's breathy moans.

Mainspring, the neighborhood we'd been staying in, was a hub for serious intellectuals and unsociable fine craftsmen. The cobbled street was lined with still, moody townhomes and luxurious, manicured hedges, most of which sealed the houses off completely from prying eyes such as ours.

"I expected the streets to be filled with artists' cottages and expensive bookstores," Mari said. "This is a little dreary."

Arwen nodded. "And too quiet." Her long dark hair had been

pulled back with an onyx ribbon and it swirled in the sharp wind. "Where is everybody?"

They were right. Despite the sunny winter's day, the winding street was silent and bare of horses and carriages. Bare of any people at all.

"They're working. Mainspring is the quarter reserved for those dedicated to the craft and nothing else."

"And those successful enough to own land here," Griffin added.

Arwen observed one of the painterly cream-white homes with its fine black detailing and picket fence. "Crafts like portraits? Sculpting?"

I shook my head. "The sculptors and artists live in a more boisterous region of Revue, where there's far more wine and women. These residents build clever mechanisms. They write dissertations and spend hours poring over philosophical texts."

"So this historian and ledger-maker is someone quite serious."

"Oleander crafts the finest tomes in Evendell," Mari said to her. "Dagan has a few of his original works back in the Shadowhold library."

"I actually sent a noble of mine here years ago to offer him a stay in Willowridge." I'd hoped the old man might bring some of his impressive young apprentices and peers. Willowridge had a bounty of artists and restaurateurs, poets and novelists . . . I thought Oleander might fit in nicely and help to draw more like him to the capital.

"But?"

I shrugged. "He refused. I never found out why."

I'd sent Lady Kleio, one of my most persuasive dignitaries. She'd returned with little more than a regretful shake of her head, and for whatever reason—perhaps I'd been distracted with the ancient Blade that had just disappeared from my vault at the time—I'd never pressed the issue.

As we neared the elderly man's home, it occurred to me how lonely living in Mainspring must've been. These men and women, working on their novels or machinery day in and day out. And I thought then how close I'd come to a similarly solitary existence—revenge my sole craft. Stealing me away from any meaningful human contact, bringing out the most brutish, selfish parts of me.

I reached for Arwen's hand and she laced her fingers between mine contentedly.

Oleander's house was a little weather-beaten and could have used a fresh coat of oxblood paint. The two-story manor was still affluent, and the wrought-iron fence and oil lamps glinted in the stark sunlight.

Griffin led the way. The ornate knocker rang out into the garden, and we waited.

Water trickled from a stone fountain. A breeze rustled Arwen's lengthy hair. Mari fidgeted with her spinach-colored velvet cloak. "Maybe he isn't home."

Griffin frowned before tramping off the stone path into the grass spotted with patches of snow like a speckled egg. He leaned against one of the bowed windows.

"There's a fire still crackling inside."

Worry flickered in Arwen's bright olive eyes. "How long until we're expected to meet with the Scarlet Queen?"

There was no clock tower for miles, but the sun had anchored itself in the middle of the clear blue sky. "A few hours at most."

Not enough time to come up with another plan. And my father would have his lighte reserves back soon—we couldn't postpone.

My heart had begun to thud. I drew a hand down my face in frustration. Nothing was easy. Nothing.

"What if someone got to him first?" Mari posed. "Found out about our plan?"

The thought of yet another betrayal . . . after Aleksander, Amelia . . . I didn't allow myself to touch that rage.

"There's no evidence of a struggle." Griffin's nose hovered against the bookmaker's window.

Without another word I moved past Arwen, Mari, and my commander and slammed the heel of my boot into the dark red door. Tendrils of smoke black as oblivion spun from my foot. The hinges of the door swung open so violently it nearly wrenched clean off.

I stalked through the warm foyer and away from the sound of Mari's squeaks.

Griffin had been right. The fireplace in the sitting room was crackling and full of life, oil lamps were hot and candles still burning. But the vaguely cluttered house was too quiet and I followed an instinct past the grand staircase and that cozy sitting room and deeper into the bowels of the home.

In the darkly tiled kitchen, a fresh kettle curled steam into the air. I made a left and my boots echoed down a hallway dotted with doors. Between them hung ornate gold-and-silver-framed glass casings with leather-bound history books on display. Fine embossing, edges sprayed with paint—work that could only have belonged to the missing bookmaker.

The doors of the hallway were all cracked open to various degrees. A peek into a spare bedroom. A sliver of a porcelain tub. Only one door was closed fully.

I yanked it open and strolled inside.

Oleander's craft room was a battlefield—hides of leather from every animal I could name, white-bone tools for folding and pressing those skins into submission. A wooden tray of awls and rulers, brushes of every size, a massive sewing frame in one corner and a stained canvas smock tossed hastily over a well-worn desk in the other.

Griffin slunk into the room behind me, Mari and Arwen surely not far behind. "If he made it like he agreed to—"

I finished the thought for him. "Then it's in here somewhere."

My hand reached for the first tome I saw—one with a tan leather binding similar to the ledger from Reaper's Cavern—and closed around nothing but air as an old man's voice bit across the disorderly room.

"Do not lay a single oily finger on that."

Griffin growled before I'd even spun.

When my eyes found Oleander, hobbled and gangly as he was, I snarled, too. His crafting knife was held to Mari's trembling throat.

"Not a *finger*," he repeated.

I moved for them—

And stopped myself. Likely for the same reason Mari hadn't spelled him into an early grave. If we killed the old man, we'd never find the decoy ledger. Griffin must have come to the same conclusion, because for all the power shared between us, nobody had used an ounce of it.

Where was Arwen?

"Let the girl go," I said once in warning. "We aren't here to steal anything, nor to harm you."

The man only pressed the knife closer to Mari's neck, and Griffin took one intent step forward. I'd never expected the day it would be *his* fury I'd have to concern myself with. I lowered my brows in strict warning.

"I know who you are, King Ravenwood," Oleander said. "I know what you seek. And I request you leave my home, *this instant*." The old man was trembling. So much so, the knife he'd pressed to Mari's throat was at risk of severing her flesh unintentionally.

"I won't ask you again," I cautioned. "Let her go, or I will be forced to hurt you. I don't *want* to hurt you, but I will."

"Listen to him," Mari urged, voice quieter than I'd ever heard. "He—"

"Out! Out of my house!" Spittle flew from the old man's cracked lips and Mari flinched and that knife—it shifted just a bit too close for Griffin's liking. Oleander was given no further notice as an arc of ruthless, glossy lighte snapped across the room and straight for the wrinkles in the old man's head.

No, no, fuck—

Griffin's lighte sputtered on impact. But not against the man's flesh. No, it was a shimmering, iridescent orb of lighte that his power smacked.

Arwen's shield.

Mari stumbled away from the deranged bookmaker and his knife as Arwen pushed through the doorway, panting. She snapped at Griffin. "What were you thinking?"

But my commander had already crossed the room to Mari and was brushing her hair from her face and checking her neck for any damage. Mari gasped in heaves as he assessed her. Oleander shook with fear, trapped inside Arwen's bubble of lighte.

"Bring him here," I said calmly, pointing to the craftsman's chair. We had to play this very carefully.

Arwen did as I instructed, dragging a protesting Oleander to his desk in her luminous bubble of lighte. She deposited him in his seat and burst the orb around him.

"You're crazy, you're . . . witches!" he muttered, eyes wild, lunging from the seat.

I seized the old man by his shirtsleeve and tossed him back into the wooden chair easily, allowing twin wisps of my power to tether his arms and legs. They coiled, spindly and black, around the horrified man.

"Where were you?" I murmured to Arwen as the old man writhed and swore at us.

"Looking for you all. Mari and I got separated and then I heard the scuffle . . ."

We both looked back at Mari, still rubbing her neck. And then to Griffin, from his spot close beside her. Studying us—my stone-faced commander showed no remorse.

Disappointment soured my expression. He'd acted on impulse, and nearly killed the old man—the only one who could retrieve the false ledger for us.

"Take her outside," I ordered him.

Not my friend, in that moment. Not my family. My commander.

"But—"

"*Now.*"

Griffin frowned, but did as he was told. I drew in a steadying breath as both his and Mari's footsteps sounded down the hallway.

"We're here for the replicated ledger that was ordered days ago," I said to Oleander, who had at least exhausted himself enough to halt his unflattering squirming. His nose was indented where spectacles usually sat. The wiry white hairs in his ears and nose long and unkempt. "The one with the false names."

"I know that," he spat.

Arwen's brows creased. "You do?"

"I told your king here I knew what you sought. And that I'd never give it to any of you."

"So you did craft it?"

"I never would have, if I'd known it was for *him*. The demon king of Onyx." Oleander spat at my shoes, some white froth dribbling down his chin.

Arwen sucked in a gasp.

My eyes fell to my dark boots, speckled with saliva, and my lips curved. I guess I knew now why he'd refused to relocate to Willowridge.

"What has he ever done to *you*?" Arwen's voice held more offense than I felt. Her ire on my behalf was quite endearing. But I'd had many lifetimes of people who barely knew me despising me regardless. Arwen herself had once looked at me that way.

"What kind of question is that? He's slaughtered good men," the old man spat, hatred in his eyes. "Sacked my lands. Raped and pillaged."

Sacked his lands . . . I'd left all of Evendell alone since I came to the continent. Frankly, it was self-serving—I didn't need anyone knowing too much about me, or putting together how slowly I aged. I'd only gone to war with Amber when they'd aligned with my father. And I'd certainly not *sacked* any Garnet land, even when they joined Amber's forces. They were a mighty kingdom with a mercenary army and armada. But . . . I raised a brow. "You're from Amber?"

Oleander's glare confirmed my suspicion.

Arwen's jaw slackened. The smell of leather and glue filled my nostrils as I attempted a steadying inhale.

"I am not a man of much patience, Oleander. I'll give you one opportunity to tell us where the replica is. My procurer paid you handsomely for it, and I'd like what's mine."

"The procurer I spoke with said it was for a book-making museum in the Pearl Mountains."

"Yes." I lowered my brow at him. "I'm sure you can imagine that was by design."

"You pompous ass," Oleander swore. "You aren't listening. I won't let my work be purchased by a man who destroyed my homeland. Kill me, if you must, but you aren't getting the ledger."

"Well, aren't you a saint?" I drawled, though my blood was beginning to simmer. "Last chance."

"Sir," Arwen pleaded. "I, too, am from Amber. I grew up in Abbington, a small town just outside of Rookvale. I never thought I'd align myself with King Ravenwood, either. In fact, I was raised to hate him. But trust me when I say he is not who he's been made out to be."

But the bookmaker only sneered at her and I ground my teeth nearly to dust. "Aren't I, though?"

Arwen's eyes slid to mine in warning. "Kane—"

Stretching my palm out to the desk beside him, all three sets of our eyes fell to the rows of paints there. Mauves and plums and mustard seed. They became dust in the air in a scattering of pitch-black night.

"*No*," the historian uttered in horror. "*Kill me.* Do not punish the work. This is all . . . It's all I have in the world."

I cracked my neck, lighte accelerating down my limbs. I spread my palms against the cluttered space in a show of violent power. Tendrils of shadow and diabolical thorns danced around my palms. "Then this will be quite unpleasant for you."

"Kane—" Arwen snapped.

Oleander's pale eyes cut around the room in dismay. The sewing frame. The rows of half-stitched books. The stained smock. Back to the sewing frame again . . . His life's work. His entire existence. Everything that made him—here in this room, and soon to be annihilated.

He opened his mouth in anguish. Then closed it again, trying, fighting, *straining* to come up with something that might save his precious, irreplaceable work.

Arwen stepped closer and murmured, "Please, don't do something you can't take back."

But I'd already gotten what I'd needed. I crossed the room toward the sewing frame and heaved it off the counter.

Underneath sat the tan ledger. Same golden embossed font as Niclas's. Same printed "Southern Legion" across the front. Same pages and pages of names.

Except these ones weren't real.

Arwen took a step back. "How . . ."

"Thank you," I said when I faced Oleander once more. With a flick of my wrist, his dark shackles misted.

He palmed his wrists and feet, thin lips clamped together in thinly veiled wrath. "Leave my home."

"Of course."

We walked out of the house into the cold, clear day and toward Griffin and Mari.

"You're just going to leave him?" Arwen asked. "He'll go straight to Ethera."

"No," I said coolly, brushing my hair back from my face. "He won't."

Not only had I spent centuries learning what terror could do to keep a man in check, but he was also an Amber Kingdom loyalist. A man who sided with the impoverished south that was so morally and visually similar—and so geographically close—to his homeland. He hated me, but only as much as he likely hated the Scarlet Queen.

"You didn't have to threaten the man," Arwen huffed as her arms tightened around the ledger. "I could have gotten it out of him. I'm *from* Amber. I have empathy. That can be an incredibly powerful motivator."

The winding street went on and on. Stark in some places under the unfiltered sunlight, but shadowed in others, lorded over by the looming faces of the vast, silent homes.

"As can fear," I replied.

28

ARWEN

BY THE TIME WE ARRIVED, QUEEN ETHERA'S PALACE WAS lit by a dusk sky of bursting blue, blushing peach, and bruising violet. Kane's cruel-king demeanor was back in full force and I couldn't tell if that was a reaction to the morning's events with Oleander or another layer of protection when entering an unpredictable situation such as this.

His usually wavy hair was pushed slightly out of his face by that dark crown of twined thorns, his sleek, sable finery and stacks of glinting rings more menacing than elegant. His lethal scowl and bored eyes somehow *still* made me want to sink to my knees before him and watch that jaded gaze unravel.

I tried to convey just that as armored guards in leather breastplates guided us through a pruned hedge tunnel and two decorative hallways that led to a tearoom. That I didn't blame him for what he felt he'd been forced to do with Oleander. That I was grateful he'd found a way to retrieve the ledger without hurting the old man or his many books.

Kane only offered me a soft dipping of his chin as we sat at a fine table covered in white lace and little baby-blue bows. The room more closely resembled a sweetshop, or maybe a nursery.

None of us spoke while we waited for the Scarlet Queen.

Mari's eyes were fastened to the eastern wall of the parlor, where a towering gilded sculpture of an elm tree sprouted so tall it grazed the domed ceiling. Constructed with vines and leaves dipped in gold, the monument was piled with books—vivid with color, some with bright white spines, others sunny yellows or rich blues. By the roots of the sculpted elm tree, all the novels wedged between branches and in the hollowed-out trunk were stained black.

Griffin appeared more concerned with the significant number of guards that crowded the room alongside us. His brutal eyes slid along them over and over again. Counting, measuring. Sizing them up. I wasn't sure why—they were all mortal. But there were about two dozen of them and only four of us.

Still, the Scarlet Queen's tearoom didn't strike me as an arena for violence. The ceiling was painstakingly painted to depict a lush, scenic meadowland, replete with rolling hills each dotted with daffodils. The white columns supporting the domed, picturesque scene above were carved with intricate detailing. An oversize floral couch lay atop warm maple floors. And the room's little details were all in lovely feminine colors: lampshades of dusky mauve, mismatched pastel yellow knobs on drawers, and candy-pink throw pillows.

Across from the table where we sat stretched a sprawling bow window divided into four equal segments that split the garden view. Outside rolled snow-flecked grass, pruned rosebushes, and robust, emerald-green hedges. A marble fountain, and some kind of wrought-iron arch sprinkled in winter holly adorned the garden, too.

Ethera was clearly a queen who liked *things*. Aside from the enormous tree of books, couch, and crackling ornate fireplace, the parlor was stuffed with girlish curiosities. Porcelain cake stands, birdcages, dice, candleholders without candles, vases bare of flowers. Peculiar feminine oddities were crammed into every nook and cranny.

None stranger than the shiny metal instrument in the corner that spouted music with no player. The machine reminded me of the rounded maw of a clam or a blooming flower. Waxy vibrating tunes emanated, and I knew it to be one of the strange inventions the north of Rose was so famous for.

The entire room reminded me of what a very rich person who'd never stepped foot into nature would guess spring looked like.

And when Ethera waltzed in, I decided my assessment was spot-on.

"Greeting, darlings, greetings!" she sang, weaving through the room to join us, wine-colored hair swaying as she moved. Her lithe body was surprisingly curvy—perky, ample chest, tight apple-shaped bottom. I averted my eyes, feeling bizarrely like a man the way I'd ogled her. She was hard *not* to look at. Her long, slinky pink dress was skintight and revealing but deceptively casual. It was like someone had lengthened my silk nightdresses and covered the bottom in bright, rosy feathers. The gauzy matching robe practically floated behind her as she waltzed to us on satin, heeled slippers.

She'd paired the ensemble with mouthwatering, colorful gems— the holy rose quartz of her kingdom's namesake looped around her neck, bright green topaz and iridescent opal hanging from her ears. The most glittering of all, her red-painted, dazzling smile.

The woman was *enchanting*.

All four of us stood out of courtesy as she drew near, and she swatted her hands at us like we were fat houseflies, her feathered sleeves swaying. "Oh, do desist, lovies. Lest you make me feel tremendously old."

Her voice surprised me. Briar was hundreds of years old, Kane and Griffin as well, but their mannerisms, their speech . . . they had maintained a youthfulness—a modernity. Their slowed aging meant they didn't just appear younger, they *were*.

But the way Ethera spoke—

She only looked about thirty or so, but if my math wasn't terrifically off base—she'd won her civil war with Aleksander's help just a year or so after Kane first arrived in Onyx, and she'd been thirty-one then . . . By my count, the young, jaw-droppingly beautiful queen with the pouty full lips and wild teal eyes was . . . over eighty.

"Seems it's the blood oath that keeps her so young."

"And so fucking crazy."

I shivered. Is that why she was mad? Because she'd not aged the way humans were supposed to? Unlike Briar or Kane, was there a crinkled, hobbling eighty-year-old woman trapped inside that flawless body?

"Your Majesty . . . your collection"—Mari gestured to the books wreathing the elm behind the queen—"it's exceptional."

"Go! Go peek," Ethera encouraged as she sat.

Ethera's long nails were painted the color of her namesake—a bright scarlet—and she ran them through her silky hair absentmindedly until she removed one hand and, with it, an entire fistful of maroon strands.

My brows shot up my face, and I worked to school them as the queen wiggled her fingers absently and allowed the entire clump to drift to the floor.

I glanced sidelong to see if Mari, too, had witnessed the strange occurrence, but she'd already bounded across the room, drawn to the towering tree of vibrant books like a bee to honey.

"Find me something suitable to peruse amid all that arboreous hodgepodge, will you?" Ethera asked.

"Crafted in Garnet?" Kane asked, his gaze still roving the shelves Mari examined.

Ethera grinned broadly. Her unblinking eyes turned my stomach. "I trade with all lands, my dear. All the clever items conceived of within my kingdom are of value someplace." Ethera whirled in her chair until her eyes landed on the metal mechanism still pumping out a twangy melody atop them. "Like that marvelous machine, over there, we've dubbed a *melograph*. My citizens are absolutely *besotted* with the doohickey. If you have a trinket of interest for me, perhaps your kingdom can be bestowed with them, too?"

"I'll have to think on that," Kane drawled.

Given Ethera's penchant for innovation, her kingdom-wide trade network made sense. My eyes crawled across the room. What else did they have here in the north that my imagination couldn't even fathom?

Surely the same upright bathing columns Citrine had. The ones that mimicked rain that Kane loved so much. And the book I'd read Mari when she'd been in a coma—*A History of War in Rose*—had spoken of wheels on thin carriages that only held one person, and using loud, repetitive sounds to communicate across long distances rather than sending ravens.

The queen clasped her hands together in anticipation as two handmaidens brought out our tea. The spread made my mouth water. Teapots and platters of spongy almond cakes and tarts piled high with cherries and currants. Sandwiches of radish and rye, mushrooms hollowed out and stuffed generously with herbs and some kind of soft cheese.

Mari found her way back to the table at the sight—the enormous tree of books would have to wait. Griffin stiffened as the food was laid before him, and while I raised a brow in silent question, I was answered only with a glare.

When none of us moved immediately for the food, the queen tutted, "Eat, eat. You're all too thin."

I did as I was told and piled my plate high with both savories and sweets. A handmaiden in pale pink poured a fragrant milky rooibos tea that swirled inside gilded porcelain cups for each of us.

"Queen Ethera," Kane purred. "I wish we were here under less dire circumstances, but we've come today to ask for your help."

Ethera plopped two cubes of sugar into her tea before dipping a dainty red-polished finger in and swirling it as Kane spoke.

"The battles I wage against King Gareth of Amber and King Thales of Garnet are not exactly as they seem."

Ethera pulled her finger out of her tea, and—

My stomach churned in revolt.

Her fingernail was missing. Not the bright red polish—the actual *nail*. It had just . . . fallen off her finger as she stirred. Unbothered, Ethera took a sip and hummed. As if she knew we'd all seen the curious occurrence, and was pleased to luxuriate in both our shock and her own delectable strangeness.

My gaze shot to Griffin's across the table, whose rarely emotive pale green eyes flared as he sipped from his cup. He'd also seen the beautiful queen decay right before our eyes.

"Yes, lovely," Ethera said to Kane, pursing her full red lips. "You needn't offer me a history lesson. I know of your diabolical father and your otherworldly heritage. But I must confess, I can't envision my humble kingdom assisting much at all."

Ever since Hart had told us of Ethera's blood oath with Aleksander, we'd assumed that she'd know more of the Fae Realm than other mortal monarchs.

"Are you aware of the seer's prophecy?"

Ethera nodded, and then, as an afterthought, flashed another dazzling, wide-eyed smile that made me shudder.

"Through magic beyond any of our comprehensions," Kane continued after a sip, a little put off, "I have been reborn as full-blooded Fae. Arwen here is full-blooded as well. That makes not one but *two* opportunities to slay Lazarus with the Blade of the Sun."

"Which you've located?"

Kane didn't falter. "Yes."

I held my tongue as I drank, steam curling around my nose. The tea was thick with milk and honey. More sugar than anything else. Kane's words weren't a lie but . . . if she agreed to work with us, we'd have to tell her where the blade was currently being held.

"We have my entire army positioned at the ready, but without Peridot or Citrine, and knowing no other kingdom has comparable legions, we will not have enough men to face Lazarus, Garnet, and Amber combined. We need your men, too, Ethera."

"Hogwash. Why must it be *my* army?"

"There is no one else," Griffin cut in, irritated. "As we've just explained."

Ethera's red hair brushed through her plate of food as she leaned forward as if we were swapping clandestine secrets. "And why," she whispered, "is it we must fight?"

Mari's eyes widened in alarm, cutting to me and then to Griffin.

"Ethera," Kane managed, not unkindly. "My father is going to sack all of Evendell. He'll kill everyone in your kingdom." When the mad queen didn't react—didn't even lift her hair from her desserts,

Kane pushed on. "What is it you need from us to pledge your armies to our cause?"

Ethera sat back and pressed long fingers to her mouth in thought. Then she smiled brightly. "Oh! Nothing, my dears."

Triumph sang in my ears at this crazy old bat, with her dementedly beautiful body and frilly tea parlor. Somehow *she* of all people would be our saving grace. Even Griffin's mouth turned upward.

"Holy Stones," Mari breathed. "That is excellent news."

"No, no, lovely." Ethera's pearly white smile glistened, and when she blinked rapidly a few eyelashes fluttered down into her peaches and cream. "There is *nothing* that could convince me to lend you my army. They are quite busy—the vexatious southern half of my kingdom remains steadfast in their hopes of unseating me from my throne. If I sacrificed even a fraction of my men in your battle, I fear the delicate tapestry of peace I've woven might unravel beyond repair."

Kane's eyes blazed. He set his cup down. But already, my gut was churning. And . . . my bones—heavy and a little weak.

"We thought you might say that," he drawled. "So we've brought one last thing."

"A gift?" Ethera's teal eyes sparkled like her jewelry. "For me?" She clapped riotously, and I braced for flying fingernails. Griffin pulled the ledger from his satchel, nearly dropping the heavy tome on a platter of apricot pastries. Mari's and my eyes met across the table in silent confusion. Griffin had the preternatural strength and precision of an ox made of steel. He did not struggle to hold *books*.

"It's the missing—"

Ethera sat up, shiny hair bouncing. "The other half! How in all the realms did you find this?"

"We know some people," Kane said with a cunning smirk.

"Well," she breathed, sitting back in a puff of pink gossamer and feathers. "Consider me flabbergasted."

"Pledge your armies to our cause, and we'll leave you with half that ledger now. The remainder will be waiting for you on the other side of our victory." Kane's features were hard. No relief in those tense shoulders quite yet. My stomach roiled.

"Naturally, my dear, naturally . . ." Ethera wound more of that thick hair into her hand as she studied the leather and fine print. "This has transformed the landscape of my predicament."

After long moments, Ethera hefted the book in her delicate hands and stood, her chair scraping on the wood floor with the movement. "I'll need to think on it. Maybe for just a little while . . ."

"You've plied us with mountains of tea and pastries and indulged us in idle chatter . . ." Kane shook his head as he braced white fingers on the lace tablecloth.

My own stomach flipped *again* and some faraway corner of my mind forced my eyes down to my teacup. It had been so milky. So thick, and pale—

Kane bared his teeth at her. "We need an answer now, Ethera."

"While I would have been absolutely bedeviled by this . . ." She waved the ledger, and the pink feathers of her sleeve fluttered. "Had you not regaled me with your new nature, I might have been persuaded. But alas . . . now I'll have to take both prizes I desire. Deepest apologies." She turned to her guards and cocked her lovely head at me. "Seize her, won't you?"

29

ARWEN

CHAOS ERUPTED IN THE PRETTY PARLOR.

Kane didn't give the first two guards a fighting chance. He flung his arms out, surely expecting his obsidian lighte to obliterate them as I did—

And nothing happened.

Without thinking, Kane drew his sword with otherworldly swiftness. I fished for my own power, but knew it wouldn't come. Memories rushed into my mind like water over a cliffside.

Maddox and a cackling Octavia . . . the lighte leaving my body. Feeling limp and weak and powerless. The uncanny ache and dizzying lethargy. Being held down, being *drained*—

No, no, *no*—

My hands had gone to my veins. I squeezed and tried to breathe. But my mouth was bone-dry and my jaw was wound so tight it was shaking, and my heart was *racing*, and I couldn't breathe—

"Liquid lilium," I managed to say, as Kane pushed me back behind him, stumbling us both into the pastel wallpaper. "In the tea."

Kane grimaced, but said nothing of the sickening sensation of lighte dwindling from his body. My only indication of his fury was his white knuckles, clenched into fists around his dagger and sword.

One overzealous guard lurched toward us and Kane's steel soared through his gut. Another parried twice before taking one of Kane's blades through the neck. Blood gurgled out onto the rug, soaking the soft threads.

"Why do you want me?" I begged the queen, drawing my own blade and hearing it sing against a shield embedded with the Quartz of Rose crest.

The queen had backed into a corner, surrounded by enough guards that I could hardly make out her shiny hair or glittering teal eyes. But I could hear her.

Hear her *laughing*.

The clatter of silverware and shattering of porcelain cut my eyes across the room as six guards took Griffin down and the tea table along with him. They'd known he was strong by his size and his title, and had clearly put the most manpower toward him.

I tried to quiet my panicked mind—we knew something the queen did not.

We had a witch.

Mari could mangle the entire room with any number of spells. She'd trained with Briar all the weeks I'd been gone.

My eyes cut to her over the fray. Her eyes were closed as static raised her curled hair around her head like a corona of fire. A guard hauled Mari away by the middle, shouting something I couldn't hear, his face a mask of horror. She continued to mutter her spell, undeterred.

I smelled the magic before I saw it—that earthy wind, like ancient moss and rain drying on primeval stone. When Mari's eyes opened, the room, already teeming with guards and swords and screaming handmaidens, had crowded with a dozen more bodies.

No, not bodies—*shadows*.

Human forms, made entirely of poisonous black silhouettes. Not like Kane's pitch-black power, which shot out of him like wisps of curling, violent smoke. These magic-fueled soldiers were the absence of light altogether. Muscle and sinew hewn from pitch-darkness. Ghoulish, eyeless faces born of night.

They attacked like a tempest, twisting violently through the room. Slashing Rose soldiers' necks with whatever weapon fit the fight—a baton to club one man, which became a phantom axe for the next. Cutting men down two, three, *four* at a time with little effort.

Ethera screamed and I maneuvered past the soldier before me to see if she'd been gobbled up by one of the apparitions. Victory should have rung in my ears. Success—our way out.

But it was too . . . vehement. Too unnatural. The phantom soldiers were mindless. They didn't seem like they killed for Mari. These shadow soldiers killed to *kill*.

And then it was Mari who screamed.

I craned my neck to find her and my blood *chilled*.

Mari's red hair was swallowed in a blur of gloomy black. They'd converged on their own witch. On Kane, on Griffin. On all of us. The specters saw no creed or color, only warm bodies. I knew it wasn't a soldier that held me back as I lunged for her. As I shrieked—

It was Kane's hand that coiled like a manacle around my wrist, yanking my shoulder nearly from its socket as he battled Rose men and spectres, halting me from throwing myself between her and those ghastly things.

The dark phantom drew his weapon. Raised it high—a ghoulish cleaver carved of pure, starless night. Ready to slash Mari in half as she scuttled helplessly back across the floor on her hands. Before I could scream her name again, or watch Mari sliced to bits, the phantom sword landed on a thick, edged dagger.

Griffin's.

Griffin, who'd somehow broken free of at least ten soldiers despite being poisoned and without any of his Fae strength. Griffin, who parried the demon like a mythical hero and a fabled beast.

Kane's and my relieved sighs were short-lived, though. More phantoms headed in their direction, finished with the husks of Rose men that littered the parlor floor, looking for their next kill. Griffin wouldn't be able to hold them off for too much longer.

Kane was already straining to get there—to maneuver past Rose soldiers and aid his commander.

And Mari—Mari was *screaming*. Lunging for Griffin, the pleats of her warm-colored dress tearing as two Rose guards fought to subdue her, though she thrashed and bit and sobbed.

And those phantoms, those shadows, converging on him—

Griffin barely cut down one apparition only to be throttled by the next.

They'd kill him.

"Mari, stop the spell!"

But fear had swallowed her whole. I'd never seen her so stunned. So frozen.

"You can send them back," I called to her, grunting as I conceded another step to a snarling guard without meaning to.

But she wasn't listening, or couldn't hear, her panic taking hold—

"Somebody help him," Mari croaked, though a shadow had already slain the Rose guard who held her to get its thick hands around her neck and—

I just had to get to her.

Griffin's sudden, pained groan was gut-churning.

I knew from the sound—even before I'd seen all the blood—how bad it was.

But Mari's silence, the horror in her eyes as she watched the gleaming phantom slide his broadsword deeper into the groaning commander's rib cage— Somehow, what she saw in that moment—it was enough.

The whirl of magic stung the air even as we continued to fight.

Fallen book pages fluttered, the hairs on my arms stood on end—

And then the phantoms were gone.

My gaze clawed across the turmoil. Griffin gnashing his teeth against the floor, bright red blood seeping through his Onyx armor and into the fallen cakes and biscuits. Rose soldiers still swarming us all, more and more and *more* guards. Drawn to the chaos, to their queen—

Far too many for us to get through.

Kane's brow dripped sweat as his blade sailed through six men at a time. Fighting to get to his wounded commander.

But more soldiers were coming, hauling Mari back despite her pleas. More and more and more . . .

And it was futile.

This was all . . . *futile.*

"We need to run," I said to Kane under my breath.

"How?" Kane grunted, blocking an elbow to his face and sinking his sword into a man's thigh. The guard groaned in agony and crumpled to the floor.

My eyes found the wide glass bow window. "We need—" I cut myself off, dodging a fist. But the next one connected with my temple and I flew backward into the solid gold trunk of the mighty sculpted tree.

Leather-bound tomes toppled and smacked me and my assailant

both. Metal fasteners at the base of the sculpture creaked and snapped. Delicate golden branches thudded to the carpeted floor.

Kane's quicksilver eyes locked on mine. We'd had the idea simultaneously.

He gave me a single steadfast nod. "I'll cover you."

Despite the lilium still sagging my limbs and clouding my mind, I threw myself into the trunk of the behemoth sculpture. Two guards lunged for me, catching on. I dodged, faster than them even as my entire body felt as if it were wading through a thick bog.

I flung myself into the teetering gold elm tree once more. Pain sang in my shoulder, my side, my *teeth*, but I only slammed the gilded trunk again. Then again. All the while Kane blocked each shrieking blow and lunging strike that sailed toward me.

Until a mighty, near-deafening creaking sounded—

An earsplitting *crack* as the towering work of art teetered, groaned, and . . . came crashing down across the parlor and through that massive bow window.

I covered my head as glass and pages and gilded petals rained down upon us all.

A barrage of colorful leather-bound books and branches of fine metal. Ethera screamed so loudly I wondered if her fragile, antique lungs would collapse.

I could only hope.

Cold winter air scented with hydrangea and freshly cut grass whipped at my face. The window was gone, and in its place, an escape route through the palace garden.

"Go," I yelled past Kane to Mari and Griffin. Even in his bloodied state, the commander still sliced his sword through any guard that even breathed near them. Mari shot a single agonized look in my direction as she ran, and then they leapt together from the second-story room.

"Arwen." Kane sounded like he was chewing through cast iron.

When I turned, I saw that I hadn't been far off. The blades near his throat were dangerously close to making irreversible contact. I lunged with my sword.

The soldier gurgled, steel clattering.

And Kane and I leapt over the body to sprint for the gaping hole where the parlor windows had once been. But I knew from his labored pants—and my own heavy breathing—we'd never make it. Not when I could see the energy draining from Kane's eyes, his wrath only flickering as his body grew weak and tired. Being drained was grueling—we wouldn't have the fight in us much longer. And all the Rose men—they only wanted *me*. Ethera had called for them to seize *me*.

And I thought I'd screamed it, but maybe I'd only whispered the words, *"Keep going,"* before taking off in the opposite direction of the whipping wind and that broken window, and instead toward the interior doors of the parlor.

"Stop her!" Ethera wailed.

And as I'd hoped, the guards who were still standing—not crushed under the metal trunk of that sculpture, nor wasted by Mari's spell—did just that. They followed after me as I hurtled over the floral couch and dodged pillars, out the painted parlor doors and through the gilded, rosy hallway, lush peonies and bronze harps painted onto the walls.

I'd only seen two or three men go after Kane. Child's play for him, Griffin, and Mari. With or without their powers.

And even as my jaw careened into the floor—the crushing weight on my back telling me multiple guards now held me there—and pain bloomed in my spine and shoulder and lilium coursed through my system . . . it was relief that flooded me.

They'd gotten out.

30

KANE

WHAT THE FUCK HAPPENED BACK THERE?" I SNAPPED AT Mari as we hurtled toward the imposing wrought-iron gates that wrapped around the manicured palace garden. Griffin snarled softly, hand still pressed to his gruesome wound. I waited for Arwen's reprimand at my brusque tone.

In the split second that it didn't arrive, I whipped my head around and my heart stopped.

The swarm of guards behind us were losing ground, and we were mere feet from the palace gate. But my chest constricted with each step. She hadn't made it out.

"We have to go back," I said, halting my feet. "Arwen—"

"We can't get her like this," Griffin rasped, leaning into a rectangular hedge. "We need our lighte. Or a convoy, at least."

We never should've come without men. Ethera had insisted, always worried that our Fae nature gave us an advantage, and we'd been so desperate to please her. Ridiculous.

But the guards were drawing nearer—

And there were too many of them for us to best, powerless, injured, and saddled with a malfunctioning witch. Though it nearly killed me to admit it, he was right. We had to get out first and retrieve Arwen after. "Fine," I barked. "Hurry."

Mari's feet slapped one after the other along the brick path until we reached the gates and hauled ourselves over them. Griffin first with a pained groan, then myself, then Mari, who we pulled down after us. On the other side, deposited into the heart of the capital city of Revue, we ran.

It was barely night and the sky was free of both stars and clouds. An empty, forlorn blue that did not match the urgency warring in my bones.

We rounded the nearest corner—heavy footfalls and horns still sounding behind us—and barreled down a narrow street. Swerving to avoid a neighing steed drawing a carriage, I led us through one more thin alley between two brick buildings.

Silence sounded in my ears, minus the clopping of hooves and our panting, haggard breaths. Above us, wet crepe dresses hung over an ornate teal balcony that mimicked latticework.

Griffin shoved two fingers down his throat and retched against the bricks. His back and arms had been carved with those phantom blades and he was dripping blood on the cobblestone from his ribs as he purged.

"That won't work," I breathed, but it didn't stop him from gagging himself once more. "It's already in your bloodstream." We'd need Fae lighte to heal. Or time for the lilium to leave our bodies.

Mari spoke for the first time since we'd left Ethera's parlor. "I'm sorry . . ." Her voice was small. "I thought . . . I'd been trying—"

"Later," I said to her. "We need to get back in there and with some brute force before Ethera—" I wouldn't finish the thought. I wouldn't lose faith in Arwen, either. She was savvy, and skilled, and a full-blooded Fae, and . . . she'd be fine. Until we could reach her, she'd have to be fine. "How fast can we get back to Shadowhold?"

Mari ripped part of her skirt and used it to stanch the bleeding in Griffin's ribs as he looked back toward the busy city center that surrounded Ethera's sprawling urban palace. "Without our lighte?" He worked his jaw, weighing. "Twelve hours. Eleven, if the horses we steal are very fast."

Fuck. We didn't have enough time for that.

"A long shot, but—" Mari produced an ornate leather-bound book from her sack. Griffin's brows rose weakly. "I took this from Ethera's tree. It's the mate of the real ledger."

My brow furrowed. "I don't understand."

Mari chewed her bottom lip. "When I saw the similar spine, I knew this one must be the twin Niclas had told us of. The one that contains the names of those who fought for the *north*, not the south. So I took it. This ledger has family names, home cities, known businesses and affiliates of every single person who fought for Ethera. If Aleksander and all his people helped her—"

"Then his name will be in there . . ." Griffin finished, massaging his bruised jaw.

My mind had begun to whirl. "If Aleksander is still in Rose like the rebel king told us, he'd be the closest Fae for miles."

"I've read Blood Fae have all kinds of healing powers," Mari said. "His fixing you both might be our fastest way to get Arwen out."

She was right. Hemolichs could do a number of unpleasant but valuable tricks with blood, including removing toxins. If we convinced him to aid us, we'd be able to shift and fly back here far faster than if we traveled all the way to Shadowhold for aid. If anyone could help us now, and swiftly, it might actually be him. "Mari, you're brilliant."

The look on her rosy cheeks was one of meager redemption.

Griffin added, "It's the least he could do, given how much he owes us."

Regardless of my disdain for him, we'd use Aleksander to free Arwen. And then, I'd tear the deranged Scarlet Queen delicate limb from delicate fucking limb.

Mari was already prying open the ledger and searching for his name.

"What's Aleksander's last name?" she asked.

I came to stand behind her. "Hale."

"*H, H, H . . .*" Mari repeated, flipping through the pages.

"Nothing came up under *A*?" Griffin asked, hovering over her, eyes squinted at the fine print.

"No," she said, leaning into his chest a bit. "Unfortunately not."

Griffin froze with the contact and his face flushed. He stepped back from the witch in an instant and she nearly toppled over.

"Is it listed by last name?" I asked.

Mari remained silent, her cheeks now a matching pink before emitting a low, "Nope . . ."

And she was well past the *A*'s.

Gods damn it.

I peered out to see nightfall cloak the city inch by inch. What was the best way to go about stealing a horse? Would I reveal myself as the king of Onyx, or would it be faster, and avoid time-wasting questions, to simply threaten—

"Go back," Griffin said, voice low. "I know that name."

I turned back and peered over the ledger, Mari squished between the two of us. "Which one?"

"Hearken Sadella," Griffin said. "He owns the Neck Romancer."

"What's that?" Mari asked.

"A theater in a seedy port town called Rotter's End." Griffin winced as he held Mari's ripped skirt to the wound at his ribs. "Only an hour from here by horseback. A strange place . . . It's in one of the most dangerous towns in northern Rose but caters to some of the kingdom's highest-end clientele. Somewhere the rich can find decadence as well as anonymity. Quite the operation—prostitution, banned spirits and drugs, and apparently some mighty fine theater."

When Mari made a face of surprise, Griffin added, "Kane and I hunted for the Blade of the Sun for five years. I know of every criminal operation in Evendell."

I ran a hand down my face, attempting to maintain my waning patience. "How is that relevant to Aleksander?"

"I'm not sure . . ." Griffin admitted. "It was the only name I recognized." He looked back down at the ledger and squinted again. "All the columns for Hearken Sadella's known associates and locations have been left blank."

I opened my mouth to respond. To tell them we were wasting time and needed to go abduct two horses immediately, but Mari's gaze stopped me cold.

Her focused eyes, bottom lip caught between her teeth—

"Hearken Sadella . . . *H-E-A*— I need some parchment."

I gestured to the snowy alleyway. "Afraid we're all out."

"Turn around," she ordered Griffin, and my enormous bleeding, cold-as-ice commander whirled like a well-trained dog. Mari began to draw her pointed finger across his broad back as if she were writing something. He bristled with each movement of her tiny finger.

"It's an anagram," she whispered after a long moment, her voice a blend of awe and triumph.

Griffin spoke into the brick before him. "A what?"

"A word formed by rearranging the letters of another word. He was hiding from you, right?" she asked me. "When he first came to Evendell with all of his people? He likely fought under an alias and then adopted the pseudonym to live in anonymity. But he used all the letters of his real name. Aleksander Hale and Hearken Sadella." She grinned, that fire back in her eyes. "One and the same."

IT TURNED OUT THE EASIEST WAY TO STEAL TWO HORSES WAS for Mari to distract a carriage owner who had stopped to fix his broken spoke, and for Griffin and me to free his horses and take off for Rotter's End, swiping Mari from her conversation on our way. She insisted on leaving the man a satchel of coin, to which my commander grudgingly agreed.

Griffin had been right. The ride was less than an hour, as our horses were quick, and we arrived in Rotter's End before the dilapidated clock tower in the town square rang seven. We'd made good time.

Still, the entire ride, steed racing at a bone-crunching gallop, my mind ached with the image of Arwen chained somewhere in Ethera's palace. I'd filtered through every possible reason the queen might have wanted her. Her lighte, to trade her to Lazarus, to hurt me in some way. None of it made any real sense. Ethera knew my army could slaughter hers. She couldn't withstand another war, not with the south of Rose already breathing down her neck.

I was still driving myself mad with the possibilities as a bistro somewhere pumped out the notes of a deep, brassy saxophone and patrons whooped and hollered. We'd arrived.

Rotter's End reeked of booze. Not just the fresh liquor, but the smell of it once someone had failed to keep the stuff down. And it was oppressively dark—not many streetlamps or lanterns, and the few the town did have were dimmed or caked in frozen snow. One watering hole was growing boisterous with the coming night, but even that establishment near the riverbed was so encrusted in snow and dirt I couldn't make out much.

And yet the shuttered-up windows and closed-down harbor, each knackered barn and splash of horse hooves through cold sludge, was illuminated by a vivid, glowing *red*. As if the rising moon had first been doused in fresh blood.

I searched for the source of the ruddy glow and found it swiftly.

"The Neck Romancer," displayed in vibrant flashing lights of red and white and gold—either Aleksander's lighte or quite the spell. The theater, shaped like a circus tent, with panels of striped fabric and flags at the top of each peak, presided over Rotter's End like a harlequin on a palace throne.

As we approached, we found the doors barred off with long planks of wood. A lone fish-eyed man sat on a repurposed barstool, bundled in a fur hat and coat, his eyes on a weathered novel grasped between cracked leather gloves.

"We don't open until nightfall," he said, before we'd even reached him.

Mari gestured wildly at the cerulean blue dusk all around us. "That's now!"

The doorman didn't lift an eye. "No, wench. It ain't."

"Listen," I said, voice low. "We—"

"I'm not saying it again," the doorman grunted. Finally his eyes found mine. They held the will of a human bull.

My body prickled and instant fatigue flooded my veins.

Gods-damned lilium . . .

"Please," Mari tried again. "If I may, nightfall is a very confusing time to open an establishment. Is it simply the moment the sun falls and it becomes night? Because that would have been hours ago. Is it once the sky is pitch-black? That's tricky, too, because that might be midnight, and then the show would be long over, right? So, you see, we could bother you with all these complex ramifications of your operating hours, or you could just let us inside and be back to your book." Mari beamed at him before peeking down at the pages in his hand. "And that's such a great one. I love Baudaire's use of color."

The doorman and his scraggly goatee loosed one unimpressed laugh. Mari laughed, too, and then unexpectedly rushed him, trying to dodge past his hulking torso for the doors.

Before either Griffin or I could move for them, the man caught Mari around the middle and threw her back into the snowy ground. She went down hard, taking a spool of rope and a broken chair along with her. "Your woman," the maggot spit toward Griffin and me as he sat back down, "is insufferable."

Rage forced my tongue against my teeth. *Breathe . . .* We could not fuck this—

Griffin laughed once. Still bleeding from his ribs and brow, that laugh blunt and mean. His eyes found the fading sky as if in apology before his fist slammed so hard into the man's jaw, it wasn't just spit that flew as he toppled from his chair. It was *teeth*.

Even without his Fae strength, the entire building trembled with the force of the man's body smacking the brick façade, and snow tumbled down in heaps.

In two hundred years, Griffin had successfully stopped me from clocking at least two dozen men. He'd failed at holding me back more than double that. And in all those years—all those tavern fights and violent brawls, men who deserved it and those who didn't—I'd never seen my commander strike someone out of impulse. The man couldn't even buy a new pair of boots without debating it for weeks.

"Holy Stones!" Mari shrieked from the ground. Griffin offered her his mangled hand—our lilium tea meant those fractured fingers weren't righting themselves anytime soon—and then, noting the damage, offered her his other one instead.

Mari allowed him to yank her up as she yelped, "You *killed him*."

"No," Griffin bit out, flexing his hand when she released it. "I didn't."

I leaned over the body, out cold and leaking blood into the stone and snow. His chest rose and fell, and I sighed. "When he wakes, he'll wish you had, though." I looked back up to my beleaguered friends. "Come on."

Per Griffin, on any given night, the Neck Romancer was a glamorous kaleidoscope of light and color and skin and song. Clinking glasses and alluring peals of laughter and enough decadent food and liquor to flood Willowridge twice over.

But the theater we walked into was empty and quiet.

The vaulted ceiling was shadowed, its hundreds of dangling crystal chandeliers still unlit. Heavy, bloodred velvet curtains framed the main stage, pulled off to the side by gilded rope. The balconies above and tables below, all of which surrounded that broad stage, sat empty, though some had a yet-to-be-dressed performer dozing off inside them.

Stale tobacco smoke and perfume thickened the air in my nose, and to our right a coughing man replaced one risqué poster of a blushing woman hiding her breasts with another one of virtually the same image.

Somewhere, one of Ethera's melographs oozed out a slow metallic accordion tune, and behind the curtains a sultry voice vocalized low, easy warm-ups.

Across the stage, lit only by oil lamps and candles, dancers practiced a provocative performance in various stages of undress. Some twirled in faded, ruffled petticoats clearly worn just for practice, while others leapt in sensual lace silhouettes, with tights that criss-crossed up their legs and silky satin gloves. The troupe rehearsed before a woman whose face had been painted to resemble a pouty jester. She tapped her leather-bound foot in a rhythm for them to follow.

"Hey," I called to her, pushing past shiny red booths and high wooden tables. "We need to speak with your proprietor. Urgently."

The entire stage's attention fell to me and I watched as most faces lit with fear while a scarce few sparked with lust. Those women offered heavy-lidded, finger-twinkling waves; one who was lacing herself into a harness tethered to some sort of trapeze blew me a kiss.

I grimaced.

"Anya will know where he is," the head dancer replied, jerking her painted chin toward a woman over by the tables.

I maneuvered past two men hefting an ornate theatrical mirror through the booths and found Anya bent over a dining table, flattening out a tablecloth. She wore nothing but puffed, frilly bloomers that offered a scandalous peek at her curved bottom and hosiery that resembled a fisherman's net, climbing up her legs and stopping in the middle of her thighs. Her lean back was expertly cinched in a corset of rich indigo.

"Anya? We're looking for—"

When she turned to face me, I was greeted with two supple, bouncing breasts.

Tiny circles of fabric dotted with a single tassel carefully concealed Anya's nipples. That velvet corset dipped low in the front beneath both breasts, which struck me as senseless—supporting the woman's chest was the very purpose of the garment.

"Me?" she purred, rolling a single finger down my shoulder to my waistband. "Certainly *I* have what you're looking for?"

"Not even close," I admitted. "Hearken Sadella. Where is he?"

Anya rolled her eyes, which had gone from heavy-lidded with interest to morosely bored. "Who's asking?"

"An investor. And longtime admirer of his establishment."

Those long-lashed eyes, lids doused with a glittering sheen, popped right back open. "A *patron* of the *arts* . . . Oh, la, la," she sang. "Stay right there. Sir will be glad to meet you."

He made all these women call him *sir*? It was already going to be a phenomenal effort not to relieve Aleksander of his fingernails before asking him to help us. I didn't know how many more reasons to revile him I could take.

"This place is kind of magical, isn't it?" Mari asked, returning to us with a fresh rag she'd swiped from somewhere. She pressed it to Griffin's ribs and then dabbed his brow and sliced arms.

"I don't know, I guess." Griffin rubbed his hand across the back of his neck as she worked, blushing like a schoolgirl. "Thank you, for this. I can probably take it from—"

"It's just the chandeliers, I think," Mari continued, grinning up at him. "I love their intricacy. I wonder what they look like all lit up."

"Yeah." Griffin nodded, eyes on the crystals above us. "It would definitely be . . . bright."

Evidently, my commander had been woefully underprepared for what he'd do if Mari ever stopped harassing him and showed him even an ounce of interest. She tapped her foot a bit, waiting for him to say more—anything else at all—but he didn't.

I fought the urge to knock their heads together.

The provocative dancer returned from behind a single dark satin curtain with a frown.

"Apologies, Sir is a tad indisposed. May I suggest you return when we open in a few hours?" Anya leaned closer once she reached me, her candy-apple breath whispering against my chin. "For you, patron, I'll open whenever you tell me to."

Irritation prickled along my skin. Wrapping my hands around the woman's slender shoulders, I hefted her up and deposited her a foot away from me. Her disgruntled *humph* didn't even register as I made for the still-swaying curtain.

"*You can't go down there. Excuse me! Hello!*"

Anya didn't do much else to stop us slipping behind the roped-off fabric. The girl had likely seen enough unsavory acts in this place that she knew when to steer clear. She hadn't even balked at Griffin's blood-soaked body.

We hurried down an old wooden staircase adorned with little twinkling elvish lights. If I squinted, the corridor almost resembled a night sky.

Breathy, pleading moans echoed through the darkened stairwell and a sneer warped my face.

Mari's feet stalled, her voice echoing a similar distaste. "That better not be—"

"It is," Griffin grunted behind us.

The low ceiling at the bottom of the stairs told me we were standing just below the Neck Romancer's main stage. The shallow basement had been converted into some kind of tiring-room, and candles dousing their votives in melting wax flooded the space in flickering shadow. The scents of sex and tobacco mingled with old wood and oily makeup. On a tufted, red leather couch that sagged in the corner, a kneeling man was tongue-deep in a very vocal performer.

"Fuck," the woman groaned, face wound tightly. "Fuck, *fuck* do *not* stop—"

"Or do," I offered, leaning against the stairs.

Her wanton whimper warped into a shrill cry of surprise as her eyes sprang open to find myself, Griffin, and a stunned, pale-faced Mari. I unleashed a chilling grin that I hoped said, *Correct. Now scram.*

The still-panting woman snapped her legs shut so fast she nearly took Aleksander's infamous head with her as she yanked her checkered skirt and its many layers of tulle down and scrambled off the couch. Breezing past us in a cloud of flustered apologies, I only caught a flash of those eerie, glowing red eyes as they lingered on Griffin's body before she careened up the stairs.

Aleksander stood, his back still to us, and I worked my jaw free of its iron vise on my teeth. Then I unfurled my fists and flexed my taut palms. And then, for good measure, I breathed. Deeply.

"Aleksander," I tried. It did not come out friendly. Not by a mile.

Aleksander's long shock-white hair swayed at his back as he stood. When he turned, he was wiping blood off his lips, grave red eyes glowing. "What have you done to yourself, Ravenwood?"

Griffin's head snapped sidelong toward me and I tensed my jaw. Aleksander, like all Hemolichs, could scent quite a bit from someone's blood. Their fear, arousal, health. And, clearly, that I had been made full-blooded.

When I didn't answer, Aleksander leaned his long neck to the side until a *crack* sounded loudly across the hidden den. "Are you here to kill me?"

"Actually," I gritted out, my smirk laced with venom, "I need a favor."

31

ARWEN

My stomach flipped so riotously I was sure I'd be spewing radishes and cherries soon.

The oblong birdcage was too short for me to stand, but too narrow to lay down, and hugging my knees in to contort myself had resulted in close to full-body numbness.

If there'd ever been an exotic bird that fit inside this cage or any of the other empty, bent-out-of-shape cages in here, they were long gone now. Not even the few fossilized feathers dotting the floor told me anything about what kind of creatures Ethera had once kept.

It didn't matter. I needed *air*.

It was late, and the glass panes around me had grown dark, but I could tell by the mossy scent and coiled, twining vines that I was in a greenhouse. A stuffy, suffocating greenhouse. And a very neglected one, given all the shriveled blooms and prickly thorns. Overrun with vines and withered leaves that slithered along the floor and up the glass walls, curving themselves around the potted plants and twisting around the legs of raised wooden plant beds. The deterioration wasn't due to the wintertime—all the soil I could see was dry as bone, no cover crops or shrubbery to keep it moist. Maybe nobody had been in here for years.

Years . . .

I counted my inhales and exhales as my hands twined in my blouse.

One, two. One, two.

In, out. In, out.

That was making it worse. Now all I could think about *was* my breathing—or lack thereof. My heart—it was beating too fast. I was going to have a heart attack. I was going to die of a heart attack before I could escape.

No, I told myself. *You cannot die from fear.*

"Anxiety lives only in the mind. If your thoughts are elsewhere, you can't panic."

How many times had I conjured Kane to take over as the voice in my head and distract me when I was held captive in Lumera? How many times had I allowed him to flirt with me or anger me inside my mind so I could lose track of how long Octavia had been reaping lighte from my veins?

I could do that again.

Three things. *Find and focus on three things you can name, bird.* I could do that much.

One. A long-since-withered, rancid pomegranate. Rolled to the side of a dusty ceramic pot. Desiccated, kind of like a—

Bleeding Stones, I couldn't think. Not as my blood lurched in my veins with the urge to run or move or breathe *more* or breathe *harder—*

No. No—

Three things, Arwen.

That voice in my head. My own this time. Urging myself to unclench my hands and slow my rapid breathing.

What was two? Two marble pots, both overrun with stinging nettles. I knew from my *Evendell Flora* book that despite the sting, that nettle could be brewed to make the sweetest summer tea. I conjured my mother, and her patience as it brewed while I waited on tippy toes for my cup.

"What ailment has you so deeply discomposed?" Ethera's voice chimed. I knew only from the singsong tone as my vision continued to tunnel.

No words formed.

Three, three . . . In the heart of the greenhouse was a low tiled pool half-filled with fetid water, now sage green with algae. At its center a copper fountain of a woman with a scaled tail, long since oxidized and now matching the water's teal hue. I tried to imagine myself becoming very small, walking through the bars of this cage, and taking a mossy dip.

By the time Ethera bent over before me, beautiful head cocked, I was actually breathing. My heart rate had slowed.

The queen was bundled in a deep vermillion fur and matching hat that looked like feather grass, with two hulking guards behind her. She frowned, drawing her hands up to her face. "Dear, are you all right? This whole endeavor has given me the collywobbles."

Her eclectic capriciousness had surpassed grating. I glowered at her, still catching my breath. "Pity."

She sank to her knees. "I must ask you a question, darling, and I require your utmost truthfulness."

"Why would I give you anything you ask for?"

"I do not wish to execute you," she said, nodding to one of her guards who knelt as well, brandishing a serrated hunting knife and sending a vicious chill down my spine. "But I haven't the luxury of sparing you unless you do indeed answer me."

I swallowed hard, eyes still on that jagged blade.

Ethera's beautiful brows rose. "Have you and the king yet borne a child?"

My shock, confusion, or both must have been written clear across my face, because the queen sighed as if my expression alone served as her answer. "How truly fortuitous."

I sighed as well. "It is? Well, we haven't, I swear."

Ethera nodded. "Yes, darling, for me, very fortuitous indeed. Delightful, really. For you, not quite as splendid, I'm afraid."

Before I could shriek, Ethera's guard wrapped a calloused hand around my blouse and yanked me into the bars of the cage. He drew his dagger back and moved to drive it through the slats and into my chest.

"Wait!" I wailed, scrambling my aching limbs backward and going nowhere. "Wait—"

I needed to buy time. I needed— "Please, I just have one question!"

The guard hesitated, and Ethera's painfully stunning head cocked to him, gleaming hair spilling across her shoulder.

"Why?" I breathed, making use of his moment of indecision. "If you're going to kill me, at least tell me that. Why would my life have been spared if I'd had a child?"

"Well, there would be nothing I could do about it then, would there?"

My mind reeled faster than my lips could keep up. "You are killing me to . . . ensure that I *don't* have a child with Kane?"

Ethera grinned again, those teal eyes surrounded by the expansive bright whites of her eyes. She clapped her hands. "Yes, yes, very good!"

Why in the world—

She was a mad, *mad* woman. Out of her mind.

I needed to stall her. To distract her until some kind of help arrived. Or I came up with something more clever.

And I didn't know, even as I said, "But I have something you need . . ." if this might work. If she would even allow me to utter the words.

Ethera narrowed her lovely eyes at me, long dark lashes lowering. "Do you take me for a dunderhead?"

"No, Your Majesty. Of course not."

Ethera's guard's dagger hovered between the bars of the cage. He watched as she considered me. I was sure I wasn't breathing.

Eventually the corner of her mouth quirked up, and with it, a small crack tore at her lips and up her cheek. A fissure, like in sedimentary rock.

I must have made a terrible face because she waved her elegant hand at me and said, "Oh, hush. Do share whatever it was you felt so inclined to." Then she nodded at her guard, who sheathed his serrated knife, releasing me back into the bars.

"I don't want to imply anything improper, but . . ." I let my eyes trail over her nailless finger and the thin crack along her cheek. "It seems to me you have an ailment, Your Majesty. You know the power that I hold . . . I could help you. Could *heal* you. Make you healthy again."

Ethera's eyes had grown so wide I was worried they might pop right out. She seemed the type. The queen tapped a long, painted finger along her heart-shaped chin. "But you've been ensnared by the lilium. You cannot perform any benevolent acts with your lighte now, can you?"

I swallowed my nausea. "We'll have to wait until it's left my system."

Ethera's teal eyes burned, and I cowered against my better judgment. "And allow you to annihilate my home with me and all my lovelies inside it?"

"No," I swore. "Never. If you wish to stop decomposing, Your Majesty, you'll have to trust me."

Ethera considered me, her mouth a tight knot.

I forced my gaze anywhere but Ethera's guard's sheathed knife. "I am not an advocate for violence. I allowed your men to capture me just to set my friends free. I helped you put an end to that bloodbath. I don't wish to see your home destroyed or to take your life. I just want to spare my own."

"Very well," she said in the end as she stood. "I shall be back to inspect you tomorrow morning."

And then she left in a whirl of fur and wine-colored hair. I exhaled thoroughly.

The greenhouse was cold, and I knew the coming night would only bring more snow atop the glass roof. I wrapped my arms around myself as best I could given the angle and tried not to shiver.

All I could really discern in the stifling darkness were cobwebs and drying brown vines that climbed along the glass and across the dusty floor. And I was unfocused. My mind dissecting over and over again why Ethera would want to prohibit Kane and I from bearing a child . . .

Before I came up with a single halfway-decent theory, the glass door creaked open. A pink-clad housemaid strolled in with a bowl of something meaty and warm and a hot mug billowing steam into the chilly greenhouse.

The handmaiden knelt and threaded the supper steadily through the birdcage. But before I could take the bowl and mug from her, a commotion sounded from beyond the greenhouse doors.

My eyes shot up.

The handmaiden's expression had blossomed into one of true fear as the shouts and slamming doors intensified somewhere outside. She offered me one last stricken look before she ran, knocking hot soup across the greenhouse floor.

Not just ran—this woman *sprinted* for the doors, her footfalls on the floor reverberating into my stiff bones. In her haste she threw the glass wide open, dousing me in a blast of snow-flecked night. The wind set my teeth on edge as she deserted me in a frozen greenhouse clearly destined for some kind of violence.

And there was nothing I could do but sit and listen as that shouting only drew nearer. The squawk of the queen rang out, alongside the low rumble of someone—not Kane. Not any voice I'd heard before.

More shrieking . . .

My hands braced around the wire of the birdcage. If I hadn't been doped with lilium I could have torn the wiry iron bars apart enough to squeeze through. Instead I shattered the fallen mug on the hard ground and brandished one ceramic sliver like a dagger.

"We are not finished here!" Ethera's voice warbled from right outside the greenhouse.

The glass doors swung open and my blood—

The striking, *harrowing* man that stood before me turned my blood to ice.

Pale, near-translucent skin as if he avoided all sunlight, ice-white hair, glaring expression on that carved, elegant face—all of it aligned with the expected beauty of Fae males. It was the glowing, sinister, bloodred eyes that stole the breath from my chest. Their razor focus. Their *need*.

Aleksander Hale. I knew it in my bones.

And, knowing what I did of the Hemolich, he could sense the way the chilling sensation of beholding him coursed through my veins. The slight uptick of his elegant dark brow told me as much.

He was like a hound. He could *smell* my fear.

"You must be Arwen."

"Where's Kane?"

Without answering me he strode toward my cage and flicked the ironclad latch open with a single menacing finger.

When I didn't scramble out immediately, the Blood Fae lowered his brows. "I won't bite."

I didn't laugh. Neither did he.

In the end I scooted out of the birdcage about as ungracefully as a gangly newborn lamb. By the time I was standing he'd already walked out.

Night had drowned the palace courtyard in darkness and the few mermagic lamps that decorated the garden's arches and fountains cast the blades of grass and clumps of frost in hazy blue.

Where I expected slain Rose men I found untouched, fresh snow. I'd only heard yelling, but assumed Aleksander had slaughtered them all when he'd arrived.

My boots crunched as I raced to keep up with the Blood Fae's long legs. Terrifying or not, the man was tall and lean and graceful and made me feel like a scurrying rat beside him. The weakness in my bones didn't help.

"Why didn't Kane come free me?"

He said nothing and my heart slammed into my ribs.

"Where is he?"

Aleksander didn't turn at my question even as he said, "I told him to wait outside."

"And he obeyed?"

At a gilded arch wreathed in snowy vines, the Hemolich finally turned to face me. Those bloodred eyes simmered. "I owed your king a debt. He cashed it in. But that required doing this my way."

Kane had gone to Aleksander to free me. Besides his father, I wasn't sure Kane despised anyone as much as the ice-cold man that stood before me. Warmth flickered through my chest.

At the end of the garden path, Aleksander opened a heavy palace door with one hand and I dashed in after him before it could slam in my face. The long hallway was empty, and I couldn't hear any voices in the neighboring rooms. The eerie quiet turned the watercolor wallpaper and gilded moldings ominous, the cherubic faces in the paintings like ghosts, watching us.

Was the palace empty? Had he killed everyone inside? Did Ethera's men know I'd been freed, or would they be after me the minute they found my cage empty? I was still too drained to defend myself against much of anyone, even mortal soldiers.

For now at least, I had my white-haired Hemolich bodyguard. Whatever he'd done—or *not* done, given the lack of gore or bodies— I was grateful.

"Thank you for—"

"Don't." Aleksander's voice was low as he his stalked through the next passage, his hands lodged in his pockets.

"Why can't I thank you for your kindness?"

"I'm not kind." Each word seemed an effort not to tear into my throat, and I swallowed audibly. Aleksander's nostrils flared.

"Kane was riddled with lilium when he found you," I said as we rounded a corner into a hallway dripping in chandeliers. Some so low I had to dodge past the dangling crystal. "You could have killed him, but you didn't. Is that not kindness? Or mercy, at least?"

Aleksander didn't respond, trudging through as if he knew the place well, turning here and pushing a door open there. His eyes never met mine, his hands never left his pockets, and I didn't spy one guard or handmaiden.

"Are they all dead?"

His throat bobbed though he didn't answer me. I paled, regretting the question.

"They're hiding," he said, voice like venom, as he nudged the door to the grand hall open with his shoulder. "Like mice."

The grand hall was off the parlor, and I could just make out the shattered window, which funneled freezing night air into the room. The towering golden elm tree and its priceless branches were still lodged through the broken glass, halfway hanging outside the now-vacant bow frame.

Though servants had clearly tried to tidy up, there were still stray books, shards of glass, and smears of blood on the floor. I spied still-wet rags and buckets of soapy water left haphazardly across the room, as if everyone who'd been cleaning had up and left in an instant.

My eyes cut back to Aleksander, his bloodred gaze on me intently. I hadn't realized I'd stopped walking. "You frighten them."

His eyes burned. "I frighten you, too."

I swallowed hard. "No, you don't."

His nostrils flared as he scented the air. Then he cocked his head at me pitilessly. "She lies."

"Fine." I inhaled sharply, resuming our walk. Maybe this would be my only chance at an honest conversation with this man who held so much fury and yet so much power. Whom we'd need if we had any chance of winning this war. "You frighten me, yes. But I feel sorry for you, too. I . . . have empathy for you." His jaw tensed, and I shivered, an unpleasant reaction to his severity. "You've suffered. Is all I mean. You—"

"Subtlety is not your strong suit, full-blood. My men will not be used as weapons again. You'd be wise to keep any other pesky thoughts to yourself."

But I couldn't. Not when I hoped there was a chance. A slim one that—

"Don't you see? If Lazarus wins, they'll—"

"*Do not argue with me,*" Aleksander hissed, stepping toward me with intent. I pressed myself so far up against an oil painting to get away from his wrath that I could smell the fresh varnish.

But he only folded his hands back into his pants and continued toward the foyer. I caught my breath and tried in vain to still my racing heart as we passed more decorative arches and luxe pastel furniture in tense silence.

Finally, we arrived at the castle entrance. A single guard stood there, the first we'd seen in the palace all night.

"I did mean it," I murmured, so quietly I wasn't sure I'd said it aloud. "That you don't deserve the suffering you and your people have endured. And I'm sorry for it. Whether you fight with us or not."

"Don't you despise me? The blood of your king's family is on my hands."

"I must believe there is some light buried inside everyone. Even those who appear at their darkest."

"You *must*?" he asked, incredulous.

Mocking or simply arrogant, I didn't care. I nodded at him just the same. "It's the only way I can live in this world. Compassion must be born out of all this cruelty, otherwise I just can't see my way through. What would be the point of any of it?"

Aleksander said nothing, eyes desolate as he stalked onward.

The Rose guard stood taller and opened the wide, gilded white doors for us with a grimace. A chilly breeze kissed my face. There, in the bustling city center, beyond the palace gates, were Kane, Mari, and Griffin.

Before I could race down the polished stairs to them, the Rose guard spat at Aleksander, muttering, *"Filthy fucking viper."*

I froze—ready for a fight, a *disembowelment* . . . whatever it was unpredictable, violent Hemolichs like Aleksander did when disrespected with such a slur—

But he only clicked down the stairs past me, hands still lodged in his pockets, cold red eyes on the falling snow.

32

ARWEN

THE FREEZING AIR WOVE THROUGH MY LUNGS AS I LAUNCHED myself into Kane's arms.

"My bird," he murmured, pulling me into him. I inhaled at his neck, savoring his scent and warmth as he stroked his fingers through my hair. He only pulled me from him to kiss me once and ask, "Are you—"

"I'm fine," I said, refusing to let go. Gripping his shoulders more tightly. "I'm fine."

I pulled Kane even closer, relishing the fresh air outside the vast castle gates, amid the hustle and bustle of Revue bathed in snowy starlight.

"Holy Stones, Arwen, I am so sorry," Mari said from behind us.

When I finally released Kane and got a decent look at her, my throat tightened. Mari's eyes were ringed in red. She looked stricken.

Griffin watched her carefully, backlit by the glowing, rosy lights of the city center. I couldn't tell if his scowl was from disappointment or the discomfort of empathy.

"Don't do that to yourself," I said, reaching for her hand. "You didn't—"

"There's no excuse." Mari shook her head vehemently. "I never should have tried something so . . . My magic has a mind of its own, I fear. And—"

"You didn't know Ethera would have lilium. Or that we'd end up relying on you so soon after you left Briar's."

Mari nodded once but I knew that look. Knew the shame in her eyes. Knew how it affected her to have let us down. I pulled her into my arms. "I love you. Be kind to yourself, please."

"That's my cue," Aleksander deadpanned.

"Not so fast," Kane growled at him.

I released Mari, sagging a bit with the movement. Too quick. I'd moved too quickly . . .

Kane motioned to me. "Heal her of the lilium."

Aleksander sighed, and without another word, shining black claws—long, razor-sharp, not of any creature I could describe—sprouted from his fingers and slashed gently against my wrist. The pain was brief. Just a bloodletting—

But not like any I'd done before as a healer. Aleksander waved a still-clawed hand across the wound and little specs of white alloy—the lilium—lifted from my blood. I flinched but felt no further discomfort, even as drops of red fell from my wrist into the snow at my feet.

That lighte he used—he wasn't as Fae as Kane and I—I didn't know if he could even shift. But those claws—something beastly, immortal, ancient as ammonite . . . I would have recoiled from them if they hadn't brought me such relief.

Energy funneled through my entire body as he removed each fragment. Liberation and *power*—I nearly purred.

Aleksander's jaw had gone to rigid steel. He kept his eyes on the city before us even as he used his strange power. Those elegant nostrils flared until enough lighte had returned that I healed the small incision on my wrist myself. It would be a bit longer before I'd recovered enough to heal Griffin's wounds.

I uttered my thanks, and Aleksander paced farther away from us. I wondered if my blood or Griffin's was bothering him.

"Are we done here?"

Murder glinted in Kane's eyes, but he nodded once.

Aleksander pursed his lips, as if debating whether to press his luck. He must've decided it was worth asking, because he said, in a low voice, "And you and I—we're . . ."

"If I was planning to kill you, you'd be dead."

Aleksander dipped his head as if to say, *Fair enough*, and turned to leave us.

"Wait," I called after him.

The Hemolich whirled, those illuminated eyes as bloody as the magical glowing signs and streetlights behind us.

Kane groaned in frustration. "Leave him."

"You and Griffin were weakened when you found him," I said under my breath, glaring. "He could have killed you, but he *didn't*."

I hurried toward Aleksander before he could change his mind. "How did you convince Ethera to let me go?"

"Does it matter?"

"It does to me." I was desperate for any shred of information he'd spare regarding my future child.

"I told her the truth," Aleksander said, red eyes studying the place on my wrist where I'd bled. I tucked the offending limb behind my back. "Your lighte can't heal a spell," he said.

My jaw slackened. "It can't? How do you know?"

"You aren't the only Fae with healing abilities."

Though my eyes hadn't left Aleksander's pale, chiseled face, I knew Kane had come to stand beside me, his cedar and leather scent heightened by the winter snow, both calming and fortifying at once.

"She still could have killed me," I pressed.

"No," he said, eyes brightening to an even more vibrant shade of crimson as they held mine. "She couldn't have. I told her that as well."

"Why not?"

Aleksander sighed, plunging his hands into his pockets and looking around the lively square. Citizens bundled in dyed furs and sheepskin gloves were hurrying in and out of a nearby tented market that pumped nutmeg and coffee-scented steam into the night air. His eyes were stark with how much he despised it all. "You ask a lot of questions."

Kane released a warning growl beside me. "Answer her."

Aleksander's face contorted, as if Kane's protection of me sickened him.

In the end, he said, "We made a blood oath, Ethera and I. Fifty years ago. They're similar to spells, presided over by powerful sorcerers to ensure their binding ability. But, unlike a common spell, every blood oath requires . . ." He fished for the right words. "An escape clause for both parties—a way out, should either of us need one. Ethera thought killing you would destroy *my* way out, leaving me bound to our deal for eternity. But Ethera is impulsive and uninformed: One cannot affect their own oath. The sorcerer's magic won't let you. Ethera just didn't know."

"So by killing me, Ethera would ensure Kane and I never bore children . . ." I worked the ramifications over in my mind. "How does our future child have anything to do with your 'way out' of a decades-old blood oath?"

If Kane was startled by my words, he didn't give anything away. He hardly bristled at my side.

"It doesn't," Aleksander said to me, and then again to Kane, more emphatically, "It *doesn't*. Like I just told you, she was wrong. She's not right in the head, if you can't tell."

Kane chewed through the words as he said, "What was the nature of your oath?"

"I pledged my people to her cause against the south. The last war they'd ever fight for someone else."

"And in return?"

Aleksander's eyes flashed. "Any Hemolich would be permitted to reside within her kingdom. As free men."

Kane's brows rose with interest. "You're saying your people face no persecution here in Rose?"

"Of course not." His tone told me continued discrimination toward himself, toward his people, had wounded him so thoroughly he was numb to it now. "But they aren't in chains."

"That was fifty years ago," I said. The queen had dropped her entire plot to kill me tonight at his behest. "Why do you still have such power over her?"

"We talk." Aleksander couldn't hide the way whatever he was leaving out soured on his tongue. "Occasionally."

I wouldn't get more information out of Aleksander. He was a vault. I spun on my heel to be rid of his lethal eyes and their punishing glare.

"Your people," I heard Kane say. And I wanted to stop him. To tell him I'd already tried and nearly had my head bitten off, but—

"I won't ask them to fight someone else's battle. I don't wish to purchase or force them. But *this* war . . . it is all of ours to fight. We've likely only got a fortnight before we leave for Lumera. Come with us."

Any exhaustion or revulsion eddied from my mind, replaced by surprise. Kane had all but sworn not to ask Aleksander for his army. He was too angry, too proud.

"I can't," Aleksander seethed at Kane.

"There is no price we could pay?" I asked. "Nothing at all we could offer you?"

"You have nothing of value to me," Aleksander snarled.

"Defeating the man who enslaved your people isn't of value? Saving the human lands that housed you and all other Hemolichs for half a century, after you *swore* to fight Lazarus alongside Kane and the rest of them and then *lied* to flee Lumera like a *coward* isn't payment enough?"

"Arwen." A note of caution.

"No," the Blood Fae hissed. "It's not."

It wasn't anger that filtered through my body, but something else. Something more sorrowful that fueled me as I said to him, "They're wrong to assume you're a monster. They *are*. But if you continue to behave as one . . . why should they ever stop?"

I wrapped my hand through Kane's and pulled him backward toward Griffin and Mari.

I was done with all of them. Aleksander. Ethera. Amelia. I understood just as well as they did the brutality of war. I didn't want our people, all those warm faces back in Shadowhold, to be slaughtered, either. Of course I didn't. But we couldn't all sit on the sidelines while—

"There is one deal I would broker with you both," that unfeeling voice called into the winter night.

I whirled first.

Kane, with his many years of life experience and knowledge of Aleksander, had the good sense to keep walking. Keep moving toward

Griffin and Mari. Usher them away from whatever might come out of the Blood Fae's mouth. Had I not pulled his arm back, our hands still intertwined, we both might have left before Aleksander could have said—

"When your firstborn daughter comes of age, send her to live with me, here in Rose."

I coughed on nothing, choking on sheer incomprehension.

Aleksander only plowed on, drifting closer, like a shadow across a wall. "A fair deal. My army, my *people*, thousands and thousands of lives at stake, for the mere company of your daughter. I will not hurt the girl. You have my word. Will not touch her. But—"

Kane unleashed a predatory growl. "You must be as mad as the queen you serve." Visceral fury rippled across his shoulders and jaw. He'd dropped my hand, and I knew if my eyes dipped I'd find thorns and curling smoke twined across his fists. I was shocked they hadn't already sliced through Aleksander's pale flesh.

"Get out of my sight," Kane seethed. "Before I rip you apart as I should have years ago."

"Hear me out—"

"You think anything you could say would convince me to give you my *child*? You, who would wish to drink her true Fae blood like a fucking fine wine?"

"You know my restraint, Kane. Any other Hemolich standing before not one but *two* full-blooded Fae . . ." He sniffed the air with lupine poise. "They'd be rabid for your blood. Foaming at the mouth. I could actually protect the girl—"

"You said the queen was wrong . . ." My head was reeling. He was hiding something. Some connection between our future offspring and his deal with the mad queen. "You said our child, if we even *had one*, would have nothing to do with your age-old oath."

Aleksander bared his teeth. "I lied."

Ablaze with unbridled rage, Kane's fist sprang forward and collided against Aleksander's jaw with a jarring *crunch*. I gasped, more shocked than afraid, as they flew into the snow.

Aleksander's blood sprayed, painting the white frost beneath them like a canvas. Kane's, too, as his knuckles split open, pounding the Hemolich's face and jaw relentlessly.

"You fucking *betrayed* us. They're dead because of you, and now"—he panted between blows—"now you fucking ask—"

Before he could deliver the next punch, I yanked Kane backward and off the fair-haired man. Kane's eyes were feral when they found mine, but there was a great sorrow behind the fury, and my chest caved in at the sight.

Behind us, Griffin had begun to stalk over but I shook my head as if to say *We're fine*. The last thing we needed was a brawl.

"We would never, *ever* allow our child anywhere near your filthy kind," Kane seethed. "Over my *dead* fucking *body*."

Aleksander groaned as he worked his jaw back into place. Bright red blood painted his lips and nose and the dirtied snow beneath him. Then, with a grace I'd never seen from any creature—Fae or otherwise—he knelt lower to the ground and dragged his tongue across the wet snow, licking up both his and Kane's blood. His glowing red eyes never left us.

I gagged at the sight, hauling Kane backward before he well and truly killed the man.

"What was that—" Griffin started, Mari hidden behind his hulking form.

"Nothing," I fired back, cutting him off. "We're leaving."

When Kane shifted into his dragon form, he released a roar so violent, the snow shook from the buildings below us.

33

⸻❧⸻

ARWEN

WE'D MESSAGED WORD OF THE COMING WAR TO THE VAR-
ious territory leaders of Opal and the highest priest in Pearl.
We'd even sent a raven to the Jade Islands, in case the inhabitants
that were fabled to live there could somehow be reached. We knew
it was a long shot, but we were out of options.

Still, every day since we'd returned from our failed mission to
Rose I'd checked the ravens at Shadowhold both at first light and
dusk. But today, like all days, the raven house was empty of messages.

My eyes scanned up to the fading sun, melting behind the bare
trees of the Shadow Woods, the sentries' towers doubled in manpower since our return.

Dinner would be served soon.

I shut the worm-holed wooden door, drowning out the flapping
of wings and feathered coos in favor of my boots crunching in snow.
Barney was escorting Briar back to Willowridge tomorrow to gather
a few spell books before we set off for Lumera as planned with Hart.
Just us, the Onyx men, and Hart's rebel army. I'd convinced Kane to

let us host everyone in his private dining quarters tonight as a send-off. A goodbye dinner, of sorts.

Though I wasn't sure Mari would even join us. She'd been quiet this past week. Her father told me he'd found all her grimoires in their wastebasket. I'd tried visiting Mari bearing treats—cloverbread and her favorite romantic novels. With Kane's help I'd found her a first edition copy of *Onyx's Most Foul*—a Mari classic.

She'd told me she was busy.

Mari was *always* busy. It had never stopped her from speaking to me before.

The warmth of Shadowhold enveloped me as I strolled inside, past guards and soldiers and children. I climbed the well-worn stairs, my hand running up a banister twined in holly.

The sound the apothecary door made when I swung it open was a tonic to my anxious mind. I'd met the new healer a few days ago. Eardley told me they'd hired her from a small village outside of Sandstone. She wasn't Fae, but she did have a knack for sutures and salves. Dagan had only called her by the wrong name twice, so I knew he liked her just fine.

The familiar wood floors creaked under my feet and I inhaled lemongrass and antiseptic. Familiarity warmed my limbs and I shed my fox fur, tossing it onto a lambskin chair.

I only needed sunflower oil. It helped keep my dry hands from cracking after training with Dagan in the winter air, which I did every morning. My aching quads never ceased to remind me. I massaged one such protesting limb as I hobbled around the counter. Maybe I'd grab some arnica root as well.

My hands stilled at the movement in the infirmary around the corner. I'd thought both rooms were empty . . .

"Hello?"

Nothing.

"Anyone there?"

Despite the rational part of my mind that knew no Fae mercenary was going to begin its pillage of Shadowhold in the infirmary's bandage drawer, a welcome rush of lighte zipped down my veins and into the tips of my fingers.

I stalked inside and a gasp shuddered through me.

"It's fine," Mari said, before I could form words. "Arwen, I'm fine."

But she wasn't. The blood was everywhere.

All over the crinkly daybed, drying brown and stiff on freshly washed sheets. Pooling in her skirts, trickling in between the cracks in the floorboards . . .

My hands flared with lighte as I seized her arm and ripped the plump leech from it. "Bleeding Stones, Mari, what did you do?"

"Bloodletting is supposed to help with certain abilities . . ." She was too pale.

But I could feel the blood she'd lost replenishing beneath my glowing fingers, and once she didn't look so woozy, I inspected the leech's entry point.

"You slashed yourself?" I twisted the arm a bit. "With a straight razor?"

"It wasn't taking enough blood . . . I thought I could it speed up."

I stanched the blood with a nearby rag and held tightly. "Herbalists have suggested leeches can remove toxins to help with abilities like *sight* or *mobility*. Not *magic*. It's more of an old wives' tale." Shaking my head, I tossed the rag to the ground and brought my lighte back to seal up her cuts. "You, of all people, didn't do your research?"

Mari didn't answer, only lifting her eyes to the wood panels of the ceiling. But tears pooled in them anyway, and her lips trembled as they spilled down her temples into her hair.

I kicked myself internally for berating her.

"Mari." I softened my tone. "Why are you being so hard on yourself? We've all told you . . . Nobody blames you for what happened with Ethera."

"I couldn't help when you needed me," she snapped, wounded eyes on mine, voice raw. "And you suffered because of it. *Griffin* suffered."

I shook my head emphatically. "You made a *mistake*."

Mari used the heel of her other hand to wipe her dripping eyes, and I opened the infirmary window to let the fat little leech out onto the roof tiles. A soft winter night swam inside and cold air brushed across my face.

When I turned, Mari was wiping down the floors.

"Let me do that."

"Don't even think about it. Yet another one of my *literal* messes you have to clean up."

"Right," I said, dropping to the floor with a rag to help her. "As if you've never had to do the same for me."

"It's different."

"Why?" I sat back on my heels. "Because you decided at some point that your value to people is how perfect you are?"

Mari said nothing as she scrubbed.

"It's not your job to protect us. Or to be the smartest, or the best witch. You didn't even know you could *do* magic six months ago."

"You don't get it. You can't imagine the pressure—you had the blessed luck of being the last person anyone expected greatness from."

I frowned at her.

"You know what I mean."

"You've put all these expectations on yourself for so long and I have no idea why. Who made you feel like you couldn't make mistakes?" It was something about Mari I'd never understood. Her father adored Mari more than the moon and the stars, and told her often.

"I don't know, nobody did."

"The boys who bullied you growing up? Maybe you felt like you had to prove something to them? I want to understand. Did someone—"

"I lived and she didn't, Arwen."

My heart constricted at the words.

Her mother. Who had died giving birth to her. Who by all accounts had been the most talented, warmhearted, lovely woman and witch. Who had been rendered perfect by the pedestal she inhabited in everyone's memories.

"That has to be worth something," Mari murmured. "*I* have to be worth something."

"You are worth *everything*, Mar."

"So you think. But one day, people will realize that I'm not as talented, or clever, or . . . That I'm not anything special. I'll disappoint all of you."

I swallowed the emotion in my throat. I had no idea how to explain to the smartest person I knew how wrong she was.

"It was the worst moment of my life," she whispered. "Watching you all struggle in that parlor."

"What even was that spell?"

"They're called Delusions. Briar told me they were difficult to master but I didn't know what else to do. We needed the manpower."

I tried to replay the situation in my mind. "But they went after *you*."

"I know. You think I haven't pored over the exact sequence of events a dozen times?" Mari rolled her wet eyes and sniffed. "I can't control it, Arwen. Sometimes my magic wants to *hurt* everything. Even me."

"*Maybe there's something in my lineage that shouldn't be touched.*" That's what she'd said when her powers had disappeared. And then, in Revue, she'd told me her magic had a mind of its own.

I was terrified to ask the question, and yet I found myself doing so anyway. "What do you think is wrong with them? Your powers?"

Mari's brows knit inward. "I have these dreams. Horrible, horrible dreams. I can't even tell you—" She shuddered. "I think I'm from something tremendously *bad*. My lineage. My coven . . ."

It wasn't the winter air that set my very bones on edge.

"And then, even worse than being unskilled or being unstable, I'm too scared to practice. So I'm a failure and a *coward*."

"No, no," I said, though I knew it was terribly unhelpful. I crawled across the floor and looped my arms around her neck, pulling her close.

"And I can't tell Briar," she said through her tears into my shoulder. "Because it's her coven, too. I know she already knows. She's holding back in our lessons. I can feel it."

I didn't know what to say that would help her. How to offer guidance on a system of beliefs she'd had about herself since childhood. Or what advice to offer on her magic and its origin, ominous or otherwise. "Will you please join us for dinner?" I said in the end. "I don't think isolation is helping anything."

"Really?" she sniffed. "I think it's doing wonders."

My lips twitched with a weak smile as I pulled Mari closer, feeling her tears slide down the back of my shirt, quiet as a prayer in the dead of night.

34

ARWEN

Kane's private dining quarters were surely designed for hosting dignitaries, plotting conquests, or impressing royals with masterfully sliced garnishes, not ale spewed from Ryder's nose in an uproarious fit of laughter—yet our motley group was absolutely defiling the stately room.

Hot buttered rum spilled across the polished wood as I reached for Kane's arm in hysterics, gripping it to keep from falling out of my chair at the sight. I fished for a napkin to mop up the mess through my tearing eyes.

Barney cackled alongside my brother, pressing his mouth to the crook of his elbow to make sure he didn't suffer a similar fate.

"Suffice to say," Briar continued, smirking, "it was the last time a peddler tried to sell me 'witches' brew.'"

Kane raised his mug to cover the grin tugging at his dimpled cheek. His shoulders were relaxed. His eyes crinkling.

We'd needed this. All of us. The Quartz of Rose had been a loss on every front. Failing to secure Ethera's army, Mari's setback, and of course, Aleksander . . .

I'd asked Kane this morning, curled in his arms, what he thought of Aleksander and Ethera's blood oath. If he had any knowledge what their agreement all those decades ago might mean for us if we were to somehow bear a child. Kane only told me he'd have his spies travel to Rose when this was all over and uncover what they could. I knew he thought it was useless now. He'd never allow us to have a child in a world his father still lived in. And once Lazarus was gone . . .

To stave off tears before breakfast I'd then asked how his generals were feeling about laying siege to Solaris without first hearing from Hart or Amelia—clearly they hadn't been able to secure the blade.

Kane had said if Briar could fix Mari's magic, maybe we'd wait another few days—four at the most—and try to portal to Hart's enclave first and see if he had news. But it had been three weeks since we'd blown Lazarus's lighte reserves. Surely he would be ready for war soon. Either way, we both knew time was running out.

I'd only wished Mari would have joined us tonight. Only wished she could have—

The mahogany doors peeled open and I turned in my seat, expecting another round of warm rum and fizzy ale. A shock of curled red hair filed in instead, bringing a fresh grin to my cheeks.

"You came." I almost sang the words.

Mari only nodded, a little shyly, and walked past my side of the table to take the last empty seat next to Griffin.

I might have gasped when he peered up at her with those usually unfeeling pale green eyes and said, "Hello, Mari." And then, swallowing, "You look very well."

Her answering grin was faint, but warmed my heart all the same.

Since our return, I'd caught Griffin not once but *twice* strolling past the woodcutter's cottage where Mari and her father lived. I was sure he'd made his way up to the library daily, hoping she'd found solace in between her favorite stacks. And now she was seated beside him—the commander practically glowed.

The jovial conversation and rich spirit continued to flow, and while Mari hadn't laughed yet, I did catch a smirk working its way across her face as Dagan regaled us with a story about finding her hiding under his counter in the apothecary when she was six.

"I told the kids hunting for her that I'd transformed Mari into a newt." Dagan's eyes lit with the memory. "And if they didn't bolt, they'd be next."

Apparently Dagan had known for years that the entire keep thought he was a wizard and simply chose not to correct anyone. Everything I learned about the man made me love him more.

"I wish I'd been there," Briar lilted. "I would have made good on such a promise." Her eyes simmered on Mari's warming cheeks. "Nobody harasses our little witch."

"Well," Mari said, her voice still a bit small. "About half the castle did. I could write you an essay on how too much free time in an army stronghold with no role models other than burly soldiers can turn little boys into monsters."

"Poor Red." Ryder hummed. "Too brainy and cute. The boys had no idea what to do with themselves."

I fought the urge to roll my eyes. I had no doubt Ryder and Halden would have aided the little creeps in filling Mari's lunch pail with snails.

"If I'd been there," Ryder continued, "I bet we could have taken them."

Griffin wasn't smiling. "If I'd been there, they'd have been butchered."

Mari's eyes went wide as she peered up at him. Ironically, outside of his armor Griffin looked a little stiff. Like a lion in a dress suit, attempting to sip from a chalice without crushing it.

Barney's eyes might have gone even wider. "These were six-year-olds."

"I said what I said," Griffin replied.

"Is that how you first met?" I asked Dagan. "When you found her under there?"

Dagan nodded, sipping his wine. "Quite the first impression."

"Dagan asked me to dance with him when we first met," Briar said from across the table. "Do you remember? You looked very handsome in that velvet jacket."

Dagan loosed a wry smile as he chewed. But there was something a little somber wending through his eyes at the memory, too.

I shot a sidelong glance at Kane, who only listened gently, as if he'd heard the story before.

"At the Lumerian Solstice." Briar smiled. "He'd been the seventh man to ask, but the first one I said yes to."

I couldn't help myself. "You were *courting* Briar?"

"No," Dagan said around a bite of meat. "I was foolishly trying to make someone jealous."

"Who?" Mari asked, her russet eyes lighting. Nothing—truly, *nothing*—would ever curb Mari's ravenous curiosity.

Dagan took another sip of wine. "My wife."

The air left my lungs in one single breath. Kane entwined his hand in mine.

"Of course," Dagan said down to his dinner, "she wasn't my wife at the time. I'd only hoped."

Dagan never spoke of his wife or infant daughter, both of whom had been killed by Lazarus. The memory sent my dinner crawling back up my throat and I reached for a glass of cool water.

Briar saved us all the same train of thought by adding, "I might've fallen in love had you not been a little young for me." Her violet eyes twinkled.

I breathed out a quiet laugh as Ryder and Barney both leaned imperceptibly toward her. Briar tucked a pitch-black slice of hair behind her ear demurely.

"And yet," Kane drawled, questioning eyes on the sorceress, "you apparently *danced* quite a bit with the young rebel king, Hart Renwick."

Despite her dry laugh, I knew my cheeks had gone red. I wasn't even sure why. Briar didn't strike me as a woman who had been embarrassed once in her life.

"He's only fifty years younger than you two." She motioned to Kane and Griffin. "And very charming."

Hart's dazzling smile popped into my mind. "He seems a bit of a . . ."

"Whore?" Kane offered.

"I was going to say *free spirit*."

"He is," Briar agreed. "Both. I wonder how he'll take his impending nuptials."

"He's betrothed?" I asked. "To who?"

Griffin made a gruff noise as Kane cringed, leaning back in his chair. "It was the only way Citrine would grant us refuge back in Azurine. I promised Isolde and Broderick I'd wed their daughter, Sera, to whomever takes the Lumerian throne."

Meat practically lodged itself in my esophagus and I coughed wildly. "You promised him to *Fedrik's sister*? That meek girl who's clearly still hung up on you?"

Kane shrugged. "Perhaps she has a type?"

"What—gorgeous, power-hungry womanizers with swoopy hair and a sideways grin?"

Kane pinned me with a rakish smile. "I was going to say *kings*."

"What does swoopy hair consist of?" Ryder asked, downing his ale.

As Barney pointed to Kane's dark chin-length locks and tried to mime how he would rake his hand through it from time to time, Kane returned to our game. "When I first met Griffin, he punched me for a butterscotch." My eyes darted to him, and Kane added, "We were four."

I snorted into my wineglass. I loved these stories. The links between us all—how this family of sorts was held together through memory and history and laughter.

And that, I realized, was what this was. Somehow, despite all the odds that stood before us, all the pain and suffering we'd endured, this was my family. And as with Leigh or Ryder, I'd do anything for the people sitting around this table.

Though the knowledge fed my soul, it also chilled my blood. It was a weakness, to know I'd give anything to keep every person seated here tonight alive tomorrow.

"When I first met Griffin," Mari said, mood brightened by wine and company, "he was looking for a book in the library on stonework. He told me his quarters in Shadowhold were too close to *all the people*, and he intended to build himself a cottage, like a mumbling bearded recluse."

"Yeah, yeah." Griffin shook his head. "Wish I'd never climbed those Gods-forsaken stairs."

He said it playfully, and we all laughed, and the conversation continued—Ryder ruminating on the first time he met Kane and knew the Onyx king was gone for his sister; Kane recalling his first encounter with Dagan, when he was the only mortal kingsguard in Solaris and still bested half the regiment.

But I couldn't tear my eyes from the rapidly declining situation to my right. Mari's cheeks had pinkened—even the tips of her ears had gone red.

Griffin turned his entire body toward her, uninterested in the rest of the dining room. "Witch, that is not what I—"

"No, it's fine." Mari kept her eyes on her napkin. She folded it twice in her lap.

"*Mari,*" Griffin mumbled to her. "I didn't mean—"

But whatever else he'd hoped to clear up was lost with the slamming open of the dining room doors.

I knew I was friends with too many soldiers because in an instant Kane, Griffin, Barney, and Dagan were all on their feet, lighte and swords shining, plates and wineglasses jumping with their movements.

"Help! Please—" Leigh was repeating as she dragged Beth inside. "I don't know what to . . . What's happening to her?"

Beth was convulsing, shaggy brown hair rustling with her movements, eyes glazed over as her little body shook with tremors.

Briar rushed to her at the same time I did. Immediately my lighte knew she wasn't seizing. At least, not for any medical reason.

"She's having a vision," Briar said, hushed.

Barney peered over the table. "What can be done?"

"Nothing." Briar helped Leigh and me lay Beth on her side. "We must let it pass."

As she spoke, the jolting slowed and Beth's bloodshot eyes blinked open. My selfish, twisted heart hammered.

Please not the deal. Not the deal—

It had kept me up more nights than I could count. Beth's harrowing promise: *"You'll have to make the deal. When the time comes, you'll have to."* She'd sworn my face would be wet with tears, and Kane's hands coated in blood. I looked to Kane's clear palms now, braced on the table, and was soothed.

Leigh brought Beth a glass of water and she sat up to sip it slowly.

"What did you see?" Briar asked when the little seer had regained her composure.

Beth took in the crowded dining room. The half-melted candles. The spread of steak and cloverbread rolls and rum. She swallowed twice and I debated telling everyone to leave so she wouldn't have to speak before them all.

But then she said, "Lazarus and his witch . . ."

"Octavia," I supplied, though the name was like mold growing over my tongue.

"They've cast some kind of spell. Or, they will, soon."

"What spell?" Briar asked.

"Lumera. The Fae Realm—if Lazarus dies in battle it will be sealed shut. He's tethered his own lighte to the realm itself to keep it from collapsing. If he is killed . . ."

Horror threatened to topple me like a lone ship on a windswept sea. I cut my eyes back to Kane, who was still standing in place at the dining table. His glare gave nothing away as he listened.

"If he is killed," Beth continued, Leigh holding her hand tightly, "the roads and seas that lead to Evendell—the *entire* channel—will crumble . . . The skies themselves will fall. There will be no way in or out of the realm."

"And all those people," I found myself saying.

"They will spend eternity trapped there."

In that withering realm. I shook my head.

We could not take any more terrible news. *I* couldn't.

"Can the realm be saved somehow?" Leigh asked her friend.

Beth shook her head. "I don't know. I only know what I saw."

"With time," Kane said. "It can be restored with time. We'd need to move at least a third of the Fae population here, to Evendell. Right now there are too many resources being used at once."

"What about the portals?" Mari tried from the table. "If we kill Lazarus, can the realm still be accessed by portal?"

"Portals are magic," Briar weighed. "They aren't tied to the lighte that built the channel."

I held Briar's violet eyes. "That's good, right?"

"But there are very few witches alive who can open portals between realms. Even I have struggled. Sometimes an entire coven can, if they're incredibly strong. I only know of one."

The Antler coven. Valery's family.

Octavia. And Briar.

Briar could do it.

"We need to open one tonight. Begin to get people out," I said to her, and to Kane.

But Briar shook her head. "Lazarus's men will be on us immediately. They monitor the most populated cities. If we were to try to funnel people out of them . . ."

"The war will begin before we're ready," Kane said.

"So what do we do?" Griffin finally asked, eyes steadfast on his friend. His king.

"We can't just win by killing him anymore," Kane managed. "Now we have to win on our own terms."

When none of us said anything—Ryder, Mari, even Dagan—silenced by the grim reality expanding before us, Kane continued.

"We beat his army. We defeat Amber and Garnet, too. We end his life without losing our manpower or our witches. Then we free the innocents of Lumera, work with Hart, and start a new era here in Evendell: Fae and mortal alike, living as one. We'll fight like all the lives in all the realms depend on it, because they do." Illuminated by the guttering candelabra above and muted stained-glass lamps, Kane pushed his broad shoulders back and shook his head.

"We can't approach this war with this . . . fear that's seized us any longer. We have to fight *for something*." Kane's eyes found mine and my heart opened up just a little. "We'll fight armed with hope. Hope for something better than just his death. And when that hope feels out of reach . . ." Kane studied the quiet, dimly lit dining room. All the faces latched on to his every word. Briar's small smile. Dagan's crinkled eyes, Leigh's youthful ones. All the age and experience and loss and fear and joy and love that we shared, collectively. "We rely on one another.

"Lazarus has never had real allies. For too long I thought that coldness was his strength. But each of you . . . you've shown me what it means to fight with more than vengeance. That nobody can triumph alone. That's why Lazarus won't win." Kane looked back down to me. "And why we must."

35

⟡

ARWEN

WATER SLOSHED OVER THE LIP OF THE TUB AS I LEANED back into Kane's chest. I reached for a towel to blot the sudsy puddle on the stone floor, but Kane pulled me back.

"Leave it," he ordered gently, drawing me into him as more water spilled and more steam curled through our washroom. We sighed in unison as my back met his muscled torso, his powerful thighs spread around me.

"It had been such a nice dinner," I said quietly.

Kane hummed his agreement, stroking idle fingers through my wet hair. The water was just shy of too hot, and each muscle in my body relaxed with the generous feel of it.

Two fat waxy candles lit our bath in dim violet light, flickering from the moisture in the air. That flicker reflected the swirling, soapy water against dark walls. Lavender and jasmine soap filled my nose. Moonlight filtered in from the closed window, dulled by snowfall, and cast Kane's long legs in silver slants.

"I'm sorry," he said after a long while, that broad hand still moving softly through my hair and at my temples. I hadn't realized I'd closed my eyes.

"What for?" I murmured.

"Everything. That we have so little time together. So little joy. Not even one dinner."

My throat tightened and I shut my eyes tighter. "Let's feel joy right now."

Kane hummed again.

In this moment, we were together. Not joyful, admittedly, but we had some sort of resigned peace shared between us. A bare, honest intimacy.

We had to appreciate these moments before they were snatched from our grasp. It was like Kane had said—the love we all shared was what made us strong. We couldn't let moments like these pass us by when we had so few left. I fished through the water for Kane's hand and threaded it through my own, placing it atop my chest.

Kane's thumb rubbed lazily across my skin until he grazed my nipple. The bud tightened with the simple, tranquil touch.

"So," Kane said, his voice a little devious. "You think Hart Renwick is gorgeous?"

I barked out a laugh. Clearly, the word had been lingering around in his mind all evening. "Did I say gorgeous?"

Kane's thumb continued its soft strokes. His other hand skated casually down my arm, pebbling the flesh despite being submerged in hot water. His cock hardened, pressing against my back. "You did."

"Look who's jealous now," I purred, letting my fingers drift across his thighs, grazing the fine hairs there.

"Yes." I could hear the unapologetic envy in that deep voice. "And you've all but conquered that, haven't you?"

It was true—that voice in my head that told me I wasn't enough had become more of a pest than a mantra. "Maybe I should be rewarded," I said, arching my body up so that his fingers floated closer to my stomach.

"Perhaps so." His voice did riotous things to me. "What is it you'd like, bird?"

His fingers traced across my inner thighs, along my lips and my entrance, but no matter how I spread my legs, how I arched up into him, he avoided any meaningful contact.

I sighed, my fingernails scraping against his thigh in frustration.

He hummed in satisfaction, grazing a thumb across that sensitive bundle of nerves and eliciting a choked breath from me. "How will I know if you don't tell me . . ."

Kane pressed a single finger firmly between my legs. When he found proof of my near-painful desire, even in the water, he growled against my neck and held my breast in his other hand, squeezing softly until I whimpered. "And yet, you're terribly needy, aren't you?"

My head nearly jerked into Kane's chin with my nod. The heat from the water, the flush of my cheeks—I was feverish with how badly I wanted him.

Kane pressed his finger inside just an inch. Less than that.

And I *mewled*.

He chuckled, his cock now throbbing against my spine. "Yeah?"

I whined plaintively in answer.

He withdrew his finger and resumed his indolent tracing across my swollen lips, watching as I writhed.

It was decadent, the leisure. But my skin was on fire and I was losing my mind. "Please," I practically slurred.

Through my wetness and the warm bathwater, he relented,

reaching the spot I needed so, so desperately. I pitched upward, splashing us both, and he growled in satisfaction, pinching the nub lightly. When I moaned, Kane's cock twitched behind me.

"Kane," I whined, squirming.

"All right, all right." He began a slow, excruciating massage between his thumb and forefinger of that one overly sensitive spot. I convulsed and cried out, frantically building toward a climax I knew would be the end of my sanity. Stars danced across my vision. My limbs sparkled. My body like a weightless cloud in the water, forcing Kane to heft me up him just a little so he could use one hand to hold me open and run the other through my plump, aching core.

"You are breathtaking," he murmured.

I couldn't even breathe, let alone respond. He dipped a finger inside me, the other hand continuing its gentle assault at the apex of my thighs.

And then he curled that finger, pressing against the spot that so often led to my unraveling. Acute pleasure coiled tight in my core and I clawed at the porcelain tub.

"Kane, *Kane*," I babbled. "Oh, *Stones*, Kane—"

"Shh," he murmured. "You're all right."

I wasn't—I couldn't take much more.

But Kane only ran his nose along the shell of my ear and the side of my neck. Licking and sucking and murmuring how beautiful I looked spread open for him like this, how tight, and wet, and warm. How mesmerizing my breasts were, how my face, pinched in near agony awaiting release would fuel his fantasies for years to come.

But my bones had turned to scalding liquid. I was surely melting in his arms.

I must have said as much because Kane's throaty laugh accompanied his eventual acquiescence. Freeing himself of restraint, Kane pushed a second finger inside me until I was so full of him, stretched so tightly around his long, broad fingers, I released a purely animal groan that sent Kane swearing and grinding himself, *straining* against my back as I moved with his fingers, pliant and aching and, all the while, that other hand circling rhythmically, delivering glorious pressure—

Bright colors burst across my vision. Water sloshed from the tub. I could barely contain the ragged, wanton screams—it was enough to keep myself from levitating out of the bath completely, or shooting firelighte out of my fingertips and burning the keep to the ground.

By the time I could breathe again Kane was nearly panting himself.

One of his hands had left my body to grasp the porcelain of the tub. Tiny fissures spider-webbed down the sides where his grip held firm. He had . . . cracked it. He'd *cracked* our tub. And his cock—

Thick, taut, and painfully hard. I sat up and Kane groaned with the lack of contact.

"Stand," I told him.

Kane's lust-dazed face—those flushed, sharp cheekbones and near-feral silver eyes—contorted in confusion.

I nodded, letting the provocative ideas filtering through my mind color my expression.

He stood inside the tub, sending water careening in waves like a creature of the sea. So large, so powerful. I cast my eyes up at his controlled, possessive, thoroughly *male* expression. A little smug as he towered over me—

My core heated again. It was getting ridiculous—would I never be rid of this *need* for him? Kane's erection was long and painfully hard, and my mouth watered with anticipation.

He grunted as I knelt before him. Now that he was standing, the water barely covered my navel, and the cool air tightened my nipples.

"Arwen." His voice was a little guttural. "You don't have to."

It was wild to me that after everything, he still said this every time. As if his pleasure was less important than mine. Or that this act, this giving of myself to him, was somehow more than he deserved.

I ignored him, wrapping my hands around his thick length. He weaved his fingers through my wet hair, and I worked him over with my hand, reveling in his hoarse groans. His skin was soft from the bathwater, and warm in contrast to the slight, pleasant chill of the washroom.

I pumped him slower, harder, until the head of his cock had begun to drip and his ab muscles were contracting.

"Put me in your mouth," he said, as if the words had seized control. "Please," he added quickly and with a low groan, his fingers tightening along my scalp and down my neck. And then he said it again on a single broken breath.

Overwhelming pride coursed through me and I moaned a little as I pressed his head against my tongue, continuing to stroke him with both my hands.

Kane's eyes shuttered as he swore. I suckled him until his hips twitched—his need was my fuel, that undercurrent of barely tethered dominance lighting me up from the inside like a lantern in the dark.

I knew what swirled inside the basest parts of him. That primal craving to hold me still and thrust into my mouth and make a mess all over me. And yet there he stood, solid as a mighty oak, grinding his jaw, fisting his hands as gently as he could, *enduring* whatever I desired to give him, at whatever pace I chose. I knew he would have stood there and allowed me to lick him slowly, *mercilessly*, for hours and hours and hours on end.

I opened my mouth and enveloped his hardness as best I could. He was thick and long, and I had found through trial and error the other night that if I brought him too far back into my throat I would gag and cough and my cheeks would turn a very unsensual shade of pink as little beaded tears collected in my eyes. Kane had withdrawn himself from me with such haste I'd nearly fallen into his abdomen from my position bent over him in bed. He'd cursed softly and wiped the tears from my eyes with a look of such regret my heart had twisted nearly in two.

I'd asked him to let me try again but he insisted it was his turn and had spent the rest of the night making me sob through crest after crest of merciless pleasure on his tongue until finally, when I was loose and pliant and delirious, he'd nudged inside of me and finished within seconds.

I wanted to do better this time. I opened my mouth wider, and allowed him to guide me. To work my jaw and chin around his fullness. I swallowed and licked as he grunted. Moaned when he brushed a reverent thumb across my full, wet lips stretched around his heft.

Our eyes locked. His were a little pained. "Can I—? Down your throat?"

We'd never made it this far. Always in too much haste to knot ourselves together. Needy to become one shared soul. I nodded, his words wringing a slight, unexpected whimper from me. As if that was all it took, Kane's thrusts picked up speed and he groaned loudly, his voice echoing off the mirror and wet stone floor of the washroom.

He spurted into my mouth and I hummed with the masculine taste. I swallowed his release eagerly, and continued to suck him until he purred, "Easy, easy," and withdrew himself from between my lips.

When our gazes met, he released a breath of such deep satisfaction my eyes burned. Sinking slowly back into the water, he brought my bruised lips to his. The kiss was soft as he brought me back between his open legs and under the warm water.

Satiated and buoyant, I relaxed in Kane's arms. The water softened the sharp edges of desire that had built back up inside me while I'd pleasured him.

Night blossomed outside. Owls hooted, crickets chirped.

A loud knock snapped my eyes open and I turned back to Kane, a little dazed. I wasn't sure how long had passed.

"I'll go," he murmured.

I didn't argue as he stood from the tub with a mighty push and surged water all over the floor. I also didn't hesitate to admire his perfect round backside as he reached for a towel. Those lean yet powerful hamstrings, sculpted calves, tan, boyish feet . . . He was a masterpiece.

"Always staring." His laugh was rough as he wrapped the fabric low around his waist and slipped out the washroom door.

I only heard muffled murmurs, but when Kane poked his head back inside his mood had changed slightly. Not quite dampened but . . .

"I'm needed by Eardley. Shouldn't be long. Keep the water warm for me?"

"I'll come, too," I said, moving to stand.

"No," he said with more urgency than I expected. "No need."

Despite a nagging feeling in my gut, I nodded. Kane and I didn't keep secrets anymore. If he needed me to come with him, he would have said so.

The door snicked shut and then I was alone.

~⚬~

THE WATER HAD TURNED LUKEWARM, RESULTING IN GOOSE-flesh across my arms and thighs. And my heart was pounding awkwardly. Not panic, exactly. But . . . I wasn't calm.

He'd been gone too long.

I stood from the bath and dressed quickly in a silky golden nightgown.

And then, without really thinking, threw on my now-beloved fox fur and leather boots and hurried into the hallway.

My palms began to itch with unease.

"Is the king still with Eardley?" I asked the two guards on duty outside our quarters.

"I haven't seen him, Lady Arwen," one said, kind enough not to make a face at my bizarre clothing.

"Not in a while," the other confirmed.

Calm down. If something were wrong, the whole castle would know it.

And it was true. It had to be almost midnight, and the castle was quiet. If someone had come for him, I'd hear the thunder of his wings, the torrent of soldiers running, the screech of Griffin's shifted form . . .

Right?

I sped through the candlelit hall, that shred of doubt driving me faster and faster. Past the locked throne room doors and down that sprawling stone staircase. Along the hallway filled with statues, past those shadowed, haunting enclaves. Past shimmering cobwebs and sturdy wrought iron and delicate, snow-flecked stained glass.

Barney was walking out of the great hall right as I ran by, a loaf of cloverbread in one hand, mug of something warm and steaming in the other.

"Where is Kane?" I asked, my voice a whip through the silent night.

Barney studied me, hesitant to say anything at all.

"Barney."

"He should be in the gardens." Something like sympathy laced his words, but I was running again before I could ask. My mind had flashed to the last time Barney told me the same.

When Kane had been planning to leave.

Oh, Stones.

Barney's face. He'd looked so . . . guilty.

Kane would not be so moronic as to attempt some kind of suicide mission . . . Would he?

Don't you dare leave me, my brain begged, despite all logic that told me nothing was wrong. Barney wasn't scared. No guards appeared concerned . . .

So why was I sprinting like my very life depended on it?

I couldn't answer myself as I raced across darkened halls, trying my best not to cry, not to crumble at the thought of searching this entire keep and finding it empty of him. Hurtling over stairs and slipping under railings, I reached the heavy doors and nearly screamed as I waited for the guards to wrench them open for me.

Panting, I careened out into the ice-cold night, the falling snow harsh against my still-damp skin and wet hair. I listened to the acute silence—even as the barracks were noisy with soldiers' laughter and merriment—it was the absence of *his* voice. His footsteps. That was silence to me.

My hands shook.

Don't do this, Kane. Do not do this.

I could barely see the moon through the clouds and the thick trees that rose overhead. I ran through the courtyards and fields for those gloomy, ethereal flowers.

Barreling, sprinting, lungs in my throat—

And stopped short, my heart stilling, too.

To find the entire garden—every hedge and arch and pathway—illuminated in twinkling, flickering firelight.

Trees adorned with hanging glass bulbs that glowed. Verdant, despite the season. Tiny candles placed around the gazebos and verandas. Bouquets of flowers that I knew for certain did not bloom in the winter, tinged with glittering magic. Lilies—those black, spindly ones that grew only here, tied beside the white ones Kane had brought to Onyx just for me—as well as roses and orchids, pansies and lilacs. Fragrant lavender and night-blooming jasmine wreathed the central arch, moonlight and all that dainty, flickering fire casting the curved structure in an otherworldly glow. Like the sun, risen in the dead of night.

And below it, Kane.

Lighting a few lingering candles.

"What . . ." I had no words. I was still catching my breath when emotion closed my throat completely.

"I thought you'd still be bathing. I was about to send for you," he said in that low, sensual voice before turning to face me. His brows knit together. "Did you run here?"

I responded only with, "This is . . . for me?"

"Who else?" He placed the final candle along the brick beneath his feet. "Everything . . . it's all for you."

My feet carried me to him without thought until I was grasping his hands in mine. Both were chilled from snow, but I hadn't even noticed until I saw the little flakes decorate his thick brows.

"Are you cold?"

I shook my head. "Kane, what is all this?"

With no fanfare or theatrics, Kane knelt on one knee before me and said, "You deserve far more. You deserve a long life and children if you'd like them and days upon days without fear. Acres of flowers and all the cloverbread that can be baked."

A quiet, tearful laugh tumbled out of me.

"It kills me, bird, that I cannot promise you any of it. All I can promise you is myself—my love, my respect, my devotion—every day that we have together, and every day that exists beyond then." Kane's eyes gleamed. "In life, in death, my soul is yours. Arwen, will you be my wife?"

My chest expanded. I could hardly breathe past the swell of it.

"I love you," I whispered.

"Is that a yes?" he whispered back, roguish smile melting my heart.

I nodded vigorously.

Kane's mouth was on mine faster than I'd seen him stand. His warm lips enveloped me, and I pulled myself against him so tightly I felt the breath leave his lungs in a rush. His tongue licked against mine and I shivered.

I had barely pulled away, could still taste his breath as I uttered, "But . . ."

Kane's shoulders stilled beneath my hands. "But."

The words nearly doubled me over. "But aren't you afraid? Of what will come next? Aren't we . . ." I couldn't say *doomed* or *hopeless*. Not with all this beauty surrounding us and sparkling in his silver eyes.

He took my chilly hands in his and pulled me closer. His warm breath fanned over our interlocked fingertips. "I'm only afraid of being without you. In death. In life. It's all the same to me if we aren't together."

Before the tears could wreck me, I brought my lips up to his once more. Our kiss was even more hurried this time. Fiercer. More desperate. Tongues and teeth and breath.

"Inside?" he murmured into my lips.

"I'm not even cold anymore," I said, pressing my mouth under his ear and down the warm column of his neck. It was Kane's turn to shiver.

"That's not why . . ." He grunted before he could finish the words as my lips traveled along the center of his throat.

My blood heated instantly. "Yes," I mumbled. "Inside."

Kane released me, and like teenagers we raced through the iridescent, glittering snow back toward the keep.

36

KANE

"I WANT TO TRY SOMETHING," ARWEN BREATHED, AS I mouthed the soft silk of her nightdress over her stomach and ran my fingers down her slender, toned legs.

With great difficulty I lifted my mouth from her body and peered up at her. Her cheeks were still flushed from the winter snow. Rosy and feminine. Her nose a little red, too. She pushed stray hairs out of her face and I imagined what my signet ring would look like glinting on her left hand. The thought sent a near-predatory need to claim her skating across my bones.

"Mhm?" I crawled closer and trailed indulgent kisses across her warm collarbone. "My sweet wife." I brought my mouth down to her stomach, lifting the inhibiting dress up, yanking her thin cotton undergarments down—

"Kane." She laughed, weaving her hands through my hair. "Did you hear me?"

Gods, I love how she says my name . . .

"Kane?"

I sat up, a little rattled. A little ashamed. "Of course, yeah." I tried not to look at the way the strap of her nightdress had slipped and exposed her nipple. "What is it you want to try?"

Arwen shimmied up against the pillows and brought the thin silk strap back up, concealing her breast. I breathed more evenly.

"I've noticed you like to maintain control," she said. "When we're in bed. I think we should try the opposite."

I recoiled, examining her.

"Just once," she amended, as if concerned for *my* well-being.

But a sickening thought was clanging through my mind. *You've done things to her she hasn't liked. Demanded too much. Allowed your obsession with her to—*

"No, no, Kane—" Arwen grasped my hands in hers, her brows pulling together urgently at whatever was bare across my face. "Not for me. I love— I wouldn't change—" She shook her head. "I want to do this for *you*. I think you might find it . . . freeing."

"Sure," I said, a little weakly, the thought of forcing myself on her still acrid on my tongue. "Whatever you want, I'm game for."

Arwen brushed a gentle hand across my face and I closed my eyes with the touch.

"Lie down," she instructed.

I did so, and fluffed a pillow behind me to my comfort before spreading myself wide across the bed. My shirt had come off the minute we'd crashed into the bedroom, and my pants as well. I was bare save for my breeches.

Arwen's hair looked like caramel in the glimmer of soft candlelight. She moved to sit on her knees between my legs and ran her fingers over my thighs tortuously slowly. When she drifted a single finger across my low waist, I bucked up toward her.

She released a devious smile—a flash of white in the night-covered room. "Must I tether you to this bed, my king?"

Gods have mercy. "I'll be good."

Arwen seated herself more comfortably between my legs and brought her hand up to her breast. My cock tensed as she squeezed, her cheeks flushing, that evil little strap slipping down her shoulder once more. Her hand was so small, cupping herself. So delicate as she rubbed her own nipple softly. I made a low noise I didn't recognize.

My mind blanked as she brought her other hand underneath the hem of the silky fabric. I could only imagine how her fingers brushed between her legs.

I lay there helplessly as she circled in no rush at all, her breaths a little ragged. The only contact her folded legs between my own. Her eyes had shut, her beautiful lips parted, and I could *hear* the sound of her arousal. The wet, slick noises as she played with herself for me. I needed to drag my tongue across that wetness more than I needed my heart to keep beating.

And the fucking useless nightdress—I'd shred it with my teeth.

"Take it off," I said roughly.

"You're not supposed to be making demands," Arwen said, eyes fluttering open.

"I'm a little beside myself." An attempt at a joke, but it came out all too sober.

Arwen, flushed by her own ministrations, obliged, pulling the silk fabric up and over her head.

And the view . . . Exquisite. On her knees, fully bare, those heaving breasts pointed and full. Flushed cheeks and ripe, ready center glistening as she spread her legs wider for me. Arwen watched me study her, my breath husky and uneven.

My restraint was eroding. My erection painful and pleading for some relief. I was lightheaded, unable to bear another minute, another *second,* when I could see clearly her own need dripping down her smooth thighs.

You need to wind down. You are practically hissing your breaths, you lascivious bastard.

As if she could tell the pain I was in, Arwen pulled me free of my breeches and my cock sprang forth, swollen and heavy and beading moisture from the head.

"So beautiful," she murmured, appraising me.

"You have no idea," I said, watching her wet, round lips part and her tongue swipe across them.

My body twitched with ruinous need, the desire, and the difficulty of staying still, oscillating across me. Arwen didn't seem to care. She parted herself with one hand and ran her now-soaking fingers across that spot she craved. A soft moan slipped from her lips.

The sound that came out of me was crude. Debased. My mind—*empty* as she trailed her hand lower and slid a finger inside herself.

"Dear Gods," I swore.

Arwen drew the finger out and dipped it back in, wetness clinging to her hand. My mouth watered. "Please," I breathed. "I need to taste you."

All control, all dignity abandoned me—I'd take a beating twice over to lick her clean.

She only withdrew her finger again, and after a moment of thought, leaned forward to bring the hand to me. Her slickness shone on her fingers in the candlelight, her eyes molten and dark with pleasure.

My mind fragmented. I couldn't think past my pulse as it hammered. "May I?"

Arwen only nodded, squirming a bit at the unquenched desire I knew ached between her legs.

Possessive, savage need sent my cock throbbing as I wrapped my lips around her delicate, silken finger and sucked. Her heady taste altered something in my body. I might have been groaning as I held her dainty hand and shoved it deeper into my mouth, licking indecently between her fingers. If she choked me with them I'd probably come.

Arwen nearly lost herself in her moan. She withdrew her fingers and placed a single soft kiss against my sternum. My fists swallowed as much bedsheet as they could muster. The yearning to touch her again was more powerful than anything . . . I couldn't take much more of this . . . I'd erupt from my own body soon. I needed to douse myself in her.

Light honeysuckle filled my nose and my mouth watered as she licked down my chest, stopping at my hip bone to drag her teeth across my low abdomen. Her hair fell across my cock, featherlight.

"Cruelty . . . this is cruelty."

My skin was too tight on my body. My heart careening toward some kind of combustion.

"Is it?" She hummed, her tongue licking up and down the inside of my thighs. "I don't think so . . ."

I couldn't form words as Arwen climbed atop me and wrapped her hand around my cock to guide me into her.

My groan was as rough as gravel. Breathless, from both the sight of her, parting as she pushed my aching length inside, and the sensation. Perfect, silken, mind-melting tightness gripped me.

It might have ended with Arwen's sweet whimper. The carnal noise as she rocked her hips—that alone might have been enough to finish this little game and send me up and on top of her, flipping her to her back and pounding into her body like a madman. Drawing climax after climax from her, coaxing her through the savage waiting, through the begging, through the *need* . . .

But she had asked for this. And I would not be selfish with her.

So I surrendered, shutting my eyes, allowing her to move herself at whatever pace she wanted. Arwen rode me slowly, her warm slickness enveloping me. Each arch upward and lowering down, delicious and maddening and more than I could stand.

She quickened her pace. Milking me, whining a bit as she ground herself closer. I'd memorized enough of her perfect noises to know she was minutes from climax. She leaned forward, gripping my arms, fingernails jutting into my biceps, her face inches from my own, and met my gaze.

It was moments like that—the mere latching of her olive eyes onto mine almost sending me over the edge—in which I realized how utterly at this woman's mercy I was. She could have told me to throw myself off our balcony. I would have been plummeting through winter air before she'd finished the command.

The thought at one time might've terrified me. The powerlessness of loving someone with all that I had and then some. I loved Arwen with all of myself, and then all the things I hoped to be, too. But tonight, that love only made me feel rooted. Tethered to someone. Bound to them, and bound to this life because of it.

And it was that connection—the way our souls had at some point become one shared life—that racked through my bones and sang in my blood as her hot breath fanned over my mouth. As I licked her lips slowly—the taste of them like honey and sunlight. Paradise and my thorough undoing. And then I couldn't resist any longer.

I lifted my head and angled my mouth against hers. Wild and inelegant, our lips twined, my hands still fisted in the sheets, which I'd ripped clean through at some point—

"You can—" she choked out. "You can touch me, now. If you want—"

Thank the fucking Gods.

My hands shot to her body, her soft skin like warmth incarnate after eons of brutal winter. I bucked up into her—barreling, frenzied—I couldn't feel enough of her. Her hips, her breasts, her hands, grasping clumsily for my own, her cheeks and delicate chin and the spot between her legs that I circled and rolled and—

As if she hadn't realized it was happening, Arwen's climax tore through her. Ruthless contractions pulled her innermost muscles tight. She sobbed, racked by pleasure, full of me and whimpering my name in breathy, agonized, pretty little moans—

I came with a vicious roar, my hands full of Arwen's soft flesh and long hair. Thrusting up as white-hot, exquisite ecstasy spun up my spine and down my legs, spurting out of me and into her.

Arwen collapsed on top of me, heaving.

Reduced to nothing but panting breaths, I tried to re-form my fractured mind around the eternity of pleasure that had enveloped me.

After a long while, Arwen said, "Did you like it?"

"Very much so."

I could almost hear her grin, and found myself doing the same.

We had only slept together a handful of times—one of the greatest tragedies known to man—and yet in such a brief period, she'd come to understand something so deeply personal about myself, I hadn't even known it. And I'd been bedding women this way for years. "You're a perceptive little bird, aren't you?"

Arwen nodded against my chest and I laughed.

"Did *you* like it?" I asked.

"Yes," she admitted. "Not every time. Mostly I like when you . . ."

Heat simmered in my veins. "When I what?" I could hear the growl already taking root in my voice. I was useless around this woman.

"You know. When you *handle* me."

I barked a laugh. "Good Gods, I hope that's not what it is I'm doing."

"But," she said, "I did like it. It was empowering."

"You are always powerful."

Arwen nodded noncommittally against my chest.

"That thing you do, with your lighte . . ." The image of Arwen's bright white fire, blinding and scorching and nimble, soared through my mind.

"Sunfire," she murmured, and I knew her eyes were closed. "In my head I call it sunfire."

"It's not anything I've seen before."

"Really?"

"Really. That *sunfire* . . . it's just like you. Beautiful and dangerous. Soft but unbreakable. Strength and vulnerability in one." I ran my fingers tenderly along her back. "It makes sense that it's the embodiment of your lighte."

I was a lucky bastard. I'd fallen in love with a woman who opened up my mind in ways I'd never imagined. Who showed me how strength could be found in tenderness, or how the vulnerability of giving yourself over to someone could be a mighty, fortifying force. I'd fallen in love with a woman who was my friend. A light in pitch-darkness. A bird to guide me home.

Never mind that war was looming and our miserable fates were sealed and we'd already lost so much. Never mind that we might never truly be married. I was lucky just to be holding her tonight.

For a while she said nothing, only nuzzled her head closer to mine. Worming her way into the crease of my head and shoulder she called my nook. Eventually, I wondered if she'd fallen asleep.

Until she asked, "When should we be married?"

"Tonight?" I laughed faintly. "Tomorrow?"

Arwen rolled from my chest and onto her side. "You're right."

"I am?"

She sat up. "Tomorrow. Before we go back to Solaris. I want to live in this moment. Right now. Who knows what's coming . . . Like you said earlier, we deserve all the joy we can get these days."

"Did I say that?" It didn't sound like me.

"No," she said, undeterred. "But it's what you meant."

I grinned, basking in the soft glow of her positivity. "I love it in there."

Arwen's eyes narrowed. "Where?"

When I placed a finger between her brows, her bright smile lit the room like sunlight.

37

ARWEN

Mari hadn't said wearing black on my wedding day was a bad omen exactly, but she *had* brought me six different white dresses from her wardrobe, each with more detail than the last, until I physically couldn't see my way through all the lace and tulle.

Her focused expression and insistent hands, pushing eyelet lace at me like it was gospel, brightened the entire closet. It wouldn't be instantaneous, but Mari had already begun to find herself again, and I was grateful. I'd missed her spirit tremendously.

"I'm going to stick with this one," I told her. "P˙ase don't groan again."

"Fine." She sighed, propping herself against the only armoire not piled high with white chiffon. "I suppose it is *your* day."

I studied myself in the full-length mirror. My long chestnut hair, lightly curled and pulled back into my now well-worn onyx bow. The brightness in my eyes. Fullness in my cheeks. Strength in my bones and muscles. "I suppose it is."

As I looked down at the black tea-length dress I'd borrowed from Mari so long ago—the one I'd worn to Kane's forum—I couldn't deny how much I felt like *me*. It was the dress I'd worn when I'd first thought I might belong here.

Acorn's scampering sounded from Kane's attached study and I listened as he scurried into the bedroom. We glided from the large closet to greet him, his birdlike head nuzzling my palm for scratches.

"I can't believe you've befriended the beast," Mari said, though I could hear the smile in her voice.

"He's actually a big softie. *Aren't you?*"

The strix nuzzled into my legs and hummed happily.

Despite the slight apprehension she had around the creature, Mari looked sunny and luminous. Her cap-sleeved periwinkle gown had a sweetheart neckline that showed off the dusting of freckles along her collarbone, and the crepe fabric was light and easy, spilling along the floor as she walked.

Dagan surveyed us both, his embroidered, indigo tunic a welcome change from the swordsman's usual aged armor. But he hadn't matched the fine apparel with dress shoes, opting instead to keep his trusty scuffed boots on, which brought me a strange comfort.

"Ready?" he asked.

"I think so." I appraised myself. "How do I look?"

"I am rarely one for sentimentality, but . . ." Dagan cleared his throat. "Quite lovely."

Mari squealed with delight, Acorn mimicked the sound, and a grin tugged at my cheeks. "Thank you. Both."

"I have something for you," Dagan said quietly.

"A wedding gift!" Mari chimed.

I shot her a look—I got the feeling Dagan might scare easily.

The old swordsman only shook his head and pulled a creased

envelope from his pocket. I wondered if he didn't look a little embarrassed. "It's nothing fancy. Just a note."

"Thank you," I said, heart swelling with appreciation. My fingers slipped under the outer edge to tear it open, but Dagan's dry, cracked hands stilled my own. "No gifts yet. After the wedding."

"He's right," Mari added. "Another bad omen."

"Of course," I said, placing the letter on Kane's desk. "After, then."

Dagan offered a slight smile and tipped his elbow out for me to take. "Any nerves?"

And it might have been the first time I looked into Dagan's warm, wrinkled face—after months and months of so much fear and so little courage and about a thousand different variations of panic and anxiety—and shook my head. "None at all."

After making our way through a lively Shadowhold filled with children ringing bells and throwing rice, Mari, Dagan, and I made the hike up the mighty stairs to the temple, which put the library climb to shame.

Overhead, a decorated ceiling arched high and allowed for ample sunny winter light to filter in. A few thickly vined plants spilled from whitewashed ceramic pottery, and vibrant stained glass depicted all nine stones, none more prominently than the rich black onyx, which cast the room in a soft violet glow.

Between the pews, in time to the harp's poignant tune, Dagan walked me toward Kane.

And I thought then that maybe I'd always been walking toward Kane. Tethered to him in some way or another since the moment we'd met in that glade in Amber. When the most terrifying creature I'd ever seen was able to bring me comfort.

And when I couldn't walk to Kane, I'd climbed, fallen, crawled . . . I'd found my way back to him time and time again.

Kane hadn't dressed up for the wedding much, either. He faced me at the end of the aisle in simple, sophisticated trousers, his thorned crown, and a finely stitched white shirt, like the snow on the tree-tops, visible behind him from the temple's towering height. Kane didn't wear white too often, and I decided that was a misfortune for us all. The color enriched his hair to an otherworldly black—the embodiment of all colors, rather than the absence of them.

"You look . . ." Kane's words failed him and he cleared his throat.

This was the only kind of wedding I ever would have wanted. Dagan, standing beside us, no fuss or flourishes. Only our closest friends, highest-ranking generals, and few members of Kane's court in the pews. A single harp playing, a handful of lilies in my grasp—a crisp and clear morning, just for us.

And of course, I was already crying.

"Sweet bird," Kane soothed, brushing a thumb across my cheek.

"We come together today," Dagan began, sending the tittering crowd quiet and the harpist's soft melody fading away, "under the divine Stones of this great continent and before you all as witnesses, to join King Kane Ravenwood and Lady Arwen Lily Valondale in holy matrimony."

Despite his gruff tone and ever-present scowl, in another life Dagan would have made a wonderful minister. That side of him he fought so mightily—the one that was a patient teacher, a thoughtful advisor, that offered such valuable wisdom as often as crotchety barbs—it was the same side that had all the faces in the small, intimate room hanging on to his every word.

"Marriage is a partnership, a lifelong pact of trust, and an agreement to depend on each other while you navigate the often stormy seas of life. You have probably heard the word 'marriage' tethered to others like 'work,' 'commitment,' and 'sacrifice'—unfortunately, nobody knows that truth as well as these two."

Though surely Dagan wasn't joking, Kane's mouth quirked up in a half grin. I fought the urge to shake my head at him. Gallows humor until the end.

"And yet, they have found happiness in moments of despair, strength in each other's weaknesses, love when surrounded by violence. I've never seen two people have not only such a deep well of respect for each other, but also such *fun* together."

Dagan, espousing the virtues of *fun*? I narrowed my eyes at the old swordsman.

"A precious rarity," Dagan continued to the crowd, ignoring me, "in our somber world. A union such as this can only thrive when both individuals make the other stronger. In the case of Arwen and Kane, their union makes our entire realm stronger. Now, that is quite the marriage."

Kane squeezed my hand, his rings glinting in the soft pools of morning light.

"Without further ado, as I am old and my knees are already barking, let us get on with it. Kane, do you take Arwen as your wife, to love and to cherish, so long as you both shall live?"

The words held a different meaning today, for us, than they might have if our fate weren't decreed as it was. Had we not been staring into the gaping maw of a brutal war, a cursed prophecy, and a foe as impenetrable as Lazarus—and yet Kane answered with such a peaceful, "Indeed."

And when Dagan prompted me, I responded in kind.

Twin sniffles echoed against the cool stone and I knew them to be Barney and Mari, sharing one handkerchief between them both.

"Then under the Holy Stones above us, and before all who are assembled here, I am honored to pronounce you married. You may—"

Kane didn't wait for instruction. He leaned forward with catlike grace and swept me into a tasteful yet firm kiss. His lips soft as they held mine, his hands cradling my waist and neck, careful not to ruin my half-pinned-up hair nor my bow.

The cheers and hoots jostled me from the dizzying kiss and I released Kane, breathing a laugh onto his grinning mouth, inhaling his scent, that leather and cedar and masculine *Kane* smell that I could have bottled and sold for riches beyond measure.

"And," Dagan said, grinning himself, deepening the soft creases of his face, "your union sets forth another ceremony."

I lifted a brow in his direction, our friends and family quieting behind us. The harpist had begun her tune again—a less romantic one. Something a bit more ceremonial.

Dagan turned to fish something out from behind the large, dusty organ and returned with a glittering tiara.

Iridescent black gemstones—onyx itself, or maybe dark gray diamonds—had been shaped into a dainty array of flowers, adorned with clusters of pearls and silver leaves. A garden of sparkling obsidian that Dagan placed atop my head, saying softly, and more to me than anyone else, "For the rightful queen of Onyx Kingdom. May she wear it and be well."

Cheers of *"Hear, hear"* and *"Long live the queen"* echoed through the temple. Rays of unfiltered sunlight ricocheted off their smiling faces.

"Where did you find this?" I whispered to Kane, who had not stopped grinning at me since Dagan revealed the sparkling crown. Dimples in full effect.

"I had it made for you."

"When?" We'd been a little busy.

"After I had more fun trapped inside a wine cellar than I'd had in two hundred years of living."

I looped my arms around Kane's neck and kissed him again. Chaste, joyful—my feet arched in my shoes and sparks danced up my spine when his fingers curled there.

"I think," Kane murmured against my lips, "our friends may have had enough of our kissing."

But I didn't let go. I wasn't sure I could, all my focus on those simmering, silver eyes heated with unfiltered, unending love.

"Lucky for us," Kane continued with a mild shrug, "I don't give a—"

My heart surged into my throat before I knew why. Just a fraction of a second—the one in which my body knew before my mind, before my consciousness, that something was terribly, grievously wrong.

Then, with a shattering roar—the ceiling rained down.

PART IV

The Rise

38

ARWEN

FRAGMENTS OF BRICK AND STONE FELL LIKE MISSILES. ICE-cold wind cut through the room with the decimation of the temple's towering spire. Voices screeching, bodies surging, ground shaking, the blood—where was the *blood* coming from?—splattered against the old wood of the pews . . .

Leigh, I had to find *Leigh*—

And there had been no horns, no warning . . .

Dozens of men in the keep must've been precisely, carefully executed long before the wedding for this to have happened. How had I not realized . . .

Mercenaries.

My feet stumbled down the stone steps, hands frantically searching through fallen wood beams and toppled statues of the Stones. Through so many moaning in agony, the urge to heal them writhing at my fingertips.

Leigh, Leigh, Leigh—

A second blow smashed through the ceiling.

Scales of gray filled my vision as I craned my neck up while I ran.

It was a tail, slicing through the temple walls. The spiked, sickly gray of a vicious, roaring wyvern.

Lazarus—Lazarus had come for Shadowhold.

Kane was nowhere to be found amid the turmoil, and for a moment the most gut-wrenching thought imaginable sliced through me. *He's already dead.*

But the earsplitting, resonant roar from the now-gaping hole in the temple ceiling offered a twisted rush of relief. Smooth, sleek black wings clashed with veined ashy ones in a violent blur above me.

Kane's shifting had saved us time—a few minutes at most, as he dragged his father away through the skies—but we needed to get as many people to safety as possible before . . .

Mercenaries converged on the temple like a cyclone. I'd forgotten their speed. How mighty, how much *power* Lazarus's most valuable Fae assassins contained. And all their perverse, shifted forms. Multiheaded, snarling hydras; flying lizards with the razor-sharp beaks of eagles; brutal-looking women with bodies like mythical birds—harpies, those. Squawking and shrieking as they tore their claws into our soldiers like wet parchment.

My lighte shot from my fingertips and into the heart of a wolf-beast not unlike the one that had attacked me so long ago. The rabid creature flew back into an altar of unlit candles before he could rip his fangs through an Onyx guard shielding the sweet harpist, now covered in blood.

"Go," I urged them, gritting my teeth as flares of sunfire split from my wrists and twined around the creature. "Get everyone to safety. To the lower floors, now."

Griffin soared overhead, his wingspan knocking over the long-since-abandoned harp as he used his claws to scoop a feathered mercenary up by her haunches and toss her out one of the shattered stained-glass windows. Flecks of rosy glass littered the floor at his feet.

I called to him, scrambling for a discarded sword dusted in debris and nabbing it just in time to lodge it between the wide-open jaws of a hydra. The sword chipped into the enamel of its upper fangs. I fought to extricate the weapon, panting until we sprang apart. It lunged, and I swung the sword through the air once more.

This time my blade sliced clean through one writhing, hissing reptilian head, just as another carved the air toward my neck.

My lighte bloomed—

Sunfire engulfed the creature, sending agonized shrieks into the already deafening cacophony of violence around us.

Griffin landed beside me, and together—rippling steel and beastly claws—we shredded through the remaining four heads of the mercenary. Warm Fae blood splattered across my face and the fabric of my dress.

"Where's Leigh? Where's Mari?"

My power flowed from my limbs, halting creatures in traps and cages of shimmering white light long enough for swarms of Onyx soldiers to cut them down. Griffin shifted back into his human form, breathing labored, and unleashed a flash of glossy emerald energy that cut through something snarling behind me.

"Barney got the witch out," he grunted, a sprawling translucent shield blocking a claw from my face. "I haven't seen Leigh."

I meant to tell him to go find her, but any words were lost in my throat as I beheld a snarling, cackling figure—

Octavia slithered in like an adder in tall grass. Blood soaked her leather corset and the dark blouse beneath it. Wiry gray hair twisted around her head.

She prowled toward a cowering girl, hidden beneath a pew.

Beth. It was *Beth*—

Octavia's mouth split in a reptilian smile. "So you're the little seer . . ." she cooed. "If I rid you of those eyes, will you thank me?"

Hurtling over pews, I ran for her—

Only to see Leigh sprint from the opposite side of the temple. My lungs ceased to breathe as she barreled right toward a slithering scaled mercenary, oily green sheen, pink-hued teeth from all the viscera. The creature reared up on its hind legs and Leigh—

Plowed into him, deftly maneuvering her sword and slicing the thing clean through its heart. She leapt over its gurgling body and scrambled in front of Beth, bloodied sword outstretched at Octavia.

I moved faster, unable to think around the fear swelling in my heart. And the pride.

Octavia stalked forward, despite Leigh's mighty slashes with her small blade. Her strides forced the two girls back against a wall already painted in gore.

And I was jumping over wood, dodging blows—

But not fast enough.

I wouldn't get there in time. The witch unleashed a wretched cackle, lunging toward them, her white teeth sharper than razors as she grinned, magic spinning around her hands—

"NO!"

I threw myself toward them, my sister, her sword quivering—

In an instant, Griffin and I were both slammed backward by some tail, some wing, into the ancient temple organ, keys and wood and pipes bowing beneath us in a discordant, pained exhale. Agony exploded in my leg and side.

No, no, no, *Leigh*—

Scrambling to right myself, I could only see Griffin out of the corner of my eye as he took the feathered creature down in a mess of jade lighte and bloody claws, but I was already up, ignoring some agony in my calf—

Be alive be alive be alive—

When my eyes found the wall Leigh and Beth had just been glued to—I didn't see them.

Instead, I found *Ryder*.

Curled atop both girls.

Body arched over them. A human shield in wedding attire—no weapon, no powers, no armor—

Unmoving.

And my heart seized in my throat—

But he was . . . breathing. He was breathing. And I exhaled a bigger sigh than I thought possible to hold within my lungs and raced to them anew.

Ryder righted himself and brushed soot and debris from both girls' hair, his body still blocking them as he scanned the space, looking around . . .

Where had Octavia gone? How had they made it out unscathed—

Rounding the last row of pews, my eyes found her. Octavia stumbled backward, choking as she staggered, a mighty engraved sword—a pommel with vines like Shadowhold's gnarled forest—lodged perfectly in her heart. A direct hit.

Not Leigh's, nor Ryder's.

The older witch screamed, eyes down on her bloodied hands. And it was horror—genuine, bone-chilling *horror*—that fueled that noise. That beautiful song of fear.

Her expression became one of agony for just a brief moment as she fought to dislodge the mighty blade from her chest—until she spasmed once and fell to the floor, eyes dull and unfocused.

I drew nearer, my limbs carried by both awe and confusion.

Until I tripped over something—

A body. At my feet.

No.

Stones above, no—

Face slack, body twitching, blood pooling around the gaping, magic-tinged wound in his gut—

Dagan.

"No," I cried, dropping to my knees. "No, no—"

A high-pitched ringing sounded in my ears. My hands shook as violence quieted all around me, the mercenaries fleeing with the death of Lazarus's witch.

And blood. So much blood—

Ryder spoke behind me. "He . . . he saved us. He—"

Lighte flowed through my hands and pressed to Dagan's stomach. "Don't let them see," I sobbed. "Get them out of here!"

"Arwen!" Leigh cried behind me.

But then I heard three sets of footfalls take off.

"Dagan," I said, swallowing blood and sweat. "Stay with me. You're going to be fine."

The flesh resealed under my palms. The blood dried.

"Dagan," I said to him again, the temple becoming a quieting coffin of moans and wails. "I've healed you, see? You're all right. You're fine."

I allowed myself to peer at his face.

Still. Eyes open but unfocused. Mouth slack.

My stomach heaved.

My mentor. My friend. The first person to show me how to truly be brave. The closest thing I'd ever had to a . . .

I couldn't—

No, this couldn't—

"Dagan, you have to listen to me, all right?" My hands continued to move over his chest. Sealing the wound, lacing the skin together, fusing his organs into place once more. "Nothing is going to happen to you. You are my *family*. Do you hear me? I am not going to leave you—"

"Arwen." Griffin's gutted voice behind me cracked my heart in two. "It's too late."

"Don't say that, don't—"

"He's gone."

"*Please*," I cried. And cried and cried.

"Arwen," he said again, with as much warmth as I'd ever heard in his voice. "He is. We need to run while we still can."

My eyes, blurred with tears, found Griffin's grim expression. I scanned the room. Empty save for bodies and debris and that crushed altar and an entire corner of the temple charred in black soot, where a fire had been narrowly extinguished. Below me— Horror clung to my fingers as I realized the *corpse* I'd been rebuilding, as futile as plugging a hole in a sunken ship. His wrinkled, slack face. Vacant, unmoving eyes.

And his hand in mine . . . just flesh. "I'm so sorry, Dagan . . ." I'd not been fast enough. I'd not—

I collapsed on top of him as I wept. Pepper and mothballs and the iron-rich tang of fresh blood filled my nose.

Griffin's broad hands encircled my upper arms and lifted me off him. "Come on," Griffin said.

"We can't leave him!"

"All right," the commander conceded. "All right."

He released me and I fought the indescribable urge to fall back down to the soiled stone floor of the chapel. To stay there and never get up.

The clear winter day shone through where the tower had been destroyed. No Kane. No Lazarus.

"Where did they go?"

"I don't know. That's why we need to move."

Dagan had given his life for Ryder and Beth and Leigh . . .

"Arwen," Griffin said once more. When I looked over, he was carrying Dagan's lifeless body with little effort. "We have to keep going."

We hurtled down the dizzying stairs in a daze until we'd reached Shadowhold's eastern courtyard.

I knew it made me weak but I couldn't stomach the bodies that littered the snow-tufted grass. Not just our soldiers, but *innocents*. Nobles and friends who'd been in that temple to celebrate our wedding. Tossed from those gothic stained-glass windows like stale bathwater. Or maybe they'd jumped to avoid a more gruesome death at a harpy's claws.

We'd failed them either way.

I had.

We made it inside with a handful of other soldiers and residents of the keep, and while Griffin kept moving—giving Dagan's body to a cluster of soldiers, commanding his generals, his lieutenants—I stood by the castle's heavy stone doors.

Ushering terrified faces inside, calling to those still in the barracks or the cottages.

Where had all the mercenaries gone? The snow-topped tents and iron gates of the keep were silent. Empty, as everyone had been ushered inside.

I stood on shifting feet, waiting for Kane.

"He'll come," a sleek voice said.

I turned to Briar and blinked slowly. I had understood her but . . . my mind was fogged. Too much horror—

Like she was an oracle, or her very words conjured him, a lethal dragon's roar cut through the panic already clutching the castle. A roar and the pound of many beating wings.

I stumbled out the front doors. Two Onyx guards and Briar followed behind me. I craned my neck up. There, in the skies—amid a beautiful, clear morning like fresh running water—was Kane.

And all of the mercenaries.

All of them.

A celestial battle. No . . . a *slaughter*.

More mercenaries than I thought Lazarus had. Amelia . . . She'd been right. They'd used *my* power—

My shoulders itched and rippled and I shut my eyes tightly and begged the Stones.

Shift, shift—

I thought of Dagan. Of how much he'd want to see me take flight.

But I couldn't focus against the gruesome sounds of Kane's anguish as they tore at him. My concentration, fracturing as he breathed fire and clawed to no avail. His animalistic *whines*. Like rusted nails through my insides.

There were too many of them.

"Go get Griffin," I ordered the guards behind me. He was the only one who could shift. *"Go!"*

Two Onyx men took off running.

"We have to get you inside," another urged.

But I wasn't moving. Not when Kane was up there *alone*, wings beating against talons and beaks and tongues twined in fire. Each blow that crested across his chest, his tail, sent volleys of pain through my own body.

"Call to him," Briar said beside me.

"He'll never retreat," I bit through gritted teeth. "Not when he knows he'd lead them back to Shadowhold."

He'd allow himself to be ripped to shreds up there before he'd bring the mercenaries into his own keep. The agony at the thought— I nearly collapsed.

"That's the *point*."

Despite the caws and roaring, I cut my eyes to Briar's violet ones. "What are you saying?"

"He knows *you*. Knows you would never put his keep in danger. If you call to him he'll know you've planned something. I'll take care of the rest."

When I squinted back up into the skies a hydra had just ripped one of its several sets of teeth through Kane's hind leg. He howled in pain, kicking forcefully and sending the creature careening down—it landed with a thud somewhere in the Shadow Woods.

Only more mercenaries swarmed in its place.

"KANE!"

I screamed for him until I tasted blood.

Until I saw his predatory gaze cut down to me.

"KANE!" I called again, motioning for him to come back to the keep. Waving my hands in the air. Then I ran back into the castle, praying I'd placed my faith in the right witch.

The sound was like a swarm of locusts. All those mercenaries, barreling toward the keep, charging after Kane, a symphony of winged assassins.

Faster, faster, faster—

Kane's mighty dragon wings flapped as he soared, and just inside the castle doors was Briar, hands strained against the skies, wind and static and snow swirling around her and pulling her carefully coiled dark hair free. Chanting, muttering—

Magic scenting the air and thick on my tongue.

Until Kane slammed to the ground, on two human feet—

And all other mercenaries that had been nipping at his tail, snarling, savage for his death—severed.

Split in half. Blood spraying, hooves and claws and snouts falling from midair.

Cleaved.

By some ward, some guard Briar had spawned around the castle.

Those slower, and spared the same gruesome fate, slammed into the barrier and fell to the earth.

Briar slumped against the castle's innermost wall and caught her ragged breaths.

Lethal silence fell. The entire keep's eyes on Kane.

Tendrils of that obsidian power still clung to his shoulders, those dark dragon's wings still retreating tightly into his spine, when he stalked through the heavy stone doors of Shadowhold and prowled right for me.

Covered in ash and blood. Limping. Face colder, crueler than I'd ever seen it. Heartbreakingly menacing. World breaker. Eater of hearts.

They'd come for his home. Not Willowridge—not his capital— his *home.*

Our home.

They'd killed Dagan. Right before my eyes, they'd killed him.

I started to break before he'd even touched me.

Kane gathered me into his arms in one powerful movement and I crumpled against him and cried.

39

ARWEN

KANE RUBBED SLOW CIRCLES ALONG MY BACK AS I HUNCHED over the shivering, freckled soldier, stitching him closed. The claw wound was serrated. Not seamless, and my lighte would have worked better, but my power had to be conserved. Every life saved with it was a wager now.

Beyond the flesh and thread beneath my fingers, the great hall grew more and more packed with citizens, some wounded, some only terribly afraid. Moaning sounded as soldiers and residents of the keep nursed their wounds. In a crowded corner Lieutenant Eardley and Griffin were conferring around a table with a group of high-ranking Onyx officers. Their voices ratcheted up an octave and Kane murmured, "I'll be right back."

I only nodded. He pressed his lips to the crown of my head, but I could barely feel it.

They had already moved Dagan's body into the crypt. They'd told me it was the safest place, *just in case*. Just in case the main castle was breeched, and Lazarus's army decided to desecrate the bodies of the dead.

Those were the kind of monsters we stood to face.

The great hall had become a makeshift infirmary, war room, and hideout. Though I was sure Briar, Griffin, the Onyx soldiers, and I had killed at least three dozen, I knew Lazarus had more. This morning had just been the warm-up. An opening act, to dazzle us with the performance of savagery he had in store.

The tremor of heavy footfalls sounded just a moment before the massive doors to the great hall swung open.

I turned, the freckled boy whose shoulder I held turning with me, to see a handful of darkly armored Onyx soldiers stalking through. Ashy, bruised, bleak—

Silence fell as Barney, at the helm, lifted his helmet of bone and said, "They've got us surrounded. The sheer number of men . . ." I'd never seen Barney with that expression.

Defeat.

Kane's men were mortal. A handful of them halflings, maybe. We'd only be safe in here for so long, and when the ward was released . . . The walls and gates and ramparts that surrounded Shadowhold were no match for Lazarus's army.

Despair—crushing and relentless—threatened at the thought.

Not yet, I told myself, focusing on the even, rhythmic stitching at my fingertips. *Stay strong. For Dagan.*

He'd killed Octavia. They were without a witch. No way to portal home, no spells to bolster their legions. That was worth something.

Kane stood elegantly from the table he'd been hunched across and motioned over his shoulder for me to join him.

"Rest," I told the boy, standing. "And drink water."

"Fuck that." He frowned. Then, catching himself, added, "With all due respect, my queen, I have Fae bastards to kill."

He stood before I could stop him, needle slick with his blood still in my grip.

While Kane and I had been suffering from Peridot to Lumera to find the blade and then to find each other, I'd forgotten that at some point Eardley or Griffin must've informed thousands of men that a fight for their kingdom meant not only defeating Amber and Garnet but Fae soldiers, too. They'd had to explain to them that the brutal, mythic creatures that sketched our childhood nightmares were not only real but standing at the other side of the front lines.

The freckled kid that stood before me, hoisting on menacing dark leather armor with a still-bleeding shoulder, couldn't have been more than sixteen. I watched as he threaded his last strap with a wince and bounded for his fellow men.

Is this what Dagan died for?

For hundreds of young boys, if not thousands, to rush to their deaths?

Against a Fae king that *could not* be beaten without the Blade of the Sun? Which we still didn't have?

"We'll need to approach from the North Gate," Kane was saying to the group when I neared.

"I want to see," I said, before I'd even really thought the words.

Kane's and Griffin's gazes, and about seven other sets of eyes, fell to me.

"See what?" Kane asked.

"The soldiers. Our position." I made for the doors of the great hall, and the tens of guards standing menacingly before it.

"No," Kane said, not harshly, but with that cold, unwavering command. "You can't go out there." Then, his jaw working, "My study."

Exiting the great hall through the back, I realized I'd never heard Shadowhold so silent.

The castle wasn't known for its noisiness, but now that there was none, I ached for the fluttering pages of books and idle suppertime chatter. The rowdy, masculine noises from the barracks and pleasant footsteps as nobles and children shuffled up and down the sprawling stairs and across the cozy, candlelit halls.

And it was *frigid.*

Despite everything, Shadowhold was always warm. Either due to breezy summer wind or roaring winter fireplaces—the keep was nothing if not filled with life. A dark, cold shell that served to protect a warm, beating heart. The mirror image of its king.

If I lived to survive this war, I'd never scrub the image of Shadowhold like this from my mind.

And all I could hope as we climbed the narrow stairs was that I *wouldn't.*

Best-case scenario was that I'd end Lazarus, and thus myself. Otherwise it would mean we'd failed. Lazarus would take Evendell, starting with Shadowhold.

Or, it would mean Kane had taken my place. And as my eyes fell to his face, features etched in furious stone, and his hand, despite it all, clasped tightly around mine as we scaled toward his study, I couldn't imagine anything more awful than for him to lose his life protecting me.

Rather than entering Kane's study through our sleeping quarters, we circled around the back entrance and Kane uttered the spelled passcode, moving that glittering display case of treasures aside and allowing us to enter.

"Mari," I breathed, finding her and Briar hunched over a grimoire on the leather couch at the center of the room. "Bleeding Stones."

When she stood, her face was even paler than usual. Her lovely blue dress was ripped and spotted with blood. "Tell me . . ." Tears gathered in her bloodshot eyes. "Tell me it isn't true."

I swallowed hard, my chest threatening to cave in once more. "I—I can't."

Mari's face crumpled and I knew mine had done the same.

"Octavia should have burned at the stake long ago," Briar murmured from the couch.

The guttural wrath that warped Kane's face as he interlaced his fingers tighter in mine was ancient and deep-seated. For Dagan, for me, for his mother . . .

But Mari wasn't listening. "I didn't even get to say goodbye."

I faltered for words. Neither had I.

"He knew you had gotten to safety," Griffin said behind us, his voice hoarse. "He saw you flee the temple."

I didn't know if Griffin was lying, and I didn't want to. Possibly a vestige from my more naive days, but I couldn't stomach the thought that Dagan's final breaths had been occupied worrying about Mari's or my or anyone else's safety. I told myself he'd died doing what he couldn't so many years ago . . . saving children. Perhaps not *his* children, but Leigh and Ryder, even little Beth—they were as close as it came for him.

And for Dagan, I'd do the same. I'd save everyone I could.

I moved purposefully for the southern windows.

Nobody followed me.

"We've sent for reinforcements from Willowridge," Eardley told Kane behind me.

"There are fewer men there than stationed here," Griffin said, too low.

The study was on the highest floor of this wing. Though not as tall as the library or the temple, it was elevated enough that the sea of gray surrounding Shadowhold's gates looked like dirtied snow to me at first.

So much so, I'd almost felt a rush—thought Lazarus and his men might have vanished altogether.

It was like discovering your shadow was actually a cloud of buzzing flies—not snow at all, but thousands and thousands of Fae warriors. Spilling deeper into the Shadow Woods, poised on foot, on horseback, on winged mercenaries. And past them, through pockets of the forest—golden armor and rusty red as well. Amber. Garnet. All of them.

They outnumbered us at least fifty to one.

It would be a bloodbath.

"We can't fight them."

My eyes hadn't left the window, and Eardley's snort behind me shook my focus. "We sure as shit won't surrender without trying."

"Can't you see?" I turned to face the room. All the worried, dirtied faces. "We've already lost."

"How long will your wards last?" Mari asked Briar.

Briar patted down the wrinkled silk of her fine lilac skirt. She had dressed so nicely for our wedding. "A couple of hours. At most."

"And then they'll breach the walls with ease," Kane promised, ice sliding through the room with his words. "They'll take Shadowhold before nightfall."

"Can we run?" Mari asked, no shame in the question.

"There's nowhere we could go where he won't find us," I said. "And we'll just rack up more death while we delay the inevitable."

"Arwen . . ." Kane cautioned.

We were powerless.

I'd been powerless to stop Dagan's slaughter and the deaths of so, so many more. Had almost seen both Leigh and Ryder killed—the thought alone like an arrowhead to my heart. We were at the mercy of Lazarus now, and Kane knew, whether or not he could admit it.

I had one final weapon in my arsenal. "But I have an idea."

Kane stepped toward me, face drawn with bleak understanding. "Why don't we discuss—"

"I'll return to him."

"You are not *his*," Kane hissed.

"But he still wants me to be. I'll go to him, willingly."

"In what Gods-damned world?" Griffin bit out, voice rough as a cliffside.

Noticing how my hands shook, I folded them across my chest. "It's our only bargaining chip. If I offer myself up in return for a ceasefire before war even begins, maybe we can spare everyone. He still needs me to bear his heirs."

"No way," Mari said. "Absolutely not."

"It won't work," Eardley added. "He'll take you and still obliterate the keep."

"See? No chance," Mari said again. "Tell her, Kane."

But Kane said nothing. His eyes only fixed on mine, a great well of sorrow pooling in them.

My throat tightened.

"It's Arwen's life. It's her choice."

"Oh, what the fuck?" Griffin rubbed his temples.

"It's not her life if he *kills her*," Mari snapped, just as a strange wind pulled through the very fabric of the room's atmosphere and turned all our attention toward movement near a cluttered bookcase.

"We're not going to let him do anything of the sort," a surly feminine voice said.

Amelia emerged from a rippling, undulating chasm in the physical threads of the room. A portal—and with her, Hart Renwick . . . as well as a familiar face that made my shriveled heart inflate.

Wyn, smiling.

And in his arms—singing only to me a song of paradise and loss and ruin—the gleaming Blade of the Sun.

40

KANE

I WASN'T SURE WHAT HAD SHREDDED THE TWO-HUNDRED-year-old tether on Griffin's self-control these days, but upon seeing Amelia for the first time since she'd betrayed us and ensured Arwen's almost-demise, he lunged for her like a rabid dog.

Snarling, my commander had the new queen's ice-white hair in a vise grip and had forced her down to her knees within seconds.

"Gods almighty." Hart dodged back, nearly knocking over my nicest stained-glass lamp but grasping its thin shade just in time.

Amelia, whom I'd never seen shed a single tear, cried out, clutching at her scalp as Griffin forced her lower, and lower still.

The young olive-skinned man who had helped Arwen and I flee Solaris drew his sword at Griffin, and my lighte flickered at my wrists as I roared, "Enough."

But my commander didn't drop the wincing Amelia, her hands scraping at his wrist and forearm as she pleaded for him to release her.

I nearly growled at him. "I said, *enough.*"

"Griffin," Mari urged, standing from her spot beside Briar, her face a little appalled. "Let her go."

Griffin gave Amelia a lethal once-over before reluctantly releasing his hold on her hair. She fell to the floor with a groan. "She turned on us," he seethed to the witch. "She's the reason you thought your closest friend was dead."

"And I'd do it again," Amelia said from the floor, rubbing her scalp.

"Bold." Hart shrugged, impressed.

I scowled at them both.

Amelia stood, righting the slinky layers of her pale green dress. "How is what Arwen herself was just suggesting any different? If I could have offered my own life for the safety of my people, I would have without a second thought."

When none of us uttered a word, she added, "But I am sorry for the pain my actions caused. Of course I am. Perhaps procuring the sword was the first step of many I can take in earning back your trust."

"You will *never* have our trust," I gritted out. "You will be lucky to still have your own head when all of this is over."

"So be it," she said, utterly calm. "Today at least, we fight for the same side."

"She's right," Arwen said. And then, to the kingsguard, "I can't believe you're alive. After you helped us I thought . . ."

The kind-faced man shrugged, almost bashful. "Lumerians are terrified of dragons. I told them Prince Ravenwood ripped you from my grasp . . . They didn't find my story so far-fetched."

Of course they were afraid of dragons. In Onyx, my shifted form was a symbol of our power. Our strength. In Lumera, the wyvern was one of fear and brutality.

Arwen smiled at him, and when my eyes found hers I saw they shone with a new resolve. I knew she saw the same glow in my own eyes.

We had *the blade*.

Flickers of triumph rose in my veins. Everything was different now.

"How did you even get here?" Eardley asked the newcomers.

"I fight with the aid of the entire Antler coven," Hart said. "We got word to Queen Amelia that the blade needed to be salvaged from the palace wreckage. With the help of Wyn here we retrieved it, and my coven portaled us to Evendell."

"Hart told me that if I helped"—Amelia's stoic eyes fell to mine—"I might be spared upon my return."

She was right, it was the deal we'd relayed to the rebel king. Still, I couldn't look at Amelia for too long without bloodlust misting across my vision.

"Where did you find the blade?" Arwen asked Hart.

"Lazarus wouldn't risk bringing the weapon with him, knowing he'd be in such close proximity to the two of you. That only left a few of his usual traps, and I've been studying the man for decades. I had a hunch."

Whore or not, it turned out we were lucky to have the rogue on our side.

"Hart arrived once Lazarus and his army left for Onyx," Amelia continued. "It was as easy as asking Wyn to use his clearance as a kingsguard to get Hart and his coven into one of the monster's lairs."

Wyn swallowed hard, some memories of what he'd battled swimming behind his hazel eyes. "I wouldn't say *easy* . . ."

Hart laughed hard and rough and I almost couldn't help my own grin. This ludicrous team of traitors and rebels had retrieved the fucking blade.

Arwen's gaze wasn't harsh on Amelia as she shook her head, amazed. "You and Wyn. Both in Solaris, and neither knowing the other wasn't really allied with Lazarus."

"Well." Amelia smirked at the kingsguard. "After you blew up half the palace, Wyn came and found me. He said he'd seen us talking at the Lumerian Solstice and asked how he could help."

Arwen's eyes shuttered as she beheld Wyn. "You knew?"

Wyn shrugged. "I'm not as feeble as I look."

Arwen shook her head, crossing the room to embrace him. "You never looked feeble to me," she muttered into his shoulder with a half laugh. "We'll need you in the coming fight."

"You've got me." He smiled faintly. "Put me to work."

Eardley loosed a rare grin.

Hart cleared his throat. "I've put my faith in you, Kane Ravenwood, and I don't intend to yank it back now, but I can't stay. I cannot go to war with you all."

"You?" Griffin balked. "Why?" After all I'd told my commander of the battle-loving bastard, I, too, was confused.

Hart swallowed, misery cresting over his face for the first time since he'd arrived. "I'd love nothing more than to soak my hands with the blood of Lazarus's men. But getting us here . . . Some of the witches in the coven didn't survive. Briar needs to send me back. The channel will take me too long."

"She'll do so after we slaughter Lazarus," Eardley said. "You have to stay and fight—we need all the manpower we can get."

Hart's brows knit. "Who are you?"

I sighed. Too many egos in one study—mine included. "Hart, this is my lieutenant, Eardley. Eardley, Hart is the rebel king. He's the only man I trust to rule over Lumera when my father falls. We can't risk losing him."

And Beth's vision . . . Gods forbid we succeeded in slaughtering Lazarus and found even Briar couldn't get us back to Lumera to begin extraditing civilians . . . The realm couldn't be left without a leader. Now, while Lazarus was here, was the best opportunity for Hart and his battalions to successfully lay siege to Solaris and take power.

"We will free the Lumerians," Briar swore to me, as if reading my thoughts, "once we've secured the stronghold. But if I go now, the ward I've cast will dissolve. It's a constant enchantment I'm maintaining over the keep, not a completed spell."

"Then just send Hart back," I said. "But first—"

I crossed the room to the spelled door and the glass display case in the candlelit hallway on the other side. Next to King Oberon's prized harpy talon and my favorite treasure—a piece of the original map of Willowridge drawn by Evendell's founders—was the first king of Onyx's diamond-and-amethyst armor. And atop it, his cherished battle crown. Leather for comfort in wartime but artfully crafted with jewels that still sparkled a millennium later.

I jammed my elbow into the case, shattering the glass, and fished the piece out before stalking back into the study.

Arwen and Griffin shot me equally questioning looks, but I only moved for Hart.

"Kneel," I instructed when I'd come to stand before him.

Hart, a man with a thousand witty one-liners and very little dignity, knelt immediately to the ground, eyes grave on mine.

"Hart Renwick, will you solemnly promise to govern the peoples of Lumera, both Fae and mortal alike, with justice, mercy, and ferocity; to protect them as if each were your own blood; to guide the realm to peace and prosperity as long as you shall live?"

Hart's eyes never left my own, even as Mari inhaled sharply. "I solemnly promise to do so."

"Hold this throne with honor," I said after placing the ancient crown upon his unkempt head. "It is yours by the authority of the heir to the Lumerian throne, Prince Kane Ravenwood. May your righteousness and just rule endure forevermore. Gods save King Renwick."

Though quiet and embattled, bruised and broken, the entire study murmured back in perfect clarity, "Gods save King Renwick."

And I'd hoped that they would.

Before he or I could utter a word to each other, a spell-cast wind and the smell of sorcery filled the room, sending pillow tassels whirring and a wicked chill through my bones. Briar and Mari hummed in unison as the undulating, gaping maw of a pitch-black portal ringed in softly glowing violet bloomed open, separating our world from whatever magic lay beyond.

"Rule well, Hart," Briar urged her old friend. "We'll celebrate when this nightmare has ended."

"Good luck to you all." Hart nodded once. "I'll take care of your people, Kane. I swear it."

"They're your people. They always have been."

He grinned that half smile once more, then stepped through before the portal slammed shut. Like an eye, winking closed.

For a moment, my ornate study was silent.

"I almost forgot," Amelia said to me, pulling something from her skirts. My black signet ring glinted in the stained-glass-filtered afternoon light. "I thought you might want this back."

"It's hers now." I gestured at Arwen, my entire body tense. Now that Hart was gone and the people of Lumera accounted for, I knew what would need to come next.

Arwen's eyes widened a bit, but she opened her palm, allowing Amelia's small, moonstone-adorned fingers to place the ring at the center of her hand.

Her olive eyes on mine, my wife placed the signet onto her left ring finger. My heart swelled sorrowfully.

Wyn was the one to narrow his gaze at her. "Arwen, you cannot offer yourself up to Lazarus like a prize. Not after everything he's done to you."

"I agree," Briar said, deep in thought.

"No," I interjected, the plan finally forming itself in my mind.

I had meant it earlier, when I'd said it was Arwen's choice. I'd made enough mistakes trying to control Arwen, trying to control the outcome of every fate that plagued us. She was capable of making her own decisions. If she wanted to spare the kingdoms and give herself up, even if it meant going back to Solaris, *shredding* me from the inside out, I would not stand in her way. "No, she . . . has to."

Griffin's head swiveled. "What?"

"I do?" Arwen asked, a bit of dismay spilling into her voice.

That sound, her voice when she was afraid, was worse than the shriek of a knife against porcelain. But I couldn't explain just yet. Not when Lazarus would have access to all our minds. "Eardley, send a raven to Lazarus's encampment. Tell him we have an offer."

41

KANE

As we walked across the avenue that bisected the Fae encampment, I could almost hear the soldiers' snarls. Hundreds of Amber and Garnet men were stationed at the fringes of the camp with their forges and tents, studying us, sizing us up, casting venomous glares, some more lecherous ones tossed at Arwen and Briar.

The thought crossed my mind that most of these witless toads hoped our ceasefire would not hold. They longed to slice and maim—their eyes told me as much.

And the silver-clad Fae, thousands of them, positioned closer to that looming, pallid gray tent at the center, packing snow-coated wagons with spears and supplies, rolling glass barrels of stolen glowing lighte . . . they studied us with even more loathing. True contempt. The fallen prince of Lumera—Lazarus's volatile son.

Due now, for his penance.

And all of this, every crackling fire and lug of metal shields, constructed through the heart of the Shadow Woods. *My* fucking woods.

Icy, rageful fog drifted along my ankles, as if the woods themselves agreed, seeping out from the tree line and curling as we walked. I hoped at least one of these sorry pustules had been ravaged by a chimera or ogre just for taking up residence in their domain.

I might've felt the thrill of vengeance brimming in my bones. Might have relished how soon I'd rid my woods of the weasels they were teeming with.

But my plan was far from seamless.

The biggest strategic issue in any battle with my father was his ability to step inside your mind and study your schemes before you could enact them. It was safest if everyone walking behind me truly believed we were offering Arwen back to him in return for a ceasefire.

Even if Griffin knew me well enough to assume that with the blade in hand I'd never surrender my own wife. Or if Arwen wondered as much, too—knew how it would kill me to see her chained in lilium and brought back to Solaris.

But their doubts were safer than physical memories of a plan explained. That was what would dart to the front of anyone's mind when told, *Do not, under any circumstances, think of this conversation in his presence.*

But that still left the blade.

I could only hope Lazarus would have no idea that the Blade of the Sun wasn't safely locked up inside his palace anymore. Even if that were the case, he'd still likely search us.

Which was why Briar was the only one I'd told my intention to. She had lived in Solaris long enough, had spent enough years in court with the man, to know how to hide her thoughts from his prying lighte.

I'd asked her to spell the weapon. And when the moment came, the blade would reveal itself within my grasp.

The cloudless sky and beating afternoon sun had melted the top layer of snow even in the tree-covered woods, and our feet sloshed in unison as we approached. We came to a halt before the rounded, high-topped tent that rose well above the rest of the canvas lodgings, flanked by at least a dozen Fae soldiers.

Two silver-clad men approached and began the demeaning task of frisking us for weapons. Running their hands across our chests, waists, and pant legs.

"Easy there," I growled at one stocky young Fae, staring daggers into his hand as it slid up Arwen's thigh. The silver-plated soldiers outside the monstrous tent braced themselves. Some reached for weapons.

But when the young soldier's face twisted up to mine from where he knelt, he had the good sense to cower from my glare. He continued his frisking on a lower section of Arwen's leathers.

"They're clear," the nervous little pig called out to the tent. And it was true. The men had not felt a single lick of steel strapped to any of us. Even Lieutenant Eardley—the bravest mortal I'd ever known—strutted into the camp of Fae warriors without a weapon to his name.

Griffin entered the tent before me, and Eardley after him.

It was ice-cold, despite the sun permeating through the dark canvas and two roaring fires—one beside the broad topographical table that mapped Shadowhold and the surrounding woods and one beside the large down bed.

My father stood from a leather chair, setting down a book and removing his spectacles as if he were a tired parent of difficult offspring.

Briar strolled in behind me, and Arwen after her until we stood in a cluster before him. I sucked in a steadying, iron-laced breath. If everything we had worked toward for months went according to plan, I'd die in the next several minutes. If I knew it wouldn't give us away, I would have pulled my gloves off, reached my hand for Arwen's, and stroked the soft skin of her wrist one last time.

Without letting panic seep into my expression, I urged my mind free of anything related to our plot and shifted my thoughts to our impending loss, my fallen keep, fisting my hands tightly and releasing them.

Guilt, remorse, weakness—

"Son," my father said quietly.

"Father."

"I'm told you come with an offer?"

"Your numbers outweigh ours too significantly." A notched blade through my gut, each word. "I don't wish to see my men slaughtered."

"Again," he added.

And I deserved the blow. *"Again,"* I conceded.

He stood. Patient. Cold. Waiting.

"We have the only thing that you truly care about . . ." I opened my mouth to say it. To finish what we'd come here to do. But the words—

I couldn't bring myself to utter them.

Weak. I was fucking *weak*.

Before I could falter too visibly, Arwen took a tentative step forward. "Take me back with you. End this before it begins, and I'll bear the heirs you seek."

For a moment, my father said nothing. Paced once in thought as I forced my mind to empty.

"You are effectively surrendering." It was not a question.

"Yes," I bit out.

His clear silence rent the room.

Ash. Ash on my fucking tongue. "We surrender."

"Is this the leadership that convinced all those rebels to die for you?" Lazarus clucked his pointed tongue. "Personally, I don't see it."

Fire ran through my veins. If it was cold in the tent, I couldn't feel it.

"And the girl?" He didn't look at Arwen as he continued. Only me. And for whatever reason, that fueled my rage more than any other word I'd spoken since entering. Here she was, offering herself to him, *her* choice, *her* body, and he didn't care. He only wanted to hear it from me. Whether that was because he knew how it gutted me to give her up or because he didn't respect her authority, I didn't much care.

"You heard her."

"Speak the words."

Out of the corner of my eye I saw Arwen's gaze cut sidelong to me. Urging me. Soothing me. I couldn't fucking look at her. "She's yours."

Griffin shifted beside me but said nothing. Briar stood preternaturally still as she always did. I couldn't even see Eardley. Couldn't see past the venomous sheen coating my vision. The throbbing artery in my father's neck.

"That won't do you any good," he muttered.

"What won't?" Arwen asked.

"Your soon-to-be late husband is thinking about tearing into my carotid artery. Futile, childish . . . He'll never change, will he?"

"End this, Lazarus," Briar said, so low I'd hardly heard her. "End this and let's be done with it."

"And what of my new realm? Surely you can't think I'll be satisfied to stay in the wasteland that is Lumera?"

This, we'd considered. "We split the continent. Amber and Garnet have already agreed to give you their lands. Peridot, too. I believe Rose could be convinced. That's four of nine, and we both know you'd never successfully lay siege to Citrine. You can send all the mortals from your new lands here, to Onyx."

"Four kingdoms' worth of men, women, and children moving into your lands? You'll be overrun. Worse than Lumera, the overpopulation, lack of resources, the bloodshed . . ." His grin was mirthless. Joyless. Revolting.

"We'll make do."

"You would, I'd imagine. Until they overthrew you." My father paced once more, his eyes on his feet as he thought. "Might be a fitting punishment, actually . . ."

Out of the corner of my vision I saw Griffin's eyes widen and then shutter as quickly as they'd opened. I knew better than to let my thoughts dwell on whatever he'd seen or felt, lest Lazarus catch onto something shared between us. I cut my gaze back to my father before Griffin could notice that I'd seen something concern him.

The soldiers that shared the tent with us, the ones lining the back wall and flanking the entrance, monitored like hawks. Not a single blink among them. It reminded me how human I'd become in my years here in Onyx. How often I blinked and fidgeted. I stilled my tensing muscles.

"Not interested, I'm afraid," my father said in the end. "Men do not succeed as vastly as I have, rule with as much uncompromising will, make the sacrifices I have made, only to share their conquests with foolhardy, insubordinate sons."

He drew close. So close I could smell the wind and ice on him. Could hear his power rippling beneath his bones.

I grasped my hands behind my back to hide their shaking.

"Perhaps once, long ago, we could have conquered this new world together. The last two dragons in existence. Wings and ice and flame. But you, Kane"—he shook his head, though his silver eyes held mine so firmly my lungs freed themselves of all air—"have only ever disappointed me. And I have grown very tired of you."

One moment my father and I held each other's gazes with such unbearable, raw hatred I feared it might consume all of us—flesh and canvas and wood alike—into a whirlpool of cruelty and carnage. The next, the Blade of the Sun materialized behind my back, the hilt gripped between my closed fists. And—

A flash of metallic lighte shrieked across the room. Spears of ice barreling, not for me, or Arwen—

But for Briar. Whose skirts had not even fluttered with her hard-trained magic. The spell she'd used to conceal the Blade of the Sun nearly imperceptible. Briar, who's face had remained stoic on my father as we spoke. As she'd sent the blade into my hands—

But her mind . . .

It was the only way he could have known.

I didn't have time to strike before chaos split the room. Before Arwen's lighte snapped out—that magnificent, deadly sunfire ripping across the tent for my father, melting the flesh of two soldiers that dove before him. Some Fae soldier's shimmering red lighte, the crests of Griffin's malachite aura all flaming and clashing—

I conjured barrier after barrier, shield after shield of black, rippling shadow. The lighte of ten soldiers shrieking against it as I swung the weighty blade for my father. Ruthless fury and pure dark *power* surging through my bones.

"Kane!" Arwen's voice.

But I was so close now, my father within reach as he pressed back toward the now-toppled table, wooden pieces bearing both Onyx and Lumerian sigils scattering across the floor—

"KANE!"

I spun, my shield of undulating shadow with me, just narrowly knocking out a Fae soldier and his raised sword.

Briar was crumpled on the ground, leaking blood, groaning in agony. And Arwen, holding her within a tight bubble of soft, glimmering lighte.

"It's not working . . . My healing, my lighte—"

But there was no way out—Eardley, dodging blow after blow of lighte that would smoke him instantly if it made contact. Griffin, barely punching and blasting through six men his size. And those mercenaries, pulling open the canvas of the tent, Fae that would shift any moment, smiles curling at their lips as they beheld the tumult . . .

Without Briar . . . we had no witch—

"No," I breathed as the mercenaries began to shift, and I hurtled for Arwen, knowing it was over, that my father's men had too much power. Would obliterate us—

The blow exploded the tent.

No, disintegrated it.

Gone.

And half his soldiers, too. And Lazarus, thrown onto his back, hacking from some kind of wound.

"What the . . ." Griffin heaved, squinting into the blinding white all around us, eyes adjusting now that the darkness of the canvas had disappeared with its blown-off roof.

Whatever the thrum of power had been, it hadn't touched any of us.

Not from a mercenary but . . .

Mari.

Standing within the now-quiet remains of the tent, chest heaving, hands outstretched, wind around her rippling.

"Invisibility," she panted. "More useful than I thought."

The words were playful, but that look—such unwavering courage—uncertain, and all the more powerful because of it. Because of the fear I knew swirled inside her, and hope that had overcome it and forced her after us. Pride and genuine gratitude nearly bowed me to her.

Mari called down to Arwen, who was still cradling Briar. *"Run."*

Arwen didn't hesitate. She carried Briar out with that Fae strength and sprinted through the encampment, arrows and lighte that rained down on them pinging softly, uselessly, off her shield.

"After them," my father cried from his motionless position, surrounded by shredded books and furs, and one now very extinguished hearth, still steaming into the frigid air. "No mercy. Take the keep!"

The blade sang in my hands. Sang for his death, for the kill. My power funneled through it, turning the silver steel of the weapon poison-black.

I did not falter.

I stalked forward and drove the Blade of the Sun into his heart.

My father shuddered, red blood spilling from his chest. Glory—*relief*—sang in my bones.

Even as I waited for death to drown me.

Even as Mari cast more spells that drenched the encampment in destruction like rageful, rampant storm clouds.

Even as I watched him twitch and morph . . . his face, altering. *Blowing away.* His phantom eyes—

The man I'd stabbed was not my father.

He was not anything at all.

An illusion.

"A Delusion, actually," my father said, from across the encampment.

I darted through the silver bodies, slashing and blasting my obsidian lighte—for him. For his lethal gaze. Drove my sword into his chest.

And watched in horror as he faded into shadow right before my eyes again.

"How many more do you think you'll slay before one of my men strikes you down?"

Octavia's last spell. A fail-safe for her king. One she'd cast before her death at Dagan's hand.

"Kane," Griffin bit out, shaking me from my acute fury. My confusion. "It's a dirty spell. We need to *go*."

He was right. Some soldiers were clearing out. Splitting for Shadowhold. Their roars, their steeds, their armor jangling. And some taking off after Arwen and Briar and Eardley, who had run off, away from the keep, deeper into the snow-drenched forest.

And Griffin and Mari were sprinting now, too. Taking out soldiers with magic and lighte like darts through a board. Each shot a bull's-eye.

I looked once more at my father. At the hatred in his eyes. The promise buried there.

It likely wasn't even him.

So I offered a promise of my own upward. To wherever I knew he could hear my thoughts.

You will die today.

42

ARWEN

I WAS A HEALER. AND FOR THE LAST FIVE YEARS OF MY LIFE, my village had been war-torn. I'd seen death. So, *so* much death. I'd built up a strong stomach, and kind eyes. A warm comforting voice, which I used often to say *I'm so sorry* and *No, they didn't feel any pain.*

And yet every part of me that had learned to withstand the heartbreak, the devastation, of human loss disintegrated as I held Briar.

I could not quell my grief.

Not again. Not another—

Nor could I shake the images that kept scraping across my vision. My mother, lips pale and mouth coated in blood, telling my siblings and me goodbye. Dagan, gray and cold, the light I'd always found in his hooded eyes gone—

Suddenly my leathers and my boots and wool socks and gloves and fox fur weren't enough to stave off the frigid winter chill. The sun was fading, nightfall beckoning to us. And with it, more carnage . . .

Briar's slender chest shook with her uneven, labored breaths.

Her blood soaked through the leather at my knees. Mari's frantic breaths rang in my ears as she held the invisible ward around us, hidden in plain sight among the gnarled, snowcapped trees. Griffin was brushing his thumb over her hand so slowly I wondered if I'd imagined it.

Kane tried his best to stanch the bleeding, but his hands were coated in Briar's blood. There was too much—

And the ice . . . The ice that Lazarus had shot through Briar's chest had melted, and in its place gaped a ragged hole through her velvet bodice. Through her entire sternum. My lighte had just begun to pour out of shaking fingertips when Briar grasped my hand and breathed, "Stop."

"Don't stop," Kane ordered, his hands pressed once more against Briar's wound.

Fear—that was what laced his stern, unflinching words. For the loss of his friend, but also—

If we killed Lazarus but Briar didn't survive . . . all of Lumera—*millions*—plunged into an eternal abyss of poison air, bestial creatures, and suffocating violence.

My lighte delved into her chest cavity, illuminating torn muscle and pulp and gore.

Briar winced, those violet eyes almost gray. "Stop," she said again. A wet cough. "There is nothing to be done."

"Why not?" Kane thundered through gritted teeth.

But I already knew, as did Briar. She'd been around long enough. She understood what my healing power told me back in that tent. The minute my lighte reached her ancient flesh, enchanted to appear supple and young.

"Her body is held together with a spell," I murmured.

Mari's gasp of horror finished the thought for me. She understood, too, what Aleksander had told me about Ethera—I couldn't heal magic.

I could hardly think past the loss that ripped through me. Tears slid down my face and landed amid twigs and dirt in the blood-soaked snow. Griffin helped me prop Briar against the boulder's surface. We had found a small, shadowed alcove between an out-cropping of rocks and a handful of elm trees, the few Fae men who had run by looking for us rendered blind by Mari's magic.

But with Briar's impending death . . . the ward around the keep had evaporated. A spell Mari couldn't do. Likely could never do.

I knew it had fallen as I heard Lazarus's army converge on Shadowhold. Sickening sounds of slaughter rang out. Horses whin-nying in agony, boys and men—

"Hey," Kane hushed against my temple. "We're going to—"

"We aren't." I wept, wrenching away from him. "It's *over*."

The reality had sunk in the moment our plot to trick Lazarus had failed. We'd been foolish—the answer staring us in the face, ever since Aleksander made his offer back in Revue.

My eyes dipped to Kane's blood-soaked hands as another hot tear slipped down my cheek.

"Eardley," I said quietly. "You need to get back to the keep. To the raven house. Can you do that?"

He knew what I meant. Could he make it there *live*.

"Of course. Who do I send for?"

"Hearken Sadella," I answered.

"No," Kane bit out, rage roiling through him like a torrent.

"There is no other way." I held Kane's eyes with sheer, unbend-ing certainty. "Do you hear that?"

Kane fell silent. Agonized cries sounded off the trees, the clash of metal on metal, the toppling of sentry towers . . .

"That is the end of this war. That is the end of Evendell. Beth told us as much. We *have* to make the deal."

"Arwen." Kane's brows pulled together in anguish.

"We won't bear children anyway," I whispered, smiling through my grief at the wretched, twisted irony. "Because we both cannot live." More tears spilled down my cheeks. "And while we have no control over our lives, we can at least try to save everyone else's."

Kane said nothing, his mouth a grim, furious line.

I wasted no time waiting for a rebuttal. "Send word to Hearken," I said to Eardley. "The fastest raven we have. Tell him we agree to his terms. Tell him . . . to send them all."

Eardley nodded once and took off through the snow-packed forest. His urgency—and the death toll yawning before us—was at odds with the late-afternoon sun that glinted softly off his jet-black armor and warm, dark skin as he disappeared into the blur of snow and branches. I hoped for all our sakes that he'd find a weapon fast. He'd never make it to the keep without one.

Raising my head to the winter sky, I tried to brace myself. I'd never be able to take that decision back. I offered a quiet prayer that it had been the right one.

A single arrow whizzed through the trees behind us and we all ducked instinctively.

Briar coughed, fishing with a frail yet still elegant hand through our bodies until she grasped the hem of Mari's skirt. "You," she guttered.

Mari nodded, guilt already gleaming in her eyes. "I know, I shouldn't have followed after you all and I'm so—"

"You were *spectacular*, little witch."

Mari's mouth quivered until she couldn't hold in her tears a minute longer. She laid her head across Briar's chest. "Tell me what spell to do," she pleaded. "Tell me how to save you."

Briar's chest rose and fell too slowly. "One last lesson."

Mari sat up and clutched Briar's hand in both her own. "Tell me."

"Find *Adelaide*."

"Who is she?"

"You will free them," Briar said on a rattling inhale. Wet and waning.

Her pulse was slow under my fingertips as I held her wrist. My lighte ricocheted off the inner walls of my hand, the need to heal so great I worried it would slip out of me against my will. Out, with nowhere to go.

"Free them—?" Mari's brows pulled together.

"They won't know . . ." Briar's eyes dimmed. Another pained breath.

Mari gripped her shoulders. "Briar . . . What are you saying? Who?"

But she just reached for Mari, fingers settling on her arm.

More tears slipped down Mari's freckled nose. "Yes. I'll find her. And free them. It's all right, Briar . . ." Mari started to weep in earnest. "Thank you for teaching me so much. Being so patient with me . . . never making me feel—"

Without warning, a booming sound tore through our shadowed alcove, shaking the snow from the trees above us.

Cannons—

I dove for Mari. Kane braced his entire body around us.

No, not cannons. Mari—

Mari's eyes had rolled back in her head, only the ghostly whites of her eyes showing, her cheeks hollowing out, her body levitating—

"What's happening?" I yelled over the whipping, swirling wind.

Griffin lunged for her, and after a moment, with an incensed grimace, released her calf with a hiss. I watched him rub his fingers, singed as if he'd plunged them into a boiling pot.

Mari floated higher, lifeless, head hung like a ghost. And then she fell to the ground in a heap.

The wind halted.

Flakes of snow drifted down from where they hovered around her body in a column.

And on the ground—

My own gasp of horror sounded through the woods as Briar's body decomposed before our very eyes. Fair skin became leathery and wrinkled, then paper-thin, then disintegrated altogether. Tendons shriveled, bones cracked. Until all that was left was dust.

The most powerful witch in history. Mari's mentor. Our friend.

Gone, like smoke in wind.

Griffin was already kneeling, scooping Mari into his arms. Feeling her pulse and listening to her heart. When I cut my eyes sidelong to Kane, his dark brows were knotted across his forehead. "Is she—"

I could not endure losing Mari. I would—

"She's fine," Griffin breathed out in a rush. "She fainted."

Kane looked to Griffin in silent question. And then, a rasped "You don't think—?"

"Yes." Griffin cut him off. "I do." He looked down at Mari's mass of curly copper hair. Her serene expression. Her pert nose and all its sweet freckles.

I thanked every Stone for the breath that funneled softly in and out of her lungs.

But Griffin's warm, sea-green eyes . . . they brimmed with more than relief. Something else simmered there.

"What is it?" I asked, though some part of me knew. And knew in turn that I had to hear them say it. That I wouldn't believe it until they said the words.

"Briar transferred the spell to Mari," Kane said. "The one that kept her young."

About a hundred thoughts slammed through my mind at his words. But chief among them, despite everything around us, was the look on Griffin's face. It was hope wending through his eyes.

Hope that one day, if any of us made it out of this alive, and if they ever found their way to each other, they might not have varying lifespans to contend with.

We had lost everything. Dagan, Briar, Shadowhold, Kane's and my future—

And with the sounds of clashing swords and zings of lighte, only more and more and more loss stood to follow, likely long before night swept over the keep.

But that—that *hope* on Griffin's face as he cradled Mari in his arms—that was one thing we had won.

43

ARWEN

Snow fell, blanketing the raucous tumult of war in a veil of serene white. The Fae and mortal soldiers had razed at least half of the Shadow Woods between Lazarus's encampment and the stone walls of Shadowhold.

The late afternoon had bled into a violent sunset. The cries of our people growing louder, the chants and roars of the would-be victors growing more sure. I swung my sword, threw out my lighte, protected those I could but—

All I beheld now as I darted for the keep were smoking branches sizzling in the gray snow and crumbled dens of animals that would be seeking a new shelter, if they'd even made it out. And where was Lazarus while all his men fought and died for him? Hiding. Staying out of the fray now that he'd lost his precious witch. Repugnant.

Our sentries—those sturdy towers that specked the woods, the first line of defense for the stronghold—had been toppled. Onyx banners defiled, glass panes shattered, bodies of soldiers who had not been able to escape ravaged.

And those front lines I raced for . . . so rabid with violence I could hardly tell friend from foe.

It was a massacre.

One I did not allow myself to turn away from. To cringe, or heave at the awfulness. I'd never seen a battlefield. I'd been wholly unaware of the sheer brutality—of how it felt to sprint with all I had in me, freezing air funneling in and out of my lungs, and fall to the ground, ice ripping at my palms, only to realize what I'd tripped over was a human head. The flesh still warm against my exposed ankle.

Don't retch. Don't retch.

I stood and kept running.

Kane was way ahead of me. He ran with supernatural speed, his legs and arms elongating and darkening, scales spanning across him as he shifted. His vast, horned wings flared violently, taking out soldiers left and right until he leapt from the ground into the air, soaring over the clashing of steel and arcs of lighte with a deafening roar.

He landed atop the tower of soldiers that had piled high before the gates of Shadowhold. They were climbing the walls and wrought iron like ants, stepping on top of one another, swarming and blurring together.

Kane swooped down, ripping soldiers from their grasp of the pointed gates, tossing them recklessly—sometimes in two halves—into the forest.

But by then the mercenaries were upon him.

Harpies and snarling, winged wolves, ripping into Kane's haunches as he fought to keep them from soaring over the gates and into the keep. His bellows, the *flame* that split from between his razor-sharp teeth, doing hardly anything at all to deter their feathers and claws and ear-splitting screeches.

And they were here as well. On the front lines. Lashing through the men and women all around me, beaks slicing beside my face. I spun, witnessing in muted horror as Onyx armor was sheared apart like torn bread. I shouldn't look away but—I could hardly watch. Could hardly witness the faces I knew, had seen trickle through the halls of my home, gurgle out their final breaths. For our kingdom. For *my* kingdom.

And I wanted to unleash all my power as I'd done so long ago at Siren's Bay. I could feel it, that vigorous lighte rippling in my veins, charged and furious—fueled by horror and grief and loss and rage— but I had more power now than I'd had then. If I let it consume me, I'd destroy everyone. The Onyx soldiers, Shadowhold—

And even if I didn't, as evidenced by the weeks after the battle that I'd spent starved of lighte, I'd have nothing left for Lazarus.

The smell of burnt flesh brought a hideous memory to my mind.

I spun, interrupted by a fist careening into my jaw. Had barely caught my breath before another blow sent me to the ground. My sword slashed up, cutting through the Amber man's leg. He howled in agony.

When I stood, I made his death quick.

But by then the salamanders were well within my sight.

I wasn't the only one who had stopped midbattle to appraise the lizard-like creatures. Onyx, Amber, and Fae warriors alike had all halted around me, if only briefly, to witness the sheer power of the prowling, fire-breathing beasts from Garnet.

I'd never seen anything like it. Even that night in Peridot, they had attacked from so far away, and it had been the dead of night, and there had only been a few . . .

At least fifteen of the beasts laid siege to our walls now. Scales as large as the face of an axe and just as sharp. Split, slithering tongues.

Cold reptilian eyes. Frying the men who held their ground. Burning the walls, crumbling the brick.

Enough to demolish all of Shadowhold. To reduce the keep to embers.

Kane took a wretched blow of that caustic, blistering salamander flame to one beautiful outstretched wing and plummeted into half the men who had claimed the wall beneath him.

NO—

A scream ripped through my throat at the sight.

I surged for him, thighs burning, racing toward my husband, my partner, my king—

Kane's ravaged roar as the fire crawled up his sleek scales shredded my heart. Smoke and flame curling as he fell.

I watched in desperate dread as his enormous body took down half a dozen soldiers of all creeds that were halfway up the walls. And their armor, their flesh, the very snow coating their helmets lit, too, with that wicked orange and scarlet like a funeral pyre—

A whip of watery lighte wrapped around my braid and yanked me backward. I went down, the notches of my spine bruising against the icy roots of a sprawling tree. Kane's pained roars echoing through the trees . . .

A soldier in that vicious red glass visor filled my vision as I gulped frantic air back into my lungs. He kicked me down to the ground with the sole of his boot and held me there, slamming his sword into the blade of some Onyx boy—just a *boy*—fighting to reach me. Calling my name. Calling me his *queen*.

The Fae's violent, watery lighte shot down from his hands toward my neck like a razor-sharp guillotine. I didn't have time to think as bright rays of my own power met his liquid strike and evaporated the blow into winter air. My wrists and arms burned with the impact.

Our eyes met, equally shocked.

Before I could recover—make any sense of what my lighte had just done—the soldier snarled and brought down another surge of water, sharp as a meat cleaver.

This time I deflected the blow with that sunfire and allowed the lighte to crawl past his offense and up his arms until the fire turned his armor molten-hot.

He shuffled back, barking at the pain, *screaming* as he fought to rip his breastplate off, allowing me to scramble up and *run*.

Kane, Kane—

Past the still body of the Onyx boy who'd tried so valiantly to save me. That boy . . . his freckles. He'd been the soldier I'd stitched up. The one who'd wanted to fight for his home, and his people.

Dead.

I doubled back and shot my sunfire at the Fae who'd murdered him. Allowed my righteous, twisting flames to crawl up his calves and legs and groin and boil him inside his own suit of punishing reptilian armor. His screams were soil to my stems. Briefly, I languished in them.

Then I raced for Kane.

My arm flew out again and again, my steel an extension of me, my lighte an extension of that weapon, winding and dodging, bracing for the ache in my back and shoulders every time I swung, every time my sword connected.

But more and more and more soldiers came. From the trees, from their steeds—

And those salamanders—right at the keep's walls. Hurling balls of fire at the gates. Their creaking like thunder, shaking the forest floor. That wall of silver men, crawling higher and higher.

I could only watch as Onyx soldiers dove from their positions on the gates to avoid being burned alive with their castle. And some were not so lucky, blaring out their suffering—

And I could barely appreciate the reprieve as I sought out Kane now where he'd fallen, charred and bruised and back in his human form, handling himself between the blades of too many Fae soldiers. I had no idea where Griffin was. Hadn't seen Mari's red hair or clouds of ferocious magic in too long. Far too long.

And wherever I set my ropes of white fire to one soldier, two more found me. Where I ducked from one blade, another cut through my flesh. Where I deflected, each next blow connected. Too many of them, closing in. Too much smoke, too much tumult, to see or hear if the gates that separated this concentrated, bloody mangling of bodies had broken through to the innocents still housed inside the keep. Leigh and Ryder—

And the animalistic sobs, the cries, the *agony* . . .

"Stand down," I screamed at them all. "We have to stand down!"

Nobody altered a single movement.

I opened my mouth to bellow the words. To beg our army to surrender. Beg them to save the women and children who filled the keep behind us as those monstrous creatures lit the forest and iron ablaze.

Opened my mouth to beg for this just to be *over*—

Until movement broke through the tree line.

I snapped my head back at the rustling branches and falling snow. More monsters, more creatures, surely . . .

But the sound—

Not hooves or claws or wings.

Just feet.

The heavy footfalls of thousands—

Helmets turned all around me. Silver and jet-black and gold and rust—

Swords fell from midair in confusion. Even the salamanders halted, turning their heads toward the shuddering ground. Tongues lashing at the air to scent the newcomers.

And then I saw it—

The sea of glowing red dots. Pairs of two.

The eyes of the Hemolichs.

So fast—

So much faster than I thought any raven could fly.

And so *many* of them. Rows and rows and rows. Bedecked in simple, mismatched armor. Some bare-chested altogether despite the cold. Some with blunt weapons. Some with none.

And at the helm: Aleksander.

Eyes steadfast and conquering and wholly *savage* as he stalked to the front of his legions. Long white hair rippling in the winter wind.

Aleksander, who offered his men only one singular nod before they took off, thousands of them hurtling and roaring in unison. Tears burned in my eyes as the very ground beneath me shook with their weight. A riotous tidal wave of Blood Fae, prepared to pull Lazarus and his armies asunder.

And I thought I might have laughed—thought I might have actually barked out an incomprehensible cackle as I finally witnessed *fear* in the eyes of the soulless Fae soldiers who surrounded me.

Fear as our allies rolled in like an avalanche unleashed across a mountainside. Surging, snarling, roaring their determination. Fear as red-eyed Fae, as agile as they were lethal, tore through Amber and Garnet men with their bare, unarmed fists. Unleashing wild, ruthless lighte, cutting down silver-clad men, every Fae spear and wheel spoke shattering easily under their carnage-heightened power. Every drop of blood only making them stronger.

Our salvation descended on the battlefield as furious as a swarm of hornets and as powerful as the quaking of the earth.

Kane's gaze, one eye bloodred and face half-burned as it was, found mine through the fray. And it shone pitch-black with victory.

The Hemolichs had come. *Aleksander* had come.

Triumph sounded in my ears and jolted through my bones. Triumph, and hope. I blinked away the wet relief that clouded my vision and wrapped my hands more tightly around my blade.

If we were very lucky, and very, *very* smart, maybe—just maybe—this might be a fair fight.

44

KANE

IT WAS HARDLY A FAIR FIGHT.

The savage Hemolichs were untouchable. Wild and ruthless, tearing heads from spines with their bare hands. Drinking the blood, growing stronger . . . All the while precise Onyx warriors unleashed havoc on the legions of Amber and Garnet men. King Gareth's mortal soldiers hadn't stood a real chance against my battalions. Black, baleful artillery crashed into their weaker, poorly forged weapons. Golden armor fell like marigolds wilting in heat.

And together . . . an undulating wave of men charged the creatures convening on Shadowhold's gates. Hundreds of razor-sharp arrows shot on Lieutenant Eardley's command, and that savage blood lighte, their sheer *numbers*—the salamanders were no match for that kind of violence. The Hemolichs used the Onyx men's arrow wounds to strangle the beasts with their own blood.

The salamanders fell within minutes. All of them—*minutes*.

My chest nearly caved at the onslaught of reinforcements. How

Aleksander had come so quickly, I didn't know, and didn't care. They were here. They'd saved us.

A Fae soldier before me, down one helmet and bleeding from his temple, charged, and I swung the Blade of the Sun, grunting as he deflected the blow. He parried, advancing on me. Clipped my breastplate. My shoulder.

Lunging to swerve from another blow, I allowed ribbons of thorny shadow to flow from the weapon and down the miscreant's throat. The Fae choked and sputtered, falling to his knees, his neck bulging and engorging with shadows as he heaved for air that would never come.

War cries at my back, blistered skin across my shoulder healing steadily, I ran for the Fae encampment.

I hurtled past the body of a mercenary—greenish scales already turning gray, long split tongue lolling outward—past torches that had been lit by both sides as the last dregs of sunset muted to black and drowned us all in darkness, past horses on their hind legs, Garnet soldiers falling on swords.

I'd only made it a few more feet when a high-pitched shrieking split my eardrums. The unexpected sound did something traitorous to my heart, and I found I'd clutched at my chest. It was the cry of a strix.

Not Acorn, please Gods—

My eyes scanned the trees above and landed back in the direction of my keep. There, high in the sky, amid clouds and snow and rich, heavy moonlight, was the rounded face of a strix, once-scarred eyes now clear and bright. That low brow and those thick gray plumes and wild wingspan . . . Shrieking and yowling. Not in pain but in fury—

For in her gnarled clutches—

Were screaming Fae soldiers.

Clawfuls of them.

She was larger than the runt I'd adopted, but just as menacing as I'd remembered—the strix that had birthed my own pet. One my father had won from a nasty Solaris breeder decades ago.

Acorn's mother.

She squawked and swerved in midair, and Acorn took flight out of a broken stained-glass window, shooting out into the smoke-filled night to meet her.

A vengeful grin split my face.

Arwen told me how she'd freed the creature. How she could have chosen to see the darkness, the suffocating fear, but she hadn't. And now, the mighty, healed strix had flown across the channel—the single most treacherous journey that existed—to come here. To her child. To help us.

The two of them shrieked happily, devouring men left and right, and I took off once more, farther and farther away from my keep. Deeper into the night-shrouded woods. Through the gnarled trees, the snow-packed earth chilling my bones, my body, my breath—

The Blade of the Sun solid and mighty in my grasp, I could almost feel my grin as the blade and my lighte worked in tandem, slamming into anyone who was foolish enough to find themselves in my path.

Each whip of my darkness sure and swift and steady.

Each lash precise and lethal.

One such motion sliced through another Fae, already half-ravaged by a shirtless Hemolich drinking the blood from his very neck as he swung at me.

By the time I reached Lazarus's encampment, it was a mere shell of what it had been hours ago. While my men had converged on the walls of Shadowhold, cutting down the lizard beasts from Garnet and fortifying the keep, it seemed most of Aleksander's men had come here eager to partake in the gory, *gleeful* bloodletting of the Fae who had once enslaved them.

I almost felt sorry for the pitiful souls.

But not sorry enough to slow my pace. All I could see was my own blinding determination. That, and the feeble wood structure that had hastily replaced what was once my father's tent. And if he wasn't there . . .

I'd scour the earth for him.

We'd won the war. I had the blade. I wouldn't stop.

I'd hunt him down until—

"We can't find him, either."

I scanned the smoking, ashy remains of the camp, torchlit and pillaged. Relief I didn't know I'd needed wheezed from me.

Griffin. And Mari.

"What are you two doing here?"

Mari frowned. "Same as you. Looking for Lazarus. Onyx and the muscly guys who drink blood have the Fae soldiers beat."

Griffin exhaled hard, eyes on the burns down the left of my face. "I should have been fighting beside you."

Mari brushed a hand down Griffin's arm and his shoulders softened.

But all I could think was her name.

Arwen, Arwen, Arwen—

To see her face once more before I ended this. That pinched brow or elegant nose or her full lips curling in a smile.

"I'm fine," I told him. "Where's Arwen?"

Mari chewed her lip and my blood ran cold. "We haven't seen

her. Maybe she went back into the castle. For Leigh and Ryder? It was getting close out there . . ."

It had been. The walls had all but fallen.

But I knew Arwen like I knew the fabric of my own soul. She would never have retreated. "No. She's around here somewhere."

I canvassed the destruction. The overturned wheelbarrows, tents glowing a soft blaze in the darkness of the woods. Creatures had begun to prowl through the wreckage, drawn to the smoke and scent of blood and fear. Wolves and vultures sniffing at the carcasses, pawing through the dirty snow . . . Far more vile beasts would be arriving soon. The remaining soldiers didn't even move to shoo the creatures. There were so few of them now . . .

"They're fleeing," I realized. "He's likely run with his men."

"He has no witch to portal him back," Griffin said. "They'll head for the channel."

We took off north through the woods. Evendell's side of the channel was accessed in the Blade Moors, which was days and days from here, but we could track them long before they got too far. We knew these woods. We knew this land.

The sky shifted from violet to blue to black. Wind battered us as we ran. Branches whistled. Snow fell.

Until there, twined in the heavy, snow-laden woods, away from the pillaged encampment of Fae and hidden from the Hemolichs that hunted them and the scavengers that would follow, was my father and a small convoy of his men, hurrying for the channel.

One trembling moment of utter stillness as they saw us discover them—a moment of total silence before—

"I should have known you'd fight alongside the *filth*."

The promise of violence curled my lips from my teeth. I raised my hands to unleash daggers of my roiling power into him and his weakened men.

When lighte, sudden and blinding in the night-dark forest, cut through my vision and slammed into my father. Lazarus was thrown—no, *blasted*—back into the shedding trunk of a tree.

His soldiers aimed their own power and weapons at the unseen assailant, but Mari was way ahead of them. She froze the remaining men in place with a single uttered spell. I'd hardly noticed the spinning, magic-tinged wind.

Arwen emerged from the tree line.

Black onyx leathers. Loose braid down her back.

A beautiful goddess of fury, bathed in moonlight and poised to kill.

No sooner did my father move to stand, to ready his palms wide with his own power, than another blow of her lighte smashed into him. Lazarus thrashed as it cut into his chest, his neck, his arms.

Mari sucked in a ragged breath. And Griffin shot me a look. Her spell on the Fae soldiers wouldn't last much longer. We rushed the frozen convoy and made quick work of them—heads sheathed in red visors toppled to the frozen ground.

My gaze found Arwen's steadfast eyes.

Lazarus beheld us, outnumbered four to one. He stumbled backward in the snow. "You'll regret this, son," he swore, inching away from us and toward the tree line. "Just like your last rebellion."

"No." With the back of my hand I wiped Fae blood from my chin. The Blade of the Sun crested in my grip. "I don't think I will."

And then—I charged.

I didn't even see Arwen coming.

Griffin roared for her to stop, but—too late. Just as Arwen

slammed into me, Griffin struck Lazarus in the knees with his emerald lighte.

Arwen and I both went down, sailing into thick snow. Pine and orange blossom filled my nostrils. Ice in my mouth. Ringing in my ears—

"It's not your fate," she pleaded. "You need to live."

"That's," I barked out, heart pounding in my ears, "*bullshit.*"

It dawned on me—perhaps well before this moment—that I might have to subdue my own *wife* if I had any hope of saving her.

I love you, I thought as I swung my blade. *The breath in your lungs is all that matters to me*, as I slammed my sword into hers. *Now let me end this.*

And in the distance, Lazarus sent ice in a hailstorm toward us. Mari cast spell after spell, Griffin deflecting each blow, driving him back, each attack casting the night in sparks of vivid green.

I struck harder and faster, Arwen conceding step after step, fighting to maintain her footing.

I gritted my teeth, panting, shuddering with the effort—

Until my foot met hers in the snow. And I did not waste the chance.

My shadows drenched us both, a swirl of obsidian mist, suffocating her softly, lulling her into a sleep not unlike one I had offered her when she had been racked by wolfbeast poison. This, too, would be a mercy. I could only hope she would see it as such one day, many, many years from now.

Arwen struggled, but my shadows proved too strong. There was nothing she could do as her furious screams fell into whimpers. As my darkness, my wings and claws blended with the night and overpowered her like fog against the sun. I swore I heard my father's low laugh.

"Please," she begged, and my heart ripped from itself.

"Forgive me," I murmured, pulling her close, feeling consciousness slip from her. Smelling honeysuckle and orange blossom for the last time. "I love you. I'll love you wherever I am, whatever I am. Always."

45

ARWEN

A ND I, YOU," I WHISPERED, MEANING IT WITH EVERY-
thing that made me.

It was the very skill Kane had noted when we'd sparred that
doomed him. Thinking I'd weakened, that I'd be forced to succumb—
I'd thought so myself. So, so many times. Yet once again, a well of
power simmered beneath my lowest point. When I thought I had
nothing left, I rose even higher.

Kane's eyes flashed once with shock and horror before he flew
backward with the force of my rippling, shimmering lighte. My sunfire lighting the night like dawn.

He did not stand.

And I didn't cast more than a passing glance toward Griffin or
Mari—though it nearly cracked me in half not to, I couldn't waste a
moment.

I grabbed the Blade of the Sun from the snow and surged for Lazarus, held within manacles of Griffin's emerald lighte. My blade
poised—

With a blast of icy wind Lazarus blew the manacles off and took off into the forest. Through frosty branches and all that howling darkness—

Heart pounding brutally inside my chest, I hurtled after him, legs pumping pleasantly, braid a drumbeat on either side of my spine. This, I knew I could best him at.

If Griffin or Mari followed, we lost them quickly. Circling through mighty trees and rolling fog and icy snow. Around boulders and dry grass. Twigs and lightning bugs and glowing pairs of eyes.

I did not want to hurt Kane, and yet I did.

I ran so fast my feet slapped along the forest floor, my mouth dry and numb as breath shuddered from it.

I did not want to leave Leigh or Ryder, and yet I did.

Until he reached a bare clearing. Rocks and moss on one side, a river across the other. Nowhere left to run. Panting like a dog.

I unsheathed my blade from my back, and it sang to me in greeting.

I do not want to die.

And yet, I will.

"You don't have to," Lazarus called to me through the night, and I was sure fear had finally crept into his voice. "It's not too late to come with me and rebuild this useless world together."

I angled my blade. "I knew you'd be scared in the end," I snarled at him. "The greatest coward of them all."

He roared with fury as his icy arrowheads flew in my direction. So many that I could only cut the Blade of the Sun through half, the rest gouging at my skin beneath my leathers, scarring the trees behind me as they hit.

My limbs shrieked with the pain.

But my body healed before I could voice the agony. Instantaneously, gaping holes in my sides and gut fused themselves. Bone rebuilt. Skin stitched closed.

The blade's power—we were one. It could not be destroyed, and neither could I.

Even as Lazarus read my mind, anticipating my every strike—as he swept my leg from underneath me and sent me careening into the ground, the skin of my knees ripping under my leathers—I swiped my blade, flung my lighte, and darted past his blows.

Sweat dripped from my brow, stinging my eyes, my arms and legs wet with blood, the torn skin rippling as I moved, flesh weaving back together. Despite the tears that welled, I hurtled toward Lazarus and swung my blade with a heaving grunt. Each blow sent gentle rays of illumination wending through the glade. Like the reflection of a hot summer sun off a clean mirror—blinding and softly radiant.

A sword of pure ice materialized in his grasp—not a broadsword, but a heavy claymore—a punishing piece of weaponry. Stronger than any I'd ever encountered as it crashed against my own. We snapped together and sprang apart, primeval ice and sacred stone twisting and flashing in utter darkness.

The force of his blow knocked me down, my knees bending against my will, my blade arcing from my hand and skittering across the snow.

Ears ringing, pain cresting so acutely—

I could barely erect a shield around me once more as his next blow landed in a tree trunk, directly where my head would have been. Still, even under my shield, the impact made my jaw ache, and I fought to stand on trembling legs.

My blade glinted in pale light, only a foot—maybe two—from me.

But Lazarus was already there, scooping it up. He swung that blade, *my blade*, at me until I found myself dodging back and back and back, between trees and scrambling over rocks, until my spine slammed against the bark of an oak, bones screaming with the force—and I sagged beneath my own weight.

"Strike me," I pleaded. "Do it."

Lazarus narrowed his ruthless silver eyes. He, too, was winded. "You think it'll end me? That's not what the prophecy says."

But there was a chance the blade could work both ways. And that was all I had left.

My lighte was dwindling, and my lungs stung from exertion. I could taste the blood—

My limbs ached. And my skin, everywhere, raw and fresh and new.

And he was massive and so much stronger, and a very small, scared part of me was beginning to doubt I could physically best him.

With one last furious glare, fast as a viper, he drove my own blade toward my heart—

Stopped only by my trembling, outstretched hands, wrapping around the mighty Blade of the Sun, even as it sliced easily through my flesh, blood surging into my palms and onto the steel. Even as Lazarus bore down, pushing harder, wringing an agonized shout from my lips.

But my hands were healing—healing as they *ripped*—fueled by the power of *my* weapon, even held within *his* grasp. And with every step Lazarus took, forcing the sword closer to my chest, I lifted the blade higher, higher, *higher still* until Lazarus's own proximity—that gleaming, grinning hubris—condemned him. I wrenched the weapon clean from his hands.

The Fae king's pained groan might have been the most beautiful, victorious sound I'd ever heard.

A blink of horror in those insidious silver eyes, and then he retreated.

My heart hammered. And not from fear or all the pain or the adrenaline.

But from *triumph*. As I knew it in my bones—I *had* him.

"Almost," he admitted, before fishing through his own silver armor leathers and pulling out a small, glowing glass vial.

A vial that called to me. *Sang* to me.

"That's mine . . ." I breathed, before I could even articulate the meaning of the words.

Lazarus smirked, all his teeth lit by watery silver shadows. Then he downed my lighte like a shot glass full of spirits.

I squirmed against the sight. Like bearing witness as someone ate your flesh before you. The violation rent through my entire body.

Bolstered by my own traitorous lighte, the Fae king shifted in a whirlwind. Gray, veined wings crested open, his gaping reptilian jaw snapping as he bellowed so loudly the half-frozen river cracked behind him . . . and he lunged up, up, *up* into the night.

Dread oozed in me as I watched him fly away through blurred eyesight, carried on an icy, unforgiving wind. Away from me, and this blade. Away from the Shadow Woods, away from his fate—

And the future played out for me in vivid clarity: Lazarus retreating safely back to Lumera. Defeating Hart. Building up his armies once again. Replenishing his lighte reserves. History repeating—more violence, more death—because I couldn't kill him when I'd had the chance.

A sob racked through my throat at the thoughts—at all the unnecessary loss. I watched, enraged and so depleted as the wyvern sailed easily up into the sky.

I'd come so close—

It could not end like this.

And for the first time, that tingling at my shoulder blades, that prickling sensation I'd only felt when falling, wrenched up my spine and across my back.

Come on, I begged myself. No Stones. No Gods. Just me—

Come. On.

The split second it took to shift was one of utter, agonizing pain, and I was sure I'd screamed so loud I'd severed the forest itself in two.

But then the clearing was lit in incandescent golden light. And I was breathing, and nothing hurt—

And everything was lower, smaller, as I appraised it. Every critter and owl, staring up at me in awe. Every pebble, every blade of dry grass jutting through packed snow.

And my back was heavy. So heavy, and yet weightless. Buoyed by something that had sprouted from my shoulder blades.

Wings.

I had *wings*.

Glorious, massive, mighty wings of gold and red and yellow. Delicate, destructive—like burning fire, or autumn leaves, or the bright colors that painted the sky at first light.

Like a firebird of myth, my wings were those of a falcon, but my body was my own. The same as it always had been as I ran one hand across my cold lips and eyelids, the other still tightly grasping the blade, which now pulsed inside my grip in time with my heartbeat. The same, though dusted in a thin layer of insulating golden feathers, shining as I moved, casting pure light into the darkness—like I was the sun.

Without another thought I took off into the night sky.

It wasn't perfectly intuitive. My arms flailed as I flapped and wove, soaring and then plummeting a bit. But flying—how grateful I was that even if these were my last few moments in this world, I'd gotten to experience *flying*.

Though Lazarus's wingspan was twice the size of mine, I was faster, and my feathered wings were more suited for flight than his bat-like ones. Sweeping up, I barreled into him, sending us both twisting and turning through thick, moonlit clouds and down toward the clearing from whence we'd come.

Head tipped back, he ripped his vicious fangs into my wing and I clenched my fists harder around the pommel of my blade to stave off the agony. His throat was in my eyeline now. I didn't even deflect his next blow. That claw as it came barreling toward my face, tangling in my hair, and *ripping*—

I allowed it. Felt his talon carve through my skin as I plunged the Blade of the Sun deep into the Fae king's outstretched neck.

And that blade—it really was a weapon of pure sunbeams.

Of dawn and air and light.

A light that bloomed forth from Lazarus's strangled moan, consuming his throat, his bared teeth, in white-hot flame. That glorious, dazzling sunfire tore through his scales, across his outstretched wings, down his flailing, barbed tail.

And for a moment, I hoped—simply wondered—if maybe the prophecy had been wrong all along. If I might watch Lazarus—this wretched, writhing wyvern consumed by flame in the deep night sky—combust like a comet. If I might flap my brand-new feathered wings and soar down to the woods below. Feel the moss and earth beneath the snow once more. Run to my family. Run to Kane—

I allowed myself to want it. To pray and wish and beg the Stones themselves to allow me to live. To please, *please* give me one more chance at this life.

But then the blade itself lit with sunfire—and so did I.

My chest, my throat, my face.

My ears, shattering with the noise. It was my voice, that noise.

My screaming. My long, feathered hair sizzling. My eyes squeezing shut before they could melt in their sockets. My *wings*, burning as I flapped them frantically.

And as the blazing fire devoured me, as I could no longer feel any pain—

That childhood game my mother had taught me—the one used for quelling panic—shoved itself to the front of my deteriorating mind.

Find and focus on three things you can name.

One: Evendell. Freed of Lazarus. Safe, for my friends. My family. For all.

Two: The man I loved. His dark, unruly hair, so like his spirit. The truth that he had loved me, too, for whatever little time we'd had together.

Three:

46

KANE

I T WAS THE SOUND I'D WAITED OVER FIFTY YEARS FOR—AND
the most horrible one I'd ever hear.

My eyes blinked open and only Griffin knelt before me. His eyes
were ringed in red.

No.

Perhaps I'd said the word out loud. Perhaps I'd pleaded—

It didn't matter.

I couldn't think.

Not with the screeching, the roaring, the beastly skyborne howls
of pain. Not when I didn't know who they were splitting from.

I took off in the direction of that sound, Griffin bellowing after me.

The clamor of men's warfare had all but faded. But those of the
battle in the skies—those screeches and that *clashing* only grew
louder. My feet propelled me through icy fog and trampled over
packed snow and the errant branch or twig. Only pale light from a

magnanimous harvest moon lit my pursuit, gilding every leaf and trunk and frozen patch of pond water in silver.

I couldn't see much of their fight through the dense tree cover. Only flashes of a rippling gray wingspan and . . .

And something golden.

Like molten embers glowing in the dark night sky.

And through a clearing of trees—

My bird. A gleaming, feathered firebird. Mighty as the dawn, lit with rapturous fire.

A phoenix.

Of course. My heart kicked up speed as did my legs. *Faster, faster—*

A hideous rip of agony sounded through the night, shaking the trees, dousing me in snow that slid under my collar and down my neck. I hurtled around wide, old trunks.

Another wail of agony. Feminine, melodic, haunting—

The sound of a dying bird.

I knew then it was the sound I'd hear every night for the rest of my living days.

It was the sound of my soul being severed.

My roar shook the ground. Toppled oaks. Rent through the clearing and the soil and the roots beneath my knees. I craned my neck up—

I couldn't fucking *see*—

But in the end, I wouldn't have to. One moment, a roar I knew in my soul to be my father's split the night like an axe through wood, and the next . . .

The next moment the entire night sky lit as if it were a robust, crackling flame. Every corner of the world above us, where stars and moonlight and serene darkness lived, replaced by blinding white and gold and shocking red. A sunset in the dead of night.

I squinted, bringing my hand up to shield my eyes as I ran. I knew I wasn't the only one—I could hear it in the absence of metal on metal, the hush of war cries, the lack of sure footing as men halted their plunder.

Silence across the woods. Silence save for the twin deaths above us and my feet pounding on the ground.

Silence in my mind as well.

I slowed. Could not suck in a single inhale around the agony. My fists funneling wicked black lighte through the ground until trees toppled to the snowy earth.

Fury and utter *despair* straining until I could taste the pain in my throat and across my tongue. More heart-wrenching, more crippling, more *excruciating* than anything. Beyond anything. Somehow worse than when I'd lost her in Hemlock Isle. Because I'd found her again. I'd fallen *more* in love with the woman. I'd married her.

And because I'd had a single stupid glimmer of hope. A single shot at taking on the burden on her behalf. And I'd wasted it.

I roared at the injustice.

We had not exchanged enough words. Had not laughed enough. Hadn't kissed or fought or slept in too late or memorized each other enough.

We hadn't lived. We'd only ever just survived.

I hadn't realized I was weeping until salt froze upon my cheeks.

She wanted this. She wanted this—

It was no consolation. I was too selfish. Too broken. I didn't care.

My grief bent from me in wide, gruesome arcs.

Her life, her beautiful, vibrant life—extinguished.

And my soul, collapsing on itself.

And when I was spent, on my knees, hacking against the frozen, bald earth, the sky was pitch-black once more. Starless and desolate. The thunder above already faded into howling wind. Snow fell from the sky and landed across my head and nose. Smoke scented the air.

No—

Not snow. Ash.

Ash was raining from the sky.

The ashes of my father. And of the woman I loved.

Come back to me, I begged. *I'm nothing without you.*

A single ragged inhale sounded behind me. It was Griffin. His pained face, when I craned my neck back, eyes wet and churning. His mouth that muttered *I'm sorry.*

I almost told him to go back to the keep. That I'd stay out here for the next few hours. The next few months. That they could all return to the world Arwen had left for them—

But I couldn't disappear inside my grief. I owed myself to my people. Knew I had to shake the hands of the men who lived, and mourn the ones we'd lost. Lay planks of wood and plant new saplings and spread the news across the continent, on behalf of Onyx, that we'd won.

As the man they'd knelt for. Their king and their victor.

Though what victor allowed the woman he loved to deliver the dying blow and lose her life because of it, I didn't know.

All I knew was a single, ferocious desire to end my life and find her in whatever awaited us next. I'd lived too damn long.

From far behind us, a single high-pitched voice cut through my sorrow. "How . . ." Mari uttered. "I don't understand . . ."

And then Griffin, drawing closer behind me. "Kane—"

Their voices weren't consoling. Not broken, not hollow. No, they both sounded . . . overcome.

My eyes were nearly swollen shut, but I fought to pry them open.

I'd leveled the forest with my rage. The remaining gnarled tree trunks and spindly branches glowed an unearthly pale blue as the very first pools of sunlight filtered in from the east.

And through the valley of felled trees, we had a clear sight to the vision ahead.

Utter awe sang through my body at the glistening white glen before me. An iridescent sprawl rippling across the forest—one of soft, fresh snow and beads of morning dew bejeweling each branch and leaf. A pearly, eternal scene, bathed in morning light and night's still, blue shadows.

And at the very center: Arwen.

Slumped over atop the powder—eyes closed, lashes dusted in snow. Lips violet and dark hair fanned around her, pale skin brushed with ash.

Serene, silent, wholly bare—

And breathing.

47

ARWEN

M Y EYES BLINKED OPEN TO A WARM SWATH OF BLUE SKY
and a cluster of swaying autumn leaves. The air was as crisp as
an apple and just as sweet. I inhaled it through my nostrils greedily—
pumpkin seeds, damp leaves, chimney smoke.

And the ground—a grassy meadow, clean with morning dew beneath my head. Blades of grass tickling my cheeks and forearms. My
eyelids fell closed amid gentle awareness.

I knew this place.

I knew the view of the small yet bustling town square that would
greet me once I pushed myself up to sit. Knew the vibrant sunset
colors that would paint the sky in subtle gradations. Yolky yellow,
rosy pink, crystal blue.

"Is it just as you remembered it?"

The voice, though I'd never heard it before, didn't frighten me. I
moved from my back to sit comfortably atop the knoll, that view I'd
been expecting to stretch below me even smaller, but somehow more

comforting than I'd remembered. Sleepy Abbington shone under the colorful clouds. Like ripped tufts of cotton backlit by liquid gold.

The man's dark brown hair receded a bit up the crown of his head. His heart-shaped face and angular nose were handsome, kind. Inexplicably familiar.

"Do I know you?"

"A complicated question," the man said ruefully. "*No* is probably the simplest answer."

White floppy butterflies floated by on a breeze.

"I owe you many thanks," he continued, his eyes, too, on the fluttering wings, the watercolor sky, the rolling autumn hills, and the shepherds that tended to flocks grazing atop them. And then down to the town. The handful of shopkeepers and merchants closing up for the evening. Headed home to their families to sleep and eat and start anew tomorrow.

I turned to him once more. "You do?"

"I was not able to return home for a long time. I had done something foolish in the hopes of helping others. Had not used my power in the way it was meant to be used. Your bravery proved it had not been an error at all." Something brimmed in his eyes. "You conquered a mighty force. Saved many lives. Spared realms."

But I didn't feel pride. I didn't feel like a savior or a queen—I was born in this quiet, autumn town. I was just a girl. "My name is Arwen."

"I have been looking forward to this day for some time, Arwen."

Somewhere in my mind I remembered I had slain a mighty dragon. Had combusted in a hail of flame beside him. I looked down at my hands, clean, bare of dirt or blood. Pale in the violet light. "Because I killed him?"

"To meet again."

"You said I didn't know you."

The man's eyes crinkled. "You don't."

I nodded, though I didn't understand. A swallow warbled out a soft tune and a fly whizzed past my nose. The gentle wind breathed through the soft cotton of my skirts and the man's white tunic beside me.

"Your husband . . ." he said after some time, "is very devoted to you."

I smiled. "I know."

"I'm glad for it. He's been a good king to your lands."

My brows knit. "My lands?"

"Well, mine." The man's low laugh reminded me of wind chimes.

"But King Oberon—"

"If you go back to the very beginning . . . the rightful heir is the child of true Onyx. You."

Realization dawned on me. Misted in a deep contentment but realization nonetheless. Words a bright-eyed young seer had uttered to me in another life. "My father . . . the Fae God."

The man—my father—said nothing. Just appraised me curiously.

"What do they call you? Those original nine?"

He shrugged and I thought it funny. A great and powerful Fae God, shrugging. "Some have deemed us Elder Gods."

"And your power . . . it birthed Onyx?"

"Correct."

My father. A Fae Elder God. The creators of the sacred Stones, and his, Onyx. The stone of power and strength and darkness. Bequeathed to me, a healer from a farming town. I nodded to myself in deep understanding. "I think it will be wonderful."

"You take after your mother in that way."

My mother.

I smiled. "Someone once called it relentless positivity."

"And who was that?"

The town below me was blurring a bit. Trees and bricks and cobblestones becoming spotty blotches of gray and brown and green. "I . . . I can't remember."

"Ah," my father said. "Time to get you back."

He stood with a soft groan and I thought the sound very human. I stood, too, and stretched like a cat under the fading sunlight.

"We won't meet again, Arwen."

"I know," I said, though I wasn't sure how. "You can go home now, though?"

He smiled, and the light from that beaming grin warmed the hilltop we stood on and all the grass surrounding us. "Yes. And you must do the same."

My heart thumped once in my chest.

Home.

THE EMBERS SIZZLED ACROSS MY FEATHERS.

Molten and liquid—scalding and blistering and scorching each fiber and plume.

And yet it felt like cleansing rain. Soothing every ache, healing every wound, building me back together, piece by piece.

My talons tingled beneath a rising sun, my palms stretched as if awakening from a good, succulent sleep, my wings burning with white flames as they spread wide across the clearing.

I screamed—wind and light and fire burning up as it rose inside my throat. Clearing my chest, bracing myself. And then I shuddered ferociously, shifting and shaking, angling my head, flexing every tendon—

Until all was quiet.

And just a little too cold. Gooseflesh rippled along my stomach and legs as a winter wind swept across me. My face lifted gently from fresh, clean snow. It tasted rich like the morning.

"Arwen . . . ?" Kane's hoarse voice sliced through my senses and my eyes sprang open.

Watery silver filled my vision.

Tears slipped down his dirtied cheeks. My hands found them and held his face close to my own. "You're alive," I murmured.

"*Me?*" He laughed, raw and rough.

Someone chuckled behind us through tears. It sounded like Griffin.

Kane sat us both up a bit and brushed the ash and snow from my cheeks. But I couldn't let go. Couldn't stop grasping at him. When I convulsed involuntarily against the cold, Kane's eyes left mine and fell elsewhere. Whoever he'd looked at rushed over and placed a warm cloak across my bare body.

The soft reddish fur smelled of clove and cinnamon and . . .

"Mari," I croaked, sitting up a little.

Mari's brown eyes were wide. Wider than I'd ever seen them. "Welcome back."

I scrambled from Kane's lap, wrapping the cloak tighter, and threw myself at my friend.

"How is this possible?" Griffin murmured somewhere behind us. "We watched her . . ."

Mari released me long enough to turn to him and Kane. "Her shifted form—a phoenix—will always rise from its ashes."

"So I . . . can't die?" I was in too much shock to wrap my mind around the gravity of those words.

But Mari shook her head and held me to her once more. "Only in your shifted form you can't."

And this time I didn't ask her how she knew so much. I only held her tighter.

When we'd held each other so long my tears had frozen on my face, Kane insisted on taking me somewhere warmer.

Through a tumult of cries for the dead and victory songs, past barrels of ale being rolled across snow and moaning bodies hefted on stretchers, we marched home. Women cried as children embraced their fathers at the knees, and boisterous teens, hanging from the remains of the sentry towers, rained liquor down onto soldiers below.

Shadowhold had survived.

Not without loss. Not without mourners and wheelbarrows filled with fallen men. But when I couldn't tear my eyes from the blood-spattered brick walls or our beautiful wrought iron warped by salamander flame, Kane took my hand and said, "We'll rebuild."

"Ravenwood."

I turned at that familiar voice, as did Kane.

Aleksander appraised us, ice-blond hair stained red, rusty eyes glowing brighter than usual. "You look like death itself."

Kane only shrugged his shoulders smoothly.

I said nothing. Too tired to snip with the Hemolich. I knew how much power coursed through his veins with all the carnage surrounding us. I had no energy left for a fight. I wanted to see my siblings.

But Kane spoke first. "The deal we made, you must know—"

Aleksander interrupted with a raised brow. "What deal?" His ruby eyes finally left Kane's to land on my own with cold curiosity.

"The raven we sent you," I said.

"I never received a raven."

My mind emptied. Then emptied again. "Then why did you . . ." But my words trailed off with deep understanding.

Aleksander was silent, his warrior pride lurking behind that solid-ice exterior. I watched him survey the torchlit scene. The hefting bodies, the prisoners of war chained in lilium. And right alongside all the gore and pain, cries of triumph that rent the air. Cheers of merriment.

"She got to you," Kane said slowly, such pride brimming in his eyes.

"Don't paint me as some changed man. I didn't do it for either of you. I couldn't have that bigoted bastard taking over Rose."

Kane continued, unbothered, my hand still held in his. "You know what she said to me once?"

Aleksander said nothing, his mouth a flat line.

"Everyone is capable of redemption."

My heart swelled at the memory, and I peered up at my husband. He was burned and beaten half to death, his eye nearly swollen shut. His Onyx armor shredded at the sleeve, his long fingers blue with frostbite. But Kane had never looked so beautiful.

I'd said those words to him in the dim midnight light of my bedroom, after Halden's explosion had forced Kane to tell me more than he'd ever planned to. And he'd remembered, all this time.

"Good luck to you, Aleksander," I said on a sigh. "I hope we never meet again."

Inside the great hall, banners were being hammered, hung, and unfurled, and bells jangled in the hands of children. Triumph and bereavement and mourning and celebration poured out in the castle like a chalice overfilled.

My brother found me first. I inhaled the tobacco and snow on his clothes as he held me before I'd even seen him coming. He pulled back just long enough to examine my face. "I was so scared—"

"I know," I breathed. "Me, too."

Leigh found us like that and wedged her way between us easily. I couldn't stop the tears then, nor did I want to.

We stayed in that embrace for a long time. Holding one another in peaceful silence.

Peace.

That's what this feeling was. Somewhere in between the clash of blades and the loss of those I loved and the fiery death of my enemy . . . peace had found me.

Surely the joy would hit me soon. The *relief* that we had won. But right now, my still-stiff limbs and reeling, foggy mind just needed this. Tangible, unmoving, pleasantly exhausted peace.

I knew Kane had not torn his soft, quicksilver gaze from me one time since I'd awoken.

Eventually I released my family and turned to face him once more.

"Hello," he said, a crooked grin at his cheeks, tears still in his eyes.

Behind him, the sun crested steadily through the stained-glass windows of the hall and over the snow-draped forest and the peaked mountains beyond. Voices throughout the warmly lit hall rang out, no longer afraid.

"It's finally over, isn't it?" I asked, relief flooding me as I grasped his broad, calloused hand. The warmth of his palm simmered through my entire body. Despite being born of ash and snow bare as a newborn, my hand still somehow carried Kane's signet ring. *A gift from my father*, I thought.

"For us"—Kane shrugged, thumb dragging softly over my skin—"I think it's just the beginning."

Dear Arwen,

I don't expect, nor see reason, for you to give much credence to the marital counsel of an old, solitary, occasionally cankerous man, but it appears I am compelled to share with you regardless.

It is not news to me that the battle you and Kane plan to wage is unlikely to leave both of you alive. It is a truth that has plagued my thoughts, and I mourn even tonight as I write to you. No man should outlive one child, let alone two.

I was lucky enough to have been married once myself, and we, too, were not given quite as much time as I thought we deserved together. Now, I am no romantic. You know as well as anyone I won't fuss over the needs of the heart. So this is the only advice I will share with you ahead of your wedding. Cherish one another. Appreciate the moments you are given, ephemeral as they may be. Do not dwell in the past or scurry toward the looming future. And be grateful, each day, for the love that you share. I am grateful to have witnessed it.

And one last thing—perhaps not sage wisdom, but as my quill has become loose upon the page and the spirit in my glass empties, I find the words easier tonight than I think they may ever be again.

For years you've believed your fears made you cowardly, yet chose time and time again to face those fears, regardless of what might've been waiting for you on the other side.

You've saved yourself and those who matter most to you. Helped and healed so many in need. You've discovered a deep well of power within yourself. Met someone you wish to spend your life with. You've found joy in times of darkness, and helped share that joy with others.

In this war, and in the days I hope will follow, I urge you to remember this: do not equate bravery with fearlessness. If someone like you has nothing left to fear, it will be your heart I worry for. Fear is human, and only grows as we come to care deeply for others. Stones know I've become more fearful in knowing you. That's what love does to us.

You are courageous, Arwen. And I'm very proud of you.

Dagan

Epilogue

ARWEN
Ten Months Later

CRAG'S HOLLOW HAD BEEN RELUCTANT TO WELCOME autumn. The bucolic summer stretched on and on, languishing in slow, fragrant days and warm, vivid nights. But when it finally did, the seaside town blossomed in shades of gold and copper I'd never seen.

As I jogged along the cliffside, those falling leaves drifted onto the inky lake below, spindrifts from the gently crashing waves whispering up to greet them.

I came to a stroll to catch my breath a handful of feet from our cottage. Through the front windows, framed between generous white curtains, I could just make out Kane and his hefty, dust-riddled book, sprawled out on the couch, lit by sleepy rays of late-afternoon sun.

A spindly, stretching feathered leg almost clawed Kane in the face. He moved the strix gently to the side and returned to his book.

That feeling fluttered in my chest once more, as it had so many times since we'd ended what was now being referred to as the Six Years' War.

Peace.

Did it bother me that so many in Evendell would never know what fate Kane and I had narrowly saved them from? That aside from a handful of soldiers and nobles from Citrine, Amber, and Garnet, and a smattering of Blood Fae living in Rose, everyone on the continent believed Onyx to have waged war on two kingdoms for nothing but riches and coin?

Sometimes.

But we had not done any of it for glory.

The peace alone—both ours and the one we were able to bless upon Evendell with quite a bit of help—was more than worth it.

I entered the cottage to find a half-finished chess game at the kitchen table, some new art of Leigh's affixed to the halls of the small foyer—a dragon at sunrise, a portrait of the inky lake—and the smell of simmering carrots. "Carrot soup?"

Kane turned from his book and offered me a knowing smile. "This will be the one. I can feel it."

Acorn scuttled from the couch and launched at me, nuzzling his little goblin head into my knees. He'd practically become my shadow the past few months. Kane had noticed it even before I had—it'd been one of the first signs.

I attempted to soothe the strix with soft head scratches as I unlaced my boots. "You don't need to like Amber food for us to make it for him," I said to Kane.

"Or her."

I grinned. "*Or her.*"

Kane stood with a stretch, his loose cotton pants displaying a delicious sliver of low, golden abdomen. "I'd just like to find one thing from your home that I like as much as you like cloverbread."

The strix scuttled away from me on all fours, leapt onto the raised, cushioned ledge below the bay windows, and nearly slammed into the glass. Out of the corner of my eye, I just caught the mighty wingspan of Acorn's mother, soaring over the glittering, pitch-black lake as the pale sun melted into the horizon.

She'd be back soon. She didn't like the dark much.

Ryder had built a shed for her this summer, which Mari had filled with oil lamps. Only some of the citizens of Crag's Hollow had been terrified. Most were used to their dark king's strange winged beasts.

"Well, that will never happen." I stood to kiss Kane on the cheek. Cedar filled my nostrils. "I don't think anyone likes anything as much as I like cloverbread."

"I like you," Kane growled softly, pulling me close.

My lips found his in a sleepy, slightly sweaty haze, and though I'd only intended to greet him before bathing, I couldn't help the heat that bloomed in my chest and along my neck as he sucked my lip between his and tongued it with indolent care. I moaned a little, and his hands found my waist and neck, dragging me against his hardening—

"You sure you two should be doing that?"

We spun, Kane coughing a little, as Ryder pushed the front door open with his back, carrying six bottles of wine by their necks.

"Doing *what* exactly?" Kane asked him.

Ryder shrugged, unfazed, as the bottles clinked with the closing door. "Won't that, you know . . . hurt it?"

Mortification turned my face hot.

But Kane couldn't help his laugh as he ran a hand through that sable hair, pushing it back and free from his face. "Your understanding of human anatomy is concerning."

"He skipped almost all of his classes as a kid," I said.

"You'll have to amend that if you intend to mold the impressionable minds of our youth."

My brother rolled his eyes. It was still surprising that Ryder had hung up his sword and leathers to pursue teaching carpentry. But he had come to love caring for Leigh and Beth back at Shadowhold far more than he'd ever enjoyed battle strategy or dueling. And like his father, he was a natural woodworker. Maybe the profession would suit him. He certainly seemed happy.

The door pushed open again, and Griffin's sculpted frame filled it as he lugged through an armful of chopped firewood.

"Need help?" Ryder offered, though Griffin seemed to have the logs under control.

"Took you long enough," Kane said, sitting down at the kitchen table.

"The women refused to leave the sweetshop." Griffin's face revealed no trace of humor.

"They're still there now?" I asked, having moved into the kitchen to stir the soup.

"Leigh went to the seer's house. She said she'd be back before dinner."

I slid behind Ryder to pull two large trout from a crate of ice. "And Mari?"

Griffin cleared his throat, and Ryder and I exchanged a knowing glance.

"The witch—"

"I'm here, I'm here," she sang, waltzing in. "Anyone want a candied apple? I have about thirty. Who knew little girls could be so convincing?"

Kane's brows lifted and he extended a hand. Mari fished through her shopping basket for one such shiny red treat and tossed it to him. Kane caught the apple deftly and bit in.

"Why so many?" I asked Mari as I pulled plates from a low cupboard.

"They don't have these in Shadowhold. Leigh wants to stock up before we leave." She craned her neck at me. "Are you sure you should be moving so much?"

I looked down at my slightly rounded belly. Two weeks ago nobody would've even been able to tell. "Yes, everyone can stop fussing." I'd actually never felt stronger.

Kane's eyes found mine and the warmth and protectiveness that shone there heated my blood once more. *That* was the real problem. The near animalistic need that had swallowed us both whole ever since we'd realized I was expecting.

"Who else is fussing?" Mari asked.

The memory of Ryder's intrusion was a much-needed bucket of ice on whatever tension had thickened the air between Kane and me. "Nobody," I muttered. "Never mind."

"Let me guess," Mari lilted, strolling into the heart of the living room. "Your overly involved commander here." She motioned to Griffin. "You just *have* to stop caring so profoundly about others. It's clearly eating you alive."

Griffin had gotten very bad at hiding the way Mari's playful jabs affected him. He almost grinned directly at her before schooling his face and returning to his task stacking wood in the fireplace.

However, the logs roared to life as soon as Mari deposited herself into the deep-cushioned couch, sending Griffin back just barely in time.

"Sorry," she said, a little sheepish. Mari was still getting used to some of the residual magic she'd inherited when Briar had passed on.

"Don't be." Griffin grunted, brushing embers from his shirt and putting some space between him and the now-crackling fire. "Feels like she's still here."

Mari beamed at him and the commander blushed—genuinely *blushed*.

But nothing more had blossomed between the two of them, much to Kane's and my disappointment. Some part of me feared it would take a great and possibly terrible reckoning to force one of those stubborn oxen to finally bend to the other.

Still, I was going to miss all of this dreadfully—everything would be different soon.

And not just because we'd have a child come spring.

We'd been splitting our time between Willowridge and Crag's Hollow while rebuilding Shadowhold. The summer had been long and lazy; Barney, Eardley, and a freshly stationed Wyn were more than happy to oversee both the capital's palace and the stronghold while Kane and I enjoyed the last dregs of the season here in this cottage. Days were spent alternating between making love, eating too much seafood, and reading side by side as we watched the sun set over the lake.

It was like a dream. The quiet morning runs. Leigh and Beth fishing off the docks. Mari and Griffin's endless banter. All my little potted poppies and buttercups blooming marvelously, their petals pressed in Kane's dry books. The quiet seaside, which rolled into the even quieter countryside, that Kane and I would fly across, flame and shadow in the afternoon sun—

I'd made Kane promise this could be a yearly practice. Summers spent by the sea, inviting all our friends and family to come stay with us. But for now, we needed to return to the keep. There was much to do.

Besides the reconstruction, I had my work rehabilitating children born to Hemlock Isle and relocating them to families here in Evendell. We also had allies to mend fences with. Amber had ousted King Gareth quickly after he'd lost so many of their men in a pointless war, and we actually quite liked the new, young queen—a twice-removed cousin that had usurped him.

But Garnet had not followed suit, instead doubling down on their praise of King Thales, who surely had told his kingdom a different story. So, we were not without enemies.

Though Kane and Griffin fought me with equal intensity, it was one of the many reasons I was determined to reinstate our alliance with Peridot. With Eryx gone, Amelia had already done wonders for the kingdom, tripling both their coin and crops, reducing poverty and smuggling in the west, and working to restore Siren's Cove to its former glory. I'd suggested a trip to the capital in the coming winter. A nice reprieve from the snow, which I'd learned was my least favorite season and reminded me of frozen blood and fallen armor. Ryder had nearly leapt from his chair at that idea, and insisted he'd need to attend the peace meeting as well. For his students, he'd said.

Despite a letter I received from Fedrik congratulating us on our victory and wishing Kane and me well in our marriage, King Broderick and Queen Isolde still insisted on the union of their daughter, Sera, to Hart Renwick, now that he sat upon the Lumerian throne. If we had any interest in not going to war with them, we needed to deliver on that promise swiftly. Which was actually our biggest issue—

We'd yet to find a way back to Lumera. With Lazarus's death, the channel had been sealed, and without Briar there was no way to open a portal. Mari had tried tirelessly, sometimes so exhausted she'd spend a few nights in the Willowridge infirmary to recuperate. I'd stop by not only to see her but to bring Griffin his supper. He'd go days by her side without eating if I didn't.

But we'd had no luck finding magic with equal strength to Briar's in almost a year. No luck either in tracking down whoever *Adelaide* was that the sorceress had urged Mari to seek out with her dying breath.

I wasn't naive to the reality of running a kingdom. Those hurdles were just the beginning. Given Kane's and my full-blooded nature, and the long, near-eternal lives that stretched before us, the likelihood of this being our last war—Lazarus our last foe—was slim.

But despite all of it, as I surveyed the cottage before me, I didn't fear the future. As if some very young, desperately self-protective part of me had not ever been able to stop fearing Powell's work shed—to accept that I was well and truly safe—until now.

Ryder and Griffin sat down to play yet another game of chess my brother would never win, while Mari's nose hovered over Kane's shoulder as he flipped through whatever book he'd been reading before I came home. The savory smell of carrots simmered and I rotated the trout as it roasted over the hearth.

Leigh's and Beth's voices trilled outside, and I peered through the kitchen window to spy them laughing as they scaled the hillside, narrowly avoiding switchgrass and crushed leaves.

As steam filled the kitchen, I pushed that window open and watched it billow out into the evening air.

"Hurry up," I called to them, and the girls squealed in glee, caught amid some game that had them in stitches, propelling them faster toward the cottage. "Mari got you candied apples for dessert!"

All my anxiety found me less often these days. The nightmares fewer and farther between. Kane's, too.

And when that terror did find us—when Kane awoke in the silent witching hours, sweating and roaring for me, convinced I was plummeting to my death once more, or a panic so vise-tight I couldn't breathe past it gripped me in the middle of a crowded market aisle—we met that fear with sparkling hope.

That those moments were fleeting. That there was nothing in this world or beyond it that we did not have the power to face, as long as we were together. It was that knowledge, that unwavering hope, not only in myself, but in the people I was lucky enough to share my life with, that kept the fear from ruling me. And if it didn't rule me . . . well, then it didn't have to leave at all. Dagan had always said I was strong because of that fear, not in spite of it.

And later, at the dinner table, amid laughter and wine and second servings of truly terrible carrot soup, when asked my rose and my thorn, my answer came to me quicker than any other time I'd played.

"My thorn," I said, realizing I'd been gently rubbing my stomach as I'd come to do so often the past few months, "is that I don't really know what tomorrow will bring."

Kane reached across the table to lace my hand in his, and his silver eyes sparkled with encouragement. "And my rose," I said, appraising the warm, full, grateful faces before me—all that breathtaking love and bright possibility . . . "is the same."

Acknowledgments

I'm going to level with you all—I've only written three books, but this one was harder to complete than the first two combined. I have many theories on why that is, starting with the practicalities of attempting to wrap up every loose thread, character arc, and plot point that I've spent the past two and a half years ruminating on, and ending with the emotional weight of saying goodbye to two characters that feel so much like real people, I've started to wince when I edit their sex scenes because it feels like an invasion of their privacy.

All that to say, ending an era is hard. *A Dawn of Onyx, A Promise of Peridot*, and *A Reign of Rose* are my little romantasy children, and finishing this book was like watching them dawdle off to their first day of school. It was time, and it was beautiful, but it was also teary, and I struggled a bit to release them from our hug goodbye. So, if there were ever a book in desperate need of lengthy thanks, it would be this one, but I'll try my best to keep it short.

My first and most effusive thank-you will always go to my readers. Whether you read the very first indie-published version of *A Dawn of Onyx* or only heard about the series when this very book in your hands came out, your interest in Arwen and Kane's story is the only reason I get to continue writing. So when I say I never could have done any of this without you—your curiosity, enthusiasm, theories, fan art, TikToks, bookstagrams, and all-around passion—I really, really mean it.

I am forever grateful to my wonderful editor, Kristine. Writing can be a pretty solitary experience, and every time I send in a draft at 11:59 p.m. or we exchange silly DMs on Instagram, I feel a little less alone. To have you on this journey alongside me, offering encouragement, solving plot holes, and killing (necessary) darlings all in equal measure, is a true gift.

Heaps and mounds and piles of thanks must also go to my entire Root Literary team—Gabrielle and Jasmine, and of course my agents, Taylor and Samantha. Your smiling faces over Zoom or positive encouragement on all my new ideas are the constant rays of sunshine that make the dark, cloudy, publishing-three-books-in-eighteen-months-is-difficult days manageable. Thank you for believing in me.

I am super fortunate to have the greatest publishing team in existence. Kristin, Anika, Mary, Iris, and everyone else at PRH and Berkley who have touched this series with even their pinky toes— thank you for all of your tireless work, for your unbelievable creativity, and for answering all my questions over email, even when I number them like a dork.

Thank you as well to the wonderful foreign publishers who helped the Sacred Stones series reach readers all over the world. It's an honor to have my work translated into so many languages, and I am beyond appreciative for the opportunity. To Italy's Sonzogno and Jo Fletcher Books in the UK especially, thank you for your continued enthusiasm, creative marketing, and clear passion for this series.

To my unreal audiobook narrators, Ruby Cherise and Will Damron—you both brought Arwen and Kane to life in a way I didn't even know was possible. Your voices sound as much like them as they do in my own head. (This might only make sense to me; I promise it is the highest of compliments.)

None of this would have happened had a handful of curious, thoughtful folks on the r/BetaReaders subreddit not given my untitled, typo-riddled first shot at a novel a chance. Those wonderful people still read all my books before anyone else does, and I consider their feedback some of the best I receive across the board. Thank you, guys, for your honest and helpful notes, and for always working with my ridiculous turnaround times. I promise to one day say, "Take your time on this one!"

I cannot express enough gratitude to the amazing fellow authors, BookTokers, Bookstagrammers, and illustrators that consistently champion me and this series. This community has driven so many new readers to Arwen and Kane, not to mention how their messages of support, blurbs, or photos of their book clubs gleefully holding copies of *ADOO* have made the difference between a terrible writing day and a great one. Special shout-out to gremlin soulmate Lana Ferguson, ray of sunshine India Holton, and all the other wonderful Berkletes; Booksta goddesses Jourdan Gandy, Tina Marshall, Vanessa Valdez, and Daddy Kristen; TikTok queen Lauren Cox; the tireless Kate Golden Book Club admins Kristin, Krystal, Iliana, and Mikayla; concept artists of my dreams Coralie Jubénot and Sasha Lee Coleman; and creator of the best special edition I've ever owned, April McCarthy.

I owe everything that's left to my incredible support system that was here long before the books, and will (fingers crossed) still be here if they ever go away. To my friends—Aidan, Echo, Brookie, Carly, Eni, Maura, Veija, Alec, and Scott—thank you for the suggestion of "Sluts for Kate Golden" T-shirts, even though we're going to workshop that one, and the SusieCakes red velvet cake the night my first book was released. And sorry for keeping it all a secret for so long, and thank you for not holding that against me.

To my family—Mom, Dad, Lily, Fin, Isla, Michelle, Susie, Chris, and Val—thank you all for supporting me even though truly *none* of you are allowed to read my books in full. Special thanks to my mom, who is one of the best creative minds in existence. You're a lifesaver and a genius. And you're my mom! So cool.

Last (but never least), thank you to my husband, Jack, and our sweet pup, Milo. When the three of us are anywhere, that place becomes home. I love you guys with everything in me. I am so lucky to share this life with you both.

ABOUT THE AUTHOR

Kate Golden is the bestselling author of viral sensation and debut novel *A Dawn of Onyx*. She lives in Los Angeles, where she works in the film industry developing movies with screenwriters and filmmakers. When she isn't telling stories, Kate is an avid book reader, film and TV fanatic, and functioning puzzle addict. She and her husband can be found hosting cozy game nights and taking hikes with their sweet pup, Milo. You can keep up with her on Instagram at Kate GoldenAuthor and on TikTok at Kate_Golden_Author, where she is known to post both spicy and heartbreaking teasers for her upcoming books.

KATE GOLDEN'S NEW SERIES

HALF CITY

COMING SOON FROM ACE!

*Welcome to Harker Academy for Deviant Defense:
An urban university specializing in training
demon hunters, located in the heart of glittering
Astera—also known as the Half City.*